Elizabeth Lavender's

Shadowed Bonds

Book 3 of the Sunspear Series

Ebook ISBN: 978-1-951741-06-8

Paperback Print ISBN: 978-1-951741-07-5

Hardcover Print ISBN: 978-1-951741-08-2

Woven with gentle words of care and bathed in oceans of tears, this bond finds life to entwine two hearts.

A precious gift to those that discover it, for though stretched many times beyond its fragile appearance, it remains unchangeable.

Unbroken. Whole. One.

CHAPTER ONE

Stealthily weaving her way through the abandoned hallway, she hid her appearance with her cloak. A smile crept across her face upon reaching her destination. After a final check for any unaccounted for personnel, she came up empty and with minimum effort the door slid open. She quickly shut it behind her and surveyed his quarters. He left the lights dimly lit, expecting by the time he returned for night to close in on him. A good guess on his part. She made herself comfortable on his couch and found things to occupy her time. Imagining the surprise on his face when he opened the door, another smile curved on her lips in anticipation.

Dante exited the dining area of the fortress answering a chorus of goodnights from the others. He glanced one last time at his cousin, Lana, and for the millionth time wished for a way to lift her spirits. Nothing worked tonight, and the others tried too, including her husband, Caleb. Only a weak smile escaped her for their efforts. Who possibly moves past the horrible scene they saw over the past few days? His mind kept reverting to the ugliness of it as well, so he didn't fare much better. He sighed and ran his hand through his sandy brown hair, hoping an idea surfaced to help her. Nothing came. Maybe an idea comes in my sleep he thought, as he walked into his quarters and shut the door.

Another figure in the room drew his attention, and he stopped in his tracks.

"Hello, Dante." She stood in the center of the room, smiling at him.

"You're here ... really here. How did you get in?" He walked slowly towards her as if in a daze.

"Finally, I'm here, and that's the first question? Your quarters posed no challenge for me," laughed the girl.

"A silly question as I now consider it." A slight sweet fragrance from something she wore grew stronger as he drew closer to her, and it delighted his senses. However, he didn't need any urging to come to her. Her beauty alone left him in a blissfully stunned state the first time, and he couldn't take his eyes from her now. This time she stood there, not her image, and he wanted to stay in the moment.

She saw him in her visions, from her ship's cockpit, and finally they gazed at each other in the Elders Hall. Always from afar. She realized only now how she longed to meet him face to face. Nothing compared to the thrill pulsing through her as she read the emotions his soft brown eyes conveyed. "I ... uh ... there's a customary way this normally begins, but not with me. I still can't tell you who I am, Dante."

"And I can't continue going around calling you young spear-bearer."

"You're right, but I'm rather fond of the name. I suppose we could earn ourselves strange looks. Frequent name changes are a necessity with the shipping business. I've even selected ones from the dining place I sat in at the time. I'll be working frequently and closely with you, Dante," she paused, "and the others of course, so you choose a name you like."

"Seriously? I'm to give you a name?"

"Yes, Dante. Tell me your choice, before I go later." She started to move on to something else, but he stopped her.

The name came in an instant. No other possibility existed to him, as he traced her lovely smile with his eyes again. "I decided."

"Already? Okay, go ahead, Dante."

"Angelina." He saw her mind search through the visions of his past to locate the connection laid with the name, but she hunted in vain. "Wondering why I chose the name?"

"I admit I do, Dante, but I told you to choose."

He moved the final step closer as her breath caught in her throat at his nearness. His brown eyes softened as he locked eyes with her, and his voice almost whispered, "I wish to tell you. From the moment I saw you, your beauty took my breath away, your sweet spirit comforted me, a gentleness always shone in your beautiful blue eyes, and there's the softness of my name every time it leaves your lips. You're my angel, my Angelina." As he spoke the words, his hand trailed down her bare arm, gently took her hand, and kissed it.

She couldn't break away from his soft, intense brown eyes, and her heart raced as much from his caress as his words. Her eyes widened as his words poured into her, because she couldn't make sense how he meant them for her. His eyes confirmed he did though, and she stood in awe of the love reflected behind the words from him as she whispered, "Dante, I ... your words ... they ..."

He whispered back to her, "All true, Angelina. Only you, my Angelina."

His hand still clasped hers and stroked the top of it, remaining near enough to his lips for his warm breath to brush it. Heat spread to her face, and she struggled to regain her composure. Her thoughts emerged into nothing more than a string of incomprehensible jumble, after his words to her. "Uh ... sit ... sorry I mean, can I ... we sit down ... now... Dante, please?"

His eyes twinkled. "Perhaps at the table, Angelina?"

"Yes, Dante." Two words more emerged than she thought she could manage.

With their hands still clasped together, he directed her to the table and scooted the chair out for her. "Do you want something to drink?"

"No, I'm good, Dante."

"Let me try again. I'm getting something for myself, and I'm determined to be a decent host. Now what do you wish to drink?"

"Water is fine, Dante."

He shook his head as he got the two drinks, the water for her and tea for himself. He sat back down and clasped her hand again. "Where do we begin, Angelina?"

"The reason I came tonight. You."

"Me?"

"Your spirit endured much at the Elders Hall, and the last few days gave you no chance to recover from it. Yesterday you buried your father." She stroked his clasped hand. "I needed to look into your eyes and see your spirit calm after the storm you withstood, Dante."

He murmured, "Always taking care of me, Angelina." He looked down, entranced by how perfectly her hand fit inside his and returned his focus to her. "The days since the Elders Hall proved hard at times, but my spirit is at peace. The father I loved as a child is the same one whose eyes I looked in for the last time in this life. I saw peace in them too, when he met the Ancient One. I'll remember the time granted with him, and it comforts me. There'll always be times something will remind me of how much I miss him, but those are expected." An item on a side table caught his attention momentarily.

Her eyes followed his to the open locket, and their eyes met again. "Images of a happier time. Keep those close, Dante. And always remember how he loved you. I'm glad he left at peace, but the sacrifice to find it, I never thought his life lost to ... I didn't see things ending as they did," she whispered, "I'm so sorry, Dante."

Her shared grief over his father's death comforted him. She understood him in a way no one else did. Nonetheless, the other part coming through as plainly he determined to stop. "You only see the visions and deliver the messages, but you don't control how they turn out. Even my father voiced those words in his own way, and he had no regrets when he departed this world. You must not either, Angelina."

"Of course, you're right, Dante." She spoke the words for his benefit. Her furious words to Alika rang in her ears from a few days previous. "At least you're safe. I believed I sent you to your death at the Elders Hall. I thought I lost you, Dante." Her voice broke.

"You didn't, though. I came back safely, as I promised you." He stroked her hand.

"You did, Dante, and your spirit is at peace truly."

"What about you, Angelina?" He searched her eyes.

"What do you mean, Dante?"

"Who worries about you? I'm not the only one who has hurt since that day."

"Please, I came for you tonight. I'm fine." She attempted a convincing smile, because she didn't want to remember the last few days and her own struggles tonight. They were numerous, and it would get them nowhere to replay them.

"My spirit is at peace and much more since you surprised me this evening." He paused, and his eyes studied her face again. "I felt all your pain, your broken spirit reaching out to me at the Elders Hall. Everything I went through, you experienced it too. You intervened twice that day, under the Ancient One's direction, once for me and then my father. If your spirit didn't endure enough with us, the evening, Angelina, I felt your spirit utterly crushed. I figured out why now, what horror you saw. Don't try telling me you're fine. This can't be one-sided. Let me comfort you as well, to bear a part of this pain you took. So, I ask you again, how is your spirit? Talk to me, please. I'm waiting and listening, as I did that night."

He would as he proved before to her. The day at the Elders Hall roared back in a tidal wave of emotions, and she saw him fighting for his life, his spirit broken a piece at a time by the Dark Lord. She stood from a great distance, connected somehow to him, but for what seemed like an eternity desperately unable to break through to him no matter how hard she tried. "Each time I watched and thought you were going to die, either by the sword or to the darkness, I was in agony, Dante." She stopped as the wave threatened to overcome her. "Powerless to stop it, and I told you to go. The Dark Lord poured his lies into you, and I saw what he did to you a little at a time until you broke." She stopped again. "I thought he won. How I begged you to stop listening to him, but you didn't hear me at first. Dante, I couldn't lose you, but I came so close. I can't think about what almost happened. You didn't fall, and you came back safe. That's the only part which matters, Dante."

He saw in awe what laid in the depths of her mesmerizing blue eyes. "I'm here with you, and I won't leave again. There's more, and I'm still listening for the rest, Angelina."

She tried, but the words stuck in her throat as the first of many images began their assault. Her eyes darted around the room and then looked down.

Gently, his hand lifted her chin, drew her eyes back to his, and held them again. "Angelina, I'm over here, remember? Take your time. I'm not going anywhere." His eyes regarded her with such tenderness as he waited for her to finish.

After a long pause, she continued, "Before the evening arrived, upon my insistence, we traveled to one of the planets to see the devastation from the Dark Lord's device. I got the foolish idea to confirm the vision I received, hoping I saw it wrong this one time. Yet the moment we stepped on the planet ..." She stopped and struggled to force the tears at bay.

"Was the first time I felt your turmoil on the planet. The next time you couldn't escape the images from your head when you tried to sleep."

"Yeah, that covers it, but I spared the time to answer you back the first time." She slumped back into the chair at the memory.

"Are you still on that?" He shook his head. "A wise Elder once said to me, 'young Dante, you are much too hard on yourself.' Angelina, you're doing the same to yourself now."

She rewarded him with a smile. "Maybe I am. I wonder if those two secretly communicate, with how similar they sound sometimes. Don't tell me the thought never crossed your mind."

Dante laughed. "It has, but for the record these words of wisdom came from Alika. He said I reminded him of another student, that we were alike in many ways."

"My teacher is right, and you as well, Dante. I came for you, but I received more than what I gave you."

"Quite mistaken, because I waited quite impatiently to see you again, Angelina. I couldn't get you from my mind."

"Well, I came as I promised, Dante."

"Yes, so why do I sense you think I'll let you leave already, Angelina?"

"You're truly at peace as I felt, but I stayed for some time now, Dante."

"Not even for an hour, and I have waited a *long* time to see you."

"I should return to help my comrade with the information. She finished what she can, and we need to confer with Alika."

"But I wish for you to remain and confer with me for longer. Come, your comrade won't mind."

"Your conferring won't solve the puzzles before me, Dante."

"Never claimed it would, Angelina. My preference is taking your mind off those puzzles to more pleasant thoughts." Taking her clasped hand, he brushed it to his lips again as he grinned up at her.

"I ... uh ... believe you do ... can, Dante." A slight flush crept up her face.

"Allow me then. You said this visit is for me, and I'm not ready for you to leave yet. Not anywhere close."

"When will you feel ready for me to leave?"

"I collected lots of questions for you. You could be here for a considerable time, Angelina."

"That's true if it's up to you. Dante, our group is at a standstill on everything, until we speak with you and the others, so we'll return soon."

"Never idle. Seth once said that about Alika's group. You're too consumed with work. It isn't good for you. An occasional break or distraction is needed, Angelina."

"No doubt you have ideas to assist me, Dante." She rose laughing and put her cloak back on her.

"I do and will persist." He laughed too and reached over to finger the top of her cloak for a moment. "Angelina, you only gave me a minute with you. I don't want you to leave yet. Tell me the key to keep you here longer, and I'll do it."

She could sit and talk with him for many hours happily, with no thought for the passing time. She trusted him completely, even alone in his quarters. The voice of obligation, of work though, incessantly intruded louder. "Dante, I do want to stay longer. You know I enjoy being here with you. You are extremely charming this evening, and I trust you in all ways, but I must leave now."

"I can try to be less charming if it means you stay longer," he teased.

She whispered, "No, you couldn't, then you wouldn't be my Dante who I ... care for so much."

He smiled at the pause. She wanted to use another word but settled on the other. Like one afraid to use the one word too soon for fear of scaring him. Regardless, he knew and didn't fear. Quite the opposite. He loved her as well.

"I'll walk you back to your ship, Angelina." Dante sighed as his efforts to persuade her ended in failure.

"Dante, I'll draw more attention with you."

"No, my clearances will get you back unhindered."

"Clearances are not an issue for me."

He started to say something else, but she decided to admit defeat. "Alright, Dante, I wish to remain with you as long as possible too, so come and walk me back."

He grinned back at her. "All you needed to do is ask. If you want my company for longer, surely ...?"

She pulled him towards the door, laughing as she did. "Enough, Dante. Your persistence gets you no further this evening. You agreed to escort me to my ship. Now, let's go."

"I had to try." He opened the door.

"Of course, I expected nothing less from you." She winked at him.

Hand in hand, they walked to her ship.

"You said your group is stuck now and will return soon. How soon?"

"Normally I don't give days and times." She turned to him as they arrived at her ship.

"I'm thinking tomorrow. Am I right?" He ignored her statement.

"Dante, I don't want to say for sure."

His voice softened. "Come now, Angelina, I'm extremely charming this evening, and you care for me very much."

His gentle brown eyes could not be refused, and she murmured, "Oh, you are and I do, Dante. Barring any sudden circumstance, your guess is good."

"See how easy? Now for the time."

"You pulled enough information from me this evening. Get sleep tonight, but I suppose I'll let you in on something about me, Dante."

"Which is?"

"I don't go for sunrise starts. You discovered my day doesn't wind down at sunset either. I'll take watching the sunset over the sunrise any day."

"Many lunchtime appointments crowd your world?"

"I prefer them. Unfortunately, operations lean towards early starts. There's a great deal planned with our visit, so we can't keep you waiting long. Still no sunrise visit, Dante."

"I'm good with that, especially the part about not keeping me waiting for long." He took her hand and kissed it again as he happily lost himself in her beautiful blue eyes. She became the center of his world now. Just like that. No doubts. He didn't know her name, but he had never been so sure of anyone in his life. He knew her, her heart, and her spirit. "Goodnight, my Angelina," he whispered.

She met his gaze, unable to leave his soft brown eyes. What passed between them in this mere hour could not be fathomed. All created from a connection started before tonight. They prevailed through so much together already, the force of it all seeming unreal at times. No words described it, and yet his words moved her in a way which took her breath away tonight repeatedly. It was shared between them now as his eyes reassured her again of what her heart already knew to be true from him. She whispered, "Goodnight, my Dante." She brushed her open hand across his cheek as she spoke. A delightful shiver coursed through him at her caress, and he curved his head to feel her hand lightly brush over his lips. She rewarded his gesture with another beautiful smile. He longed for her to linger with him, but released her other hand anyway as she turned and boarded the ship.

A female voice from the back of the ship called, "Ready to head back?"

She responded, "Yes, Alika awaits." Before the ship door closed, she smiled at Dante one last time for the evening. He watched as the ship lifted off and disappeared through the nearest portal.

"She managed to leave without ..." He laughed to himself. "That won't happen again." Once he returned to his quarters, he found sleep came with difficulty but for a far more pleasant reason this time.

"A smiling Dante. There's a good sign," said Alena as they approached the portal.

"Yes, he's good."

"We'll talk more once we get home. Alika will want to know Dante is well."

Alika strolled out of the house at their return. "Already back?"

"I figured you expected me and Alena back sooner, Alika."

"I'm aware of your predictions for the evenings, but I assumed Dante would manage to detain you longer." Alika's eyes twinkled.

"He desired to, but we needed to get back."

Somehow he hid his unhappiness as he fixed his eyes on the girl. Additional thoughts ran through his head, but he chose to keep them silent from his student for the moment. "I suppose. How is young Dante after everything?"

"His spirit is truly calm, at peace with what transpired, Alika. I wondered, but it's as I sensed from him." She smiled for an instant but looked out at the water as though she stood a million galaxies from them.

He recognized the familiar expression from her. "Why don't the three of us take a walk out to the waterside before we retire for the evening?"

She nodded, and the three stopped once they reached the shoreline. "Tell me about the rest of your visit with Dante."

Her eyes fixated on the water as an answer slowly emerged. "Alika, I told him I couldn't give him my true name, so I let him choose a name."

"I can't imagine Dante chose a terrible name, my child."

"He chose ... Angelina."

"It's a beautiful name. I don't see the problem." He continued and glanced at Alena, who shrugged her shoulders too.

"It's the reason he chose it." The girl's reply came out almost a whisper.

He had a guess, but he waited for her confirmation.

"I remind him of an angel." She lowered her head.

"I long believed young Dante always possessed the way with words if ever inspired enough, and I assume tonight he found inspiration plenty to state it so the best poet was put to shame."

"Yes, he did." She turned from them. "I am no," her voice broke, "angel."

He didn't need to see her face. Tears fell followed by her futile attempts to wipe her face with her hands as she tried unsuccessfully to stop more sobs from escaping. Alika's soothing words came through like the undisturbed water before them. "Perhaps not quite an angel, my child. They're seldom seen." The girl turned to him, her eyes still streaming with tears as he placed his hands on her shoulders. "But you must stop seeing yourself through this blurred vision because it's not true at all. Young Dante sees an angel. Give him his angel. His vision is clear in this case, my child."

"No, you're the angel, Alika. You proved my guardian angel many times."

"I've done poorly in that role at times." His mind regressed to her rooftop fall and when he thought her and Alena dead on the other side of the portal.

She hugged him. "I won't change my mind, Alika. Since we can't agree on the two of us, we can both agree on Alena." She smiled over at Alena. "You keep me out of trouble many times."

"Now, don't get me mixed up in this discussion."

She went to Alena and hugged her too. The same lostness returned to her eyes, as she focused on the blue expanse ahead and wiped her face again. "We should get to work now. I wasted enough of our time tonight." Determined to move forward with something she considered productive, she marched back to the house.

Alika and Alena glanced at each other, shaking their heads and followed her.

The three worked until their weariness won. The girl rose from the table and stretched but realized the other two remained rooted to their seats. "Is there more?"

"No, all done. Alena and I are right behind you."

"If you say so. Goodnight, you two."

Alika watched her go into her room and turned back to Alena. "Once we touch down tomorrow, I'll signal you. I didn't wish her to cut her visit short with Dante tonight. With everything they went through together at the Elders Hall, they needed the time this evening."

"I know, but to Dante's credit he tried hard. We know he's always persistent. You saw her at the water."

"Yes, I did." he sighed. "We'll be with them starting tomorrow, but it's business too. I need to impart a lesson to her before we leave. I thought about this evening but decided against doing so. Her spirit wouldn't receive it well in its current state. Hopefully my message finds its mark when I pursue it in the morning. I wonder if she isn't trained too well that she forgets ... She worries me though we strive to comfort her."

"She pours forth comfort to others but cannot find it for herself. Alika, it isn't right." She turned to him, her eyes moist.

He patted her shoulder. "I know. This shadow which darkens her vision, perhaps Dante is the one to help her past it. The Ancient One brought them together. Already this connection protected Dante's spirit from the darkness and delivered peace to Ethan's spirit." They got up and headed to their separate rooms for the evening.

...

The Black Dragon squadron leader surveyed the bustle of activity surrounding him and rechecked a few items of data before nodding his approval. He forced the troop beside him to wait another minute, simply because he could. "You may go now. I'll supply the update he wants."

He sat on the Black Dragon command ship listening to the update provided by the squadron leader. Events continued unfolding as he expected, once the Freedom Fighters made the horrifying discovery on the three planets, after no communication from them. Well, at least the group thought they uncovered what happened. Today's update continued, showing the Freedom Fighters' vain efforts to move past their shock and respond to the devastation. It was the predicted course of action by the group. By now they had also inspected the item they worked so hard to transport back. He imagined their reaction as their hopes evaporated before their eyes, and he smiled. The path ahead of them only worsened.

CHAPTER TWO

The next morning, Dante rolled over to see the display read a little after seven. "You told me to sleep in, Angelina, but I can't. All I can think about is seeing you again." Too excited to stay in bed another instant, he jumped out of bed, showered, and dressed in record time. He arrived first in the main meeting room downstairs and sat at the table, lost in his own thoughts of the previous evening. Ryan appeared next some time later.

"What are you doing here this early?" asked Ryan.

"I know you've got all your commander duties to get back to at home, but you'll change your plans and stay."

"Easily done since this is my second home these days. Why are you hyped up this morning?" Ryan normally saw Dante cheerful. Actually, they regularly exchanged wisecracks, but the last few days Ryan watched one of his best friends weather his toughest days. The grin now on Dante's face told a different story, and his eyes shone with an added spark.

Dante didn't get to answer, because the others walked in the room that instant.

"Dante beat us down here? What's the occasion?" Caleb teased.

Ryan sat with Dante. "Still trying to get the story out of him, but whatever it is, I'm staying here today according to him."

Caleb said, "We're all sitting now, Dante. Out with it."

"I had a wonderful visitor last night when I returned to my quarters. Honestly, I don't know how I slept."

Ryan's eyes widened. "Like the image of her, as in the Elders Hall?"

"No."

"Oh, that explains it. Nice." Ryan smiled.

"She and the others are coming back today."

"She told you when to expect them?" Caleb raised his eyebrows.

"I persisted enough that she made an exception for me."

"Sounds like it, Dante." Seth smiled to see his student back to his usual self.

"Dante, she came and ..." Caleb pressed.

"Caleb." Lana shook her head at her husband.

"Sweetheart, it's Dante. Your cousin. The perfect gentleman. He probably finally kissed her a few times. After the whole near-death experiences and everything else they went through together it's about time..." Caleb glanced over at Dante and read his face, "or maybe not. Not one kiss squeezed in, Dante? Really?" Caleb shrugged his shoulders. "How long did she stay?"

"About an hour."

"I guess you two did have a lot of ground to cover. Who is she, Dante? We all want to know."

"The conversation got interesting." He proceeded to hit the high points with them.

"Still can't tell us, and she let you pick a name." Caleb rubbed his chin, as he slipped into commander mode, as if trying to make sense of a puzzling military formation in front of him.

"And whatever you said left her stumbling over her words. Smooth, cousin."

"I didn't intend to, Lana. The words just escaped when I saw her."

"I'm teasing you. It's actually sweet."

"But we won't tell Angelina you told us that part, Dante. Normally, her grasp of words is exceptional." Ryan laughed.

"Yes, Dante, you have a way with words, when it comes to her."

"I guess so, Seth." The remark from Alika made sense now.

"Sounds like they planned everything out for when they get here. They possess an intense work ethic," said Caleb.

"Yeah, I'm sure they still worked on their other operations when they left here. Her comrade went through information on the ship, and Alika did the same at their home base."

"Didn't get to meet her comrade, huh?" asked Seth.

"No, she asked Angelina if she was ready to go, but no introductions last night."

"We'll get our chance today to meet the whole gang. I can hear how she manages to keep Angelina out of trouble. Give me pointers to help with you, right, Dante?" Ryan grinned.

"I forgot. You two enjoy comparing notes."

"When do they arrive?" asked Lana.

"She indicated mid-morning at the earliest or around lunchtime. I expect a lengthy visit with everything they want to share with us."

"Ready?" asked Alena.

"Another minute," said the girl, as she emerged, showered and dressed. She managed as usual stunning, as Dante said, with little effort. She settled in a chair to put on her shoes.

Once she finished, Alika said, "Not so fast. One last thing before we leave. This will take considerable time to do everything we need to accomplish."

"Of course, Alika,"

"You understand the chaos of the galaxy won't disappear with our visit."

"Yes, Alika." She chuckled.

"You needed a reminder. The battlefields at the Elders Hall you encountered, how did you defeat them, my child?"

"With great difficulty." He still waited, so he sought a better answer. "Through grief, with truth, by the connection with Dante and Ethan which the Ancient One allowed."

"Yes. Neither involved a sunspear or a planned operation. I don't know what the future holds, but this connection and relationship growing with Dante is in motion by the Ancient One. Do not treat this bond with Dante carelessly. I know you would not intent to do so, but you must give him time. Put my words in practice for this visit and future ones."

“You made your point, Alika. A needed lesson to start my day.” She smiled.

“I say we’re ready to go now. Angelina, I believe it is?” He smiled back at her.

“Yes, I’ll answer to that name for the next few days.” Time to accept it. She did allow him to choose.

Dante’s data pad flashed with a communication, and he scrambled to answer it.

“Dante, two ships approach and those on-board request clearance to land with your permission. They won’t identify themselves and want no escort to land.”

He bolted from his seat. “Clear them to land wherever they wish, and tell them I’m headed for the hangar to meet them.”

“Yes, sir,” responded the communication center troop.

After realizing he already cleared the distance to the door, he sheepishly glanced back at the others.

“Go Dante. Take your time. See you back with them, whenever.” Caleb laughed.

“Those two will be entertaining to watch. He almost fell from his chair answering the call.” Ryan laughed too, as Dante disappeared.

“Where are you going?” asked Angelina as Alena walked to the back exit of the ship.

“Over to Alika’s ship. He asked me to come for something.” She continued towards the door.

“Does he need me too?”

“Nope. Let us know when you’re ready to see the others, and we’ll join you.”

“Wait, you’re leaving me alone with Dante?”

“Yes, same as last night. You’ll be fine.”

“I couldn’t manage complete sentences at points.” Her voice rose.

“And he probably found it amusing, he left you in such a state.” Alena giggled.

"Alena!"

"I'm going now." Her giggles continued, as she shut the door.

The girl stared at the back door and shook her head. "They planned this last night at the table. Sneaky. Both of them."

The computer's beep interrupted her ramblings, as it announced, "identity verified," and the ship door opened.

"Angelina?"

"I'm here, Dante." She walked back to the front of the ship.

He strolled into the ship and immediately approached her, as he took in the beauty of her appearance anew. She came dressed casually as last night. Today she wore a loose-fitting, ankle-length patterned skirt, yet it still showed off her stunning slender, curvy form perfectly. A silken light blue blouse complemented it and captured her piercing blue eyes, which he found himself wonderfully lost in each time he saw her. Then he focused on her radiant smile, the one causing his heart to go into overdrive. Her soft long light brown hair fell in cascading waves around her. Managing to take his eyes off her briefly, he searched the room. Then he smiled back at her. He smelled the sweet fragrance she wore again too, and he drew closer to her. "Is it just you?"

He's so close now I could ... She smelled an aftershave or cologne he wore or maybe just whatever he showered with at this point. It was something she noticed last night too. He smelled amazing as she breathed it in. He wore everyday clothes as last night, but with his good looks it didn't matter what he wore. He fit nicely into a pair of charcoal-colored pants and a comfortable red short sleeved shirt. The shirt couldn't hide his well-built chest and his broad shoulders laying beneath it, from years of training as a sunspear-bearer. Necessary training, translating into his salvation many times. As she looked up at him, she admired his sandy brown hair and resisted the urge to run her hands through it. His face drew her with the most incredible smile spread across it at the moment for her, and she appreciated again how utterly handsome he was. Then those soft brown eyes stared at her with an intensity, like he sometimes did, like now. How did she concentrate? She blinked, trying to focus. She realized he asked something. He managed to do it again to her with a mere word. If the whole visit went like this, she was sunk. What did he ask? She attempted to remember. Oh yeah. "No ... I mean yes ... Alena came here with me ... I mean on the ship ... here ... but she's gone ... now." What just happened? Knowing the question had provided her no help.

"Gone?" His eyes twinkled in amusement at her struggle.

"Um ... Not gone ... like gone ... I mean Alika ... he needed something ... she left ... she is here ... but I mean ... not here."

"You mean, at Alika's ship now?" Dante barely held his laughter.

"What you said." She finally gave up getting a complete thought spoken. A toddler could spring together something more intelligent at the moment.

"Just the two of us here." He continued gazing in her eyes.

She simply nodded. Words proved useless. His eyes held her captive, pulling her towards him further. She needed no vision to tell her what came next, but waited. He stood right there, and the space between them almost nonexistent.

Immediately, he closed the remaining gap between them. "Angelina, I wished to give you something last night before you left." As he slowly wrapped one arm around her waist, and his other hand cradled the side of her face and neck, he whispered, "I wanted to since the first time I saw you." His lips met hers tentatively for the first moment like one asking for sure, but knowing full well he need not wonder. The answer became sweetly confirmed as one of her arms curled around his waist, the other arm wound around his neck, and everything about her moved towards him. All the tentativeness instantly dissipated, as he pulled her against him, kissing her as he always dreamed of doing since the first stunning view of her. He continued savoring every second of the kiss, unwilling to let it end, as he sought and found her lips yet again. He waited so long to kiss her this first time, and now nothing compared to her being in his arms like this. She melted up against him, surrendering completely to him, lost in the sweetness of the kiss. Then his body pulsed with the delightful sensations created, with her hand running through his hair and caressing the back of his neck, as she kissed him back. When their lips finally parted, he murmured, "My Angelina, I can't believe how long you made me wait for that kiss, but that was incredible." Stroking the side of her face, he stared into her eyes and smiled at her.

She stared back up at him and returned his smile, left breathless by his kiss and her heart pounding furiously. Could he hear it? He must be able to. She thought his words left her stumbling, but his kiss ... and she couldn't wait for the next one. Nothing she imagined prepared her for the wonder, the pure thrill of her first kiss with him.

He whispered in her ear, "I won't wait long for the next kiss, my Angelina."

She whispered back, "I hope not, my Dante." Leaning up against him happily, she wound her arms around his neck. He smiled as he wrapped both of his arms around her waist. They stood there, enjoying being in each other's arms, neither caring about the time passing.

"Dante, how about we sit now?"

"As you wish, Angelina." They headed to the couch and Dante sat down. She started to sit too, but then asked, "What do you want to drink, Dante?"

"Surprise me. Whatever you bring, I'm happy," he said as his eyes traced her graceful steps.

"Easy to please today, Dante." She laughed as she brought their drinks and sat beside him.

"There's no reason for me to be otherwise. The day is starting out most pleasant thanks to you." He grinned as she handed him the drink, and he took a sip. "This is excellent."

"You'd say so no matter what I gave you."

"I won't deny that, after finally tasting your sweet lips." Caressing the side of her face, she rewarded him with a smile and a slight blush of her cheeks. "But I'm not exaggerating about the drink. It's familiar somehow." Strangely, he remained unable to place it.

"Simply a fruit tea. The raspberry is strongest in it. I always enjoyed it and guessed you might since you drank tea last night."

"Even in the smallest details. You prepared nicely to see me on the ship today." He patted the couch.

"We built it this way, to adapt to a variety of situations. Alena and I spend a fair amount of time on this ship, and substantial hours checking through information while conversing with Alika. Other times, it's all three of us, like the first visit to you, and comfort does become a real consideration. These couches are surprisingly cushy, despite the lightweight micro ball substance used inside of them. For the operations, plenty of open area is the aim. This is easily hidden with a few swipes of a button and sucked up into the floor by all appearances, but you probably already guessed."

"You must have a serious cargo hold."

"You can't imagine, Dante."

"I'm sure I can. My imagination managed well today." He smiled as she caught his double meaning. Although tempted to have further fun with it, he elected changing the subject. "Did you and ... Alena get everything done with Alika last night?" Her expression confirmed he remembered Alena's name correctly.

"Yes."

"Are you sure?" He pressed as a strange expression crossed her face.

"I am, but I received a gentle reprimand or lesson this morning from Alika after last night."

"I delayed you as you said. I should not have."

"Dante, no. He agreed with you and wanted me to stay longer, as you wished."

Dante took her hand. "Another reason to like Alika."

"He's right, Dante. I see the threats, and my first answer is another operation or sunspear battle wins it. Alika reminded me, not every battle is won that way. We didn't conquer the battle at the Elders Hall with any of those things, and if I lost that battle, I lost you." The image of a broken Dante crumbling to his knees filled her vision, but she continued as she met his eyes. "I couldn't let that happen. And your father would still find the arms of the Ancient One, but not with the tranquil spirit we witnessed. In turn, your heart would be in turmoil at his parting. I get wrapped up in the other, so I end up neglecting things, in this case a certain individual." She stroked his clasped hand.

"I'll make sure you find time for me, to ensure I'm not neglected. No worries. Caleb tells me he goes through the same thing with Lana."

"Then I'm in good company. I do like your cousin, though I've yet to meet her. Caleb is an amazing husband to her, and they're even better together."

"I agree they are. As for us, we'll work it out together, as everything else. We're amazing together too." He kissed her forehead and squeezed her clasped hand. "When I said last night I collected some questions for you, I really do have a few."

"I'm about to sound like Alika. I'll give you an answer to any question you ask, Dante."

"Even if it's you can't tell me."

"Precisely. Ask away."

"Well, when can you tell me who you are?"

"I don't know. The Ancient One will prompt me, if and when I can disclose it."

"Why must it be a, secret, Angelina?"

"My life would be in danger and anyone close to me, if it were revealed."

He thought she exaggerated, but her eyes confirmed her statement. "You're someone important ... I meant, powerful, your family somehow." He couldn't figure out how he didn't recognize her.

She hesitated, taking her time with her answer. "I wouldn't say that, Dante. Those words get thrown around often, but I'm not sure how much meaning they hold. I simply need to stay in the background."

"Is your family still living?"

"I consider Alena and Alika my family now."

"Your parents are both dead?"

"Yes, they are both gone."

"Were they killed by the Dark Lord, in one of the colony massacres?"

Again she spent a moment formulating her answer. "I don't know of any family the Dark Lord didn't touch in some way, Dante. My family was no different."

"I'm not sure what to do with your answer."

"I gave you the best answer I can. Some individuals are innocent of the havoc caused, like your family and Lana and Caleb." Her thoughts drifted to her mother. "With others, the same can't ..." She trailed off as the image of her father appeared. "Like I said, both of my parents are gone."

The usual gentleness left her eyes, and a coldness replaced them. The dramatic shift signaled to move to another subject. "When did you start training with Alika and Alena?"

"Around ten."

"Your parents were gone then?"

"No."

Dante recalled Seth indicated she trained in secret. "I thought only Alika and Alena knew about your training."

"They're the only ones remaining who did."

"Your parents commissioned your training?"

Dante watched her fidget with the edge of her shirt as she finally said, "They were not in agreement with it."

"Why? Both of them or just one of them?"

"I can't tell you."

"I feel like I interrogated you. I'm sorry, Angelina." He wrapped his arms around her.

She leaned up against him. "You didn't set out to do so, Dante. I wish I gave you more helpful answers."

He continued enjoying her cuddled up next to him. "I want to keep you safe when we're together, so I'm starting to see how to make that happen."

"If we're in a group, I can fabricate a story, and we're fine, as long as you treat me like another person in your group. Whereas when it's only you and I ..."

"We really must be alone." He grinned down at her. "I can accommodate to those arrangements, and I like them more every minute I've got you like this. This evening, I'm asking for your time. What's your answer?"

"Of course, Dante, if I'm to stay out of trouble with Alika." Her eyes twinkled.

"That's the only reason, huh? Well, you need another lecture from your teacher or how about I supply something better?" He pulled her in to enjoy another long, gentle kiss with her. "Oh, yeah, this works out nice," he murmured when their lips parted.

"Better reason found. You didn't wait long for the next kiss," she said breathlessly.

"I disagree. I showed an enormous amount of patience, considering how long I waited to meet you, my beautiful Angelina." He ran a hand through her hair as he studied her face.

"Really?"

"You told me not to wait long either, so you encouraged me."

"Now I'm to blame, Dante."

"No, because I'm wouldn't pass up the chance for another kiss, but you seem content with it. I'm willing to give you a do-over if not. As many as it takes." His finger slowly traced a line on her lip.

"We both know, I'm more than content with everything you're doing, Dante. No complaints will come from these lips."

"Good, because I love seeing you smiling and happy, my Angelina." Despite the teasing back and forth, he meant those words. They came through so much in recent days and almost lost each other in mere seconds. To go from a place of such fear to a place so completely different defied description. He finally got to meet his young spear-bearer and held her in his arms. Nothing could take her from him. She was everything he imagined and more. The Black Dragon threat continued, and stopping them from unleashing again on the colonies remained a monumental task. Yet the happiness with Angelina is as much reality, and whatever battlefield lay ahead, they would defeat it together. They had proven they could. "I admit, I enjoy making that smile come on your face." He kissed her forehead. "I realize we need to speak with the others now. After all, I'm assured of your time this evening."

"Yes, I'm all yours this evening. I'll let Alika know we're ready."

Angelina put the hooded cloak back on, and she and Dante left the ship hand in hand.

CHAPTER THREE

"Excellent seeing you again, young Dante." Alika hugged Dante.

"Always, you as well, Alika," he said, hugging Alika back.

"You must be Alena. Angelina treasures you as her sister. I'm relieved to see you both back safe after your close calls lately."

"Same to you, Dante. You gave us a few scares too." She grinned. "Finally, you and Angelina got to meet, before the two of you went insane."

Dante laughed. "That danger is over. I discovered ways to make her smile, in the short time with her."

"None of us doubted you." Alika patted Dante on the shoulder.

"I expect not, but, Alika, isn't part of an Elder's duties preparing their students? In truth, you and Seth did little to prepare me for my young spear-bearer. I almost fell over in the Elders Hall because you both withheld a key description about your student." His eyes danced.

"Did I? Well, you never asked for a description of my student, Dante." Alika winked.

"Come on, I expected a guy the whole time." He shook his head still grinning.

"Yes, I recall Seth mentioning confusion on your part, something about expecting more of a brother. You're disappointed? You would rather ..."

Dante laughed at Alika's teasing. "No, not at all. She is ..." He turned to Angelina. "You are incredible. I still can't believe ..." He kissed her on the cheek and turned back to Alika. "Curious, if I had asked, would you've told me?"

"I always gave you an answer to every question you asked." He chuckled. "But no, Dante, I would have left that question unanswered. This proved far more entertaining to watch."

"I thought all the secrecy is the Ancient One's direction. There's more than meets the eye with you, Alika."

"Mostly it's the Ancient One, Dante. However, if you knew that piece about your young spear-bearer, your tasks would be more difficult to accomplish. I witnessed firsthand even the most work-driven individual finds it a challenge focusing, if presented with enough of a distraction. Spear-bearers aren't immune to it." Casting a knowing glance at Angelina, he grinned back at Dante.

Dante leaned over to Angelina. "I'll take that as quite the compliment, Angelina."

"You should. No one affects me as you do. You are exceptional."

Angelina and Dante turned back around and Alena teased, "Angelina, your meeting Dante is as pleasant, as I told you it would go. One of our many lively discussions."

"Many lively discussions, huh? What else did you two talk about, Angelina?"

"Another time, Dante. Let's go meet with the others." Pulling Dante along, she shot a glance at a laughing Alena and said to her, "Stop, Alena. He needs no encouragement."

Alena made a motion with her hands, as though clueless about Angelina's meaning.

"How many of those discussions involved me?" Dante teased as they continued walking, and he saw Angelina unsuccessfully attempt to hide a smile.

"Alena, see what you did?" Angelina tried sounding stern, but she gave up when Alika joined the laughter. "Dante, most discussions involved you. Whether they started with you or not, they somehow ended up coming to you. Courtesy of Alena's handiwork."

"Keep telling yourself that, Angelina." Alena stammered out between laughs.

"I bet I can help, Angelina."

Although Angelina enjoyed the teasing, she determined to wrap this conversation up before they reached Lana's group. She slowed down to a stop right before the hall entrance. Alena and Alika understood and gave her space with Dante.

She ran her hand over the side of his face, as he wrapped his arm around her waist. "Dante, you became a topic of discussion since the first time you entered my visions. Some lively discussion like this and some," she paused, "more subdued discussions. You are never far from my thoughts, and I counted down the time to finally see you. This evening we can discuss it further and," she leaned closer to him, "I'll show you more, about how happy I am to finally be here with you." She kissed him on the cheek. "How does that sound?"

"Perfect. We'll table it until tonight." He engulfed her in a hug and brushed his lips with hers. "Ready to meet everyone?"

"Of course. We feel we already know them."

Dante emerged into the main hall holding Angelina's hand, followed by Alika and Alena. The two women loosened and removed their cloaks, as Dante laid the garments aside for them.

"Everyone, meet Angelina and Alena, and you remember Alika from the last visit."

The group smiled at the two. They understood now, why Dante remained speechless by the girl the first time at the Elders Hall. She was indeed breathtaking. The other student claimed her own beauty too with her slender figure, shoulder-length blond hair, and gentle brown eyes.

"My visions give us an advantage on introductions." Angelina turned to Seth. "Wonderful to see you again, Seth. As much as I enjoyed fighting at your side, I'm glad we're not doing that again today. I'm relieved all the preparations came together, and Dante returned to us safely. Thank you."

"We're all grateful, but several of us played a part. It's good to see both of you again, and you as well, Alika."

Angelina nodded and turned to Ryan. "Ryan, it's a pleasure to finally meet you. Your planet provided refuge for us, and you keep Dante out of trouble many times as Alena does me."

Ryan stepped forward. “I’m glad to finally meet you too, Angelina. We wondered how long of a wait to expect. You know, how long Dante would keep you to himself today.” He grinned, and his comment earned chuckles from the rest of the group. Then his eyes focused on Alena yet again because his eyes kept drifting back to her since she entered the room. For the first time in a while, he felt nervous, but he forced it back. “Alena, I hear your other full-time mission is making sure Angelina steers clear of too much trouble. She should be grateful to you.”

“She is, Ryan. Ensuring Dante doesn’t get in over his head and juggling your commander duties probably leave you exhausted. My compliments to you. Your fleet is the easier task to manage.” Alena laughed.

Ryan laughed too. “You’re right. The two of them present a formidable challenge.” He reached over and clasped her hand in greeting. “It’s my pleasure to finally meet you, Alena.”

“I’m glad I finally get to meet you as well, Ryan.” She smiled back at him and realized she still held his hand. Her hand slid from his, and she saw him smile again at her.

“Caleb and Lana, I know both of you well, through Dante’s eyes,” said Angelina.

“She shares, so we are eager to finally meet you two,” said Alena, turning her attention to them.

Lana smiled. “We’re fond of both of you too. I’m also relieved we’re seeing you like this, rather than scared something happened to one of you. This is a much better way to start things off.” She focused on Angelina. “My cousin is beyond happy anytime he talks about you.”

Caleb laughed. “Yes, I don’t think anything takes the smile off his face, now that you’re here.”

“I don’t mind taking credit for that one.” Her eyes twinkled, as she glanced up at Dante. He slid his arm around her waist, as he kissed her on the forehead.

They sat down on the couches and chairs around the table. Lana and Caleb sat down together, followed by Dante and Angelina, and finally Ryan and Alena. Alika and Seth sat in chairs pulled up beside each other.

Lana turned to Alika. “We’ll let your group lead.”

Alika nodded to Angelina and Alena. Alena spoke, “Go ahead, Angelina. I’ll input as I wish.”

“All right, I will,” said Angelina, her voice all business. “We want a closer examination of the retrieved item. We also are aware of the tragic events which unfolded on the three colonies.” She paused to regain her composure, and Dante gave her shoulder a comforting touch. “However, we need more specific information, which will involve a difficult trip to the colony.” Her eyes translated a silent apology to Lana. “There is also another piece to this, involving another painful trip.” This time she turned to Dante. “This one will be hard for you, but we must go there again. I’m sorry, Dante.”

His eyes showed he understood. “Angelina, we’ll manage. We already defeated that battlefield together. It can no longer hurt us.”

“I hear at least two side trips. How long do you expect to be here?” asked Seth.

“At least three full days. That could change depending on the findings.” Angelina peeked over at Alena.

“It’s on the rushed side, but we’re hoping enough to obtain the answers we need,” Alena said.

“What’s first?” asked Lana as the familiar, get to work mode kicked into gear.

Caleb and Dante exchanged a glance. Angelina started to answer, but Caleb interrupted, “Lunch first, work afterwards.”

Angelina answered, “Lana, your husband is right. I’m told some of us must be reminded of when to take breaks.”

“I’ll bring you around to my thinking yet,” Dante teased.

The group continued the light-hearted banter over lunch with no work allowed.

“I thought I dreamed when I saw Dante down here first.” Ryan laughed.

“Angelina, didn’t you tell Dante?” asked Alena.

“I told him to sleep in, I promise.”

“I tried, but I couldn’t get back to sleep this morning.”

“Then you can’t blame it on Angelina, cuz.”

“From what I see, you came out fine, Dante,” teased Caleb.

“Oh, I’m thrilled about how the day is working out so far for me.” He winked at Angelina.

Alika and Seth shared a smile at the group’s exchange.

“Now that we ate, we need to examine the item retrieved from Black Dragon,” Angelina said. A collective cloud of dismay filled the room. Her voice softened. “We’re all disappointed. Actually, that doesn’t come close to conveying how the discovery left everyone, but none of us knew.” She looked at Alena and Alika.

“She’s right,” Alena said. “Caleb and Ryan, you and the other commanders and your squadrons risked your lives to obtain it. We’re grateful you both came back safely. We all assumed one thing about the item, and everything pointed to that being right.”

Alika nodded. “We move on. You can’t let your discouragement immobilize you. We don’t know what lies ahead.”

“But it must be stopped.” Lana got up. “The building isn’t far. We’ll clear the room of personnel.”

They all got up as Dante helped Angelina with her cloak, and Ryan did the same for Alena. It would become the necessary routine anytime they went from one building to the other. The group headed for the containment room where they kept the item.

CHAPTER FOUR

They entered the massive room, and there towered the item. An item which kindled such happiness at its initial capture quickly invoked only utter despair. A symbol of victory transformed into one of defeat in a blink of eye, and a reminder of the spilled blood of many colonists over three planets. Angelina and Alena exchanged a look, as they caught the expression from Ryan and Caleb. They attempted before to console the two men, but they concluded their words didn't help in the least.

"There's where you cut into it?" asked Angelina as she spotted the small incision in the bottom of the cylinder-shaped item as she and Alena circled around it.

"Yes," answered Ryan as he came to Alena's side. "Once we realized it contained nothing, we cut the top off too and removed it. It appeared it should slide open in some way, but we couldn't find it."

"Strange. There had to be a way to get into it and control it," said Alena as she traced her hand on the outside of the metal.

"A button, panel or something." Angelina did the same, equally puzzled. "Perhaps it held a connection to stop or track the device if it controlled this too."

"Does it appear the same?" asked Dante as he stood behind her watching.

"We concentrated on blending in while in the facility and inspecting it, but it does match."

The two came full circle. "Nothing, huh?" asked Angelina, as Alena shook her head.

"I don't buy it either," said Alena. They refused to believe the item was nothing more than a storage case or launching device.

Angelina spotted a platform situated next to the cylinder-shaped object. "I want to see the top of this thing. The platform moves or lifts I'm guessing?"

"Yeah," said Dante exchanging a glance with Ryan. Ryan's eyes said, "*Good luck, she's all yours, remember?"* When he turned back, Dante found her already headed for the platform. He hurried to catch up to her with Alena and Ryan close behind them.

Caleb nudged Alika. "What's she doing?"

"We'll see, but there's three people with her so hopefully that's enough." Alika shook his head. Lana and Seth looked apprehensively at each other at the comment.

The platform reached the top with the four of them on it, and Angelina peered down into the cylinder. Had the top been open? They never got that view of it while in the facility, but the top must open somehow for the device to clear or launch from this structure. Bending over the platform railing a bit, she struggled to check for more detail inside, but she needed more light. "Any of you bring a light to shine on the inside of this thing?" Ryan handed her one, but she found she needed more to see the extent she desired. "A skirt is turning out to be a poor choice for today." She glimpsed a stretchable cord with a harness type device nearby. A voice reminded her of the similarities between the cord before her and the one from the rooftop and the resulting incident. It momentarily halted her. She became angrier with herself and forced the rooftop incident out of her mind. "*What's wrong with you? This is different. Stop being silly. There's no time for this,*" she said to herself. Her thorough mental scolding successfully quieted the voice urging her otherwise. She rapidly started attaching the harness device around her waist as Dante watched her bewildered. Then she crossed over the platform to the other side of the railing, and his eyes lit up with understanding, along with the others watching. Alika started to say something from the floor, but Dante beat him to it.

"No, absolutely not. This isn't safe."

"I'll be fine. I need to see inside."

"There's another way if you wish to this badly. I'll not watch you fall to your death. No eagle will save you this time."

"Oh, Dante, come now."

"Come back across the railing this instant, or I'll physically lift you back, Angelina."

Everyone watched. A battle of wills commenced, but one Dante determined to win.

"You wouldn't."

"I will. Don't test it."

Immediately she felt it. Her skirt and shirt were both made of a slippery, silky like fabric. The whole harness rapidly slipped completely from her waist, sliding further up until it would no longer be wrapped around her. She thought her hand could still reach the railing, but she grabbed in vain and found only air. A familiar, unpleasant memory came, with an unwelcome dizzying sensation accompanying the rising panic overtaking her. She understood too late. Dante tried to tell her, but she pushed too far this time. The horrible sensation stopped. *This must be the agonizing moment, the one right before I hit the floor,* she thought to herself. She waited for the pain to shatter her body before the darkness claimed her. It never came, because two strong arms caught her and pulled her back to the railing. An instant later her whole body lifted across it, and she found herself facing a frantic Dante. Letting out a breath she didn't realize she held, she looked into his eyes, seeing a myriad of emotions.

"What possessed you, Angelina?" His arm securely encircled her waist while his trembling other hand tipped her chin up, so her eyes remained locked on his. His words tumbled out as he tried to bring his voice under control. "You almost fell. I told you to come back across. Why didn't you listen to me? Do you know how much you scared me? Do you understand what almost happened?"

She knew and realized her foolishness. "I'm sorry, Dante. I didn't mean ..." She understood what she did to him. The look in his eyes, the one still remaining ripped through her.

"Just please don't do that again, Angelina. I can't lose you. Come here," whispered Dante, his manner softening in a second at her tears. He wrapped both arms around her waist and pulled her against him as she encircled her arms around his neck. Relief poured through him that he held her safe in his arms, rather than her being motionless on the bottom of the floor.

Seth turned to Alika. "He found his match in all ways."

"Yes, this continues to unfold in unexpected ways for the two."

Lana stared at Caleb, her eyes wide-eyed. "Did that just happen?"

"Yep. Good thing your cousin got her in time."

Dante looked over at Ryan and Alena, his arms still wound around Angelina. "Let's get back on the ground, please."

"Gladly," said Ryan, taking care of lowering the platform. He touched Alena's arm again, saying something quietly to her. She nodded at him in gratitude for his comfort, still reeling from what almost occurred.

Seth walked with the others as the four stepped off the platform. "Perhaps we leave this for a bit."

Angelina answered, "No, Seth, I'm entirely at fault." She turned to Alika. "Alika, I don't know what came over me. I know what I put you and Alena through again," then she turned to Alena, "and I'm sorry, as usual." She lowered her head.

Alika shook his head. "I'm not sure what to say. You scared yourself sufficiently and worse than anything I can say. The Ancient One rescued you again, this time by young Dante's arms."

"Yes, I'm thankful to Dante's quick actions. We'll fare better, if Alena guides us for a while. I only succeeded in getting us off track."

Alena shrugged. "If you say so. The inside of the cylinder could hold the answer. Maybe hidden controls or something. We stayed floor level in the facility, so we don't know about the top. Of course, we apparently mistook a giant case or launching pad for the device."

Alika said, "We all did. However, from the comment by the Black Dragon soldier you encountered, this contained the device inside. We made a reasonable conclusion based on that, so we can't be hard on ourselves."

Ryan agreed. "He's right. The troops were breathing down your neck, and you barely escaped from your trip there. More examination and you two don't make it out."

Caleb nodded. "Absolutely. Could the way to open and close the top be elsewhere, maybe in the facility somewhere?"

"You guys blew that up if so." Alena smiled and directed most of it at Ryan. He returned it, and she felt better. She gathered his thoughts remained on the close call at the facility. "It's probably controlled somewhere else too, but I'm not ready to let go of a connection being on this item. Perhaps it's all the effort taken to obtain it."

"You can't be blamed for needing to find a connection, and you're not the only one, Alena." Ryan paused. "There must be a fair amount of space between our item and the device for controls on the inside. Still, with the size of it, I can see it."

"I agree. It's worth checking," said Seth.

"Safely, this time?" Dante gave Angelina's shoulder a gentle squeeze. She looked up at him and nodded.

"The light issue is easily remedied by angling the spotlights in the room," said Ryan.

"What about a small speed glider to maneuver inside the cylinder?" volunteered Lana.

Alika nodded. "Should work. Since Angelina is eager for a peek into the cylinder, she can check the inside of it. Although she can't pilot safely too, so. Dante, you'll need to manage that part."

"How about it, Angelina?" Dante asked and she nodded.

"Lana and I will get the speed glider and bring it," said Caleb.

"We'll get the lights situated for you two," said Ryan. He glanced at Angelina and exchanged a troubled look with Dante before leaving the two.

Dante wasted no time. "You're still in your own world. How about letting me in? Obviously, what happened before scared you, but it's done now."

"That's all it is. I'm fine." She feigned a smile.

"You're not good at this with me. We know each other on a whole different level." He put his arms around her waist and faced her.

"I hate what I did to you back there."

"That's it?" asked Dante, searching her eyes.

"Isn't that enough, Dante?"

He studied her face, unconvinced. "In that case, Alika is right. You punished yourself enough. I long to glimpse the smile which radiates to your beautiful blue eyes." He whispered in her ear, "Tell me what I must do to show I'm not unhappy with you, my Angelina. You know I will."

He planted soft kisses on the side of her face as his hand stroked her other cheek. A delightful warmth went through her at his touch. She whispered, "I'm reassured, Dante."

"There's the smile I missed." He smiled, gazing down at her.

"We're ready, but please you two finish up first," Ryan teased.

"We're done, for now anyway." Dante winked at her and turned to Ryan.

"Yeah ... we'll be ... I mean ... we're there." She blushed.

Ryan glanced amusingly at Dante at hearing Angelina stumbling over her words.

Dante took her hand. "Let's get this done."

"I packed an extra light among other items you may need in the glider. The four of us will be on the platform for extra eyes. Seth and Alika will remain on the floor to make any needed adjustments with the lighting or anything else," explained Ryan.

"Sounds covered." Dante climbed on the speed glider with Angelina sliding behind and wrapping her arms around his waist as the glider lifted off the ground and into the cylinder. "I'll adjust this now since we're in." He wanted to still steer, but the glider could handle the propulsion work now. They wouldn't do any speeding in these tight quarters. He slowly turned his body around to face the side like Angelina. One hand stayed on the front of the glider, and his other arm wrapped firmly around her waist. "Is that close enough?"

Her eyes twinkled at his comment.

He laughed. "I meant, is the glider close enough to the side of the cylinder, for you to see?"

"It is, Dante. You're a fantastic pilot." She laughed too.

The two worked together well, chatting easily as they moved along. He quickly figured out when to move the speed glider to the next area without Angelina's prompting. Originally, when she bent over to examine a part of the cylinder, his fear mounted that she leaned too far, but he realized it unfounded. She paid close attention to her positioning even as she inspected the cylinder. Also, his arm firmly encircled her waist, and he wouldn't let loose after earlier. After about an hour, she sighed as she laid her head on his shoulder. "Angelina, are you okay?"

"Tired, but your shoulder is comfortable."

"It's yours anytime, along with the rest of me." He kissed her forehead.

"Don't I know." She snuggled closer to him.

"Should we go back up and take a break?"

"Nope, give me a minute. Actually, how about we go to the bottom and check it? We can get off the glider and stretch. We need something to mark where we stopped." A rummage in the storage container of the speed glider unearthed a batch of flaggers. She tore one off and stuck it to the side of the cylinder. "Ryan is always prepared."

Ryan and the others heard the conversation from their perch.

"Back to their normal spirits." Alena laughed.

"The close quarters suits them." Ryan chuckled.

"Your cousin may stay down there with Angelina," Caleb teased Lana.

"We'll know if there's anything found on this thing, and they can enjoy each other's company in the meantime. I say it's a fair trade." Lana grinned.

The two reached the bottom of the cylinder, and she stretched for a minute, after dismounting the vehicle. "Better?" he asked as he squeezed her shoulder.

"Definitely." She smiled at him. She stooped and examined the bottom of the cylinder with the light and her hand. After making the full circle, she got up and shook her head. "I'm losing hope of finding anything, if we didn't by now, but it doesn't make sense."

"A puzzle you can't solve, and it's driving you crazy." He took her hand and his other hand lifted her chin. "This isn't yours alone to solve."

"I forgot." She squeezed his hand.

"I'll keep reminding you." Back on the glider, they resumed their inspection of the cylinder. Almost an hour later the two emerged from it. The others walked over to them as Angelina's eyes drifted back to the cylinder. Dante caught the strange look in her eyes. "You all right?"

"Yeah, I'm fine," said Angelina as her attention remained fixed on the cylinder.

He watched her. *Maybe it's because we didn't find anything. No, there's something else. I knew it. Well, she's about to tell me.*

Alika watched Angelina too, but he also read Dante's expression.

Dante shook his head. "I'm clueless where else to search if it's there."

Ryan nodded. "Time to go back to the main area and take a breather, especially you two. Seeing the inside of a cylinder for that long can't be healthy for anybody."

"It beat me," Angelina murmured under her breath, but Dante heard her.

The others started towards the fortress. Dante purposely moved slowly, so he and Angelina ended up trailing behind the group. He peered at Alika, who indicated his understanding. The rest of the group went into the fortress. Angelina began following suit, but Dante held her back. "Let's stay out for a minute."

"Dante, the others will wonder where we are."

"No, they won't. Alika will tell them."

"Why are we out here?"

"Because we need to finish this. What's going on? You can't hide from me. Something about what happened in that room still bothers you."

"I'm disappointed we didn't find anything."

"No, there's something else. It involves the near fall."

"I scared you, Dante."

His arms wrapped around her waist, and he gently pulled her over to face him. "Please no more of this. I heard excuses, but not the truth. I can do this all day and night with you if need be. We settle this now, Angelina."

She looked up at him. His eyes searched hers. He would wait. "Would you believe me if I told you I didn't know myself? Or at least I'm not sure how to put it into words."

"Yes, I would, Angelina. I asked you after it happened what possessed you, but I was upset. I'm thinking a lot ran through your head on the platform, before everything went into motion. Go through it with me this time, please?"

"I'll try." She closed her eyes for a moment and stood on the platform. The voice in her head warned her the scene resembled the rooftop again. She replayed herself striking back angrily. Fear from the rooftop incident initially halted her, but she refused to let it stop her. Yet today she needed to heed that voice on top of the cylinder. The pieces came together as she finished. She moaned, "Oh no, Dante."

"No, this is good. It makes sense now."

"But I don't have the answer."

"Yes, we do. The hard part is done. The answer is here, and two people come to mind to help us uncover it."

"It is their area of expertise." She stared into his eyes. "How did you do that?"

"Do what?"

"Whatever you did to me? Understood me when I didn't myself?"

"I've known you for a while, remember? I know your spirit, your heart, my young spear-bearer. Were those not your words in the Elders Hall?" whispered Dante. He fingered a lock of her hair. It was soft, like everything else about her he touched. Losing himself in her beautiful blue eyes again, he glimpsed the same gentleness there he loved about her.

"Yes, Dante. You do know me," whispered Angelina, unable to leave the trance of his soft brown eyes. He didn't know her name, but that didn't matter. She'd be Angelina forever if it made him happy. The way he did know her, it seemed they had known each other a lifetime. They had shared so much already.

They needed to go in, but neither one moved. Dante leaned in and kissed her. He murmured, "We'll continue this evening." She smiled back at him, and he took her hand. "Come on. Let's join the others, and we'll talk to Seth and Alika before the evening comes."

Alika and Seth noticed first when the two rejoined the group and settled back on the couch. Alika turned to the group. "Angelina imagined an ambitious schedule, but I'm not sure if that remains the case."

"Despite my efforts, we can still make the trip to the Elders Hall today with plenty of time before the shadows begin falling there. We shouldn't be caught there once that happens." She turned to Dante and her voice softened. "It'll be difficult for you, Dante, so I don't want to go if it's too soon. We can wait even until the last day we're here."

"I'll be fine. The trip will be hard for you too. Are you up to tackling the Elders Hall today, after earlier?"

"I'm fine if you will be, Dante."

"What are you hoping to find there now?"

"I don't know, honestly. I'm prompted we need to return." Her voice sounded faraway. "There's something to be learned."

"Then let's go." Dante got up, taking Angelina's hand as she rose as well. The others followed suit.

CHAPTER FIVE

"Excellent," he said, as he listened from the Black Dragon command ship. "Continue consolidating and deploying. I'm pleased with the progress. Keep me updated."

"Yes, sir," answered the Black Dragon squadron leader.

He leaned back in the command chair and surveyed again their handiwork that in such a short time displayed on all three planets. It was incredible work. Despite the Freedom Fighters' frantic efforts, they could do little to help the situation. The planets were essentially in no better shape than a few days ago. The Black Dragon forces leveled most of the planets, but the fate of the colonists was the real gem. He laughed to himself. It struck at the heart of the Freedom Fighters, and they didn't realize the true nature yet. He wondered how long.

He checked the screen again. Nothing from the one yet. He remained wondering, and it irritated him to a degree. He figured out why the first couple of days, but by now her disappearance bordered on something else. How he detested loose ends. She didn't like him, but he preferred it so. The feeling was mutual. Her botched assignments didn't surprise him in the least. He never thought the Dark Lord should let her do as she pleased to a certain extent. Although he understood her greater freedom to do as she wished was of a more personal nature; the Dark Lord kept her on his leash. Well, those days ended with the death of the Dark Lord. He only dealt with her for strictly Black Dragon business, and those rules still applied. Once she turned up, he would reiterate those for her. She'd adjust to the new rules if she wished to continue drawing breath.

He pulled up another screen and watched. His grin broadened. Everything moved along perfectly.

"This ship is deceptively small from the outside," said Caleb as they sat inside the ship Angelina and Alena used.

"Caleb, the ship impressed you from the beginning." Ryan grinned.

"This technology entails a lot of work," defended Caleb as Lana laughed at him.

"We're glad the ship meets your approval, Caleb," Alena joked.

"We should be at the portal for the Elders Hall soon," said Dante, glancing at Angelina. He offered to copilot with her this trip, and Alena gladly let him. "You squeezed a lot into today."

"I frequently do, Dante. You couldn't miss that by now."

"Are you sure you didn't pack too much into today?"

"Dante, you sound worried about this evening."

"Of course not."

"Now who's not telling the truth?"

"Seriously, I'm not worried." He started laughing.

"Oh, but you are. Did you forget what I told you the first evening?"

"I remember, honest. Angelina, come now."

"Tell me what I said, Dante. Let me be sure you listened."

"Sunsets, not sunrises. See, I listened?"

"No worries then, Dante." She dissolved into laughter with him.

"What happened to you piloting the ship, Angelina?" teased Alena.

"Your replacement co-pilot proves quite distracting."

"I went from charming to distracting in minutes. This doesn't bode well for me."

She leaned over and whispered, "Distracting is nice from you, and be assured you lose no charm, my Dante." She kissed him on the cheek.

Then she announced to the others, "We entered the portal."

She amazed him at how quickly she switched gears, but he enjoyed it. He loved the back and forth teasing that emerged so easy between the two of them. Yet with what they came through together, they worked seriously when the moment called for it.

She turned back to him and grinned. "One of us needed to pay attention, Dante."

"I did. I'm *extremely* focused, when I wish to be."

"You definitely are." She winked at him as she shut down the ship's landing mechanism.

As they got out of the cockpit seats, he whispered to her, "Later I'll remind you how pleasant distracting and charming can be together."

"I'm eager to see it, as long as I'm the focus again."

"Count on it." He squeezed her hand.

The Elders Hall building entrance quickly came within sight as they left the ship. Everything stood abandoned this time, unlike Dante's previous trip, so they walked inside the building without incident. Dante led the group through the maze of hallways effortlessly with Angelina's hand in his. They would do this together as they said. He stopped upon touching the Elders Hall door. Days ago, his battlefield began and ended here, changing his world forever. Carrying his father's body out of the hall that day, it seemed only about what he lost. Yet the memories of what he received returned to him. He thanked the Ancient One again for the treasured moments of heartfelt words between him and his father. He experienced seeing his father leave this world to meet the Ancient One, an amazing peace pouring from his father's spirit when he said goodbye. And then there was his brother. For a moment he heard his brother's laughter again as he recalled his father's and brother's reunion, and he fondly remembered all the long afternoons spent with his brother. Of course, then there was Angelina. The Ancient One sent her to intervene, to keep him from falling to the darkness. The words she received reached his spirit and filled it, snatching him from a horrible bondage. Then he caught his first glimpse of her, and his heart raced with happiness that this angel is the one whose heart he captured. The place held many memories, and a battlefield like none he ever encountered.

As though knowing his thoughts, she squeezed his clasped hand and said, "I'm here beside you as before, my Dante."

He stared back into her eyes and whispered, "Because you have never left me, and you would not now." Without further hesitation, he pushed open the doors of the Elders Hall. He walked up the aisle with Angelina at his side, and the others slowly followed behind them. He kept expecting someone to emerge through the side door as before, but no one would. Not this time. Dante and Angelina reached the front where the majority of the battle ensued. Everything displayed the same disarray as he left it after the confrontation. Or maybe not.

His eyes searched the room. *Did it end up under something? The tapestry is big that fell, but I'm sure. Why isn't it here?* He continued asking himself as he rescanned the area.

Angelina read his face. "Dante, what is it?"

He knelt, and she joined him. He murmured, "It's gone."

At first, she thought Dante said he's gone, and referred to his father. Then she realized what he said. "What is gone, Dante?"

"The Dark Lord's sword."

They both got up and resumed searching the room. The others did too, as they comprehended Dante's words.

"This room is a wreck, to say the least. Are you sure it's not here somewhere?" asked Ryan.

Angelina studied the immediate ground around her, clearly tracking something. "I don't think so, Ryan. Dante is right. I saw through his eyes during the whole battle. It ended up in this area."

"Who would take it?" asked Caleb.

She exchanged a look with Alika and Alena, one the others didn't miss.

"What is it?" asked Lana.

"Troubling thoughts. It ties into discussions we tossed around on route to you." she sighed. "The easiest conclusion is Black Dragon soldiers returned to see what happened to the Dark Lord and carried off the sword. It's also an unlikely one, considering they didn't care enough to see what happened to him on their own. The Ancient One even said something to Dante, which confirmed they cared nothing for their leaders' fate. I noticed when we entered, there are indications of Black Dragon boot marks after Dante's confrontation. They came, but not of their own inclination. That part is troublesome. Even so, they wouldn't care about the sword, as they cared nothing for the owner. We're left with someone else entering the hall and taking it, if they didn't retrieve it."

"You have a guess," said Lana.

"The piece doesn't fit completely in our puzzle," said Angelina, as she continued walking in the area they last remembered the sword being. With Dante at her side, her eyes resumed searching. Once she and Dante reached the tapestry with the pool of dried blood beside it, her eyes looked far away. Her grip on Dante's hand tightened, she stumbled, and a shadow passed on her eyes.

"Angelina," Dante's voice rose as he grabbed her when she fell to her knees. Her body shook, and he threw a panicked look at Alika with the obvious question.

"She's seeing a vision, Dante."

"I thought those only happened when she slept."

"No, they come to her when she's awake too, Dante."

"Tell me how to stop it, Alika."

"She won't let it, until she sees what she needs of it," Alika said to Dante. Then he spoke to Angelina in the soothing voice of her teacher, of a father, "Child, you're safe. The vision cannot hurt you. I'm here," He paused. Whatever she saw, her hand fingered her sunspear for a second. He carefully took the sunspear as a precaution. "I'll keep this temporarily, until the vision passes. You don't need it. The vision can't hurt you. I'm here. I won't let anything hurt you. Dante is there with you, and he won't allow anyone to hurt you. You know that, right?" Alika nodded at Dante and stepped back. He would let Dante take over.

Dante did. Angelina didn't answer Alika, but she squeezed Dante's hand, when Alika asked if she knew Dante would keep her safe. He realized the battle still raged here, and they needed to conquer it together again. He clasped her hand, and his other arm held her, caressing her hair and back. His words quietly reassured her, "I'm here, my Angelina. Your Dante is here. I'll protect you. The vision can't hurt you. It isn't happening anymore. We'll get through this together like we said, as we did before."

Dante watched Angelina as he attempted to comfort her. Her eyes widened, her grip on his hand tightened further, and her form continued to shake. Her eyes traced something creeping closer to her down the Elders Hall's aisle as her breathing became more rushed. Then he saw her peer up, her eyes fluttering momentarily as though unable to bear seeing the image, but forced to anyway. Her eyes filled with renewed fear, and her entire frame shrunk back to hide from some hideous apparition. Her breath came in shallow struggles now, and her lips trembled. Her hand frantically grasped again for where her sunspear normally resided, eyes closed and accompanied by a fresh tremor jolting through her body.

He understood. Whatever she saw, it towered over her now. None of his words or gentle touches abated the absolute terror gripping her being. Slowly opening her eyes, she resumed watching the manifestation of her fear. It remained close, still near the front of the Elders Hall. Instantly her eyes closed tightly, but they reopened as her breathing intensified again. It passed beside her a second time. Her face left no doubt. Desperately fighting the terror which threatened to imprison her, she forced herself to endure the scene before her. Dante felt her let out a shaky breath as her eyes followed it a bit away from her finally.

The calm couldn't last. Instantly, her eyes focused on the top of the Elders Hall, acting as though the whole building began collapsing on her. She ripped her hand from Dante, and both of her hands flew to her ears, hysterically trying to cover a horrifying sound only she heard. Eyes closed, her body rocked back and forth, as the sound vibrated in painful shock waves through her body. She shook her head murmuring, half pleading, "When will it stop echoing? Make it stop, someone make it stop, please." Her head sank to the floor, as her hands still covered the side of her head.

Dante sought to comfort her as his arms encircled her, but all his efforts proved useless. Tears escaped. His eyes pleaded with the obvious question to Alika, who could only shake his head in helplessness as well. Angelina lifted her head. For a moment, Dante thought his hope fulfilled, that finally her ordeal had ended. To his dismay, she resumed watching, her eyes fixated with the same terror and her body continued to shake. She removed her hands from her ears, and her one hand clung to Dante's hand again. Her eyes focused on something directly in front of her. She saw it.

Worst of all, no one could stop it, like with another horrifying vision from the past she suffered through. "No, you can't! Please don't! Stop! Noooo!" she screamed in her mind, but the words reverberated throughout the Elders Hall. Her hand tore from Dante's hand, and this time both went across her chest. The cold metal plunged all the way through, searing pain starting in her chest, followed by excruciating agony spreading through every nerve in her body unlike she ever experienced. She gasped for air, any air but found none. Then she saw only darkness.

"Angelina, speak to me, please. You have to," Dante's voice broke, "wake up. Angelina, please." Her body went limp in his arms, and he lifted her to him. Alika ran up to them with Alena, and the others close behind. Alika attempted to check her when her body jerked awake, and she gasped, as someone after nearly drowning. "Angelina, I'm here, your Dante is here, I won't let you go, I promise," whispered Dante through his tears. He gently pulled her to him tighter and cradled her.

A series of convulsions brought her back, and she choked as she gasped for air. Lingering pain clung to her chest and throughout her body, purely from the trauma of the memory. Thankfully, she didn't actually meet the fate in the vision, but it felt real enough moments ago. Better not to dwell on what that meant. She'd faced and survived more than this near-death experience, so better to treat it as such now. She struggled to catch her breath and calm the panic still coursing through her. Unfortunately, she wouldn't get the chance, because the most frightening pieces of the vision began flashing in lightning succession. They served no useful purpose, instead becoming a fresh wave of torment of the waking nightmare she begged to end. Still held by Dante and seeking comfort from the visions, she whispered, "Please make them stop now."

Dante's steady stream of caring words reached her, as he held her tightly against him. Flinging her arms around his neck, she buried her face against him further and clung to him. He continued and knelt with her until the storm passed. His gentle words and touch soothed her spirit and heart and took the poison from the images away. Finally, her body seized shaking, and her crying quieted. Her tired eyes stared up at him.

He wanted to take away her pain and the terrible things she saw. Yet, he couldn't. "I'm so sorry. Tell me what you need, and I'll do it, my Angelina."

"You did it, Dante. You stayed and comforted me through it. It's the same as Alika and Alena find themselves doing many times."

"I wish I could stop it."

"No, you don't. We needed to see it, which is why I'm given the visions, why the Ancient One directed us back here. You say that because of how you care for me." She longed for one comfort from Dante. "If another image is in my mind now, one only you can put there..." Not making her wait another second, he drew her closer for a long, gentle kiss. The previous images were left behind, and she surrendered to his wonderful, all-consuming embrace.

"Better?" he murmured, stroking the side of her face.

"Yeah, a wonderful image now." She breathed as she opened her eyes, and a smile settled on her face.

"Plenty more where that came from, my Angelina. Are you alright?"

"A little tired, but I'll be up in a couple of minutes."

"We saw enough of here today, so we can leave now."

"No. We finish here first. I don't want to come back, but the visions are done with me today, my Dante."

"If you're sure, but I'm glad it's over." He ran a hand through her hair and kissed her again.

"Looks like Dante got the situation under control." Seth smiled at Alika, as they watched the two.

"Yes, he helps her recover nicely from part of the ugliness she saw. I'm amazed as I watch them. They act as ..."

"Two who have been in the one bond together for countless years. There is no doubt the Ancient One brings them together."

Lana took a deep breath and turned to Caleb. "She's finally calming down. Alika only hinted the first time about the visions, but to watch her go through one ... Caleb, what did she see?"

Caleb wrapped an arm around his wife's waist. "We'll know soon enough, but you're right. Nothing prepared us to watch her experience that. It's obvious why Alika shared so little." He shook his head. "For your cousin though, I can't imagine, but he's comforting her and doing fine with that part." He kissed Lana on the forehead.

Concern covered Ryan's features, and he saw it mirrored on Alena's face. He picked up on her thinking today, yet this one didn't take any guess work. They talked easily throughout the day, as though he knew her for far longer. The battle and rescue footage they saw gave him a glimpse of her, but incredible didn't come close to describing her. She, along with Angelina, almost got themselves killed to save others and played a pivotal role in defeating the Dark Lord. Prior to Dante's Elders Hall encounter, Ryan anticipated meeting someone who would become a trustworthy comrade or friend like Dante or Caleb. After learning more about the identity of Alika's students, the friendship he enjoyed with Lana came to mind. But when Alena walked through the door nothing prepared him for the instant effect she created on him. Before her entrance, he stood the confident commander, with always a smooth comeback in his arsenal. Immediately she reduced him to the shaking-in-his-boots guy, who was asking a girl out for the first time, who could hardly stumble out a whole sentence. He was long past a woman causing him to become unglued. That is until Alena today. He watched her emotional turmoil continue at Angelina's terror, and an overwhelming desire to understand and ease her heart poured over him. "Alena, she's better thanks to Dante, but you helped her through these visions before. Something is different with this one, isn't it? Tell me. I'm listening."

"Am I that apparent to you, or are you just that good, Ryan?"

"I'm not sure about that part. There's a discussion for later." He'd be happy to discuss it, or anything else she wanted, but now Angelina's state took priority. He forced himself back to topic. "What's different? Maybe more intense than usual?"

"There is something, and I'm still wondering how you picked up on that from me, Ryan." It didn't bother her. Simply a new experience to be read so quickly, but she could get comfortable if it came from Ryan. Where did that stem from? She refocused on his question. "It did feel more intense, but maybe not, since we don't know the content. It's the last bit. She sees terrible images to where she can't sleep afterwards sometimes, but one never left her like that."

"Like what, Alena?"

"Unconscious in someone's arms, Ryan. Like she was d ..." Unable to finish, she shook her head.

Ryan touched her shoulder and his voice softened. "I get it now, Alena. We'll know soon what she saw and figure it out together. We won't let anything happen to her. I know what she means to you, how close the two of you are, like Dante and Caleb for me. I can't imagine what she endured to see that vision, what you and Alika go through, to see her in pain with them. I'm sorry if today is anything like the previous times. Now Dante couldn't help her, but they'll get through it. We know they can. They showed us already, and there's no way Dante ever lets her go."

Alena smiled at him, encouraged by the strength of his words, and the knowledge he meant them. He was fiercely loyal to his friends and family, one of many things she liked about him. She got an accurate picture of him from the monitoring and through Angelina's eyes. Today, she witnessed it firsthand in the small time she spent with him. He could be serious and comforting when needed. She ended up being the recipient of it, with Angelina's earlier mishap with the cylinder, and his words found their mark again. An easygoing, wonderful humor also permeated his personality with a laughter which quickly spread through a group. He served as a top commander, but not only in name. He fought with the best of them, a sword in one hand and a blaster in the other, and held the title of one of the best pilots found. His troops were loyal, because he went into battle fighting wholeheartedly for each of them.

No wonder Dante and Caleb wanted him by their side on the battlefield, while off the battlefield they became best friends. Few guys existed like him, Alena thought. She admitted more than gratitude began surfacing for him as she found his hand on her shoulder quite comfortable and resisted the urge to lean completely against him. Suddenly, she looked forward to the next few days, because of the chance to spend time with him. She also realized, he watched her curiously, as she slipped into her own daydream about him. Her mind reverted to the previous topic. Angelina and Dante. Her concern returned full force. She looked up to check on them, but grinned as she glimpsed the two caught in a kiss. "They're happy again, aren't they?"

"They are. I'm guessing we'll see much more of that from them. Any shyness is vanished. Dante got her out of her shell fast."

"He did, but we expected nothing less. They're obviously meant to be." She paused. "When it's like that, it comes naturally, and you don't think about or realize it, I suppose."

"Yeah, once you find the right person it comes together on its own." He smiled back at her.

She stared at him as though seeing him again for the first time and returned his smile. "I see that, and sometimes it happens not as you expect, Ryan."

Angelina slowly got up with Dante's arms around her.

"You're sure, Angelina?" He brushed her hair back while studying her face.

"I'll be fine now thanks to you." She smiled at him and turned to the others, trying to reassure them. Her eyes still reflected the tiredness from the toil of the vision.

She glanced around struggling to remember. "She held something in her hand."

"Who?" asked Dante.

"The lady agent of the Dark Lord."

"She's who you saw," said Alika.

"Yes."

"She brought the troops," said Lana.

"No, she came alone. She retrieved the sword and determined someone killed her master. Once she did, she was furious." Angelina's eyes flickered with fear, and Dante noticed a slight tremor go through her. She took a few tentative steps, with her hand clasped in his hand and stopped. She sighed, as she closed her eyes.

"Angelina, you said the visions were over." Dante's voice rose.

Her eyes opened, and she gazed at him. "Oh, Dante, they are. I'm sorry I scared you. I didn't think about how that would seem to you, after what happened." She hugged him.

"I guess I overreacted."

"No just concern. I can appreciate that, after what you saw." She scanned the room again. "What is in her hand? I see it, and I should recognize it." She closed her eyes again and shook her head. Her eyes opened and began slowly tracking every inch of the room.

"What is it? What does it look like?" asked Alena.

"A box of some kind. I'm assuming it contains something, but the vision didn't show that part. It just appears in her hand, but it's not the sort of thing she carries."

"Not the sort of thing she carries?" Alika repeated.

"It's not her. Too fancy and decorative. What you see in ..." Her face lit up, and she tugged Dante's arm, as she rushed towards the toppled table. She turned back to him. "Sorry, Dante, I yanked you along there."

"I'm fine. I'll always keep up with you."

She winked at him, glad for the teasing tone and matched it. "You do like a challenge, Dante." She turned back to the others. "She took one of the little boxes that fell from the table. Strange. Usually there's something sinister with her, but maybe it simply better suited whatever she collected. She didn't know what she would uncover until she searched. She spent most of her time in the vision where the battle ended, here at the tapestry and the two pools of blood. I'm guessing she used part of that piecing together the events to realize what happened to the Dark Lord. The other part ..."

"Would be?" asked Alika.

"Unpleasant avenues to explore." She knelt with Dante over the tapestry and the pools of blood, and she shook her head. "Impossible to tell anything. There's too much traffic between her and the Black Dragon troops' visits." She spread the tapestry out further and stopped. "That doesn't look right." She turned to Dante. "You cut a large piece off to slow your father's bleeding. Another much smaller piece is gone where the tapestry is bloody. Is this from your sunspear?"

He spotted where she indicated, a precise cut, as with a knife's edge. There's no way it possibly tore in almost a perfect square. "No, it's not from my sunspear."

They got up. She noted bits of ash remaining on the ground, but scattered by the traffic through the hall. The two rejoined the others.

Dante gazed down at her. "I don't want to stay any longer after watching the pain you experienced today in this place, but I don't wish any return trips for you either. What else do you need to see?"

"We endured much here again, but we got through this battle together too. There's nothing left to learn. Are you ready to truly leave this place behind, my Dante?"

"I am, my Angelina," he whispered as he hugged her. Then he kissed her forehead and took her hand. After taking one last look at the front of the Elders Hall, the two led the way out, and the doors shut behind the group.

CHAPTER SIX

Once they returned to the ship, Alena assumed the piloting duties, and Ryan took a turn at co-piloting. Gratefully accepting the offer, Angelina and Dante sat with the others for the return trip.

Angelina sighed. "Once we're back, we'll finish going through the vision. I covered most of the first part, but I didn't touch on the end. Dante and I also need assistance from Seth and Alika later with something. Tomorrow is a full day again with visiting one of the colonies the Dark Lord hit." She paused and focused on Lana. "I'm sorry for how hard tomorrow will be for you. If there's something I can do to make it less painful for you, I will."

"Angelina, stop. Don't worry about me after your day. Our concern is you."

"Lana, there's no need. Many visions have passed through my eyes. This one will lose its hold as well, fade as all the rest." She forced a smile.

Lana knew the truth as the others did. It didn't lose its hold or fade. Angelina added it with the rest, locked it away, and hoped it stayed imprisoned. She feared it wouldn't and dreaded the next one. Lana wanted to assure her somehow yet couldn't. She didn't know what Angelina saw, but the visions Angelina bore over time were terrible, and the next one could be worse. She met Angelina's eyes, and an agonizing understanding shone in them, as she continued the lie as Angelina wished. "Of course, it will, Angelina, as it always does."

"Thank you, Lana," she whispered, touching Lana's arm in gratitude. She regained her composure before continuing. "I understand the weight you feel, how you took what happened with those colonies. I see you through Dante's eyes. Even as my concern for you falls on deaf ears, after what you saw today with me, I'll make tomorrow easier on you if I can."

The longer Lana spent with Angelina, the more she understood why her cousin cared for her as he did. "What can we do for you today?"

"There's nothing else. Your mere presence is a comfort, especially Dante. I'm unhappy with what you witnessed, but I didn't know it would unravel as it did. I wish now I had made the trip with Alika and Alena before we arrived."

Dante asked, "How can you say that? The thought of you going through it without me ..." He leaned his forehead into hers. "I needed to be there. There is nothing I won't do for you." He brushed his lips with hers.

"I don't ever doubt that." She wrapped him up in a hug. "You take such wonderful care of me." Then she turned to Alika, "Oh, mind if I get my sunspear back?"

Alika chuckled as he handed it to her. "I forgot, but I trust you to handle it safely now."

"I'm put back together again." She grinned, as she secured it and caught a look from Dante. "What is it?"

"I teased you earlier, but I saw how the vision left you, and you went unconscious ..." The image of her limp body in his arms stopped him.

"Dante, I'm sorry. I can't imagine how I frightened you, but I'm fine."

"You don't need rest? I'll understand. The vision took a lot from you."

"I get it. I'm sometimes slow, and I can't blame today's events." Angelina saw Alena and Alika exchange a grin. " I speak the truth. Even my teachers know it." She turned serious. "Dante, I need this evening with you more than ever after what happened today."

"You're sure?"

"I'm sure. Our plans won't be ruined by that dark agent and the scary vision she delivered. I won't let you cancel our evening, Dante." Her smile radiated to her beautiful blue eyes, as she leaned in close to him.

"I'm convinced, Angelina." He returned her smile as she pulled him over and kissed his cheek.

She whispered in his ear, "Good, because I looked forward all day to being your sole focus this evening."

"I won't disappoint you," he whispered back, as he slid his arm around her waist.

Once back at the fortress, they regrouped in the main room.

Alika said to Angelina, "Go slowly and stop whenever you feel the need."

"I will. I'm ready to finish this." She squeezed Dante's hand. "First I'll go through what I saw when she appeared in the Elders Hall." Angelina went through the vision and stopped at the point the agent left the hall. "I'm certain I didn't see everything she picked up in the hall. I'm convinced at the least she placed something in the box. She held the sword and the box as she left. Once she pieced together the Dark Lord's death, her scream echoed through the hall. She vowed we would all pay for what happened. Of course, Dante is the only one she knew visited the hall, so she figured out he's responsible for slaying the Dark Lord."

"Which means she's coming after Dante first chance she gets," said Caleb.

"Not especially. She prefers total revenge, hence they all will pay, which includes anyone associated with Dante."

"I put everyone in danger around me now."

Angelina shook her head. "Dante, don't do that to yourself. She doesn't forgive and forget. Everyone here already made her list of torture and kill if captured. Lana and Seth earned her fury further, when they stopped her from finishing off your mother. Caleb is on it, with being Lana's husband and having a key position with the Freedom Fighters. Strike at Caleb, and you hurt Lana or draw her out for capture. It easily goes the other way. At some point. Black Beauty figures out how close Ryan is to your circle. He's an excellent target. She's a master of disguise, as you saw. The only thing saving Alena and I thus far is our appearance remaining unknown to her. Our rescuing Abigail put us on her list to maim and pull apart. Each time one of our operations caused a new failure for her, we increased her hate for us. Alena and I manage to stay ahead of you on her torture and kill list."

"You said that like reading a meeting agenda," Ryan said.

"I suppose, but we never underestimate her and do everything possible to avoid her in every operation. One of her primary tasks is assassin, and she did it with pleasure countless times. She does still." Angelina paused. "One dead does as well as another for her, unless she caused greater pain by taking one life over another. She gets a whole other thrill from that one." She looked down, lost in her own thoughts.

Alika interjected to give her time, "Unfortunately, Angelina gives an accurate picture of the agent's cruelty."

Angelina's eyes translated a silent thanks to Alika before continuing, "Let's get to the last part." She told them the second half of the vision, hoping her recollection focused them on the vision, not another element of the incident. She failed.

Even Alika couldn't hide his alarm. "She killed someone with the dagger, but you were rendered unconscious when she did it."

"Well, yes ... I mean she's scary, and she used a dagger. Who wouldn't with seeing that?" stumbled Angelina. She wouldn't that's who, she thought to herself. She saw other visions involving a dagger. The part she tried to hold back found focus despite her efforts.

"He's right. You've seen lots of awful things in visions, but this is the only time you passed out from it. You feel intensely in your visions, but this enters a whole new realm," said Alena, watching her face.

"Your arms went across your chest before you passed out. The same place she stabbed him with the dagger, right?" Dante knew the answer even as he asked.

"In the ... uh ... same area. I mean I don't see why it's important. We need to ..." Angelina said.

"You didn't just see it like the other visions," said Alika, his alarm growing.

"It happened to you, as if you were on the table." Alena's voice registered horror, and Ryan put a comforting hand on her shoulder.

Lana and Caleb didn't say a word, but they realized with the others what Angelina tried to hide.

"You felt it go all the way in didn't you? You felt all the pain? As though you," Dante choked on the word, "died in my arms?" Lifting her chin as gently as he could muster, he stared in her eyes.

"It's only a vision. It can't hurt me. It wasn't me on the table. Dante, please I'm ..." She stopped at the look in his eyes. Not just him. The others too. She attempted to shield them, but she gave up. "Yes, I felt everything from her dagger for a moment."

"Longer than a moment." He enclosed his arms around her and pulled her against him, as a cascade of emotions crashed through him again. *She's alive, but is she okay? She felt a dagger go clean through her, and she went limp in my arms. I can still see her gasping for air, for a breath, for life. Then all the pain she experienced. I can't bear to think about how much. How can she say a moment? It was an eternity for me. Why does she even have to see the visions? Go through any of it? I couldn't do anything to stop it, to help her. Why didn't she tell me everything just now? She doesn't need to protect me. I should protect her, but I don't know how. I can't imagine losing her. It almost happened again, but how do I keep her safe from a vision? Somehow, I have to because I love her.* His arms tightened around her, while he kissed the side of her face.

Alika watched as Dante continued to embrace Angelina, and he couldn't blame Dante for his reaction. He glanced at Seth, whose eyes mirrored his own worry.

"What do you make of it?" asked Seth.

"I'm at a loss, but I understand why she didn't want to tell us."

"Do you think she's in danger?"

"Logic tells me no. Like she said, it's only a vision. It can't hurt her. She didn't appear in it, which is comforting considering the ending. These are all things I say during the visions to assure her."

"But her unconscious in Dante's arms is a powerful image."

Dante felt calm return to the two of them. "Let's try again, and this time the truth. No more protecting us by leaving out what happened."

"You don't understand how hard that is for me, Dante."

"I'm beginning to, but I need it from you anyway, Angelina."

Her shoulders slumped in defeat. "All right, Dante. The reality is as you guessed. You all did. I don't know any more or what it means, and it scares me."

"How do you feel now where the blade went through in the vision?"

"I'm fine, I promise. There's no pain."

"How? You felt it all before." He couldn't stop himself from probing, after she held back earlier.

"I don't know. In the moment, it felt beyond painful. I suppose what you'd expect with a dagger through you." Her body shuttered at the recollection.

He wrapped his arm around her again. "I'm sorry, I didn't mean to press you. I don't want you going through it again."

"No, I need to unravel it too. My chest and through my body hurt when I woke up. Not like recovering from the physical wound, but the memory lingering of what happened. In that way, it became like the other visions which explains why I'm not hurting anymore from the dagger."

"You'll say something if it does?"

"I promise I will, Dante."

"Angelina, at any point did you switch places with the man?" asked Alika.

"Never. I always watched."

"You reacted when you received the dagger. Perhaps there's another connection," said Lana.

"I see where you're going, sweetheart," said Caleb.

"Yeah, she could be on to something. Did you recognize the place or the man, Angelina?" asked Ryan.

Alena nodded. "I didn't consider that, but anything triggered, Angelina?"

"Nothing with the location. Everything moved from the Elders Hall to a facility or a ship maybe. I saw a long table, where she strapped him down. I can't place the man. Plain looking guy. I'm not saying that in a rude way, but nothing in his appearance triggered familiarly with him. He could pass for any well-built guy I encountered on the colony streets, fought on the battlefield, or met in a diner or bar in the shipping world. She stripped him of most of his clothing. There's no guarantee it gives me a clue anyway. She covered him with a sheet from the waist down, but kept his upper body bare as she used the blade on him. He came in and out of consciousness, so I doubt he knew what happened, until the blade hit."

"For someone you didn't know, to feel it to this extent makes no sense." Seth paused. "Another time you witnessed murder committed."

"Yet I didn't react the way I did today." He referred to Collin's murder. A glance at Alika and Alena confirmed another murder came to their mind, as it did hers. The vision of her own mother's slaughter didn't ignite such a severe reaction from her. Yet, a complete stranger's slaying caused her to physically experience the murder as her own and die in Dante's arms. She forced herself to reengage with the others. "All I know is what I saw. I don't know why she took his life or his identity."

Alika spoke, "Yet we know her master, and he meddled in things which should not be."

"Now the student continues where the master left off," Seth echoed the fear.

"And her fury, if she finds her means of revenge ..." Angelina trailed off and the agent with her flaming eyes hovered over her again. A tremor went through Angelina's body. The reaction prompted Dante to encircle his arms protectively around her waist and whisper to her, "I won't let her hurt you. I'll keep you safe." She leaned up against him as the image faded.

Angelina sighed. "I fear Black Beauty is only a part of this." The others stared blankly at her except for Alena and Alika. "There are pieces that don't fit. What should appear before us rather than what we see."

"Black Dragon troops should be falling apart, in complete disarray with their leadership destroyed now. The Dark Lord is dead, and the Black Dragon Commander ceased to exist," said Alena.

"Thanks to Dante and Ethan. However, the Black Dragon is functioning as though none of those events occurred," finished Angelina.

Lana replied, "We didn't eliminate all their leadership."

Caleb nodded. "This agent of the Dark Lord. She carried out a lot of ugly business for him."

Ryan shook his head. "A situation where she calls the shots? There's a scary thought after today and her past activities."

Alika sighed. "We're not necessarily convinced of that either."

"What's left?" asked Dante.

"A disturbing mystery," said Angelina, "We puzzled over it before today's vision when we took apart the day of the Dark Lord's death. The Dark Lord and the Black Dragon Commander sat back and directed the destruction and poisoning of three planets. They carried out an attack here, while your group launched a full-blown attack on one of their facilities. The Dark Lord also managed to send his lady agent to recapture or kill Abigail. Initially, we assumed the Dark Lord and Black Dragon Commander put everything in motion and watched it unfold, keeping tabs on everything as it happened. Maybe that could have worked, but Dante arrived at the Elders Hall and the Dark Lord's carefully scripted lie unraveled on him to seal his demise. Yet, as it fell apart for the Black Dragon at the Elders Hall ..." She looked at Alena.

"It never fell apart for them in any other part of the battle. We realized they retreated because they accomplished their purpose, not because they lost the battle. As Angelina stated, there's what should be and there's what is. We expect mirror images, but they're not."

"The lady agent couldn't organize it." Lana slowly spoke the unpleasant realization.

Angelina sighed. "No. The Dark Lord dispatched her to finish Abigail. Once she failed, she wouldn't rush back to face her punishment from the Dark Lord. Also, she was still seething at being foiled again. No doubt she needed to complete her task as redemption for her recent failures with the Dark Lord. With those recent failures, he would not put her in charge of anything. His memory could quickly lapse even with a record of dedicated service in the light of repeated failures. Eventually it ended in one path with him. He wouldn't hesitate once he marked someone, and she knew that about him." Angelina looked down.

"Where does that leave us?" wondered Caleb.

"With a huge missing piece in our puzzle, and a Black Dragon army which is not in pieces," said Alena, to give Angelina the needed moment with her thoughts.

"And we've no idea who's running things and how it's run, but it's as efficient as before," said Angelina, rejoining the conversation.

"And they possess this working dispersal device," said Lana.

Angelina smiled. "But we all returned safely from our battlefields, and we'll do it again as many times as the threat comes." She squeezed Dante's hand.

Dante smiled. "Our struggles make us stronger and when the day is done it's worth it, because we won our battlefield together."

"Because when you almost lose the one most precious to you ..." said Angelina as she stroked the side of Dante's face.

"You find the strength to fight whatever battlefield before you no matter how overwhelming it seems," finished Dante as he slid his arm around her waist and softly kissed her.

Seth smiled. "Well said."

Alika nodded and turned to Angelina. "You packed enough into today. Time for everyone to get dinner. You and Dante made plans this evening I insist you two keep."

CHAPTER SEVEN

Angelina and Dante approached Seth and Alika as the group got dinner. Angelina asked, “Can we speak with the two of you?”

Alika replied, “Of course. Do we need to go in another room for this?”

“No, we encountered something and need your guidance. It’s nothing the others can’t hear."

“We just think the two of you are best to help us,” finished Dante.

“I know I’m curious.” Seth laughed.

Caleb nudged Lana, and she followed his gaze across the room where the four sat speaking quietly.

Lana turned to Alena. “Is everything okay with them?”

Alena nodded. “Pretty sure. They mentioned talking to Alika and Seth about something tonight.”

Lana remembered the comment from Angelina now.

“Yeah, on the return trip,” recalled Ryan. A mischievous glint flickered in his eyes. “Oh, you don’t suppose?”

“What are you thinking, Ryan? Out with it.” Alena moved to jab him playfully in the ribs, but Ryan didn’t dodge at all. The motion ended up seating the two closer on the couch, and he smiled at the outcome. She saw him wait to see if she moved back over, or if she signaled him to move further over on the couch. She grinned at him. “You’re fine where you’re at now, Ryan. Are you going to tell me what you’re thinking or not?”

Alena surprised him again today. He enjoyed her quick wit and teasing manner from earlier, something he observed from the monitorings. He found himself struggling for words again, as he knew much more laid in her question now, and her eyes danced as she understood as well. Maybe he relished this too much, but he loved to tease also, and an undeniable closeness continued growing the more time he spent with her. He had to pursue it, and everything from her encouraged him to do so. He recovered quickly, finding his usual easy-going confident manner. "You're eager to know, and I should tell you before you try to hit me again."

"I thought you'd dodge, Ryan. Reflexes a little slow tonight."

"No, you surprised me. You've done that more than once now, Alena."

"Some people aren't fond of surprises."

"I'm not one of those people, because I remain pleasantly surprised by you, Alena."

"Though I tried to hit you?"

"We both know that wasn't your intent."

"You're right about that."

"Did you wish me to dodge, Alena?" Ryan leaned in closer to her.

"Maybe not so much, Ryan." She glanced down at the diminished space between them and grinned back up at him.

They realized it the same instant. They completely forgot about Lana and Caleb who witnessed their entire interaction. A knowing look crossed between Lana and Caleb, and a grin spread across Caleb's face. Neither Ryan nor Alena minded. Obviously, Caleb and Lana were happy at the unfolding of events. They both simply found it amusing, they became so unaware to lose track of the two being there.

"Ryan, we had our fun. What will it take to get an answer from you on the proceedings over there?"

He laughed, because she continued doing it. "If you say so. What will it take, huh?" He pretended to be in deep thought as he rubbed his chin. "I don't know yet, but I reserve the right to think of something later. It may really cost you."

She looked at him with mock consideration at his warning. "Good thing I happen to like you. It can't be anything too bad you dream up. I'll take my chances with you." She laughed. "Now, out with it."

I'm definitely redeeming it, and later comes fast. "I'll confess then. Seth and Alika both have authority to perform certain ceremonies, right? How about one in particular?"

"Yes, they do." Alena sighed as a hint of sadness crossed her features.

"I upset you. I'm sorry, Alena." He reached for her hand, and to his relief she didn't pull away.

Lana and Caleb regarded her with concern too, at her abrupt change of mood.

"You didn't say or do anything wrong, Ryan, or any of you. I wish you guessed right, but there's no possibility. She wouldn't hesitate for a second to say yes if she could, and there's no doubt of Dante's answer. Yet, it's not so simple." She turned back to Ryan and squeezed his hand. "For the record by all appearances, you volunteered a good guess."

"Sorry, it's wrong. With how happy they are together, I thought for sure I had it."

"I know. They weathered through so much already. It doesn't seem fair."

"More than that. Surrounded by such pain and chaos ..." Lana watched them momentarily, as she took Caleb's hand.

"And they find each other somehow in all this mess, but they can't be completely together." Caleb shook his head and looked at Lana. He couldn't imagine. No matter how bad it got around them, they clung to each other and together they found refuge in the Ancient One. Their marriage bond represented that anchor, the calm in the storm for them.

Alena glanced over at Angelina. "Her world is complicated. Alika and I understood the moment we began her training, but we never regretted it. Times like this I wish I could change things for her. Her heart belongs to Dante and desires to stay with him. All the same we can't remain here but for scattered days at a time."

"Surely that won't always be the case?" Ryan asked.

"Hopefully not, but there are things beyond ... I can't. The Ancient One is the only who knows. It's in His Hands."

Angelina told Alika and Seth what went through her head on the platform and her realization of how it tied into the whole rooftop fall. "Dante untangled the connection."

"No, you did all by yourself. I simply got you talking and stopped long enough, to see what you already knew."

Alika smiled. "Excellent work, whatever you did, Dante."

Seth added, "The two of you prove good for each other."

"I found no solution."

"Not true. It's as Dante said. The solution is waiting to be claimed. You must conquer the rooftop's unforeseen, lasting effects rather than feel it overcame you," said Alika.

"But it did overcome me."

"No, you're alive and returned safely to us which bears out the opposite of your conclusion," Alika replied.

Seth nodded. "He's right. Angelina, if you overcome a similar situation, you overcome the other finally. We'll work out a solution. Possibly as soon as tomorrow and speak further with you two, once we return from the colony. This is a good thing discovered. You must be able to access your situation accurately, and you can't do so if the clutter from the rooftop still clouds your vision."

Alika said, "Yes, better you realize it now, not during a battle or operation. You can remedy it now. In another situation, your life could be the price."

Dante wrapped his free arm around her waist and kissed the top of her head. "Which can't happen. I couldn't bear for something to happen to you. I told you we'd solve this together."

"I'm not sure why I doubted." She looked from Dante to Seth and Alika, "Thank you. I feel better now."

"We remain skilled counselors." Alika smiled. "Say goodnight to the others, and go spend time together as you planned. With the strange happenings lately, I trust Dante to escort you safely back to the ship for the night, when the time comes."

"I'll do so, Alika."

Seth said, "We leave you in the best care, Angelina. Enjoy each other's company this evening."

"Thank you, Seth." She turned to Dante. "We'll want to check on your mother first, and afterwards we can go from there."

Dante nodded, as they headed over to the others.

"They should enjoy whatever time they get together," said Alena.

"We'll ensure my cousin gets as much time with her, while the two of you are here."

"Yeah, quality time is a necessity." Caleb grinned and couldn't resist. "Ryan, keep that in mind too."

Angelina and Dante walked up at that moment.

"What do you need to keep in mind, Ryan?" Dante raised his eyebrow.

Caleb answered for Ryan and laughed. "You missed too much. We'll catch you two up, later."

Dante and Angelina mirrored a puzzled expression. For the two of them to be the ones in the dark was a new experience.

"Sure you don't need to tell us something, Ryan?" asked Dante.

"I'm sure, buddy. Don't keep Angelina waiting. Now, go spend the evening with your girl. I promise, I'll find a way to occupy my time this evening too."

Alena added, "He's right. You too, Angelina. You need this time with Dante. Do you want another lecture from Alika?"

"Not particularly, Alena." She laughed. "Whatever it is can wait. I guess you'll tell me later."

"I will. There's wonderful company around me, and I'm sure I can talk at least one of them into spending more quality time with me."

Lana smiled. "I believe she can. We'll see both of you tomorrow. Enjoy."

Dante assisted Angelina with the cloak. The two cast one last perplexed look at the group before proceeding to Abigail's room. After the incident a few days ago, Dante's group moved Abigail to another room and reestablished the security with the access pad too. Two guards stood at the door, as usual.

"Hello Dante," said the guard as he studied the figure beside Dante.

"We both go in tonight. She is cleared in the system."

"Sorry, Dante. We didn't know."

"This is your first meeting, so no apologies needed."

"You are understandably cautious after a few days ago. My condolences for the loss of your two comrades. Thank you for protecting Abigail. Stay vigilant. It doesn't go unnoticed."

The guards bowed their heads for a moment, but then smiled at her. The one guard whispered, "Thank you, ma'am." He pushed the keypad and the computer displayed, "Two individuals wish to enter." Next it read, "The door will not open until both identities are verified."

She perceived the guards wished her to go first. Stepping confidently over to the access pad, she spoke, "Younger spear-bearer." Without hesitation, she placed her entire hand on the access pad. Immediately the computer responded with, "Identity verified." Instant relief flooded the faces of both guards. Dante repeated the process, and the computer responded in the affirmative again. The door opened, and the two walked inside.

Dante spoke to his mother's still form as he routinely did many nights now. "Mom, just checking on you for the night, and I brought you a visitor. You remember one of the spear-bearers bringing you home to me, and she got me back to you safely too."

Angelina took Abigail's hand. "We're both glad he came back safe, huh? I'm quite charmed by him as you know by now. Abigail, I missed you, and I'm relieved you're fine after what almost happened. We'll keep you safe." After a minute, she released Abigail's hand and placed it back at her side.

"She'll awaken, Dante. Don't give up. We'll find the answer together."

"You're right, and she'll see why I care for you, once the two of you meet." Clasping his mother's hand, he watched her as though believing this evening her eyes would finally open. Angelina rubbed his back as they stared down at her. Dante sighed after a few minutes, concluding tonight ended as the others. After kissing his mother on the forehead, he whispered, "Goodnight, mom. We'll check on you tomorrow." He turned to Angelina, "Ready?"

"Only if you are."

"I am. Come on." Grabbing her hand, they left the room and said goodnight to the guards.

Once they got halfway down the hall alone, he turned to her. "Numerous places normally work for a date, but you're special like that too." He brushed a strand of her hair back. "We're a little past sunset now. There are places I can assure quiet for just the two of us, but after today I don't feel safe outside under the night sky." Despite the search his mind undertook, no amazing place came to take her safely for the night.

"Dante, stop spinning your wheels. It's not about the place. It's about being with you."

He stroked her cheek as he whispered, "That I can deliver."

CHAPTER EIGHT

Alika and Seth sat with the others after watching Angelina and Dante leave, perplexed.

"Quite the animated conversation over here," said Seth.

"Yes, everyone is in good spirits, despite the stressful day," said Alika.

"Relaxed for sure." Caleb grinned. "Right, you two?"

Lana tried to appear stern with Caleb, but gave up as usual when he leaned over and stole a kiss.

"Always count on Caleb, to keep anyone from becoming too serious." Ryan laughed.

"Like he doesn't get help from you." Alena laughed. "It's a wonder Lana gets anything out of you two."

Lana burst out laughing too. "Ryan, you won't get a break tonight from Alena."

"Appears so." He turned to Alena. "Keep going, Alena. The possibilities are running through my head about the other, and there's time."

"I'm not worried, but should I ease up on you, Ryan?"

"Maybe not so much, Alena." He laughed again. A second later he barely caught himself before he pulled her over close and encircled his arms completely around her shoulders. He turned to Alika and Seth and asked, "Uh ... did you ... I mean ... solve whatever Dante and Angelina needed help with?"

Momentarily, Seth and Alika didn't register his question as their attention diverted to the teasing banter between Ryan and Alena and his quick withdrawal from her shoulder. They recovered rapidly.

"Yes and no. They presented the situation to us, and we must figure out a solution," said Seth.

"We can create one. Then Angelina has peace of mind, and therefore so does Dante," finished Alika.

"Something from today, right? I knew it," said Alena, shaking her head as Ryan touched her arm in reassurance.

"How do we help?" asked Lana.

"Or are you sworn to secrecy? I mean there's a lot of that with her," said Caleb.

"Not this time," said Seth.

"We assumed since you four went off on your own it had to be kept quiet," explained Ryan.

Alika answered, "No, they simply felt we could best arrive at a solution. We'll tell you." He did as they listened.

"I sensed something still bothered her after the cylinder, but I brushed it aside. Why did I? I know her better than anyone here."

Ryan jumped in, "Don't do this to yourself, Alena. We all saw it from her."

Caleb agreed. "We assumed coming up empty on the cylinder riled her up, but Dante pried it from her."

"My cousin won't rest, until she feels safe again with that situation too."

"Yes, Dante is determined, and we're confident of working out something," said Seth.

"Alena, the others are right. Don't think badly of yourself. Rather, view it as helping them in this case. Dante is the one who called her on it and forced her to work through it with him. These are valuable times between them." Alika said.

After briefly enjoying more relaxed chatter, Caleb grinned and said, "It's not late yet, but I'm ready to go spend quality time with Lana this evening."

"Simply abandon them here, Caleb?" Lana said, trying to hide a smile.

"Everyone will find their way. Can I please enjoy the rest of the evening with my wife?" He leaned over closer to her.

"You asked nicely, so I can't refuse such a charming request." She laughed.

Caleb rose from the couch, gently pulled her up with his hand, wrapped his arm around her waist, and stole a kiss from her, seemingly all in a single movement. "Lana, you make me happy as always." He turned to the others. "We'll see you tomorrow, since Lana granted my request."

"Caleb, sometimes ..." She smiled up at him and then glanced at the others. "Yes, we'll see you tomorrow. Goodnight."

The two walked away to a symphony of goodnights. Lana's laughter rang out as Caleb guided her to their quarters.

Alika watched them for another moment and smiled. "Have they always been ..."

Seth and Ryan answered in union, "Yes."

They all laughed.

"I suspected," said Alika, "With everything they see, their responsibilities, what they contend with ..."

"No one would know when you see them together," said Seth.

"It's one of the things which makes them leaders. Anyone around them sees it, and it ..." Ryan trailed off, trying to find the word.

"Inspires them. They draw strength from them, as Lana and Caleb do from each other," finished Alena.

"Yeah." He looked at Alena. "Thanks, Alena. It's exactly what I wanted to say."

Alika said, "The chaos around people easily wears them down before they're aware. Many relationships are undone to its poison. Lana and Caleb have found the balance thus far. They continue to impress me."

"The two imparted a lesson without realizing it." Seth chuckled.

"They did, and it didn't involve a punishing trek in the woods. Any thoughts from you two over there?" Alika asked innocently.

"You two stated it well, right, Ryan?"

"Definitely, I got nothing to add."

"I'm sure. I believe you already put it to use." A small smile formed on Alika's face. "Seth and I need to discuss some matters, including a solution for Angelina's situation."

"Yes, we aim for their answer by tomorrow."

Ryan and Alena glanced at each other, unsure of their next move.

Ryan said, "I guess I'll head out too."

Alika grinned. "And leave your beautiful company alone, Ryan?"

"Our leaving shouldn't change any plans this evening." Seth smiled.

Alika laughed at their surprised expression. "We missed it, but we didn't miss it."

Seth laughed too. "We're not clueless. This discussion sounds familiar, but with another student."

Alena grinned. "It does, and you both show yourself to be on target."

"I'm guessing, one of those discussions I didn't hear, but I watch enough to know you two see more than you say." Ryan smiled.

Alika answered, "You're both right. Ryan, I'll advise you the same as Dante earlier this evening. Please escort my student safely back to the ship when your evening concludes. She's well-trained to manage any threat, but the last few days can't be described as normal."

"Good point. I promise Alena gets back safely this evening, Alika."

"Alena, you're in more than capable hands with Ryan."

"I'm confident you speak truth, Seth."

Alika and Seth walked off with one last smile at the two.

"Unbelievable." Ryan laughed.

"You don't begin to comprehend."

"Time to redeem my request, and the Elders gave their blessing to do so. Even better."

"You don't waste any time, do you? What's my cost?"

"This evening for starters, and I plan for every evening you're here."

"I expect a fantastic first evening, if you already scheduled me for the remaining ones. Can you do it, Ryan?"

"I'll manage, Alena." The size and formality of the room for the two of them became apparent as his eyes swept across the room now. Normally lots of places came to mind to spend time with someone, but with Alena's situation this may not be as easy as he assumed.

She seemingly read his thoughts. "Overpowering for just two, isn't it?"

"It is. Funny I didn't notice till now. We can't go see the sights together either." A glance at her confirmed his words. ""here's quiet, informal, and I vouch for its safety," he hesitated, "my home in the evenings when I'm here."

"Lead the way, Ryan."

They stepped into Ryan's quarters, at least the ones he claimed when he visited the fortress. Ryan relaxed when Alena immediately made herself comfortable on the couch. He didn't want her presuming he just met women and invited them to his quarters. Honestly, he didn't expect her to jump to such a conclusion about him. Everything with her seemed different from anyone else, but a wonderful different.

"What can I get you to drink, Alena?"

"I'll take the same as you, Ryan."

He handed her one as he sat next to her. "I hope our tastes run the same."

"I'm sure it's fine and," she took a sip, "it is. A fruit drink, right?"

"Yeah, it's a blend. In a finer establishment, it'd be real fruit. Like this, well ... one day, I'll do this right for you."

"Ryan, it's not in your control. I'll enjoy the evening. It's not about the drink." She put it back down and leaned into the couch, as she smiled over at him.

"No, it's not. It's about spending quality time with you."

She sighed and instantly she appeared tired to Ryan, as one undertaking a task threatening to drain her last energy reservoirs. Perhaps today exhausted her more than he thought, and tonight should wait. She studied him briefly and said, "You're wondering about the ground rules for this. It's only fair to tell you."

Ryan stared at her, taken aback. He questioned bringing her to his quarters though she agreed, and now he had to do whatever it took to make it right. "I'm not a spear-bearer, Alena, but I hold to the teachings of the Ancient One, since I belong to Him. Besides, my own convictions wouldn't let me. You're beyond beautiful, but I won't cross that line." He stopped as he realized his mistake and laughed, "and those aren't the ground rules you referred to?"

She grinned at him. "No, Ryan. Your words are unnecessary, but a sweet reassurance. You're right. There is an order to these things by the Ancient One, those things to be kept and shared for the one bond only. I trust you completely, or I wouldn't be in your quarters alone now. Probably Angelina is in Dante's quarters too, and she isn't concerned either as Dante can be trusted without question as well." She paused. "Ryan, you won't be as excited, once you see how this must work with our complicated situation."

"I'll adjust and make it work, Alena." He took her hand as he stared into her eyes.

"Ryan, I want to as well." She smiled back at him. "Most of it's due to Angelina and being a part of her life. The rest is we made ourselves such enemies of Black Beauty and the Black Dragon. You know little about Angelina by design. Alika gave only necessary information since her identity can't be known. Her life is in danger and everyone she cares about if the information leaks out. She'll never let that happen. At times, she doesn't worry about her own ..." Alena paused, choosing to leave the thought unfinished. "When Alika and I took on her training, we understood what we signed up for, and by association with her, at some point we would become unknown with her in a sense. We're the only two people that know who she is in the traditional sense, and she worries about our possessing that knowledge."

"Why? You two would never betray her trust."

"Having the knowledge though puts us in danger, if someone discovered we knew."

"Like if the two of you got captured."

"Which is also why she insists no one outside of our circle uncovers how close we are to your circle."

"But we don't know who she is."

"Black Dragon doesn't know that part. They'll torture first and question second or kill at the start. As Angelina alluded to earlier, they could also capture someone to trap others."

"All reasons to keep you two concealed while you're here."

"And there's no need to explain staying hidden from Black Beauty, or whoever is in charge now at Black Dragon. Today reinforced how badly that ends, if they discover how to locate us or got a description of us."

"Yeah, I wouldn't want anyone in her grip. She doesn't give a second thought to settling business with a blade."

"Somehow she's more ready to spill blood from what Angelina saw, something I didn't conceive possible." She paused. "Courting me will prove challenging with our situation. Surely there's another beautiful girl who would gladly enjoy your attention, who's a much easier claim. This is a far more difficult path."

Drawing closer to her, he whispered, "But I don't want anyone else, Alena."

"Ryan, I hoped to hear you say those words, but I wished to be certain," she whispered back. "You must keep me secret, outside of our circle. If we're out, I'm nothing more than another comrade, friend, or troop, and you must treat me as such. When we're together, it can only be the two of us like this or with our small circle of friends. No traditional dates, like you normally romance your countless other beautiful young women falling all over you. They'll be crushed now as your pursuit of them ends," she teased.

"I'll happily take your rules, and there aren't all these heartbroken ladies on the colonies swooning for me. You're sweet for thinking so."

"You're holding out, or you don't realize all your secret admirers. You're more than easy on the eyes, among your many other attractive qualities. How has someone not snatched you up yet?"

He grinned as he could say the same of her. "They try, but I'm a difficult catch in my own way. Usually, it starts under the pretense of a dinner engagement my family hosts or a meeting we attend, but ends with us trying to resolve an issue in our region. Mostly we can't since they stem from Black Dragon, and I reassure them as best I can. Somewhere in there, I catch the girl's eye, like the daughter who tagged along. It's more about my family. They're a strong presence. The other girls probably get caught up in the commander part and expect shooting stars on the first date. It never happens. They're nice, but nothing more. Whatever the reason, it wears off fast, and reality comes crashing down on them. They discover the other part about being a commander in the time of Black Dragon now is that free time is sparse. I split my time between here and home, since I'm second in command and have a close friendship with Dante and Caleb. When I'm home, I work nonstop with my father and his staff to keep the regions safe under our care, or I check in with my mom for a minute. That craziness doesn't work for quality time with someone else. The girl quickly realizes I'm not the amazing catch she envisioned, but there's plenty of other stars in the sky."

"Quite the picture you painted, but I don't buy into your theory every girl is attracted to you due to your family or commander status. You absolutely shortchange yourself, Ryan." She stroked the side of his face. "I think you have your pick, but you don't take action. Sounds like lots of excuses to me." She moved closer to him. "The Ryan I see makes the time, once he finds someone important enough to pursue."

Immediately her touch warmed him, and her increasing closeness caused his heart to skip a beat. "You're right. Just one day showed me you're the only one I want to pursue." He ran his hand lightly up her arm.

"Ryan, how do you see your pursuit of me at this moment?"

"I can't get over how beautiful you are, and I wonder how wonderful it would be to kiss you now." He gazed into her eyes as he slid his arm around her waist and pulled her closer.

"Why are you still wondering, Ryan?"

He grinned as he leaned in and waited no longer. He wound his other arm around her as she pulled in against him, winding her arms around his shoulders and neck. Her lips were soft and warm, and he took his time enjoying every second of that first kiss with her. She responded to the kiss with the same fire as infused her speech all evening, and it thrilled Ryan as he deepened the kiss. He experienced no kiss like this, because there was nothing real behind them before Alena. His search ended with her.

"Wow, Ryan," whispered Alena.

"No kidding. I definitely see more in our future," murmured Ryan in her ear.

"Oh, there will be after that one."

"The ground rule about quiet evenings, just the two of us, I'll manage those well."

"I'm sold on them, too. Maybe shooting stars do happen, Ryan."

Ryan stroked her cheek. "And anything else you want me to believe in, Alena."

CHAPTER NINE

Opening the door to his quarters, Dante motioned Angelina inside. She smiled back at him. "See, perfect."

"I made that more difficult than need be. We can put something on. Tell me what you like." He projected the screen.

"I'm up for most things, from comedy to something that keeps me in suspense. After today I had enough of mysteries and my heart racing," her eyes twinkled, "well at least due to the fear factor. We can stand to laugh some."

"Agreed," Dante grinned as he pulled something up. He planned on her heart racing more than a couple of times before the evening ended. "What do you want to drink? And don't tell me water again."

She laughed. "I'll take tea with you, Dante."

Dante got the two drinks, putting them on a side table beside the huge couch. He stretched out on the extra comfy couch cushions and guided her with his outstretched arms to do the same next to him. She smiled as she did, snuggling up next to him on it, as he started the projection and wrapped his arms around her.

"Caleb and I got into the weapons room of the Elders Hall while we played this game called Mazefinder. We decided to liven it up." Dante chuckled. The two abandoned watching the projection and exchanged stories. Strangely, only a few times occurred where Angelina couldn't tell something because of her past. She simply told Dante she couldn't say or skirted around talking about it directly.

"You almost blew up the room." She giggled.

"Close. Seth about beat us with his staff when he got a hold of us."

"You assured Seth everything worked in the arsenal."

"He didn't appreciate our efforts, but Lana still enjoys reminding us of that one. She tried stopping us, but we didn't listen."

"And she has kept you two out of trouble ever since. I'm sure Seth made you and Caleb regret it. Elders create punishing training segments after those type of stunts."

"You don't worry about that."

"That's Alena you're thinking of, Dante."

"Agreed. Things come to mind which probably earned you a lecture from Alika. Okay, more than a lecture."

"He's learned various ways to counter me, some quite sneaky."

"Alika, sneaky?"

"Yes, he can be. That's the only way he treated my arm and hand injuries when we landed on Ryan's planet. He waited until after he started the vapor treatment for the smoke inhalation because you can't talk while it's released. I tried arguing with him, and he reminded me he purposely did it in that order."

"Your injuries needed treating, so I don't know why you gave him such trouble."

"From the same one who almost got part of a tank through his back and resisted treatment."

"I got treatment."

"So did I."

They both laughed.

"Point made, Angelina."

"They both played sneaky on the trip here, too."

"What do you mean, Angelina?"

"How do you suppose I ended up alone on the ship, when you came aboard?"

"They are sneaky," he whispered in her ear, "and I don't feel one bit sorry for you. I'm happy how the day started." Nuzzling her neck, he left soft kisses on it as he ran his free hand lightly down her arm.

She snuggled closer to him as she murmured, "Yes, you gave me an incredible welcome."

Later Dante teased, "You were right about tonight."

"What part?"

"The place making no difference."

"Yes, and I couldn't tell you anything of what happened in this projection. Hopefully, you didn't have your heart set on seeing it. I ruined it for you if so." She laughed.

"No, my only heart's desire is you, wrapped up in my arms this evening, so we got it perfect." He brushed her lips with his. "I could spend time with you like this forever, and never grow tired of it."

"I with you as well, Dante."

"Although, I got something for us to enjoy tonight and want to bring it out now." His eyes danced. He slowly got up, hating to do so, as he loved her snuggled up in his arms. "Give me a minute, I promise."

She sat up, watching him curiously. "What did you do?" Her eyes shone.

"I called in a favor." He sat back down with a small dish in his hand.

"When did you find time?"

"Before you came this morning. There are advantages to giving notice of your arrival. I enlisted help from Caleb and Lana, and we can enjoy it for as long as you're here." He scooped up a bite of the dessert on the fork.

Her face lit up as it slid into her mouth. "Dante, that tastes amazing."

He took a bite himself and ate it. "It's one of my favorite desserts, and I got several slices." The expression on her face brought a smile to his face as he gave her another bite.

They finished the slice of dessert, he stretched out again on the couch, and they cuddled back together.

"The dessert was delicious. How did you know?"

"I wish I could say I read your mind but no. I mean, I can't recall meeting any girl who doesn't like something sweet."

"True. With your looks and charm, scores of girls must chase after you, Dante," she teased.

He laughed. "Not quite. My parents kept close tabs on things, and they certainly would've continued. Seth took over those responsibilities. He's kept a close watch on me, checking in to make sure I didn't get into trouble, but allowing me the freedom to navigate that area. He trusts me, and he's pleased with whom this chase, as you called it, finally led me." His fingers leisurely played with a silken lock of her hair. "I see the time spent with anyone else as nothing more than past distractions, and poor ones. None of that matters now. I made my choice. You're the only one who caught my eye and captured my heart." He kissed her forehead as he stroked her cheek. "I'm sure somewhere you left an entire planet of despondent young men, my beautiful Angelina."

"Um, my family ran their household much differently, a tighter grip or more regimented than yours, so I didn't entertain the admirers you assume. Along with the intense training schedule Alika and Alena kept, I left little time to be pursued. There are no regrets, Dante. You're the only one I want as well. Every word and touch from you leaves me in awe of your care for me. You claimed my heart, and no one else can now."

He loved hearing her say those words to him, and became enthralled by her gentle blue eyes that he stared into the depths, which reflected her heart. He caught his breath anew as he appreciated her beauty again like the first time in the Elders Hall. His fingers ran through her hair, enjoying how softly the lush strands trickled through his hand and settled back on her. His hand absently ran down her arm, and he relished the velvety smoothness of her skin, like a flower petal newly opened. The sweetness of the kiss when he greeted her on the ship called to him. Surrendering to the longing, he brought her in close for another long, tender kiss as they had shared on the ship. With one arm wrapped around her waist and the other around her shoulders and playing in her hair, he took his time, drawing out every second of the kiss with her. He felt as a man too long in a desert, and finally quenching his thirst upon the life-saving water. He waited all day to kiss her again like this, and now nothing compared to it, as he couldn't get enough. Even as their lips lingered close together and the kiss seemed to end, neither one let it do so. His lips captured hers again, and he heard a happy sigh escape her as she continued to enjoy the kiss from him. She wrapped her arms tighter around his neck as she ran a hand through his hair, and his arms pulled her tighter to him. Dante gazed in her eyes, as their lips finally parted. Being with him made her happy. He didn't begin to understand it, but she turned his world around too. He whispered as he stroked the side of her face, "How does each kiss feel as sweet as the first with you, Angelina?"

Her heart raced, and she whispered breathlessly back, "I don't know, Dante." She continued staring into his eyes as she nestled next to him. One of her arms rested across his chest, and she felt his strong and steady beating heart through his shirt. Finally, being here with him still resembled a dream.

"You tired?" asked Dante later, as he planted another light kiss on the side of face.

"Honestly, I'm not."

"But ..."

"We don't want trouble with Alika and Seth tomorrow, when I'm too late getting back. I distinctly remember Alika forcing Alena and I to stop repairs on the ship, at what he described an insane hour."

"Considering what you two lived through earlier, I agreed with Alika. When did the three of you eventually stop?"

"Around 1:00 in the morning."

"You do push it. Ease up on yourself at times."

"He feared we'd blow up the ship by mistake if we continued."

"I'm glad he stopped it." He kissed her on the cheek.

"If not, Alena's better judgement kicks in, and we stop." She hesitated. "They acted strangely before we left."

"But they laughed about whatever it was as though they knew each other all along."

"It does feel that way. I'm sure they traded stories, some at our expense. Alena recalls every time she saved my skin, and she loves teasing me."

"Ryan's memory is equally sharp for me, and he shares it with great enjoyment too."

"Yes, they could ..." Suddenly, she met Dante's eyes, and the grin on his face revealed the same thought passing through his mind.

"For once, it doesn't involve us." He laughed.

"I'm sure you're right, and I'm sorry we missed it. This will be fun."

"Not all at once now."

"You don't understand how she teased me about you. Not that I mind."

He whispered seductively, "How much do you not mind?"

Gliding her arms over his broad shoulders and around his neck, she whispered back, "This much." She pulled him over to enjoy another long, gentle kiss with him.

"That much, huh," he murmured as he continued kissing her. "Angelina, I must get you back."

"I know even though I don't want the evening to end either."

"There's tomorrow night. Work hard all day. I help you relax in the evening."

"I could get used to your arrangement, Dante."

After helping her with the cloak, he escorted her back to her ship. They found Alika and Alena awake studying. The two paused working and smiled at them.

"You two enjoy your evening?" Alika asked.

"I'm sorry, It's late, it's just ..."

"Angelina, there's no need to apologize." He motioned for them to sit. "The hours you keep are no secret. Dante, I'm not so familiar. In a few days you leave, and there's no guarantee how long before you return. You need time to answer each other's questions and simply enjoy your time together. Need I say more?"

"Guess not."

"Back to my first question then. Did you two enjoy your evening?'

"Yes, we did. She agreed to tomorrow evening as well," said Dante.

"I should hope, young Dante." He laughed. "If not, I would severely question you about this evening."

Alena glanced at Alika. He asked Angelina, "Any ill effects from the vision earlier today?"

"No, I'm still fine."

"She didn't mention anything this evening with me, Alika."

"An issue would surface by now. Quite perplexing, but I'm relieved."

A glimpse of the display reminded Angelina of the late hour, but she couldn't resist. "Alena, how about your evening? Find someone to spend more quality time with you as you put it?"

"Surely you didn't think about me all evening. You were to focus on Dante."

"Oh, I focused on Dante *plenty*." Stroking the side of his face, she winked up at him before returning her gaze to Alena.

"Are you sure? I wouldn't want him feeling slighted."

"To her defense, I didn't feel neglected at any point. I possessed all her attention." He released her clasped hand to wrap his arm snugly around her waist and pull her closer to him, as he kissed her cheek.

After rewarding him with a smile, she focused back on Alena. "He won't help you with this one. How about your evening? Who did you talk to?"

"You and Dante both just saw." She tried keeping a straight face.

Alika burst out laughing at their exchange and continued watching.

"Before that, Alena. Someone mentioned finding a way to occupy his time tonight."

"I recall that now."

"Did you help him occupy his evening, Alena?"

"Perhaps I did."

"Dante, why don't you ask Ryan if he enjoyed how he occupied his evening, when you see him tomorrow?"

"I suspect he tells me on his own."

"You suppose so, Alena?"

"I can't speak for him, but he wishes me to keep him company again tomorrow evening."

"Seems we all enjoyed a pleasant evening, and have another ahead of us." She relented her teasing. "Ryan is a great guy. Sorry, that doesn't come close. He's special, and I'm happy for you, Alena."

"We both are. Ryan has been my friend for the longest time, and there's no one truer than him and Caleb. He probably can't sleep now, because he's still floating on space thinking about you." He smiled at Angelina. "I'm the same way every time with Angelina."

"It goes both ways." She rested her head further into the curve of his neck.

"The visit is shaping up nicely," said Alena.

"Yes, a wonderful evening." She glanced at the display again.

"Not everyone runs on your limited resources." Alika noticed Alena hiding a yawn, and exhaustion catching up to Dante.

Dante turned to Angelina. "I don't wish to say goodnight, but he's right."

"We'll see each other tomorrow. Get sleep, Dante."

The two of them rose, and he instantly became the awkward schoolboy. "Guess I'll go." He began walking away, but it didn't match his ending for the night.

Alika chuckled and called to him, "Dante, come back. You and Angelina are two adults. Say goodnight as you wish. I'm sure it's more of the same from earlier. You're not shy, and there's no mystery your effect on her." Winking at Dante, he resumed work with Alena.

Laughing as he strolled back over, he pulled Angelina over to the side for more privacy and wrapped his arms around her waist. "Your teacher is something. See you tomorrow." he paused. "Sure you didn't feel anything weird after the vision today?"

"No, and I promise I'd say something."

"Your body going limp scared me. Will you sleep after that vision?"

"Yes, because you gave me a wonderful evening with images assured to bring pleasant sleep, Dante." She wrapped her arms the rest of the way around his neck.

"I enjoyed creating those images with you."

"I could tell. Goodnight, my Dante."

"Goodnight, my Angelina." He drew her close and kissed her goodnight as he wanted. Slowly releasing her, he gently squeezed her hand before walking off the ship.

Her eyes followed his retreating form as the ship door closed, while Alika and Alena chuckled.

Alika said, “Looks like Dante delivered the goodnight he wanted.”

“There’s no doubt from that face.”

Angelina grinned at them. “He’s charming. What can I say?”

CHAPTER TEN

She stomped into the room, her jet-black hair whipping behind her. "What do you need this time?"

"Full of your usual pleasantness." The man raised his eyes, undaunted.

"What do you want?"

"To chat with you."

"I don't have ..."

He cut her off. "You'll make time now, I insist." His eyes and voice matched hers. "Come sit."

Her eyes alternated between icy scorn and burning rage. "Fine, what do we need to chat about?" She almost spat the last words at him, as she remained standing.

"You did this, not me. This is your mess, so bury the attitude. Apparently, you missed a step somewhere. Try getting better at your craft." He snickered at her.

"Why you ... I should run you through where you sit!" Her eyes flamed, as her hand began retrieving something from her cloak.

He stood with a smile and grasped his sword. "Oh, I wouldn't do that. I won't hesitate to use this, since I share no personal regard for you like the Dark Lord." He stepped closer to her. "In fact, I made it clear I don't think much of you at all. Mutual though, isn't it?"

"Completely."

"As long as we understand each other. I'm working on a name for myself in anticipation for our meeting with whoever took over operations at Black Dragon. I don't expect he'll rush to greet us, but I assume the trip is soon. The long-term solution can't be hiding from him. You failed miserably, and you're thoroughly ashamed of yourself, but rightly so. I mean you churned out beyond sloppy work."

"I'm going to cleave you in half!" Rage consumed her eyes anew, and her hand moved again for the item.

"No, you won't." Positioning his sword at her midsection, his other hand effortlessly handcuffed her wrist to end the grab for her dagger. "We'll make this partnership work, no matter how painful for us. We share a common goal, to destroy the Ancient One, Freedom Fighters, and all those standing with them. That part of the Dark Lord I remember well, and I'm eager to continue. That's what it's all about for me, nothing more. You wouldn't be in your current predicament, if you already learned that lesson."

"You're nothing compared to the Dark Lord."

He laughed. "I can't help I don't look like him, but I possess most of his memories. If he had spent more time instructing you rather than other things, perhaps you wouldn't have mucked this up too." The angrier she became, the harder he laughed. "You must do something for me. Simple even for you."

"I won't help you."

Finally, his patience ran out. "Then what's your plan? You did all this for nothing? Pathetic! You didn't get what you expected, and you carry on whining like this. Are you finished now, Black Beauty, because I'm sick of listening? Liking each other is not required to accomplishing the goal." His eyes became a sea of black nothingness, revealing a cruelness she remembered. "I don't need you, and we both know it. I want this done now. You will listen and fulfill my request."

Her eyes maintained their icy glare at him, but he spoke the truth even if it sickened her. She wanted back at them for what they did. Killing the Dark Lord served as the final blow. They deserved to pay for all of it. The Dark Lord's unhappiness with her started, when those two sunspear-bearers stole his prisoner, and the multitude of trouble they incited from that point. Then Lana and Seth intervened at the last moment to save Abigail. And the one, the Black Dragon Commander's son, Dante, killed her Dark Lord and somehow convinced the Commander to help him. A murderous inferno lit inside her thinking about it.

If she got a hold of them, how they would suffer. She knew countless ways too, in her seasoned role of assassin. She worked hard to do this, so she would use this resource as planned. "Fine, what do you want?"

"A mask of some kind. Get it created for me. Complete it before we go meet with him. I told you. Simple. You can manage, right?"

"I'll try to get around to it for you."

"I'll make it clear this final time, no more." He closed the space between them, his breath on her face and sword pointed up against her again. "I can dissolve this partnership in a permanent manner immediately. I repeat, you will promptly complete my request?"

Regardless of how she hated him, she understood him. They worked by identical rules in the same cruel world. Those of the Dark Lord and the assassin. A world she knew and navigated without a second thought. "Yes, I'll get to it right away."

"Your answer is finally to my liking. See that it continues."

"You're right. We strive towards a common objective."

He studied her longer and stepped back, satisfied by whatever he saw. "We can work together and make them pay. Agreed?" He placed his sword in the space between them.

She smiled at him for the first time and crossed her dagger with it. "Agreed. I'll return with the finished mask, to discuss our upcoming meeting."

"I'll be here waiting." He put his sword away, sat back down and watched her leave. She thought she possessed such power still with Black Dragon. This promised an entertaining session with the new Black Dragon leader, and he had just given her a formidable practice session for her next round.

CHAPTER ELEVEN

Morning arrived. "You two ready?" asked Alika.

"Yes." Angelina stood after tightening her boots, as Alena gave her a final check, and Alika did his own inspection of the two to indicate his approval. They dressed differently today, in pants and shirts chosen to appear more official looking. They didn't know what trouble they might encounter, so they prepared for an operation in most regards.

Dante came to find his group there, but his face fell at seeing Alika's group still missing.

Caleb grinned. "They'll be here. I bet you got Angelina home too late, and she overslept."

Ryan laughed and Seth smiled.

Lana playfully poked Caleb. "Now stop." She turned to her cousin. "Did you enjoy your evening with Angelina?"

"I did, and the teasing doesn't bother me. I could spend hours talking and being with her, and I'm completely happy. With certain topics being off limits, I thought it might be awkward. Yet I found knowing the who in the normal sense doesn't matter. I know who she is in the way I need to, and it's enough for me."

"Dante, as long as you're satisfied. You're the one who must be comfortable, and you are," said Seth.

"Yes, you're both happy, cousin, and it's clear you care for each other deeply just from seeing you together." Lana wrapped an arm around his shoulder briefly.

"We are, and we do." He turned to the others, but focused on Ryan. "Everyone else find a way to pleasantly pass the time?"

Caleb grinned as he kissed Lana on the cheek. "Lana and I did. Yeah, how did you manage, Ryan?"

Ryan laughed. "Well enough that I'm spending the evening again with Alena, but I'm sure everyone guessed."

Dante slapped Ryan lightly on the back. "We did, and this is nothing compared to what Angelina put Alena through last night when she put it together."

"I can only imagine with those two."

Voices drifted through the back-hall entrance, and the footsteps registered heavier than yesterday.

"Speaking of ..." Dante rose from his seat.

Alika greeted them as his group came through the doorway, "Hopefully we didn't keep you waiting long."

Caleb answered, "No, we're good. Your group is outfitted different today."

"Different situation, different wardrobe. We can't have our descriptions flying around," Angelina explained.

Dante wound his arms around Angelina's waist, enjoying the closeness and admiring her beauty again. Apparently, she and Alena weren't concerned about hiding their female identity on the colony. Rather, they wanted to conceal features. Their tresses were pulled back and covered with a deceptively lightweight scarf-type item. The half visor was up to reveal their facial features for now, but that would change once they reached the planet. They appeared only armed with a blaster, but no doubt they concealed their sunspears. Dante kissed her cheek and whispered, "You still look amazing."

"I try." She winked at him before turning to the others. "Are you ready? Remember there was poison on the planet."

Lana replied, "Yes, we can use the masks on our visors if necessary to protect against any lingering issue."

"Did you sleep well?" asked Dante as they strolled to the ship with the others.

"Of course, the day started pleasantly and ended the same way with you."

"I went to sleep with pleasant images too. Perhaps this evening we repeat it."

"I'm counting on it, Dante."

"Feel up to helping me pilot again, Ryan?" asked Alena.

"Like you need to ask. Anything else?"

"I'll think of something."

"I'm sure you will." Ryan grinned.

"We need to go over some items before we arrive," Angelina began once they sat inside the ship as Alena and Ryan listened and piloted the ship simultaneously. "Lana, this is an official visit from your group. Phrase it how you wish. Our group must appear as part of your group. We want as few questions about the visit and our identity. Leave it to us to come up with a story, if our group is questioned further, but our intent is to remain in the background. Today, we're just other members of your crew." She glanced at Dante.

"Understood. I'll manage."

"Sorry, I didn't mean to sound ..." She smiled as she squeezed his hand.

"My cousin will recover." Lana laughed.

"I'm sure, and no using our names on the planet. We'll come up with new names if it gets pushed."

"What do I want to accomplish with this visit?"

"We'll start with the agenda I sent to the data pads moments ago. Once we investigate, I believe the question answers itself. Mostly to be left alone to check things out."

Lana scanned through it, as she continued listening to Angelina. It provided a promising start.

"Angelina," Alena motioned her over, and Angelina knelt beside her. "Just a few minutes more. A Freedom Fighter embassy type-ship." Alena adjusted the controls, and they were satisfied with the transformation. Alena peered down at her and touched her arm. "How about where we land? I don't want to make this any worse for you." Ryan listened, awaiting further instructions from Alena.

The others spied the pained expression cross Angelina's face. Dante turned to Alika, who replied, "We're not on the planet yet, Dante. It's fine if you wish to check on her."

He walked over. "Is everything all right?'

"It will be," said Angelina, scanning the screen with Alena. "Alena, this visit will be difficult no matter what, but I'm grateful for your effort. Don't land on the hill, whatever you do. I can't do that again."

"I already knew. The images will start in your head again."

He understood. They headed to the planet which haunted Angelina's sleep, the one she visited that evening. Why, out of three planets did she choose the one hardest for her? "Angelina, why would you do this to yourself?"

"Because it's not about me. This is the last planet they hit, so it possibly holds the most answers." She peered back at Alena and her voice softened, "I'm not the only one who will struggle today. Please don't land the ship anywhere near the home of Emily and her family." Her voice broke. "Lana couldn't bear it." She glanced sadly at Lana and her eyes dropped to something hanging from Lana's neck. Her eyes returned to meet Alena's eyes.

"I'll land far from either one of those places, but near enough to get the needed assistance." Alena whispered, "Both of you will make it through today."

"Thank you." Touching Alena on the shoulder in gratitude, she got up.

Alena smiled at her. "Always."

"Dante, let's prepare your cousin before we land."

"I had no idea this was the one. Are you sure you want to do this?"

"Honestly, I don't want to see any of them again, but this is the only one I foolishly visited." Cupping his face in her hands, she stared up at him. "This is what we're doing, Dante. Please, it's time to think of your cousin." He sighed as he took her hand, and they rejoined the others.

"Are you okay, Lana? We'll pass through the portal to the planet in a couple of minutes."

"I'm fine, Angelina."

"Once we step on the planet it'll all hit anew. You bear the extra weight of immediately taking charge when we arrive." Her focus returned to the necklace hanging from Lana's neck. "Lana, I'm sorry for how hard this will be."

"Angelina, it's not your doing. Don't worry about me. I can call on Caleb." She smiled as he kissed her on the cheek.

Alena announced, "We're through the portal." Angelina nodded and went back over to investigate their landing.

Seth recognized Dante's concern and came to him. Dante answered his unspoken question. "We're returning to the planet which grieved her spirit that evening. She saw it in the vision and came to confirm the destruction. She's found no peace since."

Seth turned to Alika who nodded in affirmation. "And she chose this one. Oh my."

As the ship landed and Alena and Ryan shut it down, Angelina came back. "Are we ready?" Everyone nodded but Dante. "It's okay, Dante." She gave him a hug and a kiss on the cheek before they set out. He smiled at her, despite his misgivings. She adjusted her visor, and Alena followed suit. "Lead us, Lana."

The first step on the planet forced them to face the sobering reality of how terrible the devastation stretched. Portions of buildings and homes were reduced to rubble. Any buildings left reasonably unscathed found use, mostly for medical needs and to coordinate the assistance efforts. Temporary structures were established after the first couple of days to provide basic services. Personnel from other places volunteered to help after the news spread or were rerouted to the planet. The most unpleasant tasks neared completion. The collection of the dead and the task of identifying them, if possible, for closure continued. Then the final terrible, but necessary, part of the process to prevent disease from spreading was completed or nearly so. Just as terrible were those still hanging between the threshold of death and life, and their cries echoed as personnel transported them to the makeshift hospital. Their agony couldn't be ignored, any more than Angelina's eyes could be blind to what lay before her. She reexperienced it all as the first time on the planet.

Then Lana's grief hit again and the burden she carried for what happened. As a leader, she must take ownership for this somehow. Angelina understood, because she always did the same with the visions. Being responsible for the outcome, but being told she shouldn't feel that way. *I'm so sorry, Lana*, she said inside.

The waves poured over her though she fought against them. Too much pain again flooded her senses as the images raced across her vision. *No, I can't do this again here.* Yet the assault continued, and she turned away. She pretended to examine something on her data pad, but the screen blurred as the first teardrop fell on the trembling screen. Thankfully, no one approached thus far. She would blow this for them, if she didn't regain her composure.

Dante watched in agony, as she struggled with the images again. She insisted no special treatment, but he noticed Alika watching too. Alika approached Dante. "Come, she needs assistance."

"She said not to."

"I overruled her. We'll be discreet."

She knelt, alternating between her data pad and adjusting her boots. The two men bent down on either side of her.

"Have you struggled enough alone?" Alika whispered.

"Check on Lana. I'll be fine."

"Caleb is checking on Lana. You're needing help now, and Dante will assist you as I asked."

"That's not a good idea. If anyone sees ..."

"They'll see Dante offering assistance to a comrade because it's his nature. He's not treating you differently than he would another in his group." Alika turned to Dante. "There's an issue with her data pad. The two of you should be capable of sorting it out."

Dante helped her up, and they turned from the group. "Hand me your data pad." He pretended to inspect it. "You'll be okay," he whispered as he leaned into her.

"Yeah, I will be."

"What can I do within the strict guidelines you provided and his adjusted ones?"

"Just stepping on the planet again. The images flooded back, everything I experienced with it, the cry of the person we heard dying." Unable to continue, she momentarily closed her eyes and let out a deep breath. "It's best not to go further. It got worse. I acted horrible to..." she stopped again.

He watched her and realized, whatever happened here that evening was uglier for her on more levels than she had shared with him. He started to respond but didn't get the chance.

"I can't mess this up for us. I must block the other and treat this like another operation and push through."

"You can't flip a switch to work mode and turn off your feelings. Quite the opposite. You feel deeply. In situations like now and during the visions, it hurts. I'm sorry for that. Other times, I admit it's one of the many things I enjoy about you. You feel intensely, and it's an incredible thing when we're together. The sweet things you say and the ways you express them to me, I wouldn't want you to stop. It draws me to you in countless pleasant ways. It makes you, you."

She smiled at Dante. He couldn't see her blue eyes, but guessed what they looked like. Too bad they were here, because he longed to pull her close for one of those sweet expressions. She took her data pad and put it away. "I'm better, and my data pad works fine again. We'll pursue this talk later, and things I wish to pleasantly express to you, Dante."

"I'll look forward to it."

"Me too. I'm not sure how you manage it. You turned it so ... You know the words to say to me, Dante."

"I'll always do so for you."

"Well?" Alika asked as they rejoined the group.

"He's a master problem solver."

"I'm happy I could help her."

"Excellent work and perfect timing."

A slender, tall man in his mid-30s with jet black hair approached. Focused on his data pad, he begrudgingly pulled himself from it and plastered a smile on his face. "Oh, it's you. I didn't realize. My apologies for your wait. What can I do for you, Lana?"

Angelina instantly gauged him, a necessary and frequent task with her shipping business cover. After proving the easiest read in ages, she decided she witnessed the most insincere apology ever. His demeanor boasted irritation at their arrival, and he made the poorest attempt at hiding it. He exhibited a singular intent to return to whatever his data pad displayed, rather than dealing with his unannounced guests. The final assessment of him created a disagreeable picture, and instincts told her it didn't stem from stress due to his many duties on the planet. Quite the opposite. Not one trace of pity emulated from him for the colonists.

"We came to see the progress and assess the condition of those being treated. Just check on things in general to see what additional help can be rendered. Such a horrible thing." Lana bowed her head.

"It is, Lana. Of course, you can roam freely with who you are. At this point, I don't know that anyone ..." He realized better not to finish the thought. "Everything is rather scattered, but what you need is mostly located in this area." He stopped, finally taking interest in them. "I recognize your husband, Caleb, with his many areas of expertise on the battlefield, the Elder Seth, your cousin Dante with his excellent mastery of the sunspear. I see you joined them today too, Commander Ryan, with your equally impressive resume. I'm not familiar with the rest of you." The man waited and stepped forward towards them.

Angelina silently sighed. The effort to stay low-profile just went flying into space, and she skillfully took control. "Yes, we're advisors and handle some of Lana's security." Done. Hopefully, he'd leave it alone. She stepped back, but he advanced again.

"What are your names?"

He's not too bright either she thought as her distaste for him grew. "Kate."

"Really, Kate, huh?"

"Yes, that's what I said." Angelina stared him down through the visor, daring a further challenge.

He peered at her another moment and shifted focus to Alena. "And your name?"

"Annabel."

"Lana needs three advisors now? Sir, you are?"

"Although I occasionally give Lana advice, I'm here to assist on the request of my friend Commander Ryan," said Alika.

"What's your name, friend of Ryan's?"

"Alexander."

"Huh, how long have ..."

Angelina cut him off, "You never told us who you are."

"Oh ... I am ... came to help from another planet, once I heard what happened. There's a meeting ... yes, a meeting that I need to leave for now."

"I can tell you're an enormous help, but we need your name." Angelina made it clear he would stay until he disclosed it.

"Drew."

"Really, Drew, huh?"

"Yes, that's what I said," he answered with an unmistakable edge.

Angelina didn't say another word, but continued glaring at him. while waiting for Lana to take back over.

Lana asked, "Drew, what planet did you say you came from to offer your assistance?"

"It's um ... in the Adrian region, as my work puts me between several places in the area. I'm already late for this meeting."

"Of course, but if we need to find you later, I'm assuming that won't present a problem?"

"Correct, Lana. Let someone know, and they'll locate me. It was... interesting meeting you." He glowered one last time at Angelina before stalking away.

Once he disappeared from sight, Ryan shook his head. "Kate, he couldn't take his eyes off you."

"Yes, but I'm not waiting on a love letter from him."

Caleb grinned. "Yeah, Dante doesn't need to worry about you having another admirer."

"True. Not a pleasure, but interesting to meet." She chuckled. "He saved that for me."

Dante frowned. "He sure didn't like dealing with you."

"No, he didn't." Angelina glanced at Alena. "When was the last time we received a reception like that?"

"A Black Dragon hangar comes to mind."

"The squadron leader seemed nicer though he threatened to torture and kill us."

"You made another friend. Lovely, Kate." Alena shook her head.

"Sorry." She shrugged her shoulders. "But we learned two things. We better watch our backs, because whoever Drew is, he doesn't like us and didn't want company today."

"What's the other thing?" pressed Ryan seeing Angelina's smile.

"I'm a failure, the first day on the job as Lana's diplomat. Next time Annabel takes a turn. My apologies, Lana."

They laughed and resumed walking. Lana smiled and came beside Angelina. "I saw no failure. You figured him out immediately, unbalancing him at the first. You're an excellent advisor and diplomat." Her eyes twinkled. "We've extra quarters, certainly three to spare, whenever you and your group decide to relocate. We can make the three of you feel welcome, right Dante?"

"Absolutely. Your best idea yet, cuz."

"Yes, quite the idea." Angelina smiled. "How are Drew and everyone else getting cleared to assist? There are three planets in this condition, and obviously, it's chaotic."

"A system was supposed to be in place to keep track of who is assisting," said Lana.

"On paper maybe. Although considering the situation, who expects them to worry about who lends a hand? What planet turns down help with this?" asked Ryan.

"They can't, and it's understandable," answered Alena.

"The assumption is no one comes to do more harm," said Caleb.

"That's debatable after our recent encounter." Dante shook his head.

"I agree. Every second I spent with Drew set me on edge." Angelina cringed.

"Do you know what that means for these planets, if you're right?" Alena murmured.

"Somehow it's worse than we imagined. How do you make these people suffer more? What else is there to do to them?"

They headed into one of the buildings still standing, which had been transformed into a medical center. They met Doctor Iban, the main doctor at the center, who proved a complete change from their encounter with Drew. The doctor rushed to leave them, but for a far different reason. His face etched with concern for his patients suffering from the effects of the Dark Lord's poison, and a weariness spoke of long hours already devoted to bringing relief to their agony. They listened, as he answered what questions he could, and they became increasingly grateful for the additional medical expertise of Seth and Alika as the full extent of the situation unfolded. The group walked through the center, observing the patients.

Alika admitted, "He's trying, but this must be disheartening. I wish we arrived with answers for him, so he could truly treat them."

"All exposed to the same thing, but everyone isn't reacting the same or may be in different stages," said Seth.

"We still don't know what the poison actually is." Angelina paused and whispered, "These poor people."

"Help me," moaned the voice. A hand touched Angelina as she passed the bedside. She stopped, taking the woman's hand as the others returned. She made a motion, and Alika closed the curtains for more privacy with the woman. Angelina lifted her visor so her blue eyes showed, and her voice turned soothing, "I'm here, and I'm sorry for your pain."

"It's dark. I'm tired, but I must fight." The woman took a deep breath. "He tells me I must."

Angelina felt it, just as before. Another time, another place, another person. The struggle carried on, so long and awful, for the other one close to her heart now. It couldn't be. If so, it meant ... It took everything to remain standing. Lana placed a comforting hand on her shoulder. Dante didn't care what she said before. He moved to her other side and placed his hand at the small of her back, determined to comfort further if needed. Regardless, the curtain encircled them and the woman. Angelina fought back her own thoughts and concentrated on providing solace for this one. "Yes, the darkness is strong, and its poison burns. The Ancient One tells you to fight though, doesn't he?"

"Yes, it's hard. So tired. I can't."

"It's all right. Rest. The Ancient One will help your spirit keep fighting. You're not the first to do this. This bondage will be broken."

"Before I do, find her. Help me."

"I will try, if it gives you peace. Who do you need to find?"

"My ... daughter ... family."

"I don't know how to begin with what happened, but I sense they belong to the Ancient One. They are safe in his hands, despite their fate in this life. This is only one part of the journey. There is," her voice broke, "no pause felt from the end of this life to the arms of the Ancient One."

"I know. My husband already," the woman paused, "part of the forces ... begged me to leave ... but I ..." her voice drifted off, "I should have listened."

Angelina understood now why the woman remained when the attack arrived. Yet only to watch her husband die defending her and the colony he loved. In the end, he couldn't stop it, but none of them could. "I'm so sorry. He loved you very much, and you'll see him again one day. The Ancient One holds him secure until that day, and let that comfort you."

"It hurts. I miss him. But I need ... if I know the other ... maybe... fight as He tells me, please," the woman begged, as her grip tightened on Angelina's hand.

The woman's anguish ripped through her, and a sob escaped her at the woman's plea. The woman knew the battle, the darkness her spirit would wage against. She felt its poison for days, but soon she faced a far worse struggle, one she sensed. Her grief for her husband, still fresh, added to her burden, threatening to overwhelm her. The woman needed Angelina to answer her desperate request somehow as she said. A second sob escaped Angelina, and Dante caressed her back. She didn't possess the answer, but she knew the One who did, and He chose to give the woman the peace she sought. Angelina heard the whisper in her mind. She whispered "Anna," and the woman tried to comprehend how the girl knew her name. Angelina brushed the hair from Anna's face, and kissed her forehead. The woman gazed straight into Angelina's eyes, and an unspoken message passed between them. Angelina whispered something in her ear. The woman began crying, throwing her arms around Angelina's neck. Angelina held the woman. After a few minutes, the woman's arms loosened from Angelina, and she gradually pulled back.

The woman, with tears still on her face, asked, "Now?"

"Yes, rest your weary eyes. The Ancient One fights this for you, Anna. The night won't last forever, I promise."

Anna's eyes fluttered and closed, as Angelina released the woman's hand and sank to the ground.

Dante and Lana knelt beside her, while Alika and Seth saw to Anna.

"We're here," whispered Dante, as he wrapped his arm around her waist.

"He's right. Let us help," said Lana as she put an arm around Angelina's shoulder again.

"How many more Annas are on this planet, on the other two planets?"

Alika and Seth turned to the group. Alika sighed. "She is alive, but asleep,"

"And we don't know how to wake her."

Alika focused on Angelina. "I'm guessing you knew?"

"Yes. The sleep is the same tortured one as Abigail's, when we found her hooked up to the black substance. The darkness so awful that gripped her. For those who serve the Ancient One, this is how their suffering is prolonged." Their pain screamed out to her again, and she put her head in her hands at the onslaught. Dante pulled her over to him and completely wrapped his arms around her. Lana found Caleb's waiting arms as the realization sunk in. Three planets full of tortured spirits like Abigail endured, and the Black Dragon held the capacity to continue it. Alena shook her head and succumbed to her own grief, as Ryan embraced her. Alika and Seth sat in the two chairs by the bedside, both at a complete loss.

Finally, Angelina felt pieced back together, as the Ancient One released the emotional turmoil from the tortured spirits from her. She took a deep breath as Dante kissed her on the forehead and held her eyes for another minute. She turned to Lana, whose face reflected their shared grief, and hugged her. "I'm sorry, Lana." Lana whispered, "I as well." They got up and Angelina turned to Alena. Words stopped being necessary between them long ago, as they hugged each other. Angelina mouthed thank you to Ryan, as he nodded sadly.

"Well?" Angelina asked as everyone focused on Seth and Alika.

"I ... we don't know," said Seth, looking at Alika whose expression reflected his own.

"On the surface, these people are sick because of their exposure to a toxin," said Alika.

"The proper treatment is given. They get better and wake up."

"Yet a whole other component is at work here, which won't respond to any traditional medical treatment."

"Maybe we still approach it like the other," said Angelina.

"Explain," said Alika.

"These people are poisoned with the same as what the Dark Lord pumped into Abigail. The identical darkness is attached with both. The dispersal is different, but ..."

"It found its entrance all the same, and now they'll war against it. We can't measure spirit, but in the medical world we take a blood sample," said Alika.

"And we can't measure darkness,, but we can examine for an unknown substance that doesn't belong there, like a black substance," said Seth.

Alika and Seth drew the sample from Anna's body, sealed, and labeled it.

Seth said, "One other sample as a point of comparison should suffice. Perhaps someone else before they go to sleep."

Angelina put her visor back down. "Let's do it."

They didn't search long to find another individual in the same condition as they found Anna. Angelina shut the curtain and raised her visor again. Together, Angelina and Lana comforted the woman.

Angelina said, "Teresa, we know you're hurting, but we want to help."

Lana asked, "May we get a blood sample from you? It could aid us in discovering how to stop this poison inside you."

The woman nodded weakly.

Lana held the woman's hand, and Angelina stroked the woman's face, as Alika and Seth worked. Angelina smiled at the woman and said, "Focus on me and Lana. Almost done, Teresa."

Alika and Seth nodded when they finished.

"Thank you, Teresa," whispered Lana, "You're tired, but you're not alone."

"It's dark. Will it still be so dark?"

Angelina continued stroking Teresa's face as she answered, "Maybe. But do not fear the darkness, for even when we must pass through it, we know the One who stands beside us. He takes us through it."

"How are you sure?"

Tears shined in Angelina's eyes. "Because the Ancient One reminded me in my dark hour, and it was the only way the darkness did not take me," she whispered. "He'll be your light in this darkness too." Dante watched Alika's and Alena's eyes moisten at the memory.

"I will sleep," the woman answered as her breathing became shallower.

"You will sleep. The Ancient One battles for you."

The woman's eyes closed. Angelina exhaled and briefly closed her eyes. Dante leaned over. "You okay?"

"I'll be fine." She remained staring down at Teresa, but finally turned to him. "We should get a sample from your mother for comparison, since she no longer receives a form of the substance. Hers came through a different medium, and her spirit doesn't struggle anymore. The sample could be of help."

"Definitely. We'll see what it shows." Dante studied her for another minute. She moved past the turmoil of the last encounter to concentrate on what she needed to do now. Initially, he felt relieved, until he realized no real shift occurred, but she forced it as she often did.

Lana checked the data pad. "Next on the agenda. You know how to make a day of it."

"We should see all the outcomes," replied Angelina.

"We're certainly seeing the last possible one with this."

After wandering for a bit without finding what they needed, Lana admitted what no one wanted to, "Seems we'll need assistance."

"Drew was so eager to help earlier too. Just can't wait." Angelina shook her head.

Dante grinned. "Your eyes said differently, Kate."

"You don't miss anything, but you'll never know for sure thanks to the visor." She grinned back at him and turned to the rest of the group. "Drew enjoys making us wait, doesn't he?" Habit took over, and she wandered around to assess her immediate surroundings further.

CHAPTER TWELVE

"They are certainly busy, and I thought they would never leave the medical center. I wish they'd get back on their ship and go already," fumed Drew watching the group from another room.

The other man continued, studying their movements too. "They won't anytime soon. They're determined with their investigation now, and you didn't help matters. You're probably the reason they extended their visit. There's a way of doing these things, and you completely messed it up."

"I won't waste time playing games with them."

"Wrong again. Sometimes you must play along to accomplish your goal. They're Freedom Fighters, and you appeal to what matters to them. Now they care about these pitiful colonists, the pain they're in, the destruction, and so on. You appear somewhat helpful, try to act kind, like you care about what's happened. That gets useful information. It's not difficult, and our day goes much smoother than I expect it will now."

"Whatever. The whole group is an annoyance." Even so, Drew's eyes concentrated on one individual.

"Yes, you told me, but she's as the rest of them, same ideals and all. She's also a woman, a fairly young one at that. I'm sure if you had spoken to her more pleasantly, she'd be more agreeable and let her guard down." He watched her. Even in her attire, she couldn't mask her attractiveness, as well as the other advisor for Lana. This could be fun. "I'll manage this. Go ahead and leave. They guessed you're not a friend. Someone will return to question what happens to them, and you'll get tracked down if you remain. Sorry you can't stick around to watch, because you could learn something for the next time. I'll be close behind you, once I undo this mess you created."

Drew scolded at him, but walked away. The other man shook his head, as he adjusted his shirt and put a smile on his face.

The group wandered in the central waiting area and connecting hallways of the building, as they continued waiting for Drew. They spoke with a couple of people, who assured them they would locate him. The blank stares the group received when they spoke his name didn't encourage confidence.

"Kate." Angelina turned at hearing her name, but didn't see anyone. A door stirred simultaneously at the end of the hallway, prompting her closer to investigate. "Excuse me, Kate, is it?" Angelina turned again. This time a well-built, handsome young man with blond hair in his early twenties greeted her with a smile. Dressed in a pair of comfortable black pants and a green polo shirt, he was clearly part of the colony staff.

"Yes," she answered, waiting.

Not a problem. He could work this. After this morning, she wanted to know who she dealt with, or at least think she did. Yes, she was quite the treat for the eyes, as he got a closer inspection of her slender, shapely form, and he couldn't even see all her features for the coverings and gear. He planned to change that soon. "I'm Trey, one of those assigned here after the attack. It's heartbreaking what happened. The suffering, I am ..." He stopped as if overcome by what he had seen, and shook his head sadly at her. "I apologize. I became aware only a short time ago of the arrival of Lana and her companions. From my understanding, you're advising her, and I'm sorry for the mix-up when you arrived. I should've met your group." He reached out and clasped her hand. "You're truly a pleasure to meet, Kate."

Angelina studied him and went along with it for the moment, allowing him to take her hand in greeting. He definitely tried making up for the earlier introductions. His confidence in his appearance was becoming apparent, as he attempted to charm his way into her good graces, but this morning alerted her. Either way, she wouldn't melt into a blushing, stumbling heap in front of him as he expected. She managed and dismissed his type constantly with her shipping cover. Anyway, she didn't do that. Well, Dante reduced her to that in an instant, but he'd always be the wonderful exception. A smile crossed her face thinking of him. Her focus reluctantly returned to Trey to play his tiresome game. "It's a pleasure to meet you as well, Trey. Why don't you direct my group where we need to be?"

He glimpsed the smile that flashed across her face, and he silently congratulated himself. She quickly tried returning to her advisor stance, but he relished a challenge as he grinned back at her. "I'd love to, Kate. You didn't receive any help today, and I desire the chance to remedy that with you, Kate. I found something to help you and your group, and I'll show you since you're Lana's advisor. Just in this room next to us."

"The others will want to see too." She began saying, but his hand on her back nudged her through the door.

"They will." He quietly locked it behind them.

After a cursory scan of the room, she concluded nothing helpful existed. It was a banquet sized meeting room, but mostly open space now. Several chairs, a couple of benches, and a few tables were all shoved to the sides. She turned to him. "Whatever you wish to show me, my companions need to see it with me. We're going back for them now." She reached to open the door, but he intercepted her hand.

"We'll bring them in soon enough."

"I'm beginning to suspect you're not any nicer than Drew this morning." She stepped back to place more space between them. Although she heard a sound behind her, she didn't dare remove her focus from Trey.

"Don't say that, Kate. I put such a friendly face on for you. Honestly, Kate, I'm hoping to spend extra time with you. You're quite attractive, though you hide it under that attire. So is the other advisor Lana keeps. We don't share the same ideals, but I can get you to come around to my thinking or persuasion easily enough. I want the chance, and it appears I'll get it."

"I won't ever come to your way of thinking, Trey, and there will be no opportunity to persuade me." She realized the source of the earlier sound. He brought backup into the room as they spoke. Other entrances existed on the far side, and the troops would close in at Trey's command unless she accepted his offer. She sighed. *The reception in the hangar again. How many times must I do this?*

Dante looked around. Where did Angelina go? He lost track, when those individuals reported they located Drew. It turned out false, so they continued waiting.

Alena and Ryan strolled over. "Where's Kate?" asked Alena.

Dante stared back at them. "I don't know. I thought I saw her talking in the hallway with someone, but she's gone."

"Something's wrong. She wouldn't disappear." Alena caught Alika's eye, and he approached immediately. He glanced around. "Where is she?"

"Missing."

Alika motioned for the others.

"Kate, I can call them off. There are much better ways for this to go." He stepped closer.

"No, and I'm warning you, Trey." She stepped back from him again.

"We can do it this way too. Actually, I'll enjoy it more." He smiled and lunged for her. Her hand already reached for her blaster, and she let the blast go as he fell to the floor before her. Immediately, she turned and aimed the blaster to begin shooting the army headed for her.

They heard it at the same second, and Dante jumped. "Blaster fire." Rushing down the hallway, he reached the door first to discover it sealed shut.

Angelina started to fire the blaster at the first troop, but her motion halted as excruciating pain sliced through her back and the sensation of an inferno ripped down her arm as it was wrenched backwards. A scream erupted from her against her will, at the surprise of the magnitude of torment her body felt at once. The blaster fell from her hand, and someone stood in front of her instantly. A blow to her midsection added its agony this time, and two arms forced her to her knees. She peered up to discover Trey kneeling close to her face, whispering seductively, "Why did you do that, Kate? I dreamt of things going so much differently." His one hand roughly fingered her neck, slid his hand all the way down her throat, and up again to wrap his hand around it. She spied his other hand grasping the blade handle behind him as his hand on her neck tightened.

Dante sliced the door open with his sunspear to disrupt the locking mechanism, and they burst inside the room. He froze. A dagger headed straight for Angelina's chest.

I'm left with no other option. I'm running out of air. Her sunspear made it the instant before his dagger plunged into her chest, knocking his weapon from his grip. The hand on her throat slightly loosened, but not enough. She needed a hit on him with her sunspear before he strangled her or retrieved the dagger, but she couldn't do it. He continued bending her back, and the pain from her back and arm blinded her. He smiled the further he stretched her, knowing the agony pouring through her. Many times she had blocked out such pain, but this time nothing worked. Her body screamed for more air, as her sunspear began sliding from her grasp. Just like she felt herself starting to slip away. No. She couldn't let him win.

"Why you ... I'm going to break you into pieces!" he roared, while his hand continued its deadly vise on her throat and spine-breaking torment on her back.

Suddenly, Dante yelled as he yanked Trey from Angelina, "Get off her now!" He delivered a single blow that sent Trey rolling on the floor groaning in agony. Dante moved to get him up, intent on pulling him apart limb from limb.

Air returned to Angelina with Trey's grip gone. Though Dante wanted to kill Trey, she must stop him. Still struggling for sufficient air, she gasped, "He may," she took a breath, "have information." Dante reluctantly acknowledged her words, ignoring his desire to rid himself of the man. She heard a blaster going off and remembered. "Dante, 'lasters don't," she took another breath, "work. Tell them."

He didn't need to, as Lana overheard. Her voice rang out, "Blasters won't keep them down. Use your swords or sunspears!"

Alika ran to them. Dante said to him above the fray, "Take and guard him, would you? The blaster doesn't work on him either. Kate says spare him for questioning, but if he gets out of line an instant, get rid of him."

"Agreed." He hauled the man up and dragged him to a corner away from the fighting.

"We must assist the others, Dante."

"He almost strangled and stabbed you. No, you sit this one out." He stooped beside her.

"I'm fine. I can breathe again." She started up.

"Kate, would you please listen to me?"

"No, I'm fine, more than fine." She stood with her sunspear ready.

He sensed it radiating from every part of her, burning in her eyes through the visor. Determination. Anger. Beyond anger. He should stay close to her for all their safety. She wouldn't sit this one out.

She ran with sunspear flashing into the middle of the battle. Three troops surrounded her, and Dante rushed to help. She surprised them when she flipped from out of their trap to cleave through them from behind, and her sunspear never stopped its deadly work now. Dante fought beside her, matching her stroke after stroke. Black Dragon troop fell repeatedly at the end of their blades until he searched the room to realize it was over. He turned to her, but she still appeared poised to strike. His hand gently rested on her shoulder while staring in her eyes through the visor as he assured her, "Kate, there's no more. Can you hear me? We got them all. Please, you can stop. It's over." For a moment, she stood in a trance, seeing a battle only she could.

Her breathing returned to normal, and she scanned the room again as though expecting new soldiers to materialize from the walls or floor to attack her. "Guess you're right." She finally stared at Dante and her voice rose, "Where is he? Where's

Trey? I'll run this interrogation." She didn't wait for an answer, before spotting Alika with Trey and marching towards him. Dante followed her, shaking his head. He had never seen her like this, but he couldn't blame her, after what happened.

Grabbing Trey by both shoulders from Alika's grasp, she slammed him into a chair, and he groaned at the impact. "Comfortable, Trey?" She sneered. She motioned to Caleb and Ryan. "Secure his hands behind his back to the chair and his feet too for me, would you? No more surprises from him today."

"Sounds fair to me," answered Caleb, as he and Ryan did so.

"I thought you got to ask the questions," said Trey to Lana.

"After your stunt today, Kate should interrogate you, if she wishes. It's best to answer her questions and cooperate." Lana turned to Angelina. "Whenever you're ready, Kate."

"Trey, or whoever you are for today, I'll play no more games with you! The poison on this planet, I want to know how to get rid of it and help the colonists suffering from it. The memory of you almost putting a dagger through me is still fresh. There's no patience left in me!" She brought the sunspear's point to Trey's chest. "Answers now, Trey!"

"Always about these colonists. Well, I'm telling you the truth, when I say I don't know the answer. You're wasting time asking me."

"I said tell me!" She stopped as well as halting her sunspear's increasing pressure on his chest. The smug, little smirk covering his face only angered her more, like he begged her to drive the sunspear straight through him. Yes, he got exactly the reaction he wanted from her. She took a few deep breaths and forced herself to radiate calm as she lowered her sunspear. She reminded herself, to do this any other way wouldn't serve them. His response sickened her, but she perceived he spoke the truth. "What can we do to help them?'

"Nothing. Once it enters them, this is their fate." He laughed.

"What about those with you? They're not normal Black Dragon soldiers. I didn't see machinery. Almost as though ..."

"Come now, Kate. You said it. I refuse to answer that one. It's at your feet. You're as smart as you are beautiful."

She gave no reaction to his comment or his eyes slowly traveling over her frame. She considered the rest of his words. A strange material came from the troops when she slayed them. Of course, she didn't piece it together at the time, because everything got clouded by the one emotion. *When will you learn?* she scolded herself. "I'm not through with you by any means," she said as she walked away from him.

He replied, "I'll be here eagerly awaiting your return, Kate."

She ignored that comment too as she motioned and said, "Dante, Annabel, Caleb, Lana, and Ryan, can we talk over here?"

"Are you sure we can't get rid of him now? I'll happily volunteer to do the honors," murmured Dante. He didn't appreciate any of the last bit from Trey.

"Not yet, Dante. Trust me, he won't smile for much longer."

They all witnessed the same thing when they eliminated the troops. They knelt over one and examined it. The troop wore a Black Dragon uniform, but no sign of machinery showed where they cleaved through. He appeared mostly human, except for one thing. They stared at the wound, where the blade ripped through him.

"I'm not seeing things, right?' asked Caleb.

"No," said Lana.

"We once said, it possessed a life of its own," Alena said looking at Angelina.

"And what a horrible thing it is."

Dante and Ryan glanced at each other. The battles would be different now.

The black slimy goo continued oozing from the wound to create a larger puddle on the floor. Alena and Angelina turned their eyes from it, but the others took longer to process what they saw.

Angelina whispered, "Like before. It cuts too deep sometimes."

Alena laid a comforting hand on Angelina's shoulder and whispered, "I know."

Angelina wasn't quiet enough, and Dante leaned over. "What's wrong? What's like before?"

"Nothing, it's fine."

"Terrible job of lying to me."

"Later, I promise. It makes no difference with this."

"Later it is."

Angelina returned her comments to the group, still avoiding looking at the fallen enemy troop further. "I wonder if this is how it turns them at first, or if the black ooze is only after they're slain?"

Caleb said, "There's a way to find out."

"My thinking too. I'll talk to Seth and Alika. I'm not asking Trey's permission, so you and Ryan will need to keep him still."

They made their way back to Trey, and Angelina spoke to Seth and Alika privately. The two returned to the group surrounding Trey with medical bag in hand. Seth and Alika took the sample from Trey's arm, as Ryan and Caleb stood on each side ready to tighten the hold on him if he caused further problems.

"A blood sample? Unusual interrogation tactic, Kate," said an amused Trey.

"Does he ever stop?" asked Alena, shaking her head.

"I got an idea that works. Say the word, Kate," growled Dante.

"Any of us would gladly do it for her, cuz."

Angelina admitted, "It does seem no one taught him proper prisoner etiquette. Not to speak unless spoken to."

"Even when he does ..." Dante scolded.

"I agree it's revolting, enduring this, for the hope of the smallest piece of helpful information coming from his mouth."

Seth and Alika finished, sealed the sample, and put a covering on the puncture site. They wouldn't take any chances of the substance getting on one of them while his interrogation resumed.

Trey continued, "A bandage and everything and you say you don't care, Kate. I should've kept the act up longer, when it was the two of us. I see now you'd warm right up to my touch."

"You're kidding yourself." It took everything to resist spearing him through now, and she knew Dante's hand kept finding his sunspear with each new suggestive comment from Trey. She continued calmly, "Those who deny the Ancient

One and serve another master, this is their fate?" She indicated towards those dead, with the black goo pouring from their body.

"Everyone serves one or the other. We simply help them with their choice."

"This is your idea of helping? They met their death, and your master is cruel. There's no rest in their death."

"You pretend the others fare better?" He laughed. "Your Ancient One speaks of peace for his children. How? While they lay suffering in their bed, their spirits finding no rest now. Is your master not cruel? It eats at all of you to see, and you can do nothing to stop it."

"You know nothing of the Ancient One and His ways. How dare you even speak like you do?" Her voice rose as she struggled to call back her anger. "Your master leads you to death, as he does all who follow him. How many more of you, throughout the colonies?"

"I don't know the number. It's happening, and you're powerless to stop it. It's already put into motion." His eyes danced with merriment.

"Who is in charge now?"

"I don't know that either."

"No more games. I warned you." Her voice rose again, and she repositioned her sunspear at his chest.

"I'm not. Until maybe a couple of days ago, we thought our orders still originated from the Dark Lord and the Black Dragon Commander. Black Dragon told us operations continue to run as normal, and the details aren't our concern. Probably for this reason."

"Get his data pad," commanded Angelina glancing at Ryan, her voice no longer hiding her anger. "He's done with useful information."

Trey smiled. "Kate, this is a shame. I'm guessing your plan for me next, and I entertained such different images for us. How I would've found it enjoyable getting to know you better, see what you kept covered. I should have persuaded you further when I wrapped my hand around your lovely neck. At least stolen a kiss when I had the chance, when I pulled you close against me. If only we had been given more time alone together, Kate, what I could have done for ... to you."

His eyes slowly roamed over her form again, to show his thoughts matched his words.

She refused to satisfy him, by reacting like he wanted. Rather, she smiled at him and said calmly, "No, more time wouldn't make any difference. I'd die from the dagger before ever finding your touch welcome. And, Trey, I speak truth when I say that. Enough talk. It's time you met your master." Without hesitation, she ran him through with her sunspear as she did the others earlier. The black substance poured out. She put her sunspear up and opened up her visor as her eyes regarded his still form with coldness. "I finished interrogating him. He won't get up this time, but I need to sit a few minutes before we head out again." She settled on a bench away from Trey's body.

Seated beside her, Dante tried hiding his concern. The calm settled back into her eyes, despite the fury which poured from her earlier. Trey's words to her proved upsetting enough to hear, but the way his eyes devoured her at every opportunity made it worse. She'd never know how close Dante came to taking his sunspear and ending the man.

CHAPTER THIRTEEN

Angelina rubbed her throat and winced. The adrenaline, anger, and whatever else wore off now, and her body reminded her of the harsh treatment received from Trey.

Dante stared at her neck when her hand slid away. Pain crossed his face, and he leaned closer to her, "Oh, An ..., Kate, he hurt you badly. We heard the blaster, your scream, and rushed in as fast as we could, but not soon enough." The hand imprint revealed where Trey grabbed her neck and held it, leaving it terribly bruised. The others came over, but Alika was closest as his eyes studied her. Dante probed, "Where else did he hurt you?"

She attempted to brush it off but too late. Unconsciously she'd reached for her arm, and Alika and Dante caught the movement. "No, you got in when I needed you. He wrenched my arm back," she sighed. Bruises were setting in from the other blows too, but she hoped nothing more. "He hit me hard in my lower back twice in succession with something, and it hurts badly now. He came around and delivered another blow to the front, but it doesn't smart too much anymore. Not like the other."

Alika said, "He held a punishing grip on your entire upper body. Are you sure nothing else?"

"He smashed down my shoulders to bring me to my knees, but my shoulder isn't hurting from that. It's from him trying to twist my arm off."

Alika caught Dante wince at the description, as Alika motioned to Alena. "We need your help, please." She knelt before Angelina and waited for Alika's directions. He handed her the small instrument from the medical kit. "Check around the shoulder and neck area. You can examine it better than me with her clothing and our current location." He noticed Dante looking at him questioningly. "You're fine, Dante."

Alena pointed the device at Angelina's neck. "Oh, Kate, the bruises are deep. I'm so sorry," she said as she moved down with the device. 'I'm loosening this a bit, so I can see easier on your shoulder and down further. Your neck certainly received the worst of it, but there's bruising on the lower part too. I suppose where he tried to get a better grip or decide ..." She didn't finish, as Dante became visibly more unhappy. They all filled in the thought as they recalled Trey's last words.

"I'm okay, Dante, I promise. Don't be so worried."

"This is far from okay." He sighed and turned to Alika. "What about the other injuries?"

"Those are next." He turned to Angelina. "Do you mind if we peek at your back? It should be easy enough without removing anything."

"Yes, it's fine."

Dante said to Alika, "I can go if ..."

Alika smiled at Dante. "There's no need. It's not in an area of a delicate nature." He confirmed with Angelina. "Kate?"

"Of course, you can stay, Dante. The others too." She leaned forward on the bench and put her head in her lap. Alika untucked the uniform shirt the rest of the way and gently slid it partly up in the back. His shoulders slumped, and he murmured, "Oh, my, that's quite ugly." They glanced at Dante, whose eyes mixed with pain and anger. Alika asked, "You said you felt two blows. Any ideas from what?"

"One I'm sure from him directly. Maybe his knee or shoe. The other felt like something he used on me, like a chair leg."

"Fair guesses." Caleb gestured to Trey's feet and two parts of an object on the ground.

Ryan followed his motion. "Those boots would leave a mark, and I'd say he broke that wood piece across her back."

"Agreed." Alika said, "Annabel, hand me the spray from my bag. It'll ease the pain from the bruising," He took the spray from Alena and turned to Dante. "Hold her shirt while I spray this, please."

'Of course," replied Dante as he stared at the broad band of darkening black and blue covering her lower back. Alika treated it, and Dante slowly lowered her shirt. She sat back up.

Alika said to her, "Your midsection as well?"

"Yes. It doesn't hurt like the other, but it's pointless to protest. Let's get to it, so we can move forward. This one won't be as easy to examine and treat sitting." She made a face as she surveyed the floor littered with puddles of black ooze from the Black Dragon bodies.

Dante whispered to her, "Lean back on me, Kate." Slowly she did and heard the steady beat of his heart, and felt his arm slid under her to keep her secure. This is where she'd stay happily. Alika and Alena pulled her shirt partway up again.

Alika sighed at the black and blue revealed. "Trey's brutality again shows, but I imagine the pain in your back demands most of your attention."

Dante winced again at the place and looked back into Angelina's eyes. "I'm so sorry for the bruises you took today."

"It isn't your fault, Dante," she whispered and smiled at him, "And thank you, Dante."

"You're welcome, Kate." It took everything in him not to lean down and kiss her, but he simply smiled back.

"You may sit up, Kate," instructed Alika as he finished treating her. Dante lifted her back up as she squeezed his hand.

Alika turned to Alena. "On her neck and shoulders too."

Angelina closed her eyes while Alena sprayed it on her neck and inside her shirt.

"Thank you. That should ward off the pain for a while. Everyone closer. We need to talk," said Angelina, as she readjusted her shirt. The others stepped forward.

Lana asked, "Are you really all right?"

"Yes, I'm," she caught Dante's look, "just bruised. Trey's manner turned rough quickly."

"Longer in here with him, and he ..." Dante began.

"I know, and he shot his mouth off every chance he got. However, he told me either of Lana's advisors would provide pleasing company. Drew probably directed him to make me first choice after my earlier impression."

"I didn't think anything would come of that." Caleb shook his head.

"Me either. I'm standing by the door, and the next instant I'm trapped in here with him."

"He forced you in here. How did we not hear?" said Dante.

"It's not how you're thinking. He tried doing cleanup after Drew's disaster performance and worked hard being pleasant and friendly. He approached me immediately with who he was and his name. Even called me by my name, with no interrogation of it, and made a point to keep calling me Kate, as though he believed my story. He said it was a pleasure to meet me and clasped my hand all sweetly. The whole presentation even included him losing his composure over the state of the colonists and a profuse apology for the mix-up this morning. He said he intended to make it right."

"I bet he did. He sounds perfect in his meeting with you, Kate." Dante's eyes flashed with anger.

"Yes, too perfect." She turned to Dante and squeezed his hand. He took a deep breath, and his eyes regained a resemblance of calm. She continued, "I realized as soon as he started talking. I admit, if we received that greeting this morning rather than what we encountered from Drew, I wouldn't have suspected anything at first. He mistakenly assumed he'd flash his smile to Lana's young advisor, and I'd be at his bidding. It didn't work. He gave me a story about showing me something in the room to help us. I told him we needed to get the rest of you, but he already nudged me through the door. Once we entered the room, he dropped the act completely, and when I refused to enjoy his company, you can fill in the rest."

"I let this happen. If I paid closer attention to you, I could have prevented all of it," said Dante, shaking his head.

"Dante, please don't. You aren't to blame."

"Cuz, she's right. We were all right there and played a part."

"That's not what I meant. I'm well-trained and frankly embarrassed by how easily he overpowered me. I didn't know about the blasters when I dealt with Trey, which cost me. When I shot him point-blank with the blaster, he fell seemingly dead. I turned my back to blast the reinforcements he brought today. I avoided using my sunspear to keep my cover as Lana's advisor, but I didn't manage the first blast off, before his blows came from behind. The next second he stood before me, and I realized too late the uselessness of the blasters. Then, you found he got me into an ugly situation." Sensing the look from Dante, she turned to him. "I know how it appeared, but I was getting it under control. I knocked the dagger from him with my sunspear, and I still had my sunspear. I'm sure I'd manage to get loose. I admit I waited the last moment to pull my sunspear ..."

"The last moment?" Dante burst out, staring at her. "Truly the last moment. Do you hear yourself? He pointed a dagger within a breath of your chest. You just got your sunspear up, and he almost strangled the life out of you! How many more last moments did you intent to wait before you stopped it?" He shook his head, while running his hand through his hair.

She gazed into his eyes. "Not a moment more than I did, Dante, I promise you. I have never left your side, and I will not now, remember?" She kissed him and whispered, "What else do you need from me to be assured, my Dante?"

He cupped her face in his hands. "I'm reassured, but you waited too long, cut it too close. Don't do it anymore. You scared me again." He took a deep breath, and then his eyes twinkled. "You just broke your rules completely."

"You needed a reminder from me, and I decided you're worth the risk. I stand by that kiss. Technically, I didn't break my rules because it's only us among our friends."

"You're right. Now I know the loopholes, and I intent to take advantage of it a few more times, if we sit longer."

"I would happily give in to you too, Dante." She laughed. "If we hope to accomplish anything further, we should get up now." She couldn't resist kissing him on the cheek before she rose. He stood too and grinned at her. She turned to the rest of the group, enjoying being spectators of the two's exchange. "We're ready now. Is everyone else?"

"I believe so," Lana smiled. "How about the samples?"

"No scope needed. Solid black ooze from the troops and Trey before and after Kate finished him. Further examination waits until we return," said Seth.

"It takes over their bloodstream," said Ryan.

"As it overcomes their spirit and heart to serve their master," said Alena.

"Until death," Angelina whispered as she surveyed the carnage on the floor, her eyes resting on the final casualty in the room. "Trey was a colonist, as all these before the poison came. He's not the first to choose this master, but it always leads to the same end."

Dante watched her. Strangely, he no longer perceived anger in her eyes as they swept over these who tried killing her, only sadness. She spoke as one who previously lived through this somehow and revisited it.

Angelina realized he studied her and forced herself to refocus. "How do we spot them if they are everywhere, like Trey said? We can't ask for a blood sample as standard greeting."

"But there's no other marker," Ryan admitted.

"We need to see if there's something more apparent," said Alika.

"Otherwise, a lot of blood samples loom ahead." Seth sighed.

"In spite of how it pains me, we must take Trey and another one of our Black Dragon soldiers back for closer examination," Angelina said.

The others stared at her.

"I said I didn't like my conclusion, but we all saw it coming."

"A ride back with them. The day keeps getting better," said Caleb.

"They're not hitching a ride with us," said Angelina. She already glimpsed Lana starting the process on the data pad.

"A ship is in route now," said Lana. "Seth and Alika, I hate it, but a new task awaits you this evening."

Alika nodded and Seth answered, "We'll do so. The rest of you dealt enough with them."

"Are we still doing the last stop?" asked Alena.

Angelina replied, "After going to all this trouble, we should finish. Maybe nothing comes of it. I don't know now."

Lana followed her eyes. "We can't leave things like this."

Ryan countered, "A couple of firestones gets this cleaned up."

"Likely this becomes the scene from here on out. The mostly machine centered troops made everything easier," said Caleb.

Lana spoke quietly, "Leaving more of these to prey on the innocent colonists sickens me."

"We need a plan, sweetheart," Caleb reminded her as he wrapped an arm around her waist.

"All three like this," Angelina whispered.

"This is not your fault," Dante said, tilting Angelina's chin up to hold her gaze, "or yours either," he glanced over at Lana. "It's in both of your faces. The others are right. We formulate a plan, or it avails us nothing. Once done, we come back and carry it out."

Alika nodded. "Returning to our agenda, I suggest asking Doctor Iban for assistance."

Lana looked up. "Yes, he probably held our answer initially, but the ship just arrived to take the two bodies."

Dante replied, "Perfect timing. Let's see to this now." He stroked Angelina's cheek. "There's no way anyone gets separated again. No one else gets hurt today. But first, let's clean this up." Pulling a firestone out, he threw it on a group of the slain troops. Ryan and Caleb did the same with another group, leaving only Trey's body and one other body.

After giving their troops instructions on the handling of their cargo, the troops carefully transported the two bodies in closed body bags suited for hazardous material. Meanwhile, Seth contacted the doctor at the fortress and updated him sufficiently on the situation to ensure the bodies were kept safely secured for later examination. The group headed back to medical to locate the doctor as the ship disappeared through the portal.

Lana pulled Angelina and Alena aside. "I know what we said, but we need to be sure here."

Alena nodded. "These people in their current condition are truly at the doctor's mercy. He appears sincere though."

"However, I just experienced how painful the other turns out. There are many to suffer if we're wrong about him."

The three walked back over and Lana approached the doctor, "Excuse me, Doctor Iban ..."

"Please just Iban, Lana. The other feels much too formal these days." He peered up from something he showed the others on his data pad in response to one of their questions.

She smiled. "Then, Iban, we need a blood sample from you before we go further."

"I don't understand, Lana."

"It's related to the poison. Will that be a problem for you?"

"No, of course not. When?"

"Now, please."

His face registered surprise, but he immediately sat. Seth and Alika went over to him.

"He didn't hesitate in giving the sample. A good sign," murmured Angelina. Lana and Alena nodded, thinking the same thing.

Alika and Seth pricked the man's finger, and the blood flowed red. A collective silent sigh of relief passed through the group.

Lana said, "All those assisting him too."

Alika and Seth nodded, and Seth said to him, "We need to talk to you. You must keep this to yourself, and we'll require your help."

Shock reflected on Iban's face when they finished. "After what happened, how do I hope to maintain my patients' safety?"

Alika sighed. “That part is still being worked out, but you can’t let anyone uncover you’re aware something is wrong. We’ll clear the medical staff.”

Seth probed, “Is there anyone we check first? Anyone acting suspiciously to you?”

“We came in two groups. I arrived with the first group, and we were just grateful to see the second group. More were in it, but we regarded it as a blessing at the time. I didn’t notice anyone acted particularly strangely in either group.”

Alika finished, “But your focus is helping your patients, as it should be. The second group was larger though."

Seth read his thoughts. “And eager to help. The situation is desperate. No time bothering with clearances. Fortunate if you get a name. Quite understandable.”

Iban accompanied them for the process, and they started with the second group. He called each one into a room. Once they got in the room, they checked the person’s blood. Lana’s group purposely found a room with a nice-sized connecting room. A prick resulting in red earned the person a reassuring smile and safe exit from the room. On the other hand, a prick resulting in black ended at the point of a sunspear or sword. The adjoining room held the bodies, as the group continued to escort a new person into the first room. Those with a red prick left the room with no idea how close the boundary between life and death stood.

“Sixty-three in the group, and twenty were bad.” Caleb shook his head as he watched the firestone finish its work.

“How many are in the first group, Iban?” asked Alika.

“Thirty-six counting myself.”

“Are you okay?” Seth asked.

“Simply stunned. I allowed these people to treat my patients, and now I wonder what they did to them.” He rubbed his forehead.

“You didn’t know. None of us did, and they infiltrated your entire planet,” said Alena.

Lana sighed. “Along with two more planets like this, Iban. Honestly, once we’re done today, your patients become the safest of anyone on the three planets.”

“I understand now. How will you sort it out?”

"We don't know." Seth took a deep breath. "Let's clear the thirty-five others assisting you."

CHAPTER FOURTEEN

"Yes sir, it's the one planet," said the Black Dragon squadron leader.

"The Freedom Fighter group arrived, one of ours greeted them, and he left just like that?" He sat on the command ship puzzling over the update.

"Yes, sir. Another recruit working the same area can't be reached either. In addition, we heard nothing from one of the small groups providing support for them. At this point, we came to one conclusion."

"Too many missing at the same time. A safe assumption they're all eliminated. What about the Freedom Fighter group?"

"There's no way to know yet of their losses."

"With our results, I expect we rid ourselves of a few of them, but there are some among their group who fight quite impressively. The runaway recruit may provide insight. His sudden departure perplexes me, but I'm certain it's linked to why the operation fared poorly for the other recruit. Tell our men to meet with our fugitive. I want to question him. Take him somewhere suitable to do so. I'm eager to hear what story he tells me, and contact me when you secure him."

"Yes sir."

Ryan shook his head. "Not one in that whole group."

"All confined to the second one." Angelina wondered aloud. "Iban, did anyone else come with the second group to help? In other departments? Perhaps a Drew or Trey?"

"Yes, but I can't recall names."

"Any list, if it ever existed probably conveniently disappeared. Not that it helps anyway. Even they wouldn't be dumb enough to give me the same name."

Alena commented, "I don't know. We dealt with pretty dull Black Dragon troops."

"These aren't the same Black Dragon soldiers. I'll give them a bit of credit, until we see more." Her hand unconsciously went to her throat, as pain began creeping back.

Iban came closer and studied her. "What happened to your neck?"

Angelina smiled. "I'm okay. It's treated." He waited, her answer leaving him unconvinced. "My close encounter today with these new breed of Black Dragon soldiers led us to discover they don't remain down with blasters. My blade worked, so he won't get up again. Thank you for your concern."

"If you're sure it's treated. That looks like it could have ended badly."

"You have no idea." Dante shook his head, glancing from Iban back to Angelina.

She rerouted the conversation to their original purpose. "Where are the bodies going when they pass? I can't imagine your grief at seeing this many patients slip away at once, so forgive me for asking."

His voice softened. "Unfortunately, with the situation, it's like one of the massacres. Colony workers buried a few quickly, but regrettably most received the other arrangement."

"I understand," whispered Angelina. He meant an incinerator or some form of it, as it was the only way to avoid disease. She reminded herself, the person no longer remained in the body or felt the pain, but abided with the Ancient One now.

"No one wishes to do it like that, but there's no way to avoid it currently." He bowed his head. "It's a terrible thing. Especially, ones fallen in battle defending the colony. I have a couple of those waiting to go."

"Where are they now?"

"Down the hall. Do you need to see them?"

"Yes. Do you mind?"

"Not at all."

"What are you searching for?" asked Alena, as the group stood before the bodies with the doctor.

"Not sure," murmured Angelina. "Mercy. Too young to be here. He reminds me of ..." she stopped, shaking her head and brushing the hair from his forehead.

Dante read her thoughts. The soldier resembled Jonathan, the one they met from the colony army, on the other planet.

"Where did he get hit?" whispered Angelina. She didn't see the wound anywhere. Someone removed his gear, and Iban redressed him in the plain paper -thin shirt and pants common to this situation.

"On his abdomen."

She turned to Iban and Alika and Seth. "I don't feel comfortable..." her voice trailed off.

Iban stepped forward with Alika and Seth, and he pulled the young man's shirt up at the waistline to reveal the entrance wound. She studied it, with Alika and Seth matching her perplexed expression. She turned to Dante, who shook his head. "The entrance wound doesn't match anything I can place either." The others mirrored their agreement.

"It's almost ..." She glanced from Dante to Alena.

Alena met her gaze. "What?"

"Disc shaped," responded Angelina, her eyes asking Alena.

"It is."

"Did you remove anything from him?" asked Alika.

"No."

"And the other one is the same?" asked Seth.

"Yes, except his wound was on the back of the neck."

Angelina wondered aloud, "Why didn't their gear stop or at least deter it?"

Ryan suggested, "Those are places where the gear breaks and the next piece takes over on the softer armor."

Caleb shook his head. "They still managed to make a small target. If they're making those shots ..."

"These are not the Black Dragon of before," Angelina whispered.

Iban spoke quietly, "Or armor can only withstand so much. From what I surmised, the armor didn't help, at the point when they received this wound. Honestly, I don't know how they continued fighting." He retrieved several pieces from a bag beside the soldier's body. "His armor." It was unrecognizable, shattered and blaster scorched. Then he removed the soldier's shirt all the way. The soldier's entire upper body, from his shoulders to his stomach, testified to wounds of one continuing to fight when his armor long failed, but his spirit refused to give up the battle. Iban had cleaned the body and washed the blood away, his way of giving something back to this one so young, who gave everything to the colony. "The other was in the same condition." He shook his head.

Angelina stared down at the gashes, blaster burns, and bruises marring the young man's chest and shoulders. He survived all that, only to have a single disc finish him. The realization chilled her. Instantly, she experienced it through his eyes. His fear and pain on that battlefield hit in a massive wave, but he endured through it. Because he saw and hoped beyond that battlefield, to a victory that yet existed. He did everything for his colony, those he cared for, and here he laid quiet now. His spirit pleaded with her to remember his wounds, the story they told, as he finally collapsed upon that battlefield before her eyes. An anguish tore through her, of failing this one who cried out to her now, and sobs of more colonists filling the night, before they stopped Black Dragon. As she watched his face, it changed before her. She saw Jonathan, then Caleb, then Ryan, and finally to her horror, Dante. She stepped back, unsteady, and stammered out, "I'm ... I'm sorry I need ..." Unable to watch any longer, she stumbled to the other side of the room.

Dante turned for a second, but he forced himself to stay rooted in place. His spirit desperately cried out at not going to her, but he couldn't with the doctor there.

Immediately, Alena answered the call. "Excuse me. I'll go check on her while you continue this."

—ꝏ—

"Hey, what happened back there? Talk to me," Alena coaxed as Angelina wiped her face.

"Why do I feel everything from everyone, at the worst times? I joined him on the battlefield, when the disc hit him."

She clasped Angelina's hands. "I don't know why, but I wish you didn't."

"He needs me ... us to stop Black Dragon. This can't happen again. But what if we can't? What if we fail another colony? This soldier?"

"We won't fail this soldier. He will not die in vain."

She whispered, "We knew the last time, and we still couldn't stop this. You know it's true."

"Don't continue doing this to yourself. You only see it, but you're not responsible for it. You must separate the two."

"I see him lying there, his face ...it kept ..." She buried her face in her hands.

Alena came closer and gently took Angelina's hands again. "What about his face?"

"It changed into Jonathan, then Caleb, then your Ryan, and then my Da ... Dante." She choked out his name, as her frame trembled.

Alena hugged her. "The things your eyes see, I'm sorry, but none of those will come to pass. It's only your fears finding form. We'll fight that battle every time and win. Death won't claim them."

"How can you," her voice broke, "be sure?"

"Because we keep battling and always hope," Alena whispered, as she hugged Angelina tighter.

—ꝏ—

"Do you mind if we transport them back for further examination?" asked Alika after he and Seth completed a further visual inspection of both bodies with Iban.

"I prefer you do. Perhaps, now, they'll get a proper burial."

"We'll make sure of it," Lana whispered.

Caleb kissed her on the top of head. "Let me take care of this one, sweetheart." He used his data pad to call for another ship.

Dante said, "The transport will be here soon, but I meant what I said earlier." He glanced over at where Angelina remained with Alena.

Ryan patted him on the back. "And you're right. They'll be back over in a minute, but the ship waits until we all go meet it. No more one person skirmishes with Black Dragon today."

"Ready?" asked Alena.

"Yeah. Thanks for putting me back together."

"Of course. What else am I to do?"

"You could leave me to be. I don't know anymore."

"Never. Now stop this crazy talk from you." She started to pat her on the back, but stopped mid stroke. "Sorry, I forgot."

"Is everybody going to treat me like I'm made of glass, for the rest of the day?"

"You didn't get a look at your back, shoulders, neck, and I won't go on. I'm amazed at how you're holding up, even for you. It must be sheer will or just to spite Trey. Let's rejoin the others."

Caleb checked the signal from his data pad. "The ship entered the portal. It lands in a couple of minutes."

"What ship? Sorry, what did we miss?" asked Alena as the two walked up.

Ryan replied, "One to pick these bodies up, for a closer inspection later."

Angelina looked apologetically at Seth and Alika. "Sounds like a long, unpleasant night for two people."

Iban focused on her. "Are you sure you're all right? I didn't mean to upset you."

"You didn't. My apologies for just now. There's been a lot to take in today. If anyone has cause to come apart, it's you, with everything you face treating your patients. Instead, you hold it together and tirelessly minister to them. We're grateful to you."

"Ship's here," announced Caleb.

Dante glanced over at Angelina, as they escorted the bodies to the ship. She didn't utter a word, and he couldn't read her this time.

Once the transport left, Lana spoke, "Iban, we'll be in touch soon, and with a plan we'll need your help to carry out. Contact me if you run into any problems beforehand, and we can be here if necessary. We'll figure out a way to determine friend from foe."

"I'm confident you will. Thank you, Lana, and the rest of you."

"Ready?" asked Alena. as she started the ship and began liftoff.

"You can't imagine how ready." Angelina shed her visor completely, sat on the ship's couch, and removed the scarf to completely free her hair.

Dante had never seen her so done with a place. "I'm sorry we couldn't leave sooner."

"You did fine, Dante." She leaned up against him, her arms encircling his waist and midsection as she managed to flash him a weak smile.

"Well, it's finally over. Relax for a bit." He started to put his arm around her, but held off when the image of her bruised back resurfaced. He settled on stroking her cheek and brushing her forehead with a kiss. They'd find out the extent of her injuries shortly.

Lana motioned up ahead, as the group strolled down the hallway of the fortress. "You remember from last time, Alika. We're at medical. It's all yours," said Lana.

"Thank you, Lana. You can all come, and I'll pull the curtain, once I begin the scan on her."

"Hop up to the table, Angelina. My apologies, no hopping." Alika shook his head at the look she shot him.

"Your spray wore off, Alika." She glanced at Dante. "You must stop worrying. This is nothing compared to the whole rooftop plunge."

"Angelina, let's get this done. Alena, come in and help." Alena closed the curtain around Angelina. "Now undress waist up, and we can scan your shoulder first. Easy now. She's here to help you. I guessed that would prove a painful reach." A couple of minutes later a faint beep sounded from a device. "What did you do this time?"

Seth studied the scan on the portal, while Dante peered anxiously next to him, waiting for one of them to say something. "Dante, she won't need surgery on it. There's the good news. What's Alika's ordering? I agree. That should do it."

Alika followed up with his assessment. "You didn't break or fracture anything, but there's massive swelling inside. We need it stopped, and to bring down the present swelling immediately."

"Fantastic. That one, huh? The powerful punch lets you know it's working, but I get the no drowsy version today."

Alena went to Seth, who had it prepared. "Thanks, Seth."

"I'm familiar with that one, Seth. It's quite the injection." Dante groaned.

"Ready, Angelina? Alena, do you have a secure hold on her? You'll need to once it finds its mark."

"Hopefully secure enough for when it hits her system. With the bruising from the other, I'll try to be careful."

"It's fine, Alena," Angelina murmured softly. Immediately, a stifled cry escaped, followed by several deep breaths as Alika administered it.

"You still with us?" asked Alika.

"Yeah, I'm fine I guess."

"Are you sure?" His student sounded faraway.

"Always the arm. Ironic. The other one tried to take it off too. They gravitate towards that punishment."

"Yes, you're right."

"The level of pain even rivaled it, though with him I never wondered. Where I stood with him was always apparent."

"Yes, the one left no room for doubt. I'm not sure if that's better. There is always such a painful path set before you. I'm sorry, child."

"It makes no difference to my arm. It's not your fault, Alika. I chose this, right?" she paused. "Yes, I forgot, Alena."

Dante stared over at Seth, whose face reflected equal puzzlement and sadness at the conversation.

"Is there anything else?' asked Angelina.

"Yes, your back and midsection."

"Do I need to take the rest off?"

"Not all the way, but enough we get a total scan of both areas." A few minutes of movement, unclasping, and shuffling commenced. "Far enough."

Seth inspected the completed scan on his end, and immediately prepared another injection. Dante turned to him with a pained face. "Really?"

"I'm sure, Dante."

"Your back shows the same swelling. You'll be in greater pain later, if we don't stop it."

"I understand, Alika. You're my teacher, my friend, and my doctor, all in one, so I trust you without question. Do what you must."

Alena retrieved the injection from Seth, as she placed a reassuring hand on Dante's arm. "She won't hurt later, because of the treatment given now, and she's almost done, Dante."

Dante winced, as he heard her held down for the second injection. Subsequently, he heard Alika say, "Whenever you're ready to get up, we're here."

Several minutes later, a smiling Angelina emerged from the curtain, as if it progressed as a normal day in her world. She came to Dante first. "Still, with the same worry on your face, Dante. Honestly, I feel better, and I don't mind proving it to you." She softly kissed him, and then took his hand. Despite his lingering worry, a smile escaped at enjoying a kiss from her. She turned to the others. "Let's regroup to the other area and get started again. I saw enough of medical facilities for one day." She laughed as she led the way.

They sat down in the hall, with an uncomfortable silence hanging in the air. The group remained unconvinced of Angelina's recovery, prompting her to speak first to force them past their misgivings, "Lana, where do we go from here?"

Momentarily, Lana hesitated before plunging forward, "At least those in medical are safe, but I don't see eight of us sorting out three whole planets."

Caleb replied, "No, but it's a start, a blueprint to create a process from."

"Only larger scale. Like three-planet size," said Ryan.

A shadow crossed Angelina's face. "Or more. I believe it's spread beyond the three planets. It's already in motion. Those were Trey's words, and I fear he spoke the truth."

Dante turned to her. "He said many things today, all awful to you. It's impossible to judge what truth, if any came from him. I won't let him hurt you any further than what he already did today." He kissed her on the forehead. "We're doing this together now."

"He did say many things for the sole purpose of hurting me or making me angry, but he confirmed things we began piecing together. The Black Dragon army remains functioning efficiently, with a capable leadership of some sort. They plan to continue wreaking havoc, where the Dark Lord left off, and it must be discovered as before. Within a few days, we'll need to divide again to unravel it."

"No, we work better as a team. Today showed that." He didn't care about the arrangement before.

"We can't be seen working together continuously. You're not thinking about what's best now."

"Maybe I'm not, but after today I'm not comfortable anymore working separately. It's just not safe." Dante got up and walked over to the drink dispenser, but he didn't get a drink.

"I should go to him." She got up, and the others nodded. Coming up behind him, she laid her hands gently on his shoulders and leaned up against him whispering, "Please, Dante, talk to me. I can't bear you being upset with me."

Without a word, he turned around to clasp both her hands and guided her to sit on the nearby couch. Only then did he speak. "I'm not upset with you, and I could never be so. I was unbelievably scared today, and I can't forget it like you wish me to, Angelina. I thought I lost you again."

She saw it in the depths of his soft brown eyes and heard it in the trembling of his voice. "Oh, Dante, you're right. I constantly told you not to worry, brushing aside how you felt, and I made everything worse for you. I'm sorry. I know that fear. It almost consumed me before you went to the Elders Hall, and when I watched you dying in front of me." Tears filled her eyes. "I keep putting you through that agony."

"I couldn't bear if something happened to you, Angelina, but you're unconcerned about your life I hold so dear." He continued gazing at her as he brushed one of her clasped hands to his lips.

"I couldn't bear losing you either, Dante. It scares me too." She leaned in closer as she wound her arms around his neck. "You know, we're not on the planet anymore."

"You're right," he whispered, before he instantly answered her invitation for a long, gentle kiss. He didn't think anymore about what could happen and what almost happened. Now, he only enjoyed the feel of her safe in his arms, and he loved holding her, kissing her. He stayed in this moment, and nothing else mattered for the two of them. He murmured when their lips parted, "Every time I kiss you, Angelina..."

She whispered, "I know. The places you take me, Dante." He did too. She forgot the images, the fear, and the past, when he had her in his arms.

"If only we could stay there." He paused. "I want to see you this evening, but are you sure you don't need to rest from the injuries?"

"I rest most comfortably spending the evening with you, Dante, and I'll be sad if I miss that time with you."

"As long as you're feeling well enough. I don't wish to send you away sad this evening, and I'd be sadder." He grinned.

"Are you sure you're ready to continue?" Seth asked, as the two sat back down.

Angelina replied, "Yes. I mean, no, I hate to ask, but can we take a break? Maybe it's the encounter with Trey still in my head, or more comfortable clothing with the injuries would help. My head would be in a better place. Only if it wouldn't put us too far behind." she glanced apologetically at the group.

Alena added, "I'm with Angelina, and I didn't endure Trey as she did, by any stretch. Yet I'll work better too, if I'm not still dressed to expect a Black Dragon company."

Lana nodded. "Everyone back in about an hour."

"Sure you're okay?" asked Dante, surprised by her sudden shift.

"Absolutely, Dante. A shower and looser clothing will do wonders for the injuries, and Alena can reapply the medicine before we return. That's all it is, Dante."

He searched her eyes, and she told him the truth. "See you back here."

She hugged him. "You do wonderful talking sense into me. Besides, I didn't want to still be in these clothes, for my evening with you." Winking at him, she quickened her pace to catch up with Alena and Alika.

He grinned and decided a shower sounded perfect after today and headed for his quarters to do the same.

CHAPTER FIFTEEN

"Sir, we tracked him down, and he's ready for you," said the Black Dragon squadron leader.

"Excellent. I'll speak with him now," he said.

The recruit sat in a chair inside the locked room. His shirt stuck to him uncomfortably, as sweat poured down his back. He tried controlling the fidgeting, but his legs and hands wouldn't rest. His eyes refused to focus on any one thing in the room, but darted everywhere at once. Surrounded by four Black Dragon troops and at least another couple outside the door, he couldn't win. They directed his attention to a pitch-black screen on the wall, and a voice emerged from it. He understood, and a fresh wave of terror quaked through him. The person spoke to him from a darkened room.

"Good evening, recruit. I have questions concerning what occurred today on the planet, and you'll answer them now."

"I'll try, but I'm not sure ..."

"I don't believe you heard me clearly. I took charge of Black Dragon, and your answers need improvement rapidly. Thus far, I'm displeased with your work. Let's begin again. Enlighten me on why you left the planet, after the Freedom Fighter group arrived."

"The other recruit told me to do so."

"You're receiving your orders from another recruit? Who is this recruit taking over my leadership?"

"No ... that's ... not what I meant." His voice rose in panic.

"What exactly did you mean, because I expected you'd come up with better, given the time afforded you. I'm losing patience with your babble. Why did you leave the planet and allow the other recruit to take over for you?"

"He felt more capable of handling it, and he said I didn't manage it well so far."

"Now we reach the truth. Tell me recruit, how did he explain you didn't manage it right in his eyes? Let me see if I concur with his assessment."

"He said the way I greeted them aroused their suspicions." He stopped, but gathered that bit wouldn't work, so swallowing hard he continued, "I asked a couple of them too many questions, because I didn't recognize them. I didn't appear concerned about the hurt colonists and the destruction. In his opinion, I needed to be more ..."

"Like you belonged to the Freedom Fighter side. I agree with him. You play a part, they trust you, and then you plunge the dagger in their back. Usually, it's not hard work if it's well played, but you ruined it. He paid the price, along with the rest of the group, because of your incompetence. What a shame, because it sounds like the other recruit was much more useful than you."

"He said he could fix it. I'm sure they were not who they said."

"Who?" He should salvage something useful from the recruit.

"Lana came, along with her husband Caleb, Seth the Elder, Dante, and Commander Ryan. However, I didn't recognize the three others accompanying them. The two women claimed to be advisors for Lana, and the male said that Ryan asked him to come assist."

"Lana does sporadically take advisors to a planet with her, and considering the destruction we left, it's plausible. Same with the commander. Did they give you names? What of their appearance?"

"They gave me names, but I'm certain they were fake. They didn't want to tell me anything and obscured their features beneath gear. The women had their hair up and covered, and visors over their eyes."

"None of that surprising, since you forgot to put your best behavior on display for them. Such pleasantries aren't important to us, but it goes a long way with these Freedom Fighters. Clearly, the other recruit tried to drill the point, unsuccessfully, through your thick skull. Now we won't ever know if they lied, or if they simply didn't care to converse with you."

"Don't you want to know their names?"

"No, it won't matter. Obviously, they're smarter than you demonstrated, even if they aren't advisors. They won't use the same names, and from the outcome today, if they still live, they're every bit as practiced with a blade as the rest of Lana's crew. Is there anything else you wish to tell me? Anything you believe might be remotely useful?"

Silence engulfed the room. The recruit struggled in vain to come up with a worthy contribution.

"As I thought." He laughed. "There will be no more opportunities for you to fail me. I'm glad we chatted. You should've listened to the other recruit before you greeted the Freedom Fighter group, and I believe things would turn out differently. Too late to fix it now. It's too bad."

"Sir, you wish us to finish with him?" asked the Black Dragon squadron leader.

"Yes, I despise loose ends. Ensure this one is tied up. Good evening," He ended the communication.

"No, please! I learned my lesson!" yelled the recruit to no use as the Black Dragon squadron leader's sword silenced him permanently.

CHAPTER SIXTEEN

Dante came down the same time as Ryan. Seth, Caleb, and Lana were already down. Ryan came beside him. "How are you doing after earlier?"

"I'd be better if I enjoyed one day with Angelina, which didn't involve her approaching death staring at me."

"The two of you find a way to bring out the best in each other every time." Ryan smiled as he patted Dante on the back. "Sounds like you need to put that part out of your mind, and enjoy the time tonight with her."

Three familiar figures walked into the room. Angelina and Alena were in casual clothes again, skirts and blouses.

"Better?" asked Dante, as he gently pulled Angelina up against him. The familiar sweet fragrance reached him, which accompanied her.

"Better," she smiled, as she kissed his cheek.

"We can't go in with too large a group to weed out our impostors, or Black Dragon will figure out something is up," said Caleb as they all got comfortable.

"They may piece together more than we realize after today. Drew must be long gone now." Angelina sighed. "I wonder ... Where's Trey's data pad?"

Ryan passed it to Dante.

"Dante, I bet Trey and Drew conversed. Maybe there's a clue to where Drew headed. Do you see anything?" She leaned in, studying the display as Dante started scrolling and promptly stopped.

"Wait a minute. I'm not helping you set up your next dangerous operation."

"Go back there. They're talking." She ignored his comment, and he reluctantly scrolled back as she wished. "Not helpful. It only confirms Drew influenced the attack today. We can delve into it more later. Wherever he went, it'll be there in a few days."

"You and Alena could walk straight into a whole army of Drews or Treys or their leader. You get that right?"

"We'll go in with plan, but I want to find out how things run now at Black Dragon. We'll try less direct ways first. Alika, you got an extra transfer device?" She took it from him. "The data pad, Dante."

She inserted the device into the Black Dragon data pad. Dante watched her fingers move with lightning speed across it, without yielding what she hoped.

"It won't let you into everything. What do you need?"

"A key. Hold the data pad again."

"Sure. A key?"

"Yep, a key." She moved from screen to screen on her own data pad. "There it is. Let's try again." While taking back over the Black Dragon data pad, she scanned her data pad with it. "Quickest way to do it." Instantly a couple of hidden screens appeared, and she moved between them. Rapidly she went from screen to screen on the Black Dragon data pad. "Still not securing those locks tight enough." She chuckled, as she made one last motion on the data pad and pulled the device out of the Black Dragon data pad. Handing the transfer device over to Alika for safekeeping, she passed the Black Dragon data pad back to Dante. "In case they deactivate it soon. Sorry if I got us off track again. Anyway, one of the challenges is how to keep someone cleared once we do."

"A clearance on a badge could work," said Caleb.

"Easily compromised. I do it consistently for Alena and me to gain access. Hacking into a system and switching a badge takes no time at all." Everyone looked at her. "What?"

"How many of those times were Black Dragon systems?" Alika grinned.

"Numerous. Their locks are surprisingly flimsy with certain areas of information, as I demonstrated."

"He's saying not everyone is as talented with that as you. For most of us, this presents a challenge." Dante's eyes twinkled.

"You're right. Of course, you couldn't get past me sneaking into your quarters the first evening, so I didn't need to impress you much." The wonderful memories from that evening floated back to her.

"I recovered rapidly, as I recall, Angelina. Should we review that first evening further?" He leaned in close to her.

"You did recover nicely. Your review wouldn't serve me well, since my words didn't come as smoothly as I normally like. The evening turned out pleasant even so." The brush of his lips found hers, and she smiled at him as she murmured, "Very pleasant." After a moment, she turned back to the group and refocused on the original topic. "I understand your reasoning, but we're dealing with different Black Dragon soldiers and leadership. Security may not remain so easily manipulated for me."

Lana hid a smile at watching her cousin briefly distract Angelina and said, "True, and didn't you encounter trouble with the security access where they held Abigail?"

"I did. We concluded the Dark Lord outsourced it. He didn't have his Black Dragon troops guarding it, but they weren't the mutated Black Dragon agents yet either. They stayed down for us when we shot them. Our blasters worked to clear the room where they kept Abigail. Then, I took care of another bunch with a blaster and my sunspear before the whole rooftop fall. I didn't have any other options, but it all stained red. All the red everywhere. It started in the room with Abigail, but with using the sunspear, the red ... it covered the rooftop, then covered me, all over me." she gave a vacant stare to Alena before bowing her head.

Dante whispered, "Angelina."

She continued, like he didn't say anything. "Just like now. Except the blood is black, but it was red. It's not cleaving through something that on the outside appears flesh like, but its core will be machine. Its core is flesh and bones that we'll cleave through now. They're colonists, corrupted by the Black Dragon, as those at the facility chose to serve Black Dragon. It will be ..." She stopped.

He understood, and finished it, "Like before."

She stared back at him and whispered, "Like before." She paused. "The Black Dragon favors their half machine troops to do their bidding to the galaxy's public. Yet the Black Dragon always used multiple resources to carry out their plans, so they forced us to shed blood to defend the innocent. Evil comes in many forms. Its cruelty has no bounds. It spreads over every segment. It's found from the poorest beggar in the streets, to those in the more questionable establishments, to the average person, to the one holding the highest position on a planet. The Black Dragon, or whatever evil calls itself at the time, has them all serve the same in the end." She paused. "We answer it, as many times as we must, mostly at the end of a blade. It's been the path we're accustomed to, but the one continuously before us with the Black Dragon's new corruption. But sometimes the blade point, you feel it more than..."

Dante whispered, "It cuts too deep."

She squeezed his hand. "Yes, even as you must do it, the sunspear cuts both ways." She took a deep breath. "I remember making it back from the rooftop fall. Alika had barely started treating my injuries. I couldn't stand unaided, because I was so weak. Yet I refused further treatment, until I got a shower. At first, it didn't make sense. Then I realized the debris from the rooftop, the sweat from the day, or the scorch burns from the blaster didn't eat at me. Rather, the blood all over me desperately cried out to be gone. Most of it probably belonged to me, but I only saw the blood of others clinging to me. I tried the only way I knew of erasing it from me, but I couldn't forget."

Dante didn't know how to make it better, to protect her from everything she felt at once. So he loosely and carefully wrapped his arms around her and held her. She sighed as she wrapped her arms around his waist and leaned against him.

Lana spoke up, "Enough for tonight. Alika and Seth have an examination to do which may uncover more answers, but everyone needs dinner."

Seth and Alika came to Dante and Angelina, as the group sat to eat.

Alika asked, "May we speak with you two?"

"Of course," answered Angelina.

"Are you all right, Angelina?" asked Seth.

"This is how everyone feels compelled to start conversations with me. It isn't always like this. I'm not falling apart. Seth, I'm sorry, I didn't mean to sound so awful to you. That was wrong." She bit her lip. "I'm fine, Seth. I always am."

Seth reached over and clasped her hand. "No offense taken. I imagine it does feel like that lately, but you endured quite a beating today, I'm more than aware, this isn't the normal. The image of you fighting masterfully with your sunspear beside me on another colony remains rooted in my mind, especially cutting the squadron leader down."

She grinned. "I did enjoy getting rid of him, despite my exhaustion."

Dante laughed. "I'm sorry I missed it and only got to see the replay."

"A shame, Dante. What did you two need to speak with us about?"

Alika answered, "Your cylinder and rooftop connection situation, Angelina. Understandably, you forgot about it after today's events."

"You can work out the solution tomorrow at day's end, if you're up to it," said Seth.

"I'll do what needs to be done."

"What is she to do?"

"Conquer the cylinder, conquer the rooftop, Dante. There are other ways to master it safely," replied Seth.

She nodded. "I get it. What do I need?"

Alika responded, "To be dressed for an operation like today, including any equipment you take for one. Whatever additional items you need to safely accomplish your task, retrieve them either from the ship or from someone around you. That is the only way the others assist you. You alone must figure out the how."

"Maybe I should've done it this evening."

"How would that end after today's events, my child?"

"With it overcoming me again, Alika."

"Tomorrow gives another day for your injuries to heal."

"Tomorrow it is. Thank you." She turned to Dante. "You too, Dante. You helped me piece it together."

"I wish I felt better about that now."

"I overcome it now, so it doesn't bring me grief later, Dante."

"I suppose so." He kissed her on the forehead.

Seth smiled. "You two go, and we'll be there momentarily."

Alika watched them rejoin the others. "They're fine with the solution, but I'm surprised no further questions."

"I expected a few specific ones too. They trust us though, which is why they came to us."

"I don't like the solution we put before her, Seth. There's no margin for error, no safety net. I wished for some form of it, in the solution."

"Yet, it's the answer given. Remember, my friend, we do not follow our own counsel entirely in this."

"Yes, we both heard it, and He wouldn't lead us astray. We must exercise trust as well, and join them before they wonder what keeps us."

CHAPTER SEVENTEEN

"What is it?" he asked, as he sat on the command ship.

"Sir, a ship approaches, and it's one of ours. The individual wishes to see you and says you're expecting them," said the Black Dragon squadron leader.

"Interesting. I don't recall any appointment, but I'm curious. Put the ship onscreen."

It was indeed one of their ships, and he understood instantly.

"What are your instructions, sir? Do you know the individual? We await your orders."

He laughed. "Yes, I know who it is. It's my loose end, and I mean to tighten it. Tell Black Beauty, Duvessa, whatever she calls herself these days I'll see her. I can't wait to hear her tale of what kept her. Oh, and be sure it's right here. No more private briefings as she is accustomed. She'll learn things changed in her absence."

"The ship landed, and we're escorting them to you."

"Excellent." He remained puzzled by the squadron leader's continued reference to them, but not curious enough to delve further. The mystery would unravel itself.

Minutes later Duvessa approached. Beside her stood a man dressed all in black, including a black hooded cloak with a matching armored mask on his face.

"Finally, you turned up. I began wondering. Where have you been?"

"Taking care of things."

"Those type of answers no longer suffice. You can no longer do as you please. The sooner you realize that, the smoother things go. I repeat, where have you been?"

"Our master is returned to us." With a smile, she moved aside to reveal the hooded figure beside her.

He glanced from her to the hooded figure, back to her, and laughed. "Now I see. You're out of your mind. This is the explanation for your absence? I don't know what ploy you're engineering, but it won't work. I tried reaching the Dark Lord and the Black Dragon Commander for several days, to no avail. The Dark Lord would've made himself known within the first bit to me, if he still lived. Who did you get to agree to such a foolish ruse with you?"

"It's no ruse. Here stands the Dark Lord again."

"This is not the Dark Lord, and I'm in control now. He left me in control that day much to your dismay, and in large part due to your recent disappointing work. With both of their deaths, my control became permanent. A necessary promotion. You will address me as the Premier Black Dragon. Let me see this poor sap you recruited to help you."

"I can't believe you. It's him. You ..."

He continued with the same undeniable edge to his voice, "I'm in command now, and you're not. This man before me isn't the Dark Lord." He turned to the cloaked figure. "Remove your mask. I will see the face of the one Duvessa convinced for this trickery."

The cloaked figure smiled. He expected it to go like this since he possessed the Dark Lord's memories and placed this man in charge for a reason. He removed his mask and stood silently.

The Black Dragon Premier turned from the cloaked man and back to Duvessa. "My first question remains. Who is this man? I met with the Dark Lord and the Black Dragon Commander on a number of occasions. This man is neither. His appearance matches neither." His voice turned harsh. "What do you take me for, Duvessa? I won't be toyed with. I'm not amused by this."

"You're a fool not to see ..." began Duvessa.

Instantly, he rose from his chair and marched to her. The edge of his sword found her midsection, and his other hand tightened around her wrist. "Don't finish those words, Duvessa. I won't take orders from this man, and you'll convince no one else from Black Dragon to do so. He's not the Dark Lord. This charade stops now. I'm the leader of Black Dragon. I give the orders, and you and your friend will do as I say. This current path puts you as an enemy of Black Dragon, and you know what happens to those individuals. Consider you answer carefully, Duvessa." He moved the sword closer to her, so she felt the blade touch her skin through her clothing.

"I would take the Premier Black Dragon's generous offer, Duvessa. I see only advantages in working with him, especially at the present." The cloaked man barely held back his laughter at her predicament.

"Your friend gives you sound advice. Are you smart enough to heed it?"

Duvessa forced the fire to calm raging through her. She hated both of them, but she had to work with them. They shared a common goal, and again she reminded herself of that detail. "Yes, I'll cooperate."

"Excellent, because I won't have this conversation again with you, Duvessa." He removed the sword from her midsection and released the hold on her hand, before returning to the command chair. "I'll come back to you, Duvessa." He turned to the cloaked man. "You provided her wise counsel. We should work together nicely as you possess a better grasp of things than she does at the moment. What is your name?"

"I'm called Destroyer. My sole desire is eliminating the Ancient One and all those serving him. I share the goal of you and the rest of Black Dragon."

"Worthy ambitions. I like the name and your answer." He turned back to Duvessa. "Learn from him. This is what I expect to hear from you."

"My answers will comply in the future." She needed to play along, because she couldn't afford to make him angry anymore.

"It's time we discussed how things operate now, Duvessa. I believe you're the only one needing further clarification. You no longer share a privileged position with Black Dragon, as you enjoyed with the Dark Lord. You're as another Black

Dragon troop, nothing more, nothing less, and have no command over anyone else anymore. You will serve and follow orders. You have no other business here unless summoned, which means no evening or unannounced visits. If you're given an assignment to complete, I expect it done. You piled up many failures lately, and it stops today. No more wondering where you are or being allowed to do whatever you please. Can you follow these rules? If not..."

"I can," said Duvessa coldly.

"Destroyer, I believe we'll get along fine. In fact, please help Duvessa become accustomed to the new rules, to ensure she doesn't run into any misfortune. Who knows? You could find yourself with tasks to do before her." He laughed.

"I look forward to it. I wish to see the Freedom Fighters crushed, and it will give me pleasure to be a part of it."

"I'll contact you further. You're dismissed now." He turned to Duvessa, "You also, and you'll do well following Destroyer's example. It'll keep you out of trouble."

Duvessa nodded at the Premier Black Dragon and walked away. Destroyer smiled at the Premier Black Dragon and followed suit. Duvessa barely contained her anger, but Destroyer only grew more amused. The whole scene unfolded as he anticipated. He retained the memories of the Dark Lord, and the Dark Lord picked someone more than capable of taking control, if something happened to him and the Black Dragon Commander.

The Premier Black Dragon watched their departure. In reality, he doubted Duvessa's cooperation. He cared far less than he sounded, and planned on giving her little to do. He didn't trust her to successfully carry out much beyond simple assassin jobs, but he wanted her clear she held no control anymore. As long as she fulfilled the few tasks handed her and stayed out of the way the rest of the time, he'd be satisfied. His mind turned to Destroyer, and instinct said that one would prove helpful. Destroyer lacked the singular devotion to the person of the Dark Lord, as Duvessa did. Instead, his loyalty focused on the cause of the Dark Lord. Then even if Destroyer didn't receive a direct task from him, any activity he engaged in would still further the Black Dragon cause. The one would also keep

Duvessa in line, one less irritation for him. The meeting proved a win-win today, at least for him and Destroyer. Duvessa could stay unhappy. He laughed.

CHAPTER EIGHTEEN

Dante opened the door to his quarters, and Angelina walked in with him after just leaving from visiting Abigail for the evening. He poured them drinks, as the previous evening.

His eyes fixed on something in the room. "That should work perfectly for your back. It'll keep it from hurting as much."

She watched him trying so intensely driven by his concern for her. She knew it wouldn't work, but she didn't have the heart to stop his sweet gesture.

He stretched out on the couch, like the previous night. She nestled beside him, or attempted to do so. He started to wrap his arm around her and stopped. "I'm sorry, your back. I don't want to cause it to hurt more."

She got up and smiled. "I need to do some rearranging, Dante." Clearing the oversized body pillow off the couch, she replaced it back where he found it, and reclined again next to him.

"I thought the pillow would help."

"I know you did. You tried taking care of me again, but I'm comfortable stretched out as last night, next to you. We can't do this all evening, with you afraid to touch me for fear of hurting me. You won't."

"What should I do?"

"Treat me as you did last night, like none of today happened. You started to before." She laughed as she guided his arms around her. Then she cuddled into him and looked up at him. "Much better."

"It doesn't hurt?"

"Nope. Dante, you would never hurt me. You have only one way with me, and it's always gentle."

"I can't say that, when I grabbed you on top of the cylinder."

"Yes, you can, considering the situation. I needed to be safe most of all that instant. I felt safe in your arms as I always do."

He kissed her forehead in response.

They talked for about twenty minutes, but something felt different. He seemed sidetracked or worried, but he didn't mention anything. Finally, she asked, "Dante, are you, okay?"

"Of course."

"No, you're not. What are you thinking?"

"It's about earlier, so I didn't want to bring it up."

"I thought as much. We need to talk about whatever is bothering you from today."

"You're sure?"

She nodded and stared up at him.

"A couple of things you said stayed with me all day. Something happened which worried me too, but I couldn't talk to you at the time."

"Go ahead, Dante."

He twirled one of her silky tresses absently in his fingers. "You told Teresa not to fear, because the Ancient One walks through the darkness with us. You said you knew because He came to you in your dark hour, and kept you safe from it." He paused. "What happened to you? I saw you tearing up when you recalled it."

She answered, but slowly and with difficulty, "I can't tell you what happened, because it's a part of my past. I found myself at a juncture, which many do at a point in this life, many of us more than once, Dante. It's a scary, lonely place to dwell. Everyone faces this darkness, in reality daily. There are times the battle is one not forgotten, leaving such a mark on one." Her eyes were faraway for an instant, but then she returned his gaze. "You fought such a battle with it, when you struggled against the Dark Lord. Those are the ones that stay with you because you come face to face with how powerful the darkness is. How quickly it can take you and destroy you and all those around you, before you realize what is done. Yet you also discover how strong the One is who stands beside you, and that must be your refuge."

"Which is how you knew, and why you were so afraid for me."

"And it already took your father and destroyed your family."

"I didn't fall to it, and you didn't succumb to it either." He put his hand under her chin, lifting it to gaze in her eyes. Several emotions played across her features, most of which he expected. Yet he saw something else. Was it shame and failure mixed in? Why? Clearly, she won her battle too, since she fought on the same side with him.

"I received the help from the Ancient One when the time came. He didn't fail me in my hour of need." She struggled, unsure of her answer, and looked away briefly before returning her gaze to Dante. "What else troubles you?"

"Today isn't the first time someone wrenched your arm back, is it? We heard you telling Alika."

"You know the answer then. What are you really asking, Dante?"

"Is it true? Did someone hurt you many times, Angelina?"

She sighed as her mind traveled back. When didn't he hurt her? Twisting her arm was the least of it. She remembered running in the room as he got up, his laughter as he poured her mother's lifeblood on the floor. The sting of the slap across the face. The hard, cold floor beneath her as she knelt before him. His mocking laughter continuing as he jested, she could be taught after all. All his words of hate that day hit her. That was the worst day. Everyday though, he made it clear he hated her and wished to be rid of her. She recounted all the ways throughout the years he toyed with her, keeping a constant state of fear ingrained in her. Finally, she stared up at Dante and whispered, "Yes, Dante, there were many times."

His heart broke at the pain etched across her face, and he whispered, "Who hurt you, Angelina?"

"I can't tell you."

"Is he still alive?"

It would be simple to say no, but she couldn't. He might guess it was her father, and she didn't dare start down that road. "I can't tell you that either, Dante."

"Would he hurt you again if he found you?"

Angelina answered without hesitation, "He'd kill me in an instant."

"Oh Angelina, is that why you can't be known? Will he find you?"

"I can't answer about my identity, but I'm not concerned about him reaching me again."

"There's one more question. You must answer it, though I ..." He struggled to ask. He didn't want to think about it, consider the possibility, but he had to know.

"Dante, whatever it is, ask, and I'll answer if I can." She must be able to answer him. He was coming apart in front of her because of it.

Tears sprung in his eyes. "This person who hurt you, did he ever hurt you like Trey wished to be with you, to hurt you today, when he wanted to be alone with you because he ...?" He couldn't finish.

She understood now and held his face in her hands, as she gazed into his eyes. "My Dante, never did he hurt me like that. No wonder your spirit is troubled. Come here." She pulled him over and wrapped her arms around him.

Relief flooded through Dante. The sick feeling had stayed with him when he heard Trey speak to Angelina. Later, he couldn't shake the fear after the conversation between her and Alika. He wrapped his arms further around her, as his tears fell in her hair. "Someone still hurt you so much. I don't understand how someone could do such a thing."

"It's in the past now."

He stared in her eyes again, as he stroked her cheek. Today, he witnessed her injured, almost killed, and immediately back up fighting. He saw her absorb all the toil the visions wrought and forge ahead. Then, he watched her poured out yet again, giving comfort to those who felt the touch of darkness, and ready to continue doing it as many times as needed without question. Although she tried to be this one-person fortress, he beheld this beautiful, delicate one he longed to protect. "I wish I could spare you. You're hurt so much, but you always try to be strong, Angelina."

"No, we are strong, Dante. I said to you before there's no one the Dark Lord, the darkness left untouched in some way. It's true. I see my share of pain, but I'm not special in that. We all endured it. You lost most of your family. Lana and Caleb lost theirs. The trail of heartache is long, Dante. My pain is no worse than what surrounds me."

"That's what you tell me, but I keep seeing you in pain, and it's hard to watch." He stroked her hair. "Today, I couldn't go to you when you got upset, though everything urged me to. That's the other thing worrying me. What happened with the colony soldier? Did the images start again?"

"No, I mean, not images from before."

"Are you sure? The soldier reminded you of the one we met, Jonathan?"

"Yes he did." She closed her eyes for a moment and stared back at him. "I saw the soldier's last stand on the battlefield."

"Saw ... your seeing is all in, every last feeling and thought and with the condition of his armor and his body ... oh, Angelina." He leaned his forehead into hers as his mind understood.

"We can't allow another soldier slaughtered like that. He begged me to stop it, and next time it could be one of ..." her voice broke, and she bowed her head.

He cradled her chin up to him as she struggled to regain her composure. "Could be one of what?"

"Death's face changed on him to reflect the fear of my spirit. His face bore those I know, like Jonathan, others I care for like family now, Caleb and Ryan." She stroked the side of Dante's face. "And my heart," her voice broke, "you, my Dante."

"My Angelina, I'm so sorry," he whispered. He still held her chin with his hand and his thumb stroked one of her cheeks. "None of that will happen. You're my heart as well. No disc, blaster, blade, tanks, or anything else Black Dragon brings could separate us, not today or any day to come. We fought hard battles together already, to be here with each other. I finally found you, and I have you right where I want you, in my arms. I'm not ever giving you up now." He planted soft kisses on her cheeks to caress away her tears. While being careful of her injuries, he encircled his arms around her and coaxed her up against him. He needed her as near as possible for a bit, to feel her steady heartbeat. He found comfort in it, after what she feared and saw.

She soaked in his reassuring embrace like balm for her spirit. Her head laid on his well built shoulder, reminding her of his strength and protection. At the same time, her face nestled in the soft crook of his neck, soothing her with the gentleness and care he always gave her. Time passed, as the sweet calm poured through her spirit that came with him, and she smiled up at him. His eyes regarded her with a familiar expression, a mixture of love and concern. She realized how much she cared for him anew. "Dante, you worried about me nonstop today. You always comfort me, whether it be your words or touch. Time you took your own advice."

"Which is?"

"Enough of these discussions for tonight."

"What do you suggest instead?"

Her eyes twinkled as she took her time running one hand up his arm, over his broad shoulder, and finally to stroke the side of his face. With an equally calculated motion, she brushed her other hand through his hair as she whispered in his ear, "Oh, let me manage that. You're the one needing to be distracted this evening, Dante. Tell me how I do."

He grinned at her. He didn't how, but every sense in him awakened at her touch and yet relaxed in the same instant. "I ..." He never got another word out. She pulled him over and kissed him, a tender long kiss, like he yearned to get from her. He sank into the kiss, aware of nothing else but the intense pleasure pulsing through him from the tantalizing play of her tongue with his. Their lips parted for only a moment as Dante murmured, "Sweet ..."

"My Dante," She pulled him close again, urging him for another gentle, long kiss. Delight surged through him at being drawn into enjoying another kiss, more intoxicating than the last. He wrapped his arms around her completely as she wound her arms around his neck as they continued to be lost only in the kiss, finding their corner of bliss for as long as they could.

He whispered in her ear, "Feel free to distract me any time you wish."

"You said I needed to learn the art of distraction, while I was here." Her hand stroked the back of his neck.

"Did I? We'll say I did, because if I experienced the first lesson, bring on the rest. You're a fast learner."

"You've proved an excellent teacher, and made all the training most enjoyable, Dante."

"Actually, I doubt you needed any training. From what I've seen, you're just exceptional at whatever you touch, Angelina."

"Think so? Still, they say more training is the only way to master skills. In this case I only want to master these skills," she whispered in his ear, "with you, my Dante."

His heart skipped a beat, and he ran his hand through her hair. "I'll gladly put in whatever time you want from me, to get it perfect, my Angelina." He smiled as the warmth of her lips found his again.

CHAPTER NINETEEN

Ryan opened his quarter doors for Alena as they stepped inside, and she plopped down on the couch. He smiled at her. "We share the same taste of drink, right?"

"We do." She smiled back, as he handed her the drink and sat next to her with his own.

"Today, still ..."

"Refusing to leave my head. Something like that." She took a sip, put it down, and turned to him.

"After yesterday, I thought we'd get some calm too."

"He was upset, Ryan."

"Do you blame him? I'd react the same if it happened to you."

"No, I don't blame him."

"It was bad enough what happened, but you know what else caused him to come apart."

"Yes, it almost ended her. Another second of waiting, and it would have." Alena sighed. "Although I love her, I want to shake her sometimes."

"She could have leveled Trey and half the room with her sunspear, before it got that bad."

"But she was getting loose, remember?" Alena shook her head. "Yeah, I didn't believe it either, and you're right about her ability to annihilate half the room with her sunspear. Or there's the option of alerting us for help or finding a way to get to the door. The list goes on. Yet, she didn't do any of those things. She's so ..."

He prompted, "So ..."

"Angelina. Impossible at times."

"But she's like your sister, and you won't let anything happen to her."

"Yes, and she worries me at times. She realized the blaster didn't work only after the situation turned ugly. It came down to the same thing it does frequently." She bowed her head.

"What is it? This thing? I'm here, I promise." He gently lifted her face.

"She admitted it. The sunspear didn't come out until the last, to keep her cover as Lana's advisor. Her life was almost lost today to maintain her cover, to keep her identity secret. She deems it that important."

"Alena, she wouldn't carry it that far." Yet Alena's face told a different story.

"This isn't the first time she almost threw her life aside. In her eyes, it's the means to keep everyone safe, or she decides better her life forfeit than whoever is with her."

"Yes, with the dispersal device, she tried to stay for the download."

"And when we tried to get to the hangar. Then, there's the whole rooftop incident."

"The rooftop is different. The Ancient One closed the ship door."

"But if He didn't close it, Ryan, would it matter? I don't believe so. It was a relief for her. She didn't need to choose."

"Why, Alena?"

"The reasons are many. Some she only understands because of the way she sees things. Others are tied to what Alika and I know with her. We're the only family she has now. At times, she's alone, no matter how we try. You read it in her eyes."

"No, she has more family now, Alena. You all do here with us, and no one is letting her throw her life aside. Dante certainly won't. She's fortunate you're always there for her."

"She's always there for me too, and she'd be upset with me because of how I'm passing the evening with you so far. Don't tell her. I'll hear about it from her." She laughed.

"Your secret is safe with me. Dante said she gave you quite the time, when she figured out you spent yesterday evening with me, so I'll spare you more from her."

"She's only paying me back for my teasing her about Dante, but it's time to refocus this evening."

"But you needed to talk this other out, and we did which is a good thing. I know you're there to listen too if something worries me." His arms wrapped around her waist, and he smiled at her.

He listened with such patience and had the words she needed though they spent such a short time together. She couldn't wrap her head around it. "Do you know how incredible you are, Ryan?"

"Incredible, huh? I like how you refocus."

"Strange I took so long to see it."

"Long? What do you mean? I convinced you the first day you got here." His eyes twinkled.

"Now you're just rubbing it in."

"Great, you're going to hit me again." He laughed.

"No, I thought of something else." She put her arms around his neck.

"I'm incredible again, huh?"

"Oh, you never stop being incredible."

"You're going to tell me more about it, huh?" he murmured as she moved closer to him.

"I intend to show you, Ryan," she whispered as she pulled him over, and he wrapped his arms tighter around her waist. They forgot about Angelina and Dante for the evening. It was only about the two of them, and the kiss they found themselves in.

Caleb watched Lana as he sat up in bed. "Do you need help with anything, like finding your way over here to me?"

"I don't, and a bit impatient, aren't you?" she teased.

"It's been a long day, and you help me relax."

"You're right. The day did stretch out." She finally rewarded his patience by climbing in bed. "Despite everything that happened today and yesterday, they're happy somehow. Dante and Angelina. Alena and Ryan too."

He reached over and wrapped his arms around her. "Hey, it's scary what they've gone through, but they're stronger together every time and genuinely happy with each other. Black Dragon can take away a lot of things, but we still find what matters, in spite of what they bring. We'll always be able to. It's there to be found, even as bad as it sometimes gets."

"Quite the passion in that, Caleb."

"One thing you bring out in me every time." He kissed her forehead and gazed at her with a new intensity.

"Me? Surely not."

"You know what you do to me. All the wonderful ways you inspire me." He guided her down to a laying position on the bed and leaned over her.

"What are you inspired to do at the moment, Caleb?" whispered Lana as she wound her arms around his shoulders and pulled him closer.

"Oh, way too easy, my sweet Lana," he murmured as he brought her against him and began kissing her.

Dante and Angelina finished another piece of the dessert, and he put his arms back around her as they settled back down on the couch. She laughed. "Alena has teased me without mercy."

He laughed too. "I observed and find it as amusing as I did the first evening. We can't forget on the ship."

"You enjoy watching me stumble over my words too." Something dawned on her. "I meant to do something and keep forgetting."

"What is it?"

"The message I let you keep. It needs to disappear, and I told Alena it would be the first thing I did, when I finally met you."

"Did you now? The first thing, huh?" He couldn't contain his laughter again.

"She reacted the same when I said it."

"I can't imagine why. What happened?"

"You happened, with how you distract me."

"I'm not one bit sorry for all my distractions to you. I took pleasure in each one thoroughly, and I'll continue to." He couldn't resist doing so again. Then he murmured, "You could've made the message disappear from afar, anytime you wished."

She didn't know how he returned to topic that easily, as her mind lingered in the happy spell his kiss just put her. After a moment, she caught up to him. "I wanted to tell you before I did it. You probably didn't look at it anymore."

"Actually, I do. I'll be sad to see it go."

"It's not safe for it to stay. You'd be in danger because of me, if someone got your data pad and broke into it."

"If you say so," He paused. "Wait. Part of the message puzzled me, and you said you'd explain it to me."

"I don't recall now. A lot happened since that message, but it'll come back to me." She motioned for her data pad from the table.

He handed it to her, watching as she touched something on it, and the screen burst to life as the device recognized its owner. It began opening up a wealth of information. She started examining something further, but mumbled, "No, that's from the other operation, but I need to do something with those." He noticed the date stamp of all the correspondences covered the few days approaching the confrontation at the Elders Hall. "Way before those anyway." She moved to a different screen. "Here it is. What puzzled you, Dante?"

The date stamp on the other messages caused new questions to form, but they could wait for later. "You said it was different from your other operations, and you still felt the effects from it. I wondered what happened."

"At the time I didn't dare say more." She chuckled. "The short answer is, I asked someone to poison me."

"You did what!" A mixture of disbelief and horror came from Dante.

"I met with our key source we do most of our shipping business to get help with sneaking into the floating Black Dragon facility. He did the fake supplies for us to pass inspection. We had to test out the chemical fakes somehow, Dante."

"They were fake and shouldn't have hurt you."

"They didn't. The real chemicals are strong if you come in contact with them, so the fakes had to mimic the effects, for anyone encountering them. I made it worse, because with our time factor I tested several in a row. They were excellent fakes as needed, but I felt the effects during the testing and afterwards."

"How sick did it make you exactly?"

"Dante, he sat beside me during the testing. Even if I passed out on his ship, I was safe with him. One chemical came close to doing so. The others were minor, like burning eyes, coughing, and nausea. It wore off." She pushed something on her data pad. The screen flickered, and Dante saw an identical flash from his own data pad, signaling the message would be gone now.

"A successful operation involved you miserable, during and after it."

"You saw the footage and the supplies being inspected. Alena and I would have ended up dead as we stood, if they weren't perfect. He stayed up a couple of nights getting it done for us in time, and remained beyond worried for us. We all understood, my discomfort that day ensured Alena and I survived the operation."

"I get it, and I'm grateful you located such a trusted source. I expressed concern to Alika, but he assured me how carefully you chose your sources." He smiled. She listened to him, but her eyes wandered to the data pad again. She didn't realize it. Just habit. He slid the data pad from her hand and put it back on the table. "You won't need that anymore, Angelina."

She smiled at him. "I'll be losing my focus again."

He murmured, "Yes, you'll be distracted again, Angelina."

Her heart raced as he wrapped her up in his embrace, and his lips met hers. She lost herself again in his arms, only aware of his kiss.

"Tired?" He stroked the middle of her back through her shirt still being careful of her injuries.

"No, but ..."

"Like last night."

"We won't be sharp for the others tomorrow, if I stay longer."

After helping her with her cloak, he escorted her back to the ship. Alika and Alena were still up as before, so Dante and Angelina sat with them.

"Another nice evening, I assume?"

"Yes, it always ends too soon, Alika," said Dante.

He grinned. "Ryan said the same about a half-hour ago."

Dante chuckled. "I expect he did. Our evening company has proved enchanting, to say the least."

"I'm assuming the injuries from today didn't cause any problems this evening?"

Angelina smiled at Dante as she remembered his overzealous, but sweet efforts to ensure her comfort. "No, I was fine, Alika. I completely forgot about them with him."

"Dante, you're better than any medicine for her," Alena teased.

"I don't mind that at all." He winked at Angelina.

"I expect not, young Dante. It does me good seeing both of you happy." Alika patted Dante on the back, as he got up. "I'm returning to my ship now for the evening."

Angelina asked, "Did you and Seth find any answers?"

"It doesn't matter. You enjoyed a pleasant evening, and you'll keep it. Findings will be shared with everyone, and we'll decide what to make of it tomorrow. Goodnight to you all."

"I'm calling it a night as well. Goodnight you two."

"This is familiar," Dante whispered in her ear.

"Yes, left to stumble around in front of you. Those two."

"You don't do that anymore, at least not much. Anyway, I told you I enjoy having that effect on you."

"Mm, I suppose, Dante."

"There's no hope I manage a word if I had to say anything to you when you first appeared to us at the Elders Hall. You absolutely took my breath away that day, as you still do, Angelina." He kissed her.

She snuggled up against him. He didn't comprehend how much time passed, but as content as he sat with her engulfed in his arms, he sighed, "Angelina."

"I know, time to go, Dante."

They got up, and he wrapped his arms around her waist. "Tomorrow."

"Yes, tomorrow." She wound her arms around his neck.

"Goodnight, my Angelina."

"Goodnight, my Dante," she whispered back as he kissed her goodnight. She smiled as she watched him leave the ship for his quarters. She went right to sleep, with images of him still playing through her mind.

CHAPTER TWENTY

The next morning Dante strolled into the main room, with the previous evening still fresh in his thoughts. Such a short time with her, but he had never been this happy. She filled something in him so completely, so wonderfully.

Lana spotted him first as he came into the room. "Good morning."

Joining them at the table, he gently squeezed Lana's shoulders. "Hey, cuz."

Caleb grinned. "All smiles again, Dante. Ryan, too, this morning. Looks good on you two."

Ryan smiled. "Feels good for sure. Dante, how was Angelina? We saw how ugly those bruises were on her back and midsection, when Alika checked her on the colony. Not counting the ones on her throat. Did those injections help as much as she let on?"

Dante's manner turned solemn, as he recalled her injuries. "Surprisingly, she felt fine last night. Didn't complain at all. Initially, I feared even wrapping my arm around her with the bruises on her back, but she assured me it didn't hurt. Alika checked in with her again when we returned to the ship, and got the same response. I can tell when she's not being honest with me, and she told me the truth." He paused. "The pain I saw last night didn't come from yesterday's bruises. It went beyond that." He stopped.

Seth probed, "Dante, what is it?"

"I don't know. She won't mind me telling you though. Outside of our circle, she wouldn't answer it at all. I questioned her about the exchange we overheard, when Alika examined her in medical."

Lana nodded. "Yes, it was strange. I felt sad for her. It obviously upset her."

"Yeah, someone hurt her, and I sensed it persisted for some time. She confirmed it, but wouldn't tell me who. I asked if the person still lived, and she said she couldn't tell me that either. I feared the person would hurt her again and," he took a deep breath, "she answered he would kill her in an instant."

Silence engulfed the room.

Caleb said, "I bet that's what she's afraid of, Dante. This person finding her. Solves your whole keeping her identity secret."

"I thought that too, but she indicated he wouldn't find her. In fact, she acted unconcerned about that being an issue though she stated he would kill her on sight."

Seth mused, "Strange. Did she say anything else about what happened?"

"No, just brushed it aside as part of the past. Reminded me, everyone has been through their share of heartache, and I shouldn't feel bad for her." He remembered her face as she recalled the memory, and anguish coursed through him. "Her pain ran deep. I can still see it on her face." He shook his head. "I couldn't get the image of Trey out of my mind, the things he said to her, the way he looked at her, what he thought about doing to her because of it. I had to ask her if this other person ..."

Tears glistened in Lana's eyes. "Oh cuz, surely not."

"Not like that at least," said Dante, letting out another deep breath. "She assured me, and she told me the truth."

Lana put her arm around her cousin's shoulder. "I know you draw a small comfort that she wasn't hurt in that way. Although if it had turned out to be the case, you wouldn't falter in your care to her."

"Nothing could ever change how much I care for her. She is ..."

The sound of approaching footsteps interrupted Dante's thought.

"Everyone well?" asked Lana, as they all sat down at the couches and table.

Alena answered, "Believe so."

Dante gently clasped one of Angelina's hands and asked, "How are you feeling after the injuries from yesterday?"

"I'm fine, really, Dante."

Unconvinced by her response, more questions tumbled out, "How about as the day goes on? That type of clothing worsened it yesterday. Are you sure the bruises aren't hurting you? What about your shoulder?"

The others waited on her response as well.

She reminded herself not to dismiss his feelings, as she initially did yesterday. "Dante, this morning Alika and Alena agreed the injuries appear much better, but they put more treatment on them." He looked relieved somewhat, but still concerned. "After we finish up everything today, we'll go to medical, for Alika to do another scan."

"You'll do that?"

"It's a small thing to ease your mind, Dante. I know my body by now, so I expect nothing of the scan. Alika will give me another injection, if there's still swelling." Her tone softened, "I'll do it for you, Dante. I want to take the worry from your eyes."

"It'll ease my mind, Angelina." He forgot about everyone else in the room but her. He reached his arm over and encircled her waist.

"It'll be done. I'm in excellent hands. I have my own personal doctor in Alika, and while here I have two." She paused and wrapped an arm around his shoulder. "Then there's you. You shower me with concern, attention, and care every moment, Dante."

"Your gentle spirit inspires all those things from me and more. I wish for us to continue like this every day."

She understood his meaning, seeing it reflected in his soft brown eyes. "You know your young spear-bearer's heart. It belongs only to you. There is a time for everything. One day I hope our time comes, my Dante."

"I'll be patient until it does, my Angelina." He brushed his lips to hers and hugged her.

She hugged him back and then clasped his hand. They turned to the rest of the group as she said, "I guess it's time to begin."

"Yeah, sorry we held things up."

"No one minded." Caleb gave Lana a kiss on the forehead. The two reminded him of him and Lana in many ways.

Lana smiled. "Yes, you two are good. We'll let Alika and Seth present their findings now."

Seth began, "We brought the samples and one of the portable sample examiners from the lab with us. The blood samples and the examination of the bodies proved enlightening and puzzling."

Alika nodded. "Quite accurate. It's best to go through each sample."

Seth inserted the slide with the encased sample into the examiner, and it instantly projected before them. "The first samples we inspected were from Teresa and Anna. Those showed traces of the black substance."

Angelina asked, "Do you mind if I take a closer look?"

Seth smiled. "I expected you would."

She touched the screen connected to the examiner and a portion of the sample enlarged. "You're figuring me out, Seth, but I'm not sure how that turns out for you." She watched it critically for a couple of minutes, and glanced over at Alena.

Seth looked from Angelina to Alena. "It's smaller, but it can still be seen. We all saw movement for sure, correct?"

Angelina and Alena both nodded. Angelina said, "The darkness is connected with it too. There's a battle going on, as with Abigail in the beginning. Speaking of Abigail ..."

Alika responded as Seth changed out the sample on the device, "We did get a sample. It's similar to the other two samples in several respects. The black substance is present, but it acts different."

Angelina studied it. "No movement, like it's frozen. Did it ever move?"

"No," answered Seth.

Dante watched. They showed up as tiny black dots scattered throughout the blood sample and simply sat there as she said. "Strange that something that small causes all this pain."

Angelina squeezed his hand. "We'll figure it out, Dante. Don't give up."

Lana asked, "Do you feel anything with it?"

"No, it's as I felt from Abigail, when Alena and I unhooked the black bag from her. The sample shows it's there, but if I didn't see it, I wouldn't know."

Alika spoke, "The next piece only adds to the puzzle. We examined blood samples from the two colony soldiers."

Ryan said, "Yeah, I wondered about those with the entrance wounds being a part of the equation."

Caleb added, "Sounds like we'll be scratching our heads more."

Alika nodded. "We still found no disc shaped object in either one, but their end came from the disc shaped wound. The other wounds ensured a great deal of pain as they continued to fight. We found the black substance in their blood, but it appeared as Abigail's sample."

Lana asked, "But how does that make sense? Abigail is just asleep."

Angelina enlarged the sample at another angle on the device. "Yet, it's as they say. Strange. It's not moving, and I feel no darkness with it either. Perhaps because they're dead, and the substance loses its power. As Lana said, that doesn't explain the black substance's behavior in Abigail."

Seth agreed, "We pondered the same questions. Once we examined the colony soldiers' bodies further, we discovered they started bleeding internally and simultaneously everything shut down. Something decimated their body from the inside out in record time, but we found nothing inside to cause it."

"Except there's a disc shaped entrance wound," said Alena.

"We should've kept one of those off the assembly line for closer examination," said Angelina.

"Like it would help us. The sample of the substance we got has proved useless so far. I remember the disc shaped part felt strange."

"Yeah, the texture was squishy."

Dante said, "The substance must be in the disc."

Lana murmured, "It dissolves inside."

Caleb sighed. "That explains no disc."

Horror registered on Ryan's face. "They figured out a way to control its effects."

Angelina said quietly, "A long torturous sleep, a painful death, or anything in between. It takes expertise."

Seth and Alika glanced at each other. Seth answered, "Yes, that part remains a mystery. We have theories, as I'm sure you do."

Angelina shook her head. "So far none of them helps us." She turned to Dante, her eyes sad. "I'm sorry, Dante, I can't figure out how to awaken your mother yet. I wish so much that I could."

"You're not responsible for figuring it out. Stop making it so. I love my mom, and I want to see her awake. However, many lives are about to share her fate, many families to share my grief, as this continues." He squeezed her hand.

"You're right," Angelina whispered. "I wonder why she isn't struggling as Anna and Teresa? The substance remains in her bloodstream as well."

Alena said, "Maybe the dispersal method? Or the time it's there?"

Ryan replied, "Does that work? We're guessing they exposed Dante's mom to it for years. Angelina indicated she immediately felt Abigail no longer struggling with the darkness, when you two removed the bag from her."

Angelina replied, "Yes, and with Abigail, she kept getting reintroduced to it in a sense, because of the way they hooked it up to her. At least we surmised. We were never clear on what part the crystal mechanism played, connecting the rest of it. We assume Abigail is the first one the Dark Lord tested the substance on. Perhaps, this is the progression, as he perfected his work with the chemicals."

"You're tossing out all the things Alika and I did last night."

"The way it just sits there is perplexing." Her mind grasped for something. "Its presence is enough to keep her asleep like the others, but not sick in the sense of struggling with the darkness anymore. Like a silent alarm. No, that's not it." She shook her head.

Dante turned to her, sensing her frustration. "Like it's dormant, like when someone is in remission after an illness."

She exclaimed, "Yes, Dante, exactly!"

Alena turned to Alika and Seth. "There are a couple of possibilities in the medical world. It stays dormant, in remission. The other possibility ..."

Seth sighed. "It comes back the same as before."

"Or worse," whispered Dante. "We must consider that possibility. We can't forget what the discs did to the colony soldiers."

"Dante, we'll find the answer." She hugged him, and he hugged her back, grateful for her comforting embrace.

Alika said, "We have the medical knowledge to eliminate other conditions which acted in that manner, and hopefully, soon we discover the key to unlock the cure to this one, too."

Seth added, "We'll need to be careful of whatever cure we try on her. If it becomes active again ..."

"We could make it much worse." Alika sighed.

Seth placed the next slides in. "Lastly, we come to those of the Black Dragon agents, Trey and the troop. They are completely black."

Angelina stared at it. "I can't get over how it changes the consistency too. It takes over every ... strange. It moved. The entire sample did. Did you see it? There it goes again. They're dead, but I know what I ... I... saw." Her attention diverted to the side of the projection at eye level. Immediately, her face paled and body stiffened, while her clasped hand inside of Dante's hand tightened.

Dante followed her gaze, but glimpsed nothing. Yet, everyone else witnessed the change come over her. Dante glanced at Alika, his eyes asking the question. Alika returned Dante's look with an equally puzzled one. Could another vision be on its way?

CHAPTER TWENTY-ONE

She continued staring ahead, with coldness in her eyes. It couldn't be possible. The sunspear did its work, but she gathered no one else saw the figure in the room.

"What do you want?" Her voice matched the chill in her eyes.

They realized a confrontation had begun. Unfortunately, they could do nothing to assist her, and they were certain, they'd only hear Angelina's end of the confrontation.

"My, pleasant as before." Trey laughed. He stood with the same confidence as when she met him on the colony, with no evidence of her sunspear's deadly blow to him. His eyes filled with amusement, as her turmoil rose at seeing him again.

"This isn't possible. You're not real. Sunspears do their work, and you don't walk away from its slice, not the one you received."

Dante's alarm grew, and the others shared his unease. A couple of possibilities of those recently killed with their sunspears surfaced, and none of whom they wanted to face again.

"I suppose you're right. You did quite the carving." He smirked.

"Why appear to me? Why am I talking to you? You're dead. This is in my head."

"Oh, I think not."

"Yes, you're in my head. There is no other answer." Slowly closing her eyes, she took a deep breath as Dante squeezed her hand. She opened her eyes, but her face paled again. He remained there.

"Are you done with this futile exercise? I'm still here." He laughed again, stretching his arms out in an exaggerated motion for a moment.

She continued glaring at him, unbelieving and fuming, as she attempted to settle the panic to a manageable level, to face him. Who is he? Trey's dead, but somehow she would replay this battle with him. How? Plunging forward, she accepted the unpleasant reality. "All right, you're not my head playing a game with me, and you won't leave immediately. Why are you here, because I want you gone!"

"Always angry with me. Why must it always be?"

"What else did you expect from me?"

"I'm striving to be friendly, but you ruined it completely, like earlier."

"Friendly, huh? I missed it somewhere, maybe when the pain shot through my arm? Why are you here, and how do I get rid of you?"

"How angry I made you yesterday, and I'm doing it again. Shame on me. Quite the effect I create in you, Kate. I mean the way you went after those soldiers, it was like nothing I had seen in a while. So focused, consumed, almost possessed with your sunspear. If that wasn't enough, you went straight into the interrogation, carrying all that intensity. You tried, but we both know the truth. Tell me, how angry did I make you, Kate?"

"Stop it! You can't hurt me again. Remember, I'm not the one who had a sunspear tear through me," responded Angelina, purposely avoiding his question. Her anger steadily rose; she tried to rein it in, to no avail.

"Come now, we both know what you just did, and it won't work with me. Oh, but you're feeling it. That anger, out of control feeling, and you dislike it so, don't you? It's what you felt yesterday, what you're feeling now. What do you hate more, me or where you feel yourself going at this moment? Go back to yesterday, to the past. Come on, admit it. How angry are you?" His voice continued taunting her, savoring every syllable.

"No, I'm not going back there with you. I don't have to answer you, and I won't give you the satisfaction." She tried sounding forceful and in control, but she couldn't stop the building fury demanding release. Mixed in were echoes from somewhere else, another time she didn't want to remember. It only made it worse, and impossible to keep it bound.

"Oh, but you are. You pushed so hard to get an answer to help those colonists, but came out empty. So empty, Kate. I gave you nothing. No answers. No help. No better than when you started, for all your pain. You put a sunspear through me, but did you feel better? Do you now? To feel so helpless, so desperate, and so angry. Like now. Again. How long before you admit it? I made you feel like that, didn't I? Am I doing it now? I'll keep on. How angry? I want to hear you say it, confess it, Kate!" His voice rose, and he stepped closer to stand directly over her.

"Fine, you made me furious and all those other things, and I feel it again! I said it! I admitted it! There now!" Screaming at him, her hand ripped from Dante's as she stood with fury flashing in her eyes. Only inches separated her from Trey, and her trembling hand ignited her sunspear at her side. The others in the room jumped at the scene, and Dante watched, visibly shaken for her. She continued, her voice trembling as she no longer cared about controlling her anger, "Now, leave, before I carve you out again with my sunspear."

He stared into her eyes, grinned, and with perfect calm spoke, "Surely you know, it's not that easy to send me away, to be rid of me? Come, hasn't this exchange been done before? Something stirring, Kate?"

Instantly all the anger left her, as if the life drained from her body. Her sunspear closed and dropped from her hand, landing on the couch. She seemed as though she saw a ghost, a horrible moment from the past becoming real again before her. The last battle she almost lost herself completely. Her body took on an impossible burden, too heavy for her trembling legs to support. She sat down numbly, and forced herself to look up at him, her voice stumbling, "We did this before." Her voice broke, "It can't be. The battle was fought. Not again will I do this with you."

"Yet here we are again. I took you somewhere you claim to hate. Anger is such a strong emotion, passion, is it not Kate? Anger, Love. Those two passions, both strong, but not so far apart as one thinks, Kate. You feel the one strongly towards me, but I can have you feel the other one as easily, right?"

"They're not the same. I could never feel ... not that ... not ever for you."

He crept closer to her now, his voice soft and seductive, "Oh, I think so, because I know you, Kate. I do, even as you wish it not to be. I took you to the edge, but you pulled back on me at the last, sweet Kate. I wrapped you up in my warm embrace. It's not unattractive, as you say. You once thought so. You can't forget, can you sweet Kate? Why do you continue to fight it? Give in to me, Kate."

"No, I won't. It was a mistake." Her voice broke again. "Leave me now." She struggled to sound firm, but her voice shook along with the rest of her. The memory came back of the time, moments she could never undo. Words said, steps taken, her hand stretched out to clasp one who promised so much, clothing herself in its seduction, allowing herself to embrace it, and giving it entrance. Here she relived it, fought it again.

"Let me take you down that path, Kate. Don't pull back on me this time. I got inside your head. Under your lovely skin. You know I did, and I still do. Come, let me see what lies below the surface."

She knew, as she stared in his eyes and choked out, "No, don't touch me. I won't ..."

Trey smiled though he didn't hear her and closed the gap between them to reach over to touch her face. Her hand moved to intercept him, but he grabbed hold of her arm. Yet he didn't twist or bend it back, but kept it in place, demonstrating his control. "You don't mean that. I can be gentle. Let me make up for before. There's no need to fear me. I told you already. Come to me, sweet Kate. Don't continue resisting further. One touch, one kiss." His other hand caressed her neck as he leaned in to kiss her.

She turned her head to the side to avoid his kiss and closed her eyes. Her voice shaking, she stammered out, "I will never be yours. I will never choose you. Let me go, and leave me now."

He whispered in her ear, "So you say, Kate. We'll try again. I long for that kiss, and I can wait." He brushed his lips to the side of her face and smiled, as he heard a sob escape. His hand on her neck took its time sliding down her shoulder and traveling the side of her body, before it finally rested on her knee.

Dante watched with the others, powerless to help. He saw her arm come up and stop in midair. It seemed frozen in place when he reached over, but he felt nothing solid in the space, only a pocket of coldness. He detected a motion of someone brushing her hair back as she turned her face, and it was confirmed by the shadow of a hand print on her neck. Then he caught a crease or flutter in her clothes on one side, as a hand traced her form. He reached over again, but could do nothing to stop it either. His hand met the same coldness as before.

She waited. The hand left her knee, as did the one gripping her arm. She didn't sense his face near her anymore, and her arm fell to her side. She opened her eyes, and turned to check around the room. He was gone. There were no words, no questions now from Dante, as she met his frantic eyes. She bowed her head and covered her face with her hands, unable to hold back the flood any longer. He already wrapped her up completely in his arms, stroking her hair and back to bring comfort to her shaking form. Her hands still covered her face up against him, trying to hide her pain. He whispered, "I'm sorry, my Angelina." Taking her hands from her face and wrapping her arms tightly around his neck, she clung to him, like she expected any instant to be ripped from his grasp. In response, he held her tighter to him, as her tears soaked his shirt. "I have you and won't let go, Angelina."

Angelina couldn't get a hold of herself. The scene replayed in a continuous torturous assault in her mind. It transported her back to another scene, one she tried keeping shut away. He unlocked it, and enjoyed every moment of dredging the pain to the surface. To bury it again... could she? She had felt his touch, and he said he would return. He would too. And Dante. He held her, comforting her, and calling her his Angelina. She didn't deserve him. The image in his mind of her only caused her to sob harder. He cared for her deeply, but she was far from his angelic image. She clung to him, even as a fear spread in her. If he knew, saw what she saw ... Yet, she clutched him tighter, because she couldn't bear to let him go.

CHAPTER TWENTY-TWO

Alika watched Angelina with the others, wondering who she saw. Her initial comments pointed to two possibilities, but it didn't all fit. From her face and the fury at the beginning, a terrifying storm brewed, threatening to unleash before their eyes. Suddenly, it stopped, and briefly relief poured through him, but what replaced it was much worse in a sense. Now, he feared to see the eyes that met him.

She stopped crying, and pulled away from Dante to stare out in front of her. Did she see them at all? Her eyes were vacant and emotionless, like she felt. She heard herself speak, but didn't comprehend their source. "I'm useless. Done. Nothing to offer, to give. There's nothing left in me."

Dante didn't know what hurt worse, her words or the look in her eyes. She pulled away, and her eyes refused to turn back to him. Yet he could see them. They were a million miles away. The faraway stare from a vision seemed comforting, compared to the emptiness laying there now. Her desolation-filled eyes were only matched by the hopelessness of her words.

Alika also watched his fear confirmed. Gone from her eyes was the fire of old, as though the life was snatched from her. The encounter overwhelmed all her inner resources, leaving her imprisoned behind bars of fear and pain. How long before she found her way back? She shifted, and he knew. His next action pained him, but he couldn't let her.

"I can't anymore. I need to go to the ship to ..." She didn't bother finishing, as she moved to get up, but two people stopped her.

"Not this time, my child." Alika shook his head, and his hand stayed her movement.

Dante wrapped his arm around her waist. "He's right."

She stared at Alika. "Please, I can't stay here. Don't make me. I must do this on my own as I always have." her voice broke.

"You trust me completely. Your words only yesterday, child. Trust me in this. It's time you stopped running away. You'll stay, and do this."

Dante clasped one of her hands in his. "Yes, you're not alone, my Angelina. I meant what I said. I won't let you go."

Her eyes continued pleading with Alika. He held her gaze, his eyes filled with grief. He understood what he asked of her, yet he wouldn't relent, and spoke again in the same soothing tone, "Whenever you're ready, child."

Alika clearly intended on making her do this here. A part of her wondered what he'd do, if she tore out of his and Dante's grasp and stormed out. Unfortunately, that took another emotion. Something long gone from her, so she didn't possess the energy or drive to carry it out. "You recall how long this takes many times."

"I do."

"You believe there's time to waste, for me to become ... this?"

Alika winced at her comment. The one touch of emotion in her voice, and it resonated disgust at the end. "We'll take the time. It's not wasted. Everyone in this room cares for you, and don't speak of yourself like that, child."

"Then you do wish to punish them?"

He sighed as she disregarded his words, but continued, "The other option is you struggle alone, and that won't happen."

Dante whispered, "No, I won't let you."

Alena added quietly, "He cares for you so, Angelina. This time he's here to comfort you. Let him, please. He wishes to."

"He has no idea what he signed up for. None of them do."

Dante, for the first time in a while, didn't know how to respond. She spoke though they weren't in the room, and a whole other world existed in her head. She determined to be alone despite all their efforts. "Even so, we're listening, Angelina."

"I'm sad for you then, Dante."

Dante glanced at Alika again, and his eyes met with sadness. Alika repeated, "Whenever, you're ready, Angelina."

"Fine. What do you want to know, Alika?"

She chose the familiar path, her way of finding her bearings again in the mess left. Alika allowed her to treat it like a vision, as she wished.

"Who did you see?"

A seemingly easy question that she couldn't answer. "I don't know."

"The way you spoke to the figure indicated you knew the individual." Then Alika wondered, "or is it you can't say because of who the person was and your situation?"

"Dead people don't talk, yet he stood there."

"Who stood before you, Angelina?"

"I saw the form of Trey and heard the voice of the same. But I honestly don't know still." It stretched beyond the dead part. His words made no sense.

"Why do you doubt what your eyes and ears told you?"

"His words to me. In one sense they were what I'd expect from Trey. Just as his encounter yesterday." She heard Dante sigh, but she continued in the same detached tone. Trey's lustful words to her didn't bother her, but the other meaning behind them did. "In another sense, his words were not from Trey, because he wouldn't know the things this figure spoke today. No one does, but you and Alena."

Alena stared up at Alika in understanding.

"Did he call you by a different name, Angelina?" asked Alena.

"No, I remained Kate to him, as Trey called me."

Alika began remembering part of Angelina's exchange, and a guess formed in his mind. The guess explained her reaction, if it proved correct. He knew how he perceived those three days in her life which culminated into that moment, but his perspective didn't help. It was how she internalized those days, that moment of decision, and her view of herself from it. Despite all their efforts they couldn't convince her to see it differently. "Did he have knowledge of a moment of crisis you encountered, and your struggle with it?"

"Yes, he did."

Alena met Alika's eyes and whispered, "No wonder." Ryan wound an arm around her waist in comfort.

Alika glanced at Seth and read the question in his eyes. Seth remembered the reference to Angelina's past battle, when the two talked about Dante's upcoming battle at the Elders Hall. Alika nodded to Seth, confirming he guessed right. Whereas Seth didn't know the details of her battle, he witnessed enough from her to see the unforgettable mark it left on her spirit. Alika sighed. "I'm sorry, child. How much did he know?"

"Everything, Alika."

"Though he didn't call you by another name."

"No, he preferred Kate. It amused him."

"How are you certain he knew everything?"

"I know, as I do. Also, he used the same words at some point, and references he made ..."

"When the paths stood before you."

"Yes."

"Did he mention any events before it?"

"He didn't say remember when this horrible thing happened, but he found other equally impressive ways to bring it back for me. He concentrated on the emotions from it. Something told me there was another reason beyond yesterday's events, when he started talking. He tied it all together for me, to his enjoyment."

He kept waiting for some emotion, but even as she talked, and he knew the pain underneath, nothing escaped. "Can you tell me what he said to you?"

Could she? It would dig up questions about her past. Either way, she reached her limit. The rest would be a conversation only for Alika and Alena. She did care about the others, despite the way it seemed now, especially Dante. She couldn't let him endure it, and so her answer came with no hesitation, "No."

Alika watched her, surprised at her abrupt shutdown, but glimpsed something finally flicker in the depths of her eyes. "Why not, Angelina?"

She stared into his eyes for the first time. "Because his words still reflected the man Trey, but they held a double meaning. Since I do care, I won't repeat them."

"I understand," Alika whispered.

Dante did too, at least enough of it. Part of him didn't want to hear, but more importantly, he needed her to find the means to banish the hopelessness descended on her spirit. "Please, you can tell us. Stop thinking about us for once."

She turned to him. "No, Dante, I won't put you through his words to me. It'll only bring you grief, and his words did enough of that yesterday. I understand his double meaning, and you won't. You'll only hear the words, as Trey of yesterday meant them."

Alika nudged Seth and whispered, "His words will touch her heart, as always. Why don't we get the others started on lunch, and give the two of them time?"

Seth nodded, as they got up and approached the others.

CHAPTER TWENTY-THREE

Dante held her eyes. A struggle reflected in them, as she attempted to dispel the lingering echoes from her earlier encounter, but its tentacles coiled around her again. He needed to claim her back, as much as she needed to return to him. He encircled one arm around her waist and clasped her hand with his other hand. "Am I still your Dante?"

"Of course, unless you don't wish to be."

"That could never be the case because you know how I care for you, my Angelina. There's nothing that changes that. I'm still your Dante?"

"Yes, you're my Dante."

He unclasped her hand to stroke the side of her face. "My Angelina, you're far from me, though you're here in my arms. Trey took something precious from you today, with whatever he said to you."

"Oh, I'm not that far away. You still have me, Dante." She felt it finally, like one crawling out of a fog. She couldn't bear to cause him pain, but it reflected in his glistening eyes, and she wished to take it away.

"The light which radiates from you, it's not extinguished. I long to see it shine again in your beautiful blue eyes, my Angelina."

"It'll shine again for you. The shadow is passing." She slid her hands to his shoulders. "Why do you care for me, Dante? I'm trouble, always. Do you not see?"

"Never do I see that. You're not trouble, and I won't let you say such things about yourself. What is there not to like about you? Come now, I showed you countless times since we met." A smile played at the corner of her mouth, and he pursued it, as he grinned at her. "How about I prove it further, Angelina?"

"You're not shy about doing so, and I walked into that one, Dante." She found her arms winding around his neck, unable to resist his smile.

"You're right on both, and I won't miss an invitation from you." He eased her over to wrap her up completely and kissed her, determined to erase today's horrible encounter.

She melted under his kiss and the next one. He infused them with words of reassurance and care, with a gentle strength demonstrating he would be her anchor in the chaos, and his arms would always be open to embrace her no matter how scared or hopeless she became. She didn't comprehend how he did it, but she surrendered to it.

He gazed into her eyes, as their faces remained close together, when the kiss finally ended. "We chased the others away."

"They'll catch up to us."

"Yeah." He stroked the side of her face. She smiled, and the vacant look in her eyes was long gone. He glimpsed the light returning to them as the Angelina he loved found her way slowly back to him. " I know a couple of kisses doesn't make it all better."

"Not all better, but you're amazingly good. Besides, we both know there's more in those than just a mere kiss. There has always been."

"I feel it too." He paused. "Is it the connection?"

"I think so." She grinned and whispered, "Or perhaps your kisses are that incredible, Dante."

He couldn't be happier to hear her teasing and see the grin on her face. "Only and always for you, my Angelina."

"Better be, my Dante."

He laughed. "Definitely. You deserve another for that." And he did.

With a happy sigh, she leaned up against him and wound her arms around his waist. He snuggled her closer, as relief poured over him. She peered up at him. "I'm sorry for being distant, Dante. It was my fault."

"Stop. It's not your fault. It's his fault, this Trey person who appeared to you, but you dealt with it the best you could."

"I'm used to processing these things differently, Dante."

"I gathered. On your own. Alone. Did you consider it's not the best method?"

"Yes, but I determined it is."

"Even after today?"

"Yes."

"Why? To spare others? Because you don't. Do you know how it hurts, to watch you go through it alone, when we want to be there for you?"

"There are parts of the struggle no one can help with, Dante. It can only be done in one's own heart. It reveals things we didn't see about ourselves, or we didn't want to, because they're ..." She closed her eyes for a moment. "There's the point we can get help in our struggle."

He watched her. She believed her words wholeheartedly, and no one would convince her otherwise. "What's the longest time you spent struggling alone?"

"Start to finish?" She took a deep breath. "Probably about four, Dante."

"Four hours is a long time, Angelina."

She whispered, "Not hours."

He gazed at her in disbelief. "You can't mean what I think? You mean days?"

"Yes, days."

"Surely Alika and Alena came beside you during it?"

"They would in an instant, if I asked. After I wrestled with my part, they always came as I requested. Many times, I deserved something else besides what I received for my behavior, for my words to them. Especially Alika." Her voice broke as she bowed her head. He lifted her chin with his hand, and caught regret-filled eyes. "I found grace and forgiveness even when I delivered anger and bitterness to him. I acted as a hateful child rather than his student. It's a wonder he continues putting up with me."

"He doesn't simply put up with you. We both know he's as fond of you as Seth is of me. Whatever happened those times, there's another side of the story. You're always harder on yourself than everyone else, and there's no reason for it."

"You say, but it's as it should be. I'm ..."

"You're wonderful, and I won't believe differently, Angelina." He kissed her forehead and continued, "This is an incredibly short time period, compared to the other ones."

"Only on the surface. This wasn't a new event. He caused an old struggle to resurface, so I'm not through with it yet, only postponed. There are things I must focus on, while I'm here."

"I'll listen, Angelina. Are you sure?" he pleaded with her.

"I promise, Dante, it won't help to tell you. The double meaning is lost on you, and it's the part which left me shaken. This is a session for Alena and Alika."

"I'm sorry I can't help you."

"Not true. You help, in ways only you can. The bond we share, nothing can replace it. One day, I'm sure I'll be able to tell you everything."

"If you change your mind, I'll always listen."

"My Dante, you never fail me." She stroked the side of his face, and brought him over for another long, gentle kiss.

He murmured, "Definitely, more than a mere kiss."

They sat there for a few more minutes, wrapped up perfectly content in each other's arms. She glanced over at the others and back at Dante. "Dante, they're waiting."

"I know," he said, running his fingers through her hair.

"They gave us plenty of time."

"Never enough with you, but they won't come back until we're done, and we need lunch. Well, maybe."

"You are ..." she started as she grinned back at him.

"Escorting you to lunch because I'm charming like that, remember?" He winked at her. "Come on." He pulled her up with him.

"Finally hungry for lunch? About time," Alena teased as they set down at the table with their plates.

"I don't know. You two were pretty happy over there, so you could've passed on lunch." Ryan laughed.

"I would've, if it was me." Caleb grinned as he winked at Lana.

"We know, Caleb." Lana smiled.

"Like I couldn't persuade you."

"Oh, you can and do."

Seth smiled at Angelina and Dante. "Angelina, it's a relief to see the spark back in your eyes."

Alika grinned. "Yes, Dante, you helped with that enormously."

"I'll do whatever it takes to have her smiling again." He kissed her on the cheek.

"I do like how you persuade me, Dante." She gave him a sideways smile before turning to the others. "Not my best moment earlier, and I wish I could say you won't see it again, but I can't guarantee that."

Lana said, "There's no need for that. It's forgotten for us, and you're the one who must now."

"That's not possible. This reprieve is short-lived."

Ryan spoke up, "Then we find a way to help the next time, but maybe we saw the last of him."

"There's nothing you could do. None of you could see him. Even I don't know how to fight him. He's dead, but he's not. He's Trey, but he's not. How do I kill it? Obviously not a sunspear. I'm not through, he's... it's not through."

"What do you mean, not through, Angelina?" asked Seth. Alika studied her too at the comment.

"He made it clear he's coming back, that he could wait."

Dante's blood ran cold. "Wait for what? What does he want?"

She bit her lip and averted his gaze. She pictured Alena and Alika trying not to appear uncomfortable with her. "I don't know, Dante. He wants to bring the worst out in me. Like you said yesterday, he enjoys saying things to hurt me. It's impossible to tell for sure because he spoke in riddles half the time."

Though it pained him, he didn't believe her. "You really don't know what he wants?"

She took a deep breath and stared up at him. "Dante, I'm not certain what I battled. Whatever it wants from me, I can't ever give it, or let it take it. If it does, more than a smile on my face or a sparkle from my eye will be lost."

He understood. She didn't know what she dealt with exactly, but in another sense she realized all too well the threat to her, the cost which lay in the balance. He stroked her cheek and answered, "I won't ever allow it to claim you, to take you from me."

"I promise, I'll keep fighting, Dante, when it returns." As she hugged him, she tried not to consider the looming possibility it wouldn't be enough one day, and she'd end up on the losing side. Gently pulling back from Dante, she turned to the others. She didn't want to give him a chance to ask another question and answer it like she had. "Let's get back to what Alika and Seth found out before all this started."

Lana nodded. "You heard Angelina, but we'll let her set the pace."

"I keep a fast pace. No slacking or special treatment, Dante."

"I get this evening with you, so I'll recoup my time." He teased her back, and kissed her forehead as he rose from the table with the rest.

She smiled at him and said to them, "Before we start, I need a few minutes with Alika and Alena."

Quiet settled on the room. Dante hated this reminder, that part of her world remained hidden from him. She insisted it kept them safe, yet the not knowing bothered him. "Sure, we'll clear this, and meet you three at the couches, when you're done."

"Thank you, Dante, for understanding." She rewarded him with a kiss on the cheek.

CHAPTER TWENTY-FOUR

The three settled in a corner to talk privately.

Alena asked, "How are you really?"

"Better."

Alika studied her. "What can we do?"

"Nothing here, but I need to go through the words of the encounter with the two of you. I'll still remember it tonight, but I won't give up my time with Dante or have Alena taken from her time with Ryan."

"I will if you need me to."

"Absolutely not. We'll leave them soon, and we don't know how long between trips it could be. We can talk about my earlier encounter at midnight, as well as we can at seven this evening."

Alika nodded. "You need our time this evening, but it'll be late."

"Yes, by the time Dante leaves, even with simply repeating the words of my visitor."

"I can secure a later start for tomorrow, and we'll take as much time as you need tonight."

"Thank you both."

Alena asked, "Anything that can't wait? You said you held back because of Dante, but was that all?"

"Some of it, but it would've raised a host of questions about the night in my room, when I battled the darkness and all the events surrounding it."

"No, we can't open the floor to those questions." Alena sighed.

"The double meanings were a whole other arena. He talked about not resisting, giving into him completely this time. You get the idea. The Trey of yesterday, but completely different in that way."

"Darkness cloaked in Trey's form. The battlefield revisited, and it promises to come to you again," Alika murmured.

"Yet, it wants the same from me as the night in my room." Her eyes traveled back in that breath.

"And it can't have you now." The gentle firmness to Alika's voice commanded her gaze back to his eyes.

"Or ever. Understand?"

"Yes, I understand, you two."

"You don't sound like it. Should I get Dante to persuade you?" Alena teased.

"He needs no further encouragement." Angelina laughed.

"Neither of you does, and I thought I had fun teasing you when you only saw him in the visions. This is much more fun." Alena laughed too.

"At least there's Ryan to throw back at you now."

"Eventually you could catch up. Look at Dante though, over there sad without your company. How long will you leave him like that? Don't you have a meeting to run anyway?"

Angelina started laughing again. "You let me handle keeping a smile on Dante's handsome face, Alena. Come on, so I can direct this meeting."

"Seems the talk did her well." Dante glanced between the two laughing women, as Angelina sat next to him.

"It did, Dante. Only one topic, in particular, puts her in such a pleasant mood." Alena grinned mischievously at him.

"I see now." He grinned back as he wrapped his arm around Angelina's waist and kissed the side of her face.

"Did you hear anything I said, Alena?"

"I did, and you're right. I should let you take care of the part. He does have quite the smile on his handsome face again. See, I listen."

Angelina's laughter subsided, but Alena's last comment brought a new wave. She started reaching for her drink, but gave up.

Dante chuckled and grabbed it for her with his free hand. "Another lively discussion. I got your drink. Anything else?"

"Yes, want anything else from Dante?" Alena continued laughing.

"I didn't intend to help her, Angelina. Sorry." Dante started laughing again though.

"Alena, I can't look at you now. Would you stop?"

"Be careful. You'll spill the drink all over you and Dante, or you're going to choke on it soon."

She put the drink back, shaking her head. "If I didn't need you to keep me out of trouble ..."

"I do a lot of that for sure, but this is what you would miss."

"Yeah, I definitely would." She turned to Alika and Seth. "You better get us back to your findings."

Alika grinned back. "My gratitude for giving me and Seth the chance to continue, but we enjoyed the amusement from you two."

Alena smiled. "It's the only reason we do it, Alika."

"Yes, our way of thanking you for those long training sessions."

Alika's eyes twinkled. "You tell me on occasion how you appreciate them, so I'll ensure they continue just for you, Angelina." He saw her answer, with the laughter in her eyes. "I believe we left off discussing the differences in the samples."

Angelina sank deeper into the couch, put her arms around Dante's waist and midsection, and leaned her head on his shoulder. Usually, she didn't make herself this comfortable while they had discussions with the group, but she needed to feel safe. Trey's words promising his guaranteed return ran through her mind. Dante knew, as always. He kept one arm around her waist, and his other hand stroked her arm. Every so often he'd kiss her forehead or smile down at her, his way of checking in with her after earlier.

Lana murmured, "The sample results didn't create the clear picture I hoped."

"It's the pattern lately, one I'm sick of seeing," said Caleb.

Angelina wondered aloud, "They could've kept going, planet after planet. What prevents them?"

Dante responded, "Could be tied to differences with the substance's effects, still experimenting to get it right."

Ryan sighed. "Then the variations aren't the result of an expert process. More like crazy or haphazard. Somebody comes to mind at Black Dragon, who has a corner on that market."

Alena admitted, "Possible. It's an easy jump with how she meddles, and she did help keep Abigail imprisoned, while hooked up to the substance."

Angelina murmured aloud again, "He said he could wait."

"Still with me?" Dante smiled down at her, stroking her cheek. "Who?"

"Trey or whatever it was."

"And he's coming to you until he gets whatever from you." The thought caused him to tighten his grip on her waist. "It won't work for him ever."

"No, because he or it can't take from me. This feels similar in a way. Like it's connected, but not."

"You went through a lot today, but if you feel anything surfacing, we're listening."

"My mind is reaching, but something bothers me about it. Actually several somethings."

"One at a time. You're controlling the pace."

"We're missing a piece again. They possess a working dispersal device. They tested it, and it passed to their satisfaction. Why not all out attacks now? It's the Black Dragon standing in the room, that no one wants to acknowledge. There's nothing they need to wait on, but they do? Why?"

Lana said, "A massacre isn't their aim. Kind of like the attacks being a distraction."

Dante took a deep breath. "But they can take everything they want now."

Angelina burst out, as her mind made the connection. "No, they can't, but they can draw it out, make it terrible for those ..."

"Of the Ancient One." Alena finished the thought.

"It's the one thing they can't take, even with the black substance, because it must be given in every case. One's allegiance, loyalty."

Ryan said, "So they're figuring out how, with the black substance, to turn the unwilling."

"Could be, but I don't think they can. Yet there's one way it was successfully done for a long time."

Dante whispered, "Through deception."

Alika finished, "Taking a person's moment of weakness, such as grief, and using it cruelly. Yet, we witnessed the bondage broken too."

"Yes, we bore witness the Ancient One's hold to his own is always stronger than any deception," added Seth.

Alena shook her head. "How would they carry it out though? It took an elaborate plot to capture Ethan's loyalty."

Lana answered, "I can't imagine, but there are more Treys out in the colonies. Our cleanup yesterday proved it."

Seth said, "However, we're envisioning a massive scale deception."

"Yes, we're back to Alena's question. To accomplish it seems inconceivable." Alika leaned back in thought.

Angelina spoke, a sadness laden in her words, "The darkness people succumb to in their weakness or grief initially seems impossible to fathom. No one understood how Ethan believed what he did, but the darkness seeks those moments to gain entrance. It tried with Dante in the Elders Hall, but he withstood it. It has claimed many victims, who fell for far less than what it used on Ethan and Dante." She stared down for a moment. "Many people, finding themselves or their families at the mercy of a horrible fate all at once would be desperate, to save those closest to them from death. Is there a more vulnerable position to be placed? To give one's own life is a possibility each time we battle. But our comrade, our friend, our sister, those we count as family, the one who holds our heart," she paused again, finding her eyes drifting to Dante, "is it that easy to sacrifice them when the moment comes? What would we do to spare them if told there stood a way?"

"She's right," said Dante, staring down, as he brushed a strand of her hair back from her beautiful face. What would he do to spare her? He wouldn't give a second thought to whatever it took to keep her safe. He turned to the group. "I never imagined I'd believe the things I did at the Elders Hall, but the Dark Lord pieced lies together perfectly, to pass for truth. Only the Ancient One, allowing Angelina's words to break through to my spirit, brought me back." He kissed her on the cheek. "You don't see past the deception when it involves someone closest to you. If you believe you're losing the one you care about before your eyes, your heart takes over reason."

The terrifying time at the Elders Hall, when she thought he would breathe his last tumbled back to her. "Yes, you only see the moment, and the fear takes over." She stroked the side of his face. "Thankfully, you found your way, and I didn't lose you."

His lips brushed hers as he whispered, "And you won't lose me, Angelina."

Seth smiled. "Hopefully, we uncover how they mean to carry out such a plan. Meanwhile, we learned there'll be no need resort to blood samples as a standard greeting."

Alena said, "Good news finally."

Alika replied, "Don't get too happy. The mark isn't readily visible. It's located on the lower back of their neck."

Ryan groaned. "Terrific. If it's a woman, her hair covers it most of the time."

Caleb added, glancing at Lana. "And you try checking for a mark on a strange woman and see how that works out for you, especially if you're a guy."

"Actually, it could go different ways," Lana mused.

Alena nodded. "Depends on how they play it. You get slapped in the face at the least, or they start hanging all over you."

"Since all three of our guys aren't lacking in the looks department in the least, the second option is a fair play," said Angelina, and then caught Dante's expression mirrored by Ryan and Caleb. "Dante, stop acting like you three don't know it."

Dante kissed her on the cheek. "You do make it clear, but the other option is an equally likely reaction."

Angelina rubbed her forehead. "Yes, those serving the Black Dragon won't hesitate to kill. These are no different. The men won't be any easier to spot as Trey demonstrated. The right shirt hides the mark. Are those two bodies still in medical?"

Alika and Seth both nodded.

"Let's go visit them."

Dante shook his head. "This isn't a good idea after earlier."

"I'll be fine, and I need to see the marking."

"A projection would do just as well."

She already got up. "No, I need to see how they did it, for myself."

He rose too, finding it pointless to argue, but puzzled by her insistence.

CHAPTER TWENTY-FIVE

Angelina and Dante walked down the hall with the others, and Alena and Ryan came beside them.

Alena said, "Our operations got complicated, didn't they?"

Angelina replied, "Yeah, depending on this mark we'll see how complicated."

"We passed off fake supplies."

"And what fun as I remember."

"You think they remove helmets?"

"Seems too much time to me, Alena. Maybe peek inside the top of the armor far enough? Probably aren't gentle with it, but spot the mark and move on."

"The positive is no more worries about real skin under our armor. Half the Black Dragon soldiers will be that way now."

"True. Once colonists, still kind of human, black sludge blood."

"Think they're checking blood, Angelina?"

"Only as a confirmation thing. The time that would take if they did would border on ridiculous. Don't arouse suspicion, no reason to bother is my guess. Anyway, I don't want to envision how to fake that one. I'm already dreading the mark. We're in a lot of trouble, if we're in a situation where they need our blood samples."

"Worse than the hangar."

"Yeah, tied up, ready for interrogation."

They realized, they somehow forgot about Dante and Ryan, whose faces both reflected horror. The understanding sunk in for them of what this meant for Angelina and Alena when they undertook future operations.

Dante's voice rose, turning to Angelina, "You'll never pull it off, and you two will get yourselves killed."

"Dante, this is what we do."

Ryan joined in, staring at Alena. "He's right. This is different, you two."

"It's not. There's a way to fake it," Alena replied.

Dante continued, "Angelina, they'll make it difficult. This is insanity."

"Yesterday you said this is where I do my best work. Remember hacking system, faking accesses, and so on. You claimed no confidence in them. Now, suddenly, I can't outsmart them."

"I didn't mean it like that, and I remember you saying in the same breath we don't know about the new leadership. They could be smarter."

"Why did you remember that part?" she muttered. "Dante, we need to see the mark."

Ryan started in again. "What about the blood? You two can't go injecting yourself with black substance."

Dante's face paled. "You two wouldn't try."

"Calm down, you two. I'm not insane." Angelina shook her head.

"Neither one of us are, but Alika would intervene, which he wouldn't need to. There's a way to do this, like with the supplies."

"Alika can figure out something with all his medical knowledge."

"The consistency may be the bigger issue to replicate, Angelina. The time undercover, too."

"Dante, we were supposed to discourage them, not get them brainstorming again."

"We apparently failed, Ryan."

Angelina glanced at Alena. "The first part is simply a color change, so not too bad to manage. Actually, with the right knowledge one would dare say easy."

"Yeah, really easy." She returned her gaze, hearing the unspoken thought.

"What is it?" asked Dante. Ryan peered at them suspiciously too.

Angelina snapped out of her musings. "Nothing. Just anticipating a shadow which doesn't exist. We're here."

"Did you hear them?" Dante asked Caleb.

"Enough. They're intense when they strategize. Don't worry. Alika manages them."

"Are you sure about this?" asked Alika.

"Yeah, I'm fine." Angelina took a deep breath, and approached Trey's silent form. Alika and Seth had stripped him of his shirt, and left him as such, probably on purpose once they discovered the mark. They undressed him all the way to do the complete exam but clothed back his lower body along with a sheet pulled up to his waist. Her eyes locked on the huge gash running down his upper body from her sunspear. Two more ugly marks darkened his shoulder and midsection that he'd keep as well. Those from Dante. She felt satisfied at seeing the marks on him. He deserved them. There went his perfectly sculpted chest, in which he placed such pride.

"You don't have to do this." said Dante, coming over to her.

"I do. He's dead, so he can't do anything to me. Let's see this mark."

Alena came over as well for a closer inspection and said, "Alika, Seth, you want to do the honors?" The others followed over.

Seth and Alika turned Trey to the side, revealing the mark.

"What's the image of?" Alena asked. "Appears rather dragonish, but it's not. Perhaps it's supposed to be one of those sea creatures you read about."

"Like only the tail of it or a snake, but not even that. Ugly for sure. Something they dreamed up," said Angelina.

Alena continued studying it. "Not too intricate. I feared it being the Black Dragon symbol, but I suppose even they wouldn't be that dumb."

Ryan said, "Yeah, that does mess up the concealment angle, stamping the Black Dragon symbol on everyone."

Angelina traced the mark on Trey with her fingertips, continuing to stare down at it and murmured, "Lines across. Waves, but not. The strangest creature I've ever seen and distorted somehow, because it's meant to be. It's not a dragon, but it is." Realization flashed into her eyes. "Dragon scales over an eye."

Alena's eyes widened. "The eye is in the slits, like it's trying to see through it."

Lana continued, "But it can't, because the dragon scales blind, distort its vision."

"It never ends. Not being too intricate just flew out the ship hatch." Angelina sighed as she continued running her fingertips over Trey's mark. "Feels strange. Deeper than a body picture, and weird underneath. I can't explain it. Dante, will you see what you think?"

"Sure." He felt relieved by her request. After earlier, the less contact with Trey, the better. He didn't want it triggering any of today's encounter. His fingertips glided over the mark. Was it indented or punctured to make the picture in places? Like a connect the dots in places, but that wasn't it. The whole picture felt elevated, but it didn't look it. Like it sat on a cloud, a puff of air, squishy underneath, but that didn't work either it. "I can't explain it either, but I see your trouble with describing it." He turned to Seth and Alika. "Did you come up with how they created the imprint?"

Alika answered. "No, there's no indication of how the mark is made." He glanced at Seth.

"We aren't convinced they must make the mark."

Alena stammered, "How else would the mark be there?"

Caleb guessed, "You think it appears when they give their allegiance."

Alika nodded. "It's a working theory. If not, whatever process they masterminded, I'm sure it's painful. What you feel under the imprint is a concentration of the black sludge."

Angelina nodded. "One mystery solved. Is there anything from the body, binding the mark to Black Dragon, a way they track them?"

"We didn't decipher any," answered Seth.

"Seems too easy, but we go with it, unless we learn otherwise. We'll need to replicate this imprint, from the design to its feel on the skin in every way, including underneath the skin. Same with the black blood sludge. Please get what you can from them and preserve it, so it retains all that. We'll need it later, as we may require outside help with this. You have the means to do so?"

"We do, Angelina," Seth listened in amazement to her. Her voice reflected all business as she glanced down at Trey, seemingly unaffected by her request.

"We'll start now," agreed Alika. Although accustomed to his student's quick shifts, he still found himself impressed at her demeanor after earlier.

"Alena, you should see how the mark feels, before they cut in, since we'll be the ones judging whether it passes inspection."

"A fair assumption." Alena ran her fingers over the mark for a minute and murmured, "Odd. I sense a headache to replicate."

Angelina nodded and turned back to Seth and Alika. "They're all yours. We'll be over here till you finish."

"We don't need to watch this," said Dante, wrapping his arm around her waist.

"I'm fine. They'll be done in no time."

Seth and Alika suited up for the procedure as a precaution. They tackled the easy part first of obtaining the blood samples from the two bodies. Now came the more challenging part. They prepared two special containers with specific solution, to preserve every aspect of their two samples. After turning both bodies on their stomachs, they used the scalpel to cut into the flesh where the mark laid and removed the entire area. They placed each sample in the container and sealed them. Then they used the medical device to seal up the wounds, to keep the black sludge from dripping further and put the bodies back as they were. Alika took the two containers, and secured the samples further in two airtight metal lab containers used for contaminants. "We won't take any chances."

They pulled off the coverings, masks, and gloves, and discarded them in a pile with the scalpel.

Angelina said, "Let's take them to the room and be done with it. I want to see it through."

Alika and Seth rolled the carts down the hall with the two bodies to another room. Normally, the incinerator-type device inside eliminated things containing harmful contaminants, transforming anything into a pile of ashes in minutes.

They would find themselves expanding its use now, a sobering realization. They took care of the Black Dragon soldier first, along with the coverings and other items as the fire consumed it. Next, they prepared to send Trey's body through.

"This is where you brought me, after everything today, sweet Kate."

Angelina's hand tightened on Dante's arm as her eyes turned cold, but no panic entered them. She wouldn't allow him to overwhelm her again. Everyone guessed who stood in the room, and followed her gaze. Dante moved closer to her side, unwilling to permit a repeat either.

Alika and Seth watched Angelina too. Her glance and the quick motion of her hand told them Trey's body would still burn, but to wait for her signal. They perceived none of the fear or brokenness from earlier.

"Don't call me that, like anything pleasant exists between us. I'm not sweet Kate to you, and I'll never be sweet anything to you."

"Your mood soured considerably this afternoon."

"No, I was in good spirits again until a moment ago. The company in the room now is the cause of my mood change. Take the hint and leave."

"I couldn't do that, since I just arrived."

"Oh, you can. You came uninvited and unwelcome, as before."

"I told you to expect my return, or did you forget from earlier? Shall I remind you? I'll happily do so."

"I remember fine. You're pleased with yourself, but I won't go there again. Not today. I vented sufficient rage for one day."

"This is a different side of you, Kate."

"I'm disappointing you. You hoped to get another outburst from me this afternoon, but you'll need to find another way to amuse yourself. I won't provide it again, so there's no reason for you to stay."

"But there is. You're reducing me to ashes and didn't bother to tell me."

"Well, if you have last words for yourself, be my guest. There's time enough. Go ahead." She repeated the sweeping motion with her hands he made previously that day, and his eyes narrowed, as he failed to hide his displeasure. She hid her satisfaction. "I'm waiting, because I'm curious to hear what someone says to one's corpse." She allowed a small smile at the corners of her mouth.

Dante watched her in silent astonishment, along with the rest as she toyed with him, making him pay for his earlier visit. He doubted Trey backed down, but she remained composed, more than matching him in battle.

Trey peered down at his still form for a bit, and shook his head before staring back up at Angelina.

"Trey, quite underwhelming. I expected something mildly entertaining. Not one word of flattery for yourself? Just stare down at what's left of your form?" She laughed. "You always thought your body attractive, that any woman seeing you should fall into your arms and left no doubt the confidence you placed in it."

"You deny it, but someone undressed me. I bet you did, Kate. Couldn't help yourself. Why don't you admit it and get it over with? It'll be easier for you." He grinned at her, his voice taking the seductive tone from earlier.

She returned his gaze and smiled at him, her own voice matching his, "You continue to wish, but I didn't undress you. I admit I admired the view underneath, Trey. In fact, I enjoyed it immensely." His eyes lit up with the familiar look at her comment, as he began his slow travel over her form. She didn't care because her next words would hit another nerve. "Yes, I loved seeing my sunspear's handiwork across your chest, and you earned some other outstanding deep marks on you, when you got thrown off me. Those are a testimony to Dante's strength and years of training. I found it satisfying, but we both take great pride in our work, Trey."

She glimpsed the momentary flicker of pure rage in his eyes he couldn't hide. He assumed he pulled her in, when he heard her first words, and his thoughts took him one place. She turned it on him though, like one about to partake of the last morsel from the most delectable dessert, only to feel it snatched right from him as it reached his mouth. She had discovered a means to get to him and past his defenses, so she now pushed forward to finish it. "I gave you enough time. Say your last words, and we can be done with your form. I tire of you, Trey."

"You're certainly not the Kate of earlier," he sneered.

"Enjoyed that Kate's company more? A shame. She's gone and not returning."

"Yes, a shame. I wonder what happened to her."

She laughed. "Must I tell you, Trey? You continue to disappoint me. The answer is before you. Sound familiar. You know me right, Trey? Your words, again remember?"

"I do know you, Kate. The Kate of before is there, somewhere."

"Yet, I stand before you, nothing like the Kate of earlier. Quite the puzzle for you, Trey. You really don't see? You surprised me earlier, but no more. And I have something else to tell you." She stepped closer to him while remaining at a safe distance. Slowly and deliberately, she spoke, "I'm starting to get to know you too, Trey, but not in the way you like."

Staring back at her, he weighed her words and grasped their meaning. Once he did, he determined it best to move to another subject. "Do you think if you burn me up, you'll finally be rid of me?"

"A girl can dream, can't she? I sliced you open with a sunspear, and still you insist I endure your company. So honestly, no, I don't believe turning your physical form into a pile of ashes ends these wearisome chats from you. However, I'm willing to find out, and regardless, I look forward to you being turned to ashes. It's a win either way for me." Without taking her eyes from Trey, she made a motion to Alika and Seth. "I'll be a more active participant in this one." Alika and Seth moved Trey's body through the opening, but didn't light the fire this time. They understood her meaning perfectly. "We started this right? You possess the battle wounds from it, and it's only fitting I finish it. In this case, Dante, why don't you come help me settle what we started with Trey?" She turned to Dante and smiled.

"My pleasure, Kate," said Dante, smiling back. He stepped up to stand close beside her, so they stood outside the opening, where Trey's body laid inside.

Alika and Seth handed each of them a firestone. The two tossed the stones on the body, and it ignited. The two stepped back to where they were, and Alika and Seth followed suit.

She watched the body burn, but she kept an eye on Trey, since she alone could see him. "Dante, I liked the other view, but this is better."

"I agree. We should've done it sooner, rather than you tolerate him as long you did."

"You were right, but he wouldn't stop talking." She rolled her eyes.

"Who knew the dead could be that chatty?" He grinned.

"You're not kidding, and he's taking forever to burn. This stretched out long enough."

"Just feels that way, after two visits from him. Relax. He's almost ashes now."

"Good. Thanks for your help, Dante."

"Of course. We all have each other's backs."

She glanced up at Trey, as if she just remembered him there. "Still here? There's nothing to see. All ashes now. Aren't you bored with this?"

"I'm not sure, Kate. There'll be other times to tell you."

"You'll make certain of it."

He looked down at the ashes once more, his figure distorted, and disappeared.

She turned to Dante and took a deep breath. "He's gone. For how long is another matter."

"Hopefully for a while." His arm encircled her waist as he kissed her cheek. "You were ..."

"Amazing," finished Alena.

Ryan grinned. "We only heard your end of it too."

"Yeah, you torched him, in more than one way." Caleb chuckled.

"He deserved it." Lana nodded.

Alika placed a hand on her shoulder briefly. "Yes, well played, my dear. I admit I had concerns, after earlier."

Seth smiled. "But you kept him on the defense. Even without hearing his end, we could tell."

"We're done here finally, and can move on." Suddenly, it approached close behind her. Automatically, she spun around and moved away, stretching her arm out to maneuver Dante with her. There would be no victory for it this afternoon. "Did you forget something? You must find other entertainment today, Trey."

"I can surprise you, Kate." He grinned.

"I'll give you that one, but hardly fair sneaking up on me. I still won't amuse you, as this morning."

"If I push hard enough, you will."

"No, I won't. We've other business to attend to, and you continue wasting our time. Stay with your ashes if you wish, or find something else to do." She paused. "Yes, tell me your plans for today, which don't involve your time bothering me."

"You'd like to know, Kate?"

"It'd be the only useful thing, from the time spent with you today. Where are you off to?"

"Since you asked nicely, how about we make a deal?"

"I don't make deals with Black Dragons, because I'm smarter than that, as you're aware."

"But it's valuable. Maybe I'm willing to tell you more than you ask. There are things you need to know. I've secrets too, ones you'd love to hear. What are you willing to give?"

She stared in his eyes and didn't know how, but he possessed knowledge she needed, things Alena and she would put themselves in considerable danger to obtain. If she could spare Alena danger, she would in a heartbeat. Nevertheless, she'd never seriously consider taking his offer. He was Black Dragon, and never to be trusted. In the end, it meant one thing. "Whatever secrets you hold, I'm not willing to pay the price it'd cost me for them. I don't need to hear your offer to know it's too much, and it'll always be. I'll never give it to you. Keep your secrets, and go where you will today."

"Don't be hasty, Kate. Remember, I know you, and you wish to. You can still choose it, and it's the easier path. I don't ask as much as you say."

"Another lie. I won't take your offer. Not ever. I'll find the answers, as always. Now go and stop wasting our time, because we're leaving this room."

"Always, you choose the difficult path, when you could make it simple."

"This path comes nowhere near you, so I'll continue on it. We're done here."

He watched her, daring her to leave. She turned her attention to the others. "Let's go. There's nothing here warranting our further attention." She continued keeping one eye trained on Trey's movement. The group made their way out of the room, with Alika and Seth going last along with her and Dante. Trey grabbed her arm, as anger swirled in his eyes.

"Let go of my arm now, Trey. You're more than a mere shadow, but I'll find the means to break you." Her voice conveyed calm, and her eyes were cold and fearless.

"You heard my student. Release her now."

Seth added, "The Ancient One won't let you hold her further. Do as she says."

"I pulled her from your grasp once, and I'll do it again, even if I must tear you from limb to limb right here. I'll make you visible enough to make it happen. Now, take your hand off her, Trey." Dante's voice resounded calm but firm, and left no doubt he'd follow through with his threat, somehow. He had reached over and put his hand on the arm Trey held. The same coldness surrounded her arm as last time, but Dante kept his hand on it. He took a warning step closer to where he knew the man stood, but remained standing, unwavering at Angelina's side, ready to protect her.

The warmth of Dante's touch countered the coldness Trey's touch always brought with it. Grateful for Dante's comforting caress, she found strength in it, as she spoke again. "You hear them, Trey. I'll walk out of this room from your grasp. I'm not afraid of you, and I won't play games with you further today. Let go now."

With his eyes smothering with anger, he released his grip on her arm. With a nod to him, she walked past him with the others and shut the door behind them, leaving him standing there.

CHAPTER TWENTY-SIX

They made it back to the main room in the fortress, except for Seth and Alika, who detoured to Alika's ship, to drop off the samples.

Angelina sat with Dante, while they waited with the others for Alika and Seth to return. She hugged him. "Thank you, Dante."

He wrapped his arms around her tightly and held her. "You're welcome, but I didn't do anything. That was all you back there."

"No, Dante. You keep me anchored and bring me back."

He took his hand and lifted her chin. "I'll always be here to do that for you, my Angelina." He kissed her, then pulled her back over, and she leaned up against him again.

"None of today went as planned," said Angelina, as they all sat again.

Alena shook her head. "Name any day that has, since we arrived."

"The other day, we at least made it out to the ship, before it all came apart."

"The return trip to the planet certainly waits until tomorrow, Angelina." Alika said.

"Agreed, but there's still the other to do." She got up. "I'll prepare the rest of the way."

Alika studied her face, as he emerged with her, from her quarters on the ship. He had applied a fresh coat of medicine to her injuries from the previous day, to ensure any remaining pain didn't distract her for this task. "It has been a long day, child. You must be up for this. Otherwise, do not attempt this today."

"I'm prepared, Alika."

She stood ready in most respects as for an operation, finishing by pulling her hair up and in a lightweight scarf-like cloth. Glimpsing Dante watching her with the rest, she teased, "Don't worry, it'll be down, as you prefer, by this evening."

"I'm that obvious?" He chuckled, trying to hide his lingering concern.

"Yes, and I'm more relaxed with it down too. However, for this, I need it up."

Gathering a few other things, she concealed them inside her gear, as customary for an operation. Momentarily, she stood in the center of the room, as she ran through the checklist in her mind. Apparently satisfied, she went over to the cockpit and stared out for a minute, seeing something only she could. She took a deep breath, and turned to them. "Let's go."

Much sooner than Dante wanted, they arrived in the room with the cylinder. He remained uneasy about this solution, created after watching her almost fall to her death a couple of days ago, and longed for a way to reassure her with words alone. "Are you sure about this? There's got to be another way for you to do this, that accomplishes the same purpose."

"No, there's not. I'll finally find out which of us comes out on top." She peered at the top of the cylinder.

"Would you please not say it like that? I didn't rescue you to see you repeat the whole thing again."

"I know." She smiled as he kissed her forehead, and she squeezed his hand. Her attention moved to the others, focusing on Alika and Seth. "Any last-minute instructions for me?"

"Yes. Did you obtain everything you needed? This is your last opportunity to gather anything else," said Alika.

"There's nothing else."

"What's your plan?" asked Seth.

"I don't have one."

Silence fell on the room, at her unexpected and panic-inducing answer.

"You knew what you faced, so you could work out the solution, and retrieve the supplies you needed." Alika said.

"On the original operation, I didn't know what I would face, as with all operations. I brought the same items with me, as that day."

Seth sighed. "You're making it true to an operation, in all respects."

"I must, or it still doesn't work. My plan will form, as when I found myself thrown the unexpected curve."

Alika stared at her. Part of him pondered stopping it. He expected her to prepare one way, and now that she didn't, he dreaded the ending. Everything she said, though, made sense. If she ended up falling to her death in the process though, he would never forgive himself. Yet it wasn't his solution from the beginning. He held none of it in his hands.

"I trust you completely, Alika. Did we not say that already?" She gazed at Alika with her usual fondness, and smiled at Seth too. "You gave the needed tools to the student, and must trust the student now to find her way. Is that not what Elders do?"

He took a deep breath and smiled at her. "My child, we do. Today is no different. We'll watch your progress from one of the platforms beside the cylinder, except for Dante at the cylinder's bottom. You can only use the existing things around you and whatever you brought with you, to get safely down the cylinder. No one can help you, provide you any further equipment, or speak to you while you do this. No one will intervene. This is your task alone. We'll stand back, and let you work this out."

"Is that all?"

"Unless there's a question?"

"No, thorough as always, Alika."

"Whenever you're ready."

She nodded and walked with Dante at her side, with the others following.

"I hope I don't regret this, Seth. If the unthinkable happens, while she tries to do this." Alika shook his head.

"We can't think such things, but trust the student as she said. She is well-trained, my friend."

"Suddenly, the training seems inadequate for her task."

"Believe me, I understand." He glanced at Dante and back at Alika. "But they surprise you."

"You're right, my friend. I'm grateful our fears proved unfounded for him at the Elders Hall. He has always pleasantly surprised me, since I've known him. I'm fond of him." Alika grinned. "Not as fond as Angelina, of course."

Seth chuckled. "I don't think it's even possible, but he's as taken with her. You said it would be when they met."

The others went to one platform to watch. Dante and Angelina headed to the second platform on the speed glider. Once he balanced the speed glider next to the platform's opening, he turned to her. "Are you sure about doing this?"

"Yes, Dante."

He wrapped an arm around her waist and stared in her eyes. "I need you to find your way safely to the bottom of this cylinder. This isn't some training. You turned this into something else. I'd prefer giving you a Black Dragon army to fight with your sunspear now to this."

"Such a frightening thing to wish on me, Dante."

"You know what I mean, Angelina. Promise me, you get down safely."

"I promise I intend to, Dante."

"I'm not reassured." He sighed. "I'll be waiting when you're safely down." He stroked the side of her face.

She tried to lighten his mood. "How about you give me something for luck?" She leaned in closer to him.

"Of course." He brushed his lips with hers, whispering to her, "When you make it down safely, I'll wrap you up and give you a 'you're wonderful' on completing your task reward."

"I like the sound of that, so I better get to it."

"Just keep your promise to me." He stayed on the speed glider, as she stepped on the platform. She waited until he reached the bottom of the cylinder, and dismounted the speed glider.

She took a deep breath, as she stared down the open cylinder. It revealed a long drop, like the rooftop. One chance at it, too. Her pulse quickened. No, she must access this like any other situation, and begin treating it the same. She surveyed her surroundings. The harness hung there, same as the first day. Her clothing that day caused it to slip, which today wouldn't be an issue. Yet, as she scrutinized it, she didn't wager it would be secure enough to get her all the way down, especially in all her gear. From the time inspecting the inside of the cylinder, she didn't entertain the possibility of climbing down it straight. She pulled out the coil with the grappling hook mechanism at the end, and bit her lip as a memory resurfaced. The mechanism served her poorly the last time, coming loose from the rooftop, or maybe it never caught. However, the rooftop didn't turn out to be a solid surface. She considered hooking it on the side of the cylinder, and made a token effort to do so, but realized quickly the futility of it. One shift the wrong way, and it'd come careening off. Maybe the platform itself could work. She knelt and attempted to attach it to the platform or railing in some fashion, but stopped. It was a movable platform structure, ideal for the platform's use. Yet utilizing for her purposes it likely ended in disaster too. She pictured herself slammed up against the cylinder repeatedly when the platform moved on her, and hopelessly plunging to the bottom of the cylinder. She undid the mechanism and rose.

Alena whispered, "Alika."

He turned to her, and she didn't need to say anything further. Their eyes conveyed the same worry. "Me too, but she's still working at it."

Angelina continued her search, frustration creeping in, as she uncovered nothing to assist her. Another realization surfaced. She took too long with no solution devised. In a battle situation, the Black Dragon soldiers had long since eliminated her. She closed her eyes. Last time her help came from up high, but no eagle appearance today. She sighed, looking up, even while knowing no solution would drop from the air. Or maybe it would. Her search had missed it, because she was preoccupied with hunting eye level. Spotlights hung from several long metal beams, stretched across the length of the ceiling in the room, and one beam intersected the cylinder. She estimated the distance, and her coil would work. She chose not to dwell on how far she'd dangle over the cylinder initially. The first difficulty lay in getting the hook wrapped securely around the beam, so she ended up positioned over the cylinder. Thankfully, her arm felt better, but it could take some tries to land it. She glanced down at Dante and yelled, "Dante, watch out!"

"For what?" Soon enough he understood.

She pulled the hook mechanism back and threw. It went too low to wrap around the beam, and fell towards the bottom of the cylinder, but she caught it before it fell far enough to hit Dante. The second throw resulted in it successfully wrapping around the beam. She pulled on it, and it held true. "Here goes," She whispered. With one hand clutching the coiled steel rope, she used her other hand to steady herself as she maneuvered to the other side of the platform railing. Then she secured the rope with both hands, and balanced uneasily on the top edge of the cylinder. Nothing remained but climbing down now. The unsettling realization in seconds she'd dangle from a rope in the middle of the cylinder came back to her with renewed force. She let her feet leave the edge of the cylinder, and her body swung back and forth like one of those olden clock pendulums. It lasted less than a minute, but her head swam at the familiar sensation it conjured up. When her body finally stopped swinging, she forced herself to concentrate on her task and ignore the frightening amount of empty space below her. Slowly starting the trip down, her gloved hands perspired as she continued the steady, but careful descent to the bottom of the cylinder. She stared straight ahead, not wanting the reminder of the long drop. Relief set in, as she estimated to be about halfway to her goal.

The others watched her, stifling gasps several times. Dante watched from below, his whole body in quiet panic, as she hovered far above him. He hated this, knowing he'd be powerless to do anything, if something went awry.

Then it happened. The sound originated from above her. She only thought the mechanism secure, but everything unfolded as before. What a fool, to believe herself capable of overcoming the rooftop, the cylinder. Her heart threatened to erupt from her chest as the deafening quake echoed through the private room of her mind. Suddenly, the cylinder disappeared along with Dante and the others. The scene became replaced by a familiar one. She dangled outside in midair. Rock and debris plummeted onto her head, Black Dragon soldiers' footsteps rushed above her, the stench of her own blood overwhelmed her, her body cracked from a building's impact, and pain raced through every nerve of her frame. She couldn't hold on anymore, as she anticipated her tumble through the air. Dizziness overpowered her, wooing her to release the rope. The present and past melted together, until they became indistinguishable as a battle waged inside her head, as it often did. One hand began slipping off the rope. She was falling all along. A truth useless to deny.

Dante watched. *She's got to be tired by now, but she has to keep going*. Halfway down, she stopped to gather more for the rest of the descent and shifted her position on the rope. The shift caused the grappling mechanism and beam to make a scraping sound as they rubbed against each other. Even from his distance, Dante confirmed it remained attached securely. However, when he focused back on Angelina, her whole frame changed instantly. Full blown panic marked it. Her frame trembled, her breathing became labored, and her eyes closed. He knew she was no longer with them, and his face paled. One of her hands moved to leave the rope, and she still hung too far from the bottom to survive the drop. He stared up at Alika and Seth, pleading with them. They gazed at him with lost expressions as to what had unfolded, but they said to wait. He stared back at Angelina and whispered, "I promised her. I can't lose her."

"I will have you keep your promise to her," said a familiar whisper.

He whispered back, "Please, tell me how to help her. Whatever it is, I'll do it."

"Trust, my child. She never struggles alone, and needs only to hear me, to find her way again."

He bent to one knee, staring at her, and whispered, "Please grab the rope again, my Angelina."

Her hand continued to loosen from the rope as a faint, but comforting Whisper broke through, "You're tired. Your strength is spent. How do you find yourself in such a state, my child?"

She whispered back, "It overcame me."

"Strange what you see. You are not alone, and do not struggle alone. Why do you persist in acting as so?"

"There's too much before me."

"No, there is not. I granted you strength to finish this, as I do all the tasks set before you, and I supply what you need for each one."

"It's not holding. It's falling."

"Trust me. Your senses are clouded, my child. I provide what you need each time. I gave you an eagle at the first, Dante's arms at the second, and your hand still clings to the other."

"It fell the last time and does again."

"The first time I did not provide it, my child. I provided the eagle. Since the rope was not to be your provision, why does it surprise you it failed you the first time?"

"What do I do, now?"

"You were doing it, before you allowed your mind to become clouded. Take the provision given to you."

"I thought it starting falling. Why did I?"

"Trust, my child. It is my provision. The anchor is secure. It will hold and will not fail you, I promise."

Tears fell, but for a different reason. She knew, and yet she became confused anew. "How do I do this?"

"My child, you have everything before you. You must grab the rope again to finish this task, but you need to do so with both hands. It is much simpler than you make it."

She renewed her grip on the rope with both hands. "It's the same, repeatedly. Why can I not ..."

"Some truths must be given many times, before they take root in a child's heart. You are my child, and I will never leave you. I love every moment spent with you. Do not doubt that, ever. Time to finish this. There is one who waits anxiously for you below, my child."

A calm overtook her, and she returned to them again. The Ancient One delivered her, breaking through the storm of her own making, and showing Himself her refuge in her sea of confusion once more. Then He reminded her of the anchor He gifted her with here, who wouldn't be shaken from her side. She glimpsed Dante, watching her on bent knee. Relief showed on his face as their eyes met, and he rose and waited, saying not a word. Yet his eyes spoke sweet words of care to her, which she translated perfectly. He'd snatch her out of the air to hold her, if he could reach her now. How she longed for that at this moment. She forced herself to slowly and carefully make her way safely down the rest of the way to him. This time, it didn't bother her to look down, but she kept her eyes locked on his intense soft brown eyes.

Her feet didn't touch the ground, before he swooped under her with his arms open. She slid down into them happily, as her arms encircled his neck. He wrapped her up completely and murmured, "My Angelina," as his lips found hers instantly, to fulfill his promise of rewarding her. In one movement, he slid the scarf off to send her hair tumbling free, delighting in the feel of the silken strands now running through his fingers, as he continued kissing her. The way she melted against him and yet responded back to him with such passion, he loved it. Yet he loved her and everything about her. He couldn't do without her. All he could think about was how wonderful she felt, safe in his arms again, after such fear gripped him only minutes before.

CHAPTER TWENTY-SEVEN

Alika smiled. "How about we meet them back in the other room?"

"Yes, they'll find us when they're ready." Seth smiled back, as they all came down from the platform, and headed for the main room.

"Those two could be there for a while." Ryan grinned.

"They earned it, so they're taking advantage of it." Caleb laughed.

"My cousin lost no time with that." Lana joined her husband in his laughter.

"Angelina wouldn't want it any other way, and don't put it all on Dante." Alena grinned back.

"I'm burning up," said Angelina breathlessly, as she still glowed from his fiery kiss.

"You are certainly that." His eyes twinkled.

"Nice, Dante, but I meant the other." She laughed. "I need this gear off."

"A reasonable request. I'll let you loose for that, and help if you wish."

"So sweet." Shedding the lower half of the gear first, she handed it over to him to put in the large compartment on the speed glider. He helped her remove the top half as well as taking off the gloves for her and packed everything away with the other.

"Better?" he asked, as he folded her back in his arms.

"Much," she answered, as she ran her hands through his hair.

"You're right. You feel much better in my arms, with the gear gone."

"Then I'm glad I parted with it."

"The bottom of the cylinder, Angelina ... it's actually enjoyable down here," he murmured into her ear, as he pulled her closer again.

"How enjoyable, Dante?" she whispered, as he found her lips again.

"This is perfect," he said, as he appreciated the feel of her body leaned up against him, as she often did.

"I know. I could stay like this forever."

"Me too. Angelina, I'm glad you grabbed the rope again."

"It got cloudy for a minute, and I went somewhere else."

"But His talk got through to you."

"How did you know?"

"I reached out, and He told me you needed to hear Him."

"It still took time for me to see."

"All I care about is you got down safely to me. You need to talk about it?"

"Later. I'm just glad I went straight to your arms, Dante."

"They'll always be open and waiting for you." He kissed her forehead and grinned, as he pulled something out. "I forgot. Here's you scarf back. Technically, part of your gear."

"Yes, you have quite the moves, Dante."

"Just getting you comfortable again."

"You did that for sure. Maybe it's time ..."

"Yeah, the others are waiting on us."

"They are."

He stared down at her, realizing again how close it came for them. They should go, but not yet. Just another minute. The instant his lips found hers again, there was nothing else that mattered, but her. The rest of the galaxy could wait and wait some more.

"How long are you keeping me down here, Dante?" she teased, as his kiss continued happily humming through her senses.

"Quite tempting, but I suppose long enough." He stroked the side of her cheek. "Sorry, I needed once more before we left."

"Never say sorry for that, Dante," she whispered. "You know how anything from you will always be received."

"You're right, and I love how it's received each time. You make me so happy, and I see much more in our future, my Angelina." He kissed her forehead. "We'll head back now for real."

He guided her onto the speed glider, as he got on in front of her. She encircled her arms around his waist securely, as he flew them from the cylinder.

"You two decided to leave the cylinder. We wondered if you might stay." Caleb laughed.

Angelina and Dante sat down on the couch and grinned at the comment.

Ryan joined in. "We wouldn't hold it against you if you had decided to."

"Glad to hear because we considered it." Dante winked, as Angelina leaned against him.

"He's right, but figured we'd be missed eventually."

Alena smiled. "We'll overlook it this time, you two. Guess we get to start at it again tomorrow. Since we identified the mark, the blood sample is unnecessary now, right?"

Angelina grinned. "Appreciate you giving us a pass, Alena. As far as the other, getting the sample appears a waste, but Trey seemed normal at first too."

Alika nodded. "You earned the right to be overcautious. For a bit, we'll check the blood too, for confirmation. It's a simple finger prick."

"Hopefully, there are no more surprise welcomes," Caleb said, looking over at Angelina.

"At least I discovered about the blasters."

Dante stared down at her. "Which means you use your sunspear, if needed. No hesitation."

"But it's essential I keep my cover, as Lana's advisor. They can't discover Alena and I are the spear-bearers they're searching for."

"What you did last time isn't acceptable. I won't see it repeated, and almost lose you again. We figure out a solution, before we step foot on the planet, or we don't go." His voice left no room for discussion.

"Angelina, we don't need to use our sunspears."

She stared back at Alena. "What is wrong with me today? We do this on operations all the time. Any blade cuts them down."

Lana grinned. "We can spare two swords from weapons."

"There's a couple stashed on our ship, but we'll take the offer and return them before we leave. It's been a little while, since we dealt with a whole army of Black Dragon."

"Worried about being out of practice?" teased Alena.

"Never. But I heard a challenge. Does my teacher think I need a refresher?"

"You can always stand practice. Maybe, you wouldn't need me to bail you out of trouble as often."

"There's still daylight, and we should break those swords in."

Alika laughed at them. "Put gear on, if you insist on a training session. I can't have one of you hurt, before you even face the enemy."

"This should be interesting to observe." Seth said, as they stood outside watching, as the two began practicing with the Freedom Fighter swords.

"Remember this was your idea, when I embarrass you," Alena yelled.

"Funny. We know you can't embarrass me," Angelina shot back.

"You're kidding, right? I do it constantly and recall doing it earlier. You almost choked on your drink, all flustered."

"You're wrong, bringing Dante into it." She laughed. "Get back to this, and stop sidetracking me."

Alena joined her laughter. "It's easy, but you're right. Let's get your lesson going before you can't talk again."

"They're flawless," murmured Ryan, turning to Dante, who chuckled from the last exchange.

"And that's just with the swords."

The two continued the session, at times one appearing to get the advantage, but it never lasted. After training together for so long, they knew each other's movements, like a well-rehearsed dance.

Finally, Alika commanded, "Done, you two."

The two stopped and worked to catch their breath.

"Alena, how about a turn with our sunspears? You game?"

"There's still daylight."

Alika took their swords. "A bit with the sunspears, and you're done."

"I thought they were great with the swords." Caleb shook his head.

"Fortunately, they fight with us. They're holding back too, since they're friends." Lana looked up at him.

The sunspears flashed, and the stones in the blades caught the last bits of the sun, as it slowly dove under its nightly blanket. The two women moved with an almost catlike quickness and grace, but once again neither one could gain enough on the other.

"Time's up," called Alika. "Well done."

The two stepped back, grinning at each other. Angelina twirled her sunspear in her hand as though it were a mere pole. For most people, it would be dangerous. Yet she handled it as an extension of her arm, and the blade's edge came nowhere near touching her.

Alena teased, "Showoff."

"I'm half your student."

"I missed teaching you the lesson in humility, huh?"

"No, you taught it along with all the other valuable lessons I needed. My teachers are always excellent." Her tone became quieter, as she retreated to somewhere else. "Rather, it's a reflection of your student as usual, but that won't ever change. I'm sorry, Alena." She put her sunspear up and looked at the ground.

Alena did the same with her sunspear and reached Angelina. "I won't have you talk like that about my student." She put her arm around Angelina's shoulders. "I wouldn't part with you."

“You’re too kind to me, Alena.”

“No, in this I see clearly, where you don’t.”

“We’ll keep our separate visions on this one.”

“I won’t give up.”

“I’m grateful for your efforts, but they’re more productive elsewhere.”

Alena gave her a hug.

Seth looked at Alika. His grieved expression reflected someone who heard this exchange more than once, because he spoke similar words as Alena to his student. He was the teacher who knew what haunted his student, and despite all his efforts, couldn’t find the words to clear the mist from her eyes either. It weighed on him anew in these moments. Seth perceived it, but he held no answer for his friend, as he possessed none for Alika’s student, who bore an ever-increasing burden upon her back with each day.

Angelina and Alena walked over to the group. Angelina’s smile returned, as if none of the exchange transpired, and Alena took her cue. Everyone else followed suit, another silent agreement struck.

“Dante, I have to get a shower. I’m sweaty and disgusting now.” She made a face.

He laughed, as he wrapped one arm around her waist. “You are not. Stop.”

“You don’t lie well, and I can’t even stand being around me. Honestly, I needed one after the cylinder climbing thing, but now there’s no question."

“It’s not that bad.” He kissed her on the forehead, amused at her outburst.

“It is, and you would say that no matter what.”

“You’re right. You’re the most beautiful woman I’ve ever seen, and nothing changes my mind. “

“Such delusions, Dante. It doesn’t change the fact I need the shower, and I got you sweaty too when you pulled me over.”

He grinned mischievously at her last comment. “You’re determined about the shower. Since you’re convinced you got me sweaty, I’ll get a shower too, but I intend to make mine worth the effort and time now.” He pulled her all the way over, wrapped his arms completely around her, and took his time giving her a long, deep kiss. "Now I'm sweaty with you, but perfectly content for it," he murmured, with his lips still close to hers, and couldn't resist stealing another kiss.

Alena smiled, as Ryan wrapped his arm around her waist. "Nicely done, Alena."

"Thanks, but Angelina is right about the shower."

"Dante is right, too. We want the two of you around, no matter what. All in how you see it."

"We have you two blinded at the moment."

"I'll keep my vision like this happily." He wrapped her up, and kissed her.

"I'd say so," Alena murmured. "Give us about an hour to be back with you and the others?"

"Deal. Gives me time to get showered and ready too."

"Will you two still be standing here, when they return?" Seth teased, as he came over to Ryan and Dante. The two smiling men remained rooted to the same spot, entranced in their own musings.

Ryan replied, "Sorry, Seth. I lost track."

"No, someone gained command over you, and it's no surprise she's able to do so."

"Good thing I'm not expected to come up with a strategy for her because I'd lose that battle." He chuckled.

Dante turned to Seth. "She's special. Amazing. I never imagined being with someone could be like this. So completely, all in and perfect."

"Yet, you find yourself as you're meant to be. Some mysteries remain as such. We accept the wonder of it unfolding before us, by the Ancient One. This is another one of those times, Dante."

"I love watching this one unfold too, and I'll see where it takes me. I believe I'll be happy with the ending." Dante grinned.

Seth laughed while steering both men towards their quarters. “Come on you two. Continue your thoughts in your quarters, as you clean up and return for the two of them.”

“Did we forget something?” asked Angelina.

“No. What makes you think that?" asked Alena.

“The guys were still just standing there."

Alika grinned. “Easily explained. I’m recalling a young woman staring from a cockpit window at a certain handsome young man, tracing his every movement while she could, and denying it the entire time.”

“You believe that’s what we witnessed, Alika?”

“I do, Angelina. You two cast a wonderful spell on those men.”

“We’ll stick with your theory.” She laughed. “And I wasn’t that bad. Come on you two, the entire time?”

Alena pondered it. “You may be right.”

“Thank you. Finally!”

“Honestly, you were worse. You still denied it when we left, like now. You have stars dancing in your eyes when you look at him, and you can’t talk half the time."

“Why do I try getting help from you?” She shook her head, still laughing. “But I spot the same from you with Ryan, now.”

“The difference is, I don’t deny it.” She winked.

Alika laughed as they reached the ship. “Call when you’re ready to rejoin the others. They’ll be ready for us. I noticed Seth reviving Ryan and Dante from the trance you placed them in.”

CHAPTER TWENTY-EIGHT

Caleb looked up as Dante and Ryan walked in within moments of each other. "The two of you did leave that spot. Seth said you did, but I had my doubts."

Lana playfully jabbed her husband. "Would you behave, Caleb?"

"It's all right, Lana." Ryan laughed. "Apparently, we needed prodding."

"I've learned I'm best listening to my teacher." Dante glanced at Seth, with a smile.

"You two made excellent time." Seth said, as they heard approaching footsteps.

Angelina turned to Alika, before entering the room. "You'll arrange the other?"

"I'll speak with her now. Don't concern yourself further. You two will certainly be pulled away to more engaging conversation."

Dante's and Ryan's expressions lit up as they headed over to the two, and Alika chuckled, as he walked past, to sit with the others at the table.

"Perfect timing, Alika. The other two just made it down."

"I thought we might beat them here, Seth. At least as we left them." Alika smiled. "Lana, I need to discuss a later starting time for tomorrow."

"That shouldn't be a problem," said Lana as her eyes asked the unspoken question.

"Everything is fine, as is possible with today's events. Tonight, Angelina needs to go through the encounter with me and Alena."

"We want to help, Alika," Lana answered.

"Yeah, she knows by now, right?"

"She does, Caleb, and she cares for you all very much. The encounter today involved her past though, as you gathered."

Seth finished, "Which is why it affected her so."

"And why she can't sort it out with us." Caleb sighed.

"She also spoke truth, about how the words would leave Dante feeling."

"Then she talks with you and Alena, and she's all better." Lana knew the words false hope as she spoke them, but she wanted them to be reality for Angelina and her cousin. He loved this girl with everything in him, and it grew stronger each day, since he beheld Angelina the first time.

Alika sighed. "If only it worked like that, Lana. No, she wants to go over his exact words with us while it's fresh in her mind. She's confused, by how he knew what he did. The processing of it is a whole other animal."

"When does she tame that beast, Alika?" Lana stared over at Angelina.

"She's putting off the other part until we get back. Other matters demand our attention with our limited time with your group, and she insists on focusing on those."

"Does she tame that beast, Alika?" Caleb asked, recognizing Alika didn't answer the question.

Alika bowed his head. "I hope one day to say yes, but she'll try, as she always does."

"I wish I knew how to help her, Alika," Lana whispered, as she continued watching Angelina, who at the moment didn't seem to possess a care in the world. Angelina smiled up at Dante, lost in whatever he said, and he stared back at her with adoring eyes. "I wish she could stay too. She's happy with Dante, and I've never seen my cousin like that." Lana paused. "You give the time for tomorrow, and we'll go with it."

"Gracious as always, Lana." Alika clasped her hand for a moment. "Angelina thinks a lot of you. Abundantly more than you realize." He turned to Caleb and smiled. "Your wife is a treasure, Caleb, and you always remind her. It's refreshing to watch."

Caleb kissed Lana on the cheek. "I wouldn't know any other way to be, Alika."

Ryan teased, "You two feel better after a shower?"

"Say what you will, but yes," replied Alena.

"Dante, you can't say I don't smell better now." Angelina's eyes twinkled.

He leaned in closer, and his lips brushed the side of her face. "I do like whatever fragrance follows you, so I won't say differently."

"A safe answer."

"It's true, and hopefully I stay in your favor."

"What do you two think?"

Ryan laughed. "Keep him, Angelina. The two of you would be miserable without each other."

"Besides, we'd miss the fun of you stumbling over your words half the time, and it's the only time you're speechless."

Dante laughed. "Alena, you didn't help my case," he turned to Angelina, "but somehow I'm still okay, Angelina?'

"There will never be any doubt of that, Dante." She kissed his cheek.

"What's the plan now?" asked Ryan. "Other than this evening?" He smiled, as he kissed Alena on the forehead.

"Looks like we're about to find out," answered Dante.

Alika and the rest of the group joined them, as Alika began, "Good to see you four relaxed, but we need to go over tomorrow. We'll meet here at 10:30, and plan to depart at 11:00. Lana, Caleb, and Seth volunteered to make sure everything is in order, so we can grab something to eat and leave on time." Alika's eyes swept the room, but rested on Angelina.

Angelina sighed silently. She got the requested late start. Maybe still too late for what they must accomplish? A familiar emotion rose, but she didn't know where to place it. She started putting it on Trey for all the trouble he caused today. Yet blaming a dead person, a pile of ashes, seemed ridiculous. The next option came that some would consider. He was a ghost, but she dismissed the conclusion instantly. They didn't exist. Once dead, always dead. The veil couldn't be penetrated. Another similar option remained, a probable one. A spirit, a dark one, visited her earlier. Those did exist, and the ancient texts spoke of them. She encountered one in her room, that horrible night in her past, and experienced how powerful it could be. Even so, where did it get her? Nowhere. She was no closer to being rid of him, it, or whatever she saw than before. Finally, the obvious answer surfaced, the one she eventually arrived at in the end. Herself. Somehow this must be her fault, as always. The never-ending war waged in her head. Her eyes met Alika's eyes, as he recognized the ensuing battle. She heard a voice and anticipated his answer to her silent question. To her surprise, someone else spoke up.

Lana answered her musings, "Angelina, we'll get everything taken care of on the planet we need to, in the time we have. Please don't worry."

"Lana's right. It's covered. Relax. It's not all on your shoulders, Angelina," Caleb reassured.

"I know," she said quietly.

Lana reached over to clasp her hand momentarily. "Are you sure you do?"

She smiled up at her, and whispered, "I do, but forget sometimes. Thank you for reminding me." She bit her lip. "It means more than you know."

"Anytime, Angelina," whispered Lana.

"10:30 it is," confirmed Seth, as he focused on Angelina.

She answered back, "10:30. Thank you."

Dante didn't know completely what occurred, but something played out in her head again. She couldn't get any rest from it. His arm curled more securely around her waist, while his free hand ran up and down her arm, hoping to focus her there, rather than on whatever unpleasantness reclaimed her attention. His efforts worked, as she smiled up at him and brushed her lips to his.

He glimpsed her stretch behind her and make a face, before taking her seat when dinnertime came. How did he forget? But recalling how the day turned, the answer was apparent. Her mind and spirit had endured an all-day assault of another kind, affording her no chance to dwell on the previous day's physical blows to her body. He sighed, as he loosely wrapped his arm on her shoulder. "How's your back, shoulder, and everything else from yesterday? You didn't complain at all, but it's only been a day, since he hurt you."

"Honestly, it didn't bother me much as the day continued. Just occasionally. You shouldn't always worry about me."

"You're here now. Let me, while I've the chance, and can do something about it. You're really, okay?" His voice revealed a mixture of doubt and concern, as the image of the black and blue band of her back surfaced afresh.

"I am, but you're not, and will wonder all evening."

"I'm sorry. You said you're fine, and you did several things to show it's true." He forced confidence in the statement, as he recalled the cylinder test and the practice session with Alena. Still, the ugliness of the bruises crept into his mind.

"I also promised you this morning another scan to ease your mind, and I keep my word, especially to you. Alika and Seth won't mind doing it, Dante."

Everyone parted ways for the evening, once dinner finished. Alena and Ryan gave Angelina a puzzled look, noticing Seth and Alika standing behind her and Dante.

"Dante is still concerned about my injuries from yesterday."

"It's probably unneeded. I'm being silly."

"No, you're attempting to care for me, while I'm here. It's sweet." She smiled up at him and squeezed his hand.

Ryan teased, "Dante, you better run with it. When is the last time she let someone see about her injuries?"

"It may not happen again in this lifetime. Take it from me and Alika." Alena giggled.

"Put that way, I should hurry, before she changes her mind."

Caleb and Lana watched the four head for medical. "Your cousin certainly has a way with her. Hopefully, the visit turns up nothing."

After seeing Dante's mother, the four arrived at one of the empty medical rooms.

"Dante, I'll need Angelina briefly, but Seth can keep you company."

"Yep, I'll get that smile back on your face in a few, Dante." She winked at him, while passing him and trailing her fingertips down his arm.

"Already done." He smiled at the delightful sensation from her teasing touch.

Seth grinned. "She seems to feel fine, so I'll be surprised if anything turns up on the scan."

"Behind the curtain here, hop up to the table, and get to it. The faster you do so, the faster you return to Dante." Alika chuckled.

She laughed. "We could have a record. See what I can do when I'm properly motivated?"

"Truly amazing. If only we could summon him, when you needed to make a quick wardrobe change."

"Doesn't work. I'm changing for a mission, not to see Dante. The reward isn't there, Alika."

Seth and Dante started laughing now.

Seth turned to Dante. "Dante, you realized you got reduced to a reward."

"In any other situation, I'd be insulted. Although once I consider whose reward I am, I'll be hers happily."

Angelina's voice floated across the curtain, "I like your answer, Dante, and I imagine it working out pleasantly for you." She laughed again. "Alika, seriously, what's this scan show? Do I get held down again or what?"

"Obviously, Dante wouldn't work for that, considering your semi-dressed state." He winked at her, and studied the scans again. "And it doesn't appear Seth needs to put on his physician's coat this evening for us."

"So I'm ..."

Alika laughed as he laid the scans aside. "Free to enjoy your evening with Dante. There's no swelling anymore, therefore no more shots. I'll put additional medication on your bruises, for any lingering pain. It's easier in your current state."

"Always, such a good doctor."

He finished applying the medicine. "You were a cooperative patient, for once. Quite refreshing. How about we try for every time?"

Angelina pulled her shirt on and leapt from the table simultaneously. At his last comment, they stared at each other and laughed as though he uttered the most insane thing.

He shook his head. "What was I thinking? It'll never happen again. Go, before I take it all back."

They emerged, still laughing from the comment.

"She's all yours again, Dante. Back to her difficult self, but none of us would ever part with her."

She grinned, and entwined her hand in his. "Miss me?"

"Always," he kissed her on the forehead, "and I'm glad no injection."

"Me too. Enough of medical. I'm ready to spend the evening with you."

"All our students found their places, for a while." Alika smiled as the door shut behind their two love struck students.

"And the day brought plenty to discuss. Let's go, and do so."

CHAPTER TWENTY-NINE

Alena took a sip of her drink before laying it aside as she leaned back into the couch.

Ryan sat and wrapped his arm around her waist as she snuggled into him. “Another eventful day, Alena.”

“Who imagined a dead man changing the course of a day that drastically?”

“They also aren’t supposed to have the iron grip I witnessed today.”

“No, they’re not. Alika and I will find out tonight what went on in that exchange, but I’m not convinced it helps.”

"Tonight? Of course, the late start tomorrow. You could still be up awfully late. Are you sure you don't need to talk to her now?”

“No, she wouldn’t give up her time with Dante, and she wouldn’t hear of me cutting short our time.”

“Did she give you any idea?”

“Yes. The exchange held a particularly painful part of her past.”

“She has a lot of those, Alena.”

“And I still don’t know how to help her. She can be with those closest to her, and yet ..."

“Be completely alone, by her own doing. Yeah, I watched it.” He raised her chin up. “We’re all in this together. Somehow, we’ll keep on until she believes it.”

Alena shook her head. “A task Alika and I have yet to achieve, with all our time with her. That won’t change in the couple of days left, Ryan.”

“Unfortunately, you’re probably right.” He sighed. “How am I to occupy myself in the evenings when you leave? I can’t imagine spending the evening any other way now.”

"There are dinner dates with your family, and entertaining company they try to pair you with."

"You'll tease me every time now, won't you?"

"Maybe."

"Well, I'm taken. No matchmaking is happening." He laughed.

She laughed too, but then grew serious. "Ryan, remember what I said. No one can know about us, so you had better have a good story in your arsenal."

"I will, don't worry. I'll say I've already got my eye on someone, and they'll leave it alone."

"Just like that? They won't push for details?"

"No, I can tell them, with the current situation, I don't feel safe giving any details about the person, and for them not to say a word. They'll assume I'm worried where the next target is with this device, or about the Black Dragon getting to the person. I'll spin that story if I must, but I don't think we get there. My commander duties are about to become longer."

"Probably the case, though I wish you were wrong. Either way, you figured out how to keep us under wraps."

"I have. What about your family, Alena? Your parents? Your past?"

"I'm limited on what I can tell, because of my ties with Angelina. I was young when my parents decided I should be trained, and so they left me with Alika, to begin immediately."

"Wait, just left you? I mean, how could they?" Ryan's eyes conjured up a disturbing image, as he took her hand.

"Nothing like that. They didn't want me distracted by other things. I saw them, but I stayed primarily in the same place as Alika. From that perspective, I spent more time with Alika than my parents. I became immersed in the teachings of the Ancient One, the sunspear world, and all the training that came with it. They decided it the better route, and perhaps they sensed the safer one. When I look at the others' experiences, they were right. I mean there's Dante, Lana, and Caleb, and what happened to their families. Their stories bear out the horrible Black Dragon procedure, of leaving no loose ends. All three of them would be slaughtered, if not for the Elders getting them out in time. Anyway, my parents arranged it with Alika at the start, so I never questioned it. It was like going to school every day, but I lived at mine."

"How often did you see them?"

"Often. They came to spend time with me, and check my progress. When they couldn't, they kept in consistent contact."

He asked the remaining question, but he guessed what type of answer to expect. "Are they still alive?"

"I must stop with my telling now."

"But you must know?"

"I know many things, but I spoke all I can on that topic."

He shook his head. "You two, with all your secrets."

"I'm sorry that I can't answer all your questions, Ryan." She grinned and stroked the side of his face. "How can I make it up to you?"

"Something comes to mind."

"How about I try?" She curled her arms around his neck.

"I'm out of questions anyway, so by all means," he murmured, as her lips claimed his, and she drew him the rest of the way to her. He couldn't form a question if he tried, but now he only wanted to enjoy her being in his arms, and make the kiss last as long as possible. So he did.

CHAPTER THIRTY

Angelina laid back, content in Dante's arms on the couch. She didn't realize her exhaustion, until she cuddled up to him. It wasn't the sleepiness, or weariness from fighting Black Dragon troops with her sunspear. This spoke of a mental and emotional exhaustion, from the string of battles she encountered today. She found the rest she needed, that of being safe and cared for in his arms.

Dante knew this is what she sought, how she drew strength from it. So he held her, pulling her close, and wrapping his arms around her waist. He alternated running one hand down her back and arm and stroking her hair. She wanted to talk about the events from today, but he wished her to direct it. He'd ensure she felt calm and safe, when she started that conversation.

"That feels wonderful, Dante." She smiled up at him.

"It's supposed to." He returned her smile as he looked into her eyes.

"None of the bad parts seem so, when I'm with you. Like none of it can find me, even if it's only for a bit."

"We found our solution. You stay right here," he kissed her forehead, "and never leave my arms." Then he kissed her cheek.

"Sounds perfect," she stroked the side of his face, "yet impossible, with the state of things."

"Sometimes, you need to allow yourself to think of what it would be like, if Black Dragon didn't exist, if you could have the world you wanted."

"I can't imagine, because I've never known a world which didn't have it. At least a vision of it, in some form. Felt the darkness near somehow."

"You need to imagine the other possibility. It's there, and it's what we fight for. I see it, and you can if you seek enough too. What must I do to pull it out of you?"

"It doesn't exist, to pull."

"Angelina, I don't believe that. I should share my vision with you."

"I'm listening, Dante. Your imagination is better than mine, in this area." She laughed.

"This is better shown," he murmured. Continuing where he left off, he kissed the side of her face and moved to leave a trail of soft kisses on her neck, as a sigh of pleasure escaped her. He continued his leisurely path back up to brush her lips with his, as he ran his hands through her hair. Finally, he found her lips again, this time capturing them for a long, slow kiss as he painted the future he envisioned with her. When the kiss started to end, Angelina pulled him back, reigniting the kiss, which he eagerly did.

"Your vision is incredible," she murmured, as she continued running her hands through his hair.

"I keep telling you. And that kiss ... I feel like I waited the whole day for it. All day, going from one struggle to the other, feeling like I needed to keep you safe or bring you back to me."

"Like being an anchor all day, a calm in the chaos. I know, Dante."

"Most times I kissed you today, it's been all mixed up in that constant storm. Not that I don't enjoying kissing you."

"Dante, I get it."

"What I'm meant is it felt great to finally just kiss you again, because I wanted to."

"You're right it did, so any time you're inspired again tonight, follow it."

"It won't be long." He watched her. She was ready to talk about today, but searched for a starting point. He waited.

She held his hand, as she talked and looked at him. "I told the truth about why I didn't want to speak the exact words of Trey. The part that upset me won't make sense to you."

"Tell me, and it will."

"I can't, since that information is part of my past. Parts there's no way he should've known."

"I see." He paused. "No way he recognized you, and heard about whatever happened?"

"Not even remotely possible. There was no mistaking the participant in that part of my past."

"This not knowing is killing me, especially when I see how the encounter left you."

She grasped for an explanation, one that balanced keeping the past undercover, but still helped him, without causing him further pain. "Remember when we talked about my encounter with Teresa on the planet?"

"Yes, she was frightened about falling asleep to deal with the darkness, but you comforted her because you faced the darkness."

"We said there are battles that stay with us, like what you faced in the Elders Hall."

"Yes." He read the answer in her eyes. "Today, whatever battle from your past, he brought it again, didn't he?"

"Yes."

The encounter made more sense as he looked back, at least what he pieced together from her part. He remembered her anger spilling forth, and suddenly it seemed like a switch flipped. That must be when Trey connected yesterday and this past battle for her. He recalled her words to Alika, that Trey brought it together for her, and he couldn't forget the broken state in which it left her. "My Angelina, come here." He pulled her tighter to him. "I'm sorry you faced that again."

"But your being there helped."

"Still, it took time to get you back." He hated not knowing Trey's end of the conversation, at points when he remembered her words. "Angelina, you told him towards the end, 'I will never be yours, never choose you.' Are you sure you can't tell me what he said to you? Your response scares me, what he said to you."

Again, she performed a delicate balancing act with her answer. "Dante, it's the double meaning I spoke of. It scares you, because you're thinking in terms of Trey, the man who had certain intentions, if he got me alone for enough time.

Every comment is seen through that filter. The other requires glimpsing through a different filter, to understand the meaning."

"He didn't mean it like that?"

"Yes and no. Whatever he was, it enjoyed saying the things it did and meaning them as Trey did, purely in a physical sense to toy with me."

"But the real point is something else."

"Yes. Dante, when you fought the battle in the Elders Hall, I feared I'd lose you. There was the obvious fear which comes from a blade, but a whole other fear existed that scared me as much, if not more. The longer you listened to the Dark Lord, the worse it grew. I felt the darkness trapping you, though you didn't. I saw the chains binding you as they had your father, and it tore me apart thinking the Dark Lord would possess you, as well. Both fates terrified me for you, death by the edge of the blade, or becoming a servant to the Dark Lord. Which is worse? One automatically assumes the sword's point. Yet is bondage to such darkness not death as well? I think that's worse, Dante. Crueler, a slow horrible death, over time. Death only takes on a different appearance. These are the battles we fight. Do you understand, Dante?"

He did. Not the full story, but the connection she made. "I do, but I think I'm more concerned now. Whatever you battled, I'm glad you didn't choose it, and I won't let it claim you. I'll do whatever it takes to keep you safe, my Angelina."

"You already do, Dante. No more worrying about the exact words. Trey is a creep, but only the first of many I met."

"And not the first to take notice of your attractiveness." He groaned. "How much more of this goes on?"

"Much more than you'll like, Dante. The establishments I frequent for the shipping deals are relaxed environments, to put it nicely, and I meet ... interesting men, when I'm getting intel. The business, as a whole, is primarily a man's domain." She left out to Dante, where women normally found themselves in that world because it would upset him extremely. She was the exception in several ways.

"Wait, you only do deals with sources you know, right? Or should I see your dinner engagements, for when you leave me?" He tried, unsuccessfully, to sound teasing.

"No, remember I schedule lunchtime appointments, so they prefer buying me a drink or lunch."

"Angelina, you've got to stop. That isn't funny." He pulled her closer.

"You can't worry so, Dante. I don't let anyone buy me anything, period. It's one of the rules we decided, at the beginning, because it's too easy for somebody to slip something in before they hand it to you. I keep all my drink orders potent-free. My mind has to be clear when I'm out. If someone insists on ordering me a drink, there are ways to skirt around it, or appear to accommodate it, all which I'm a master. With the shipping deals, our practice is only to go with who we know, and it takes an unusual circumstance to do otherwise. On the flip side, there are constantly new faces in the business. Intel gathering has a different set of rules, as far as with whom you associate. There's no deal being entered into with the other party, in most cases. The key is after you walk away, they realize they learned nothing new about you, but they gave you a lot more information than they intended."

"That sounds difficult and dangerous to pull off."

"There's a skill to it, but I'm one of the best. I'm not one to usually give myself credit either. I've got practice at keeping things under wraps."

"I agree, you nailed that one. Still, I detest the idea of guys checking you out and saying things to you, like Trey, even if you get intel."

"There's been no issue yet. Half the time you're overhearing chatter. Mostly you're sitting at the group area, when you talk with someone. Nobody tries anything major there, or at least pursues it. The owner isn't going for it there. Not because he has outstanding morals. Rather, trouble is bad for business, and that part he cares about. The worst that usually happens is somebody has too many potent drinks, and causes a commotion." She received a look from Dante. "Some start their drinking day early, or push their limit too far. People get loose lips with potent drinks behind them, some fewer than others. You overhear useful things, or they're chattier with minimum prompting."

"Apparently, I can't stop you, and you stayed safe thus far."

The other still bothered him, and it amused her. "When a beautiful woman flirts with you, I won't be upset. I'll reason, she has great taste in men." Her eyes twinkled.

"Won't happen. There's only you."

"Dante, it has happened. You can't convince me otherwise, but you wouldn't notice, because of fighting Black Dragon every second. You're incredibly good-looking, to say the least." She looked him in the eyes. "And yes, you're already spoken for, but nobody can know, which is why the beautiful girl noticing you will think nothing of it, when she makes a move on you."

"I don't care who she is, how she looks, or what she says. No one compares to you, and I'll have no one but you, Angelina."

"I know. Since I own your heart, I'm not worried about another woman's words to you. Likewise, you've nothing to worry about, because you claim mine as well. I'll continue paying no attention to another man's words, and you must not either."

"You made your point." He grinned. "This notion girls are swooning over me ... I don't know where you get it."

"Either you are clueless or unappreciated." She grinned back. "I admire a lot of your qualities, but I admit you're an enticing vision I keep tucked away, that I don't hesitate to bring out."

"Is that so?"

"It is." She wrapped her arms around his neck, whispering, "I'll demonstrate." She pulled him over and kissed him, taking her time to show him what her claim felt like on him. He wrapped his arms completely around her waist, but a moment later he couldn't resist running one hand through her hair, as he kissed her back. He loved the feel of it through his fingers. Her fingers lightly rubbed the back of his neck the way she did, and it added to the delightful sensations already going through him.

"I certainly feel appreciated," he murmured, as he kissed her cheek.

"You should." She kissed the corner of his mouth and stared up at him, her arms still entwined around his neck.

"I just don't want you meeting anymore men like Trey, Angelina. He was dangerous. He wouldn't take no for an answer. With more time alone in that room with you, he does everything he said to you. When he couldn't, the other option was running you through with a dagger. You can't tell me not to worry. He went beyond words."

"I'll admit he's in another league. I felt the same way, when the Dark Lord's agent bragged to Seth and Lana about what she would do if she got hold of you to give you special training. The thought of her near you, putting her hands on you made my skin crawl in all kinds of awful ways. It still does."

"She's got the creepy element going, but she didn't come near me, and won't. Any personal training like that, I'll insist you give me those sessions." He kissed her forehead.

"I'm there." She paused. "Trey's dead, despite whatever showed up today. The difference is Black Beauty remains alive and extremely dangerous. She killed your little brother, without hesitation. You still don't comprehend how much she delights in her role as assassin. She's ..." Angelina stopped, biting her lip. "I hope she doesn't make good on her threat. I can't have something happen to you."

She knew more of Black Beauty's work than she told him, and he couldn't shake the terrible feeling it was personal somehow. "Nothing will happen to me. We know her tactics, that she changes her appearance, and we're alerted now." He paused. "I'm just sorry you endured Trey saying those things to you. I had enough of him being anywhere near you, real or spirit or whatever."

Despite the situation, she smiled. "You must move past it, Dante."

He tried hiding his smile. "I should've sunspeared him through, as I wished, when we burst through the door. None of your silly interrogation stuff."

She laughed. "His comments bounced off me. I couldn't care less he found me attractive, and it amused him to tell me."

"He made no effort to hide it, with his words or his eyes or any other way," he grumbled.

"It does him no good. There's only one person I care about, having all his attention and affections. Do I have it, my Dante?" She ran her hand through his hair.

He whispered, "You do as always, my beautiful Angelina, and how I enjoy showing you." He began kissing her again, delighting in how perfect she felt in his arms and content to keep her that way.

She curled back up to Dante on the couch, as they finished a piece of dessert. He waited again, with one arm wrapped around her waist, and the other stroking her arm. She finally said, "I'm sorry I scared you with the cylinder earlier, Dante."

"You do get my heart racing, Angelina."

"Not my intended way of doing it."

"I know."

"Once I heard the end of the harpoon mechanism shift on the beam, my mind leapt to one possible conclusion based on last time. I decided it came undone, and I was falling as before. Everything fell into place to match."

"All of it?" He searched her eyes.

"Yeah, debris coming down, Black Dragon soldiers, pain through my body, smell of my blood, the ..."

"Complete reenactment. Let's not have you replay it again. Once is enough for you today." He kissed her forehead. "Fortunately for us, someone broke through your view, and showed you a different one." He pulled her up, and their faces were only a breath apart. "You conquered the rooftop, the cylinder. My Angelina, have you truly done so in your heart?"

"I have, Dante, I promise you."

"Good, because my heart can't take you coming up with another challenge, to retest it."

"I know. I remember your face, as you got up." She stroked his cheek. "You're my anchor here, Dante. The one whose words bring calm to my heart."

"I couldn't say anything to you, though I longed to." He brushed a strand of her hair back over her shoulder.

"You did, Dante. After the Ancient One spoke to me, I locked onto your eyes. I read it all in them, and felt it in your waiting arms, in your amazing kiss." She whispered, "You have a way with words, my Dante."

He gazed at her, his heart overflowing again with love for her. "You inspire them from me, my Angelina. I care for you so much." He closed the gap between them and caught her up in another kiss that took her breath away.

She heard and felt it again as he kissed her. Words of love, of reassurance, of safety, and more infused his embrace. She let it pour through her, touch her heart, and responded back to him with the same. She loved him, and she let it reach back to him.

"Angelina."

"Yes, I know."

"We've tomorrow evening, right?"

"Yes."

"After that..." He pulled her chin up, to see her eyes.

"We can't risk staying longer. It'd take a real game changer, which demands we stay to investigate, and I don't see that happening. Rather, more things beckon us to leave, to seek answers."

"Surely, there's a way ..."

"I won't put you and your group in danger, by my presence here. I couldn't live with the knowledge, if something happened, because I did so."

"I'll be miserable, between times until I see you."

"I'm certain, each time I return, you'll find ways to make up for the missed time. You're skilled at that." She grinned.

He chuckled. "That part comes naturally." He kissed her forehead. "Time to get you back to the ship, even as it pains me. Tomorrow, it's odd, with the much later start time."

"It's due to me, Dante."

"You?"

"Yes, I've business to sort out this evening with Alena and Alika, from the encounter today, with this one who came as Trey."

"You're doing that tonight? You seemed better."

"I am, but I need to share what he said exactly, with them, while I can remember it. They'll understand what he meant, including the double meanings. I'll pursue the rest when we leave here."

He helped her up and with her cloak. "Let's get you back to the ship."

Alika and Alena glanced up as the two walked in and sat.

"Enjoyable evening?" Alika smiled.

"Yes. I talked through a couple of things with him, after today. He's a wonderful listener."

"Not that it helps, like she claims."

Alena whispered, "It does, Dante. We all see it."

"Yes, she's right, young Dante. Don't dismiss that."

"I told him so."

"I tried comforting her, but it's like seeing everything through a fog. I only see parts of the image through the mists because she can't tell the rest." Shrugging his shoulders, he looked over at her, with sadness in his eyes.

Angelina looked down, knowing she couldn't fill in the gaps like he wanted.

Alika's voice softened. "Dante, I understand you think it would help to know that information. Alena and I do, but I grant you, though we endeavor to comfort Angelina, we fall short repeatedly. We find possessing the information is of little use, in assisting her the way we wish. You soothe her without that knowledge, when we cannot in the least. There is something much more important than the record of her past, these pieces which remain a mystery to you. Do you not see that, Dante?"

"I do, Alika, although it's better if you have the whole picture."

"Normally, yes, but if you can only see a part, isn't it better to have the more valuable of the two? I believe so, and you have the better to aid her. You reach her in ways we can't hope to, that touch her heart's core, and with words to sway her hurting spirit. She does the same for you and has in your hour of desperation. No one else could speak those words to you at the Elders Hall and keep your spirit safe from the Dark Lord's bondage as she did." He whispered, "Come young Dante, you truly care for her as no one else can."

"You're right, Alika." He turned to Angelina. "This connection with you is everything. None of the rest matters. I know you, my young spear-bearer." She'd never stop being his young spear-bearer, no matter what other name he gave her. "Your heart has not changed, since I knew you at the first, my Angelina." He engulfed her in a hug.

"It won't ever for you, my Dante." She returned his hug. and leaned into him again.

Alika smiled. "Despite a couple of topics, it sounds like an enjoyable evening."

"It was, but she says the three of you aren't done."

"Are you sure, Dante?" asked Angelina.

"Not ever with you, but this is the usual time I head back." She followed him to the door, and he wrapped her up in his arms. "If you change your mind, and you need me, I'm here."

"I wouldn't get you out of bed."

"You're stubborn. I don't care about the time. Did you hear what I said?"

"Yes, Dante."

He frowned at her response.

"Yes, *my* Dante. Is that better?" she grinned.

"I do like that better," He nuzzled her neck. "Still not what I hoped for, but you knew that. You're impossibly irresistible, you know that?"

"You made that clear."

"I do try, my sweet Angelina." He paused. "If I sense I should return, I will, whatever the hour."

"I get it. You're persistent. Goodnight, my Dante."

"I am that. Goodnight, my Angelina." He gave her a long, slow kiss goodnight, before leaving for his quarters.

She sat back on the couch and grinned. "He is incredible beyond words. I won't ever get enough of him."

"Good thing he already left." Alena laughed.

"Yes, he may not have, if he heard you say that." Alika laughed, too.

"Probably not." She continued for another minute, wrapped up in her own pleasant thoughts. "It's not getting earlier. I'm ready." Taking a deep breath, she began.

CHAPTER THIRTY-ONE

Despite getting into bed, Dante couldn't sleep. He wished to stay with her, while she recounted the encounter. The night he felt her hurt so, and he couldn't be there, rushed painfully back to him. Once she left again, he'd be unable to comfort her. Tonight she stayed close, but she seemed a million miles away again. What in her past created this intense fear? It didn't matter. He wouldn't let her go, and somehow he'd make her understand. Suddenly, he felt her emotions swirling around, as she went through the account with Alika and Alena. There were spells of turmoil, followed by calm. It switched back and forth, like the steady tides of the ocean. Many beginning large, but as the waves spilled ashore, they only made a gentle caress on the sandy coastline. As he felt through the connection, it continued the same ebb and flow. Thus far, he sensed none of the utter brokenness, as the one evening which brought him to tears with her. He thanked the Ancient One, for the gift of allowing him to remain present with her this evening.

She struggled more through the account in places, as memories washed over her that couldn't help but stir. Alika and Alena alternated, reaching over to remind her they were there, and stemming the tide of emotions surging to the surface. Finally, she persevered through the hardest parts of the encounter.

"What about the second appearance of Trey? It appeared completely different," asked Alena.

"I don't recall anything useful in the first part. He became frustrated when he couldn't get to me like earlier, but he tried not to show it. Once I found the hole in his defenses, I pushed it. He reappeared and talked about choosing the different, easier path like before. I asked for his itinerary for the day, and he offered an exchange for the information."

"Which you wisely declined," said Alika.

"Yes ... I did."

"Whatever he is, he's Black Dragon at his core." Alena studied her face.

"I know, but ..."

"There are no buts, my dear. Your answer must be no each time," Alika commanded.

"It will be, but he spoke the truth, when he said he knew things I wished to know. How he knows is as much mystery, as all this information about my past. Yet the cost is too great for the knowledge, and he wouldn't tell me the truth. You're right that he's Black Dragon at his core."

"Do you wish to tell us what happened, over the cylinder?" Alena whispered.

"I'm sure you both figured it out. My mind merged the two events and convinced me it was happening again."

"Back at the rooftop?" asked Alika.

"Yes. Thankfully, though I didn't know what I needed for the challenge, He did, as always." She recounted to them her conversation with the Ancient One, as she dangled over the cylinder.

"He provided the help and words, as always, to you."

"He did." Her eyes darkened, and a weight settled back on her.

"Something else?" asked Alika.

"The first encounter this morning with Trey. He reduced me to nothing. Everybody saw it. I fought better against the flesh and blood Trey. What does that say about me, since he left me on my knees, covered in bruises, and a dagger headed for me? What am I going to do? How do I fight him, this thing? What about the next time, when I can't fight, and there's no one to rescue me? I'm trained better than this. None of it should have happened."

"We'll figure out how to defeat him," Alika said.

"Yes, and you won't do it on your own. The second time, you got to him," said Alena.

"I found a weak point, and handled him better. That's a far cry from defeating him. There's a limited number of those performances in me. It brings up things I can't face again. It took so much from me, this crazy game he's playing. He can come, whenever he pleases, to toy with me." It began building, though she willed it to stop. She saw herself sitting there, unable to do anything against him, and she hated allowing him to exert such control over her. Inside, she screamed at herself to get up, to not be such a weakling. In rage, she yanked her image up, but the girl remained rooted to the seat by unseen coils binding her there. The image only increased her fury. "I couldn't help anyone, not the colonists, not myself, not anyone as before, just like with my mother." She paused only for a second. "How did I just sit there? How can he do that to me? How did I let him?"

"You didn't let him do anything. You fought him," said Alika.

"We saw you held, somehow."

"It doesn't matter, because I should be stronger. He's dead. How am I defeated by a dead man?" She sprang up from the couch. "How does a dead man still hold such power over me? Answer me. How?"

Alika and Alena recognized it, as she turned back to them. Anger, erupting to the surface. This was about more than Trey. The past's wounds blazed, with a vengeance.

"Perhaps he's given the power." Alika met her eyes.

"Any suggestions on taking it away?" Her voice became encased in sarcasm.

"The one who gave knows how to take it away, child," Alika answered, undaunted by her tone.

"I'm told, it's not so easy to get rid of." Of course, she understood his meaning. However, she couldn't stop herself, and her voice rose uncontrollably, as the tide threatened to overcome her. "Don't you think I would by now? I can't go back and undo that mess. I gave it what it wanted, and somehow, I always find that bloody path again, don't I?"

Dante felt the change. No longer following the predictable flow, her emotions transformed into crashing waves. in a raging storm, in danger of drowning her in its bottomless depths. He started to call her on the data pad, but it served only for one-way communication again. Her inner turmoil made reaching her through their connection a futile effort. A thought surfaced, but he feared only making matters worse. She said not to come. Immediately a whisper eliminated his fear, "Go to her, Dante." He dashed from his quarters to her ship.

"We've been through this, child. Don't do this to yourself."

"He's right. You didn't go on that path, but rightfully rejected it."

"None of us believes those lies! That day in my room marked my formal crowning failure. It was already over, when I confronted him, days before. He won, and he knew when he saw my eyes, after he laughed over her spilled blood. He's still winning. Still laughing. A dead man. If I gave him power, forgive me, if I don't have a clue how to get it back! He was right." She turned away and clenched her hands.

"Stop it! Don't you dare!" Alena yelled. "You can't believe those things he said about you."

She spun back around. "Why not? I continue proving him right and the other one today, too. He knew me, even as I hated it. If that didn't sound like my father's words. Trey knew everything about me, but what did he latch onto? This one emotion I always return to. The one poured out on that day, which consumed me before my father, and drove me straight to the darkness. The same one Trey enjoyed seeing explode out and take over, yesterday in that room. I couldn't stop, just like before, and it will always be that way!"

"No, it won't. Yet you conclude you're nothing more than a slave to the one emotion, because you choose to remember only that part. Can you not see the deception, before your own eyes?" Alika's voice spoke calm.

"I see fine!" she yelled back. The door opened, and Dante ran in. She didn't register it, but continued her tirade. "I can't always be justified. We all know it too, don't we? Come on, say it! You're thinking it, because you've seen that look before from me. I should've been unable to fight, after the beating I took. Yet I didn't feel an ounce of it, because I felt only one thing, the anger rushing through me. Nothing else mattered. It carried me, and I could've taken out that whole room single-handedly. They were all coming down for sure, but not like I did it. Trey knew it. We all did, but he had the guts to say it, instead of excusing me. He was right, and the sooner we admit it, the easier this becomes."

"Child, you're not seeing things clearly. The man would kill you, but you still believe his lies. This is not who you are."

Her scream echoed off the walls of the ship, "Yes, this is who I am! We know it's true! That's the problem! Just give up already." Her breaths came in short, shallow increments. This time, as her eyes spanned the room, she finally comprehended Dante stood there too. "Like this couldn't get worse. Guess it's better you see it now. I told you not to come, Dante. Why don't you listen?" She turned and stomped towards her quarters.

Dante ran and wrapped his arms around her from behind, ending her retreat. He whispered in her ear, "Because you needed me, my Angelina." Her entire frame trembled, and her breath still came in shallow, uneven breaks. He turned her in his arms to face him and whispered, "Look at me." Slowly, she lifted her head and stared in his eyes. The storm of emotions continued raging in them. "I have not left your side, and I will not start now, I promise you."

"How? After what you saw? This is the," her voice broke, "real me. Do you still see one who reminds you of an angel, your Angelina? There is no angel." A sob escaped, as she bowed her head.

"Yes, there is. How can you think that?" He pulled her to him, as he fought to control the wave of emotion overwhelming him. How could she wonder? It was craziness. He'd do whatever it took to convince her, but she wouldn't leave his embrace until he was sure. He allowed her to pull back enough, so he could gaze in her eyes again and recognized the question remaining there. "I'll always see my Angelina. I know you, and I've always known you. Why would you doubt that, my young spear-bearer? Yes, tonight is you as well. I'll tell you what I saw. I saw anger. There's no denying that part." She attempted to turn away, but his hand gently kept her from doing it, "but underneath it, pain, anguish, brokenness crying out, and I couldn't bear standing by, while you hurt. I'm here where I belong with you, as I said I would." He whispered, "Now stop fighting me, my Angelina. Let me be your anchor, your Dante."

An anguished cry erupted from her, as she began sinking to the ground, her heart surrendering to this one, who held a power over her, which melted her every defense. He prevented her from descending to the floor by holding her against him, keeping his word of being her stronghold in this latest storm. In one effortless motion, he swooped her up in his arms and carried her to the couch. He sat beside her and continued where he left off, pulling her form close, while stroking her hair and back. He glanced over at Alika and Alena, who watched sadly in silence.

A calm pervaded her, with a familiar spent feeling following. She untangled herself slightly from Dante and turned to Alika and Alena in another accustomed scene. "Alena, I didn't mean to be so terrible. You tried to help and, Alika, there's no excuse for it. You deserve none of the abuse I heaped upon you. My words to you, I'm ashamed, and sorry for my behavior." Her voice broke at the last.

Alika clasped her hand. "Child, there's no need. Have I not told you before?"

"You shouldn't endure this from me, Alika. Neither one of you. How many times do you forgive this awful behavior from me, before you walk away? You should."

"I wouldn't be much of a teacher if I did so, would I?" Alika smiled at her.

"But your student is hopeless, to learn the lessons before her."

"Your teachers refuse to believe that." He squeezed her hand.

"We won't give up on our student," Alena added.

Alika perceived her still distraught state, over her anger spilling out at him. “Angelina, stop punishing yourself. This is not a student unable to grasp a lesson. Nor is it something read and absorbed or practiced repeatedly and mastered, as movements with a weapon. These are hard lessons. They are ones fought through, struggled with countless times, and challenged by the fires of your heart’s battlefield. The path before you, my child, has been a difficult one to say the least, and it continues to be.”

“I’ll never understand the patience you two show for me.”

“An unproductive exercise trying to figure it out, so don’t waste time on it.” Alika winked at her. “Tonight, my child, you did what you intended. You shared the words of the encounter with us, and we agreed, delving further into it can wait until we get back, correct?”

“Yes, we did.”

“Lay it aside for the night.”

Alena said, “He’s right. We won’t find further answers tonight.”

She sighed and nodded her agreement.

“I’ll head to my ship for sleep, and leave you with Alena and Dante. Perhaps try the end of your evening again with Dante, but it’s late.” He turned to Dante. “If you get too tired, you’re welcome to stay here. There are extra quarters in the back with a small bed or the couch here. In the morning, you can head back to get ready. Of course, it may prove unnecessary.”

“I appreciate the offer, in case, Alika.”

“You’ll be all right now?” Alika stood, looking down at her.

“I will. At least for you to go to bed. Goodnight, Alika.”

“Goodnight, my child.” He kissed her forehead, as he nodded at Dante.

Alena walked Alika out and returned. “Dante, we’re glad you came back tonight, despite the hour.” She smiled and turned to Angelina. “I’ll follow Alika’s lead for the evening, but if you need me, just holler." She gave her a hug.

“I know. Thank you for putting up with me.”

“Always. Goodnight you two.” She disappeared into her quarters, with one last look at the pair.

CHAPTER THIRTY-TWO

Dante knew their thoughts realms apart, as she waited for his next words. He spoke quietly, "I need to see your eyes."

"Not a pleasant thing tonight, Dante."

"Please, Angelina."

"If you insist."

Her eyes indicated calm again, as she looked up at him, but the rest reflected there pained his heart. She directed it all herself too, and he glimpsed something else, in that sea to her heart. There was a fear she couldn't conceal. One that broke his heart, and he couldn't fathom her fear, with how he loved her. The question burst from him, his voice trembling with emotion. "Do you honestly believe I'm chased from your side, that I would ever leave you?"

"I made it easy to do so," she whispered.

"You're wrong." He caressed her cheek. "After everything that's happened between us, how can you believe that? Nothing, no one, could ever make me wish to part with you."

"I ... suppose." She started to look down, but he made it impossible, as he cradled her face.

"Some angry outburst and you seriously believe that? What happened in your past that makes you doubt so, my Angelina? I won't allow it to win. I'll drive it out yet, for you to be convinced of the truth of my words, for they reflect my heart." He pulled her over, engulfed her in his arms, and kissed her. Not just any kiss. She felt as though he put everything into the kiss, as a fiery passion infused it. She thought to catch her breath, but he used the second to deepen the kiss, and continue his unrelenting pursuit of her lips. He determined, no matter what, to persuade her, to drive out any uncertainties she still harbored. Finally, his lips moved to her ear, and he whispered, "I'll never let you go, my Angelina." Leaning his forehead on hers, he met her eyes again.

She nodded.

"Persuaded yet?" He grinned, as he ran a hand through her hair.

She nodded again and smiled back at him.

"Trouble catching your breath?"

"Yeah."

"Well, I'm not sorry, and you're not either," he continued, "I'm taking Alika's offer, but not due to tiredness. I want to be close, in case you need me again, because you won't call, even if you should." From anyone else, it would come off as a reprimand, but from Dante, it was a dilemma now resolved.

"A fair conclusion from earlier, but you didn't listen to me anyway."

"You didn't listen first." He chuckled. "Honestly, I did listen, and you got overruled. He told me to come."

"How? I was arguing with him, so he couldn't call you."

"Not Alika."

"Oh." She paused. "His Voice certainly won't be ignored. I am relieved you came back, even though I'm still ashamed of what you saw."

"No more of that. I came when you needed me. The times I can't are what I'll hate. I'll take this to the other any day. I also could happily remain, with you curled up in my arms like this, but you need sleep. Show me these extra quarters, so I can decide where to settle." He pulled her up with him.

She led him towards the back of the ship. "Ironic. I spent evenings in your quarters, but you didn't get a tour of the other half of the ship yet. My home away from home." She opened a door. "Here's the room Alika spoke of. It's what he said. There a bed that pulls out, a compartment underneath for storing a few things, and a small fold out tray for laying items on top."

Dante walked into the room. She followed behind and leaned against the wall due to the limited space. He came to her, his face full of mischief. "It's compact, close quarters in here, huh?"

"What are you suggesting?"

"Nothing. Just an observance." But he moved closer to her, and his arm wound around her waist.

"If you say so."

"It's cozy and calls up another time of pleasant memories with you." He leaned down and kissed her. He pulled her from the room, murmuring, "Give me the rest of the tour."

"Of course, Dante." The grin on his face confirmed their shared thought of staying longer, to make more pleasant memories. "That door leads to Alena's quarters. This next one goes to the bathroom." She slid her hand on the wall panel device as before, and the door opened. "The décor doesn't scream masculine, but you can overlook that if you need it."

He laughed. "I'll manage." There were pleasing colors in it. It favored blues and conjured up images of clear skies and water, as he spent a minute surveying it. "Actually, not bad. I meant it's not overflowing with what I'd picture with two women. Let me stop, before I land into trouble."

She grinned. "You in trouble? Never. I get your point, and you're right. Neither one of us are overly frilly, girly types and considering how we spend our time ..."

"Prefer not to think about it, but it explains the other."

"These are my quarters." She opened the next door and entered. He walked in too, eager to glimpse this small slice of her world, and wondered how it compared to her room at home. The mini space showcased a fair amount of blue too, but one wall caught his attention. It was an ocean blue, reminding him of her eyes he found himself happily lost. Intermixed in the blue, and particularly on the top, it possessed a sheen or a sparkle, like flecks of light radiating from it. Fascinated by it, he tried to decipher the image as he inspected it closer and ran his hand over it. His examination discovered nothing remarkable about the feel, but something about it spoke to him. It called up emerald blue water, a majestic sunset painted across a perfect sky, and gentle waves lapping on white sandy shorelines. This other he couldn't figure out, the dancing lights spread on the top of the whole blue expanse. He turned to her. "It's beautiful. What is it?"

She sat on the bed, and he settled beside her. "You know, Dante. You see it."

"It's a water scene, a sunset, an incredible one, but there are beams of light, flickers or something everywhere. What are they?"

She stared at it. "That part is when the moonlight and stars shine on the water, I imagine it's the light reflecting off the stone in the sunspear. I suppose it would be like a diamond shimmering on the top of the water."

"That would be quite the sight to behold. I can't imagine."

As she continued to stare at the scene, she whispered, "A spectacular sight to behold, indeed." She turned to him, with that beautiful smile which reached her eyes.

It reflected in her eyes, and she looked stunning anew in that instant. None of the day's battles manifested on her face. He wound his arm around her waist, and his other hand brushed the side of her cheek. "It calms you, doesn't it?"

"Yes, Dante."

"In your room at home, you have the same scene or something similar?"

"I do. How did you guess?"

"It made sense." He paused. "Regardless, you and the others don't need to stay in the ship when you're here. We've plenty guest quarters for you all. It'd give you more room, and you'd be more comfortable." He saw her look. "Yes, you'd be closer to my quarters. I like that part, but I can still behave." He grinned.

"Despite all your teasing, you'd manage to. However, the surest way to start questions is staying in the quarters when we come, and I won't put you or the others in danger."

"Okay. The picture is amazing though. It's no mystery why it comforts you. Surrounded by such beauty ..." He wrapped his other arm around her waist, and drew her to him. She already moved to him, wrapping her arms around his neck. He kissed her, his hand delighting in finding her hair to run thorough, and a happy sigh escaped her. When their lips parted, she leaned up against him with one arm around his waist, and the other stroking his hand. He sat there too, enjoying the closeness for longer. Eventually, he kissed her on the forehead, as he sighed. "I wish we could stay like this, but I'm afraid not." He untangled himself from her enough to stand, and eased her up too. “I’d better decide where I’m sleeping tonight.”

They stepped from her quarters.

“I’ll be back in a few while you sort it out, Dante.” On cue, she returned. “Where do you want to sleep tonight?” His eyes twinkled at her choice of words. “Out of your two options, Dante?” She laughed.

“The extra quarters.”

“The ship is locked down for the night. I’ll wake you in the morning.”

“I can handle you being my wake-up call.” He kissed her on the cheek.

“Bet so. Let’s be sure you can get into everything.” She motioned toward the door pad.

He swiped his hand over it, and the door opened. The computer announced, “Verified, one of nine authorized individuals activated the door entry.”

“Why did it do that?” asked Dante as he sat on the side of the bed.

“First time accessing this area of the ship. It’s double-checking, but you’re fine now.” She sat beside him.

He didn’t count nine. “Who’s the nine?”

“What do you mean?”

“I count eight in our group. You three, and five of us.”

“The ninth is our contact we work with the most.”

“I forgot about him, since normally you avoid doing business on the ship.”

“But he’s different. The Ancient One specifically led us to him. He’s more like a close friend now, who happens to be an excellent business connection. Some things he helped us with weren’t safe discussing in the colony’s diners or bars. The operation with the supplies alone comes to mind.”

“Yeah, one better discussed in private. It’s strange for you to trust someone this much that I don’t know.”

“You know you’ve nothing to worry about, right? He’s protective of me, in the same way Alena is.”

Dante smiled. "It's not that. I'm used to your past being mysterious to me, but I'm reminded again there's this present world you navigate in I'm clueless about, too. What's his name?"

"I don't know. There's the name he goes by with me, as I do with him."

"Which you won't tell me." He shook his head, still smiling.

"Constant name changes are a trademark of the shipping business, but I trust you. Still, the reality is, the more you know, the more danger in which you're placed. If you don't know, there's nothing to tell."

"One way to see it." He watched her. "What is it?"

"He's our first contact when we return. I'm worried we don't reach him with our discovery, before he has ugly dealings with these blaster-immune Black Dragon."

"Can you send a message to him?"

"No, it's the same as with your group. I find him when necessary."

"He's fine, until you reach him, Angelina. He operates within a dangerous realm constantly, which takes doing, from your indications."

"You're right, and we need sleep if we're to manage tomorrow. We can't afford to make mistakes with Black Dragon."

"I'll see you get into bed. We're doing goodnight all the way this time." He pulled her up with him.

"This isn't necessary, Dante."

"But I want to." He winked at her as her quarter's door opened for him with a slide of his hand. "You need anything before you climb in?"

"No, I did everything earlier, while you decided the other. We don't change into nightwear while here. Always a possibility we need to leave immediately."

"Get in bed then. It's not getting earlier."

"You're seriously tucking me in?" she laughed, as she laid down.

"That's my plan." He grinned as he sat on the side of the bed and pulled the covers up to her. "Comfortable?"

"Yes. Will waking you up about 9:15 give you ample time to get back over, shower, and all that?"

"Unless I'm held up, by my lovely wake-up call."

"I'll not let that happen."

"But I anticipate taking considerable time to wake up," he teased, as he leaned down and caressed her cheek. "Goodnight, my Angelina."

Her arms encircled his neck as she smiled up at him. "Goodnight, my Dante."

Reaching down the rest of the way, he kissed her and murmured, "Aren't you glad I tucked you in?" Her eyes gave the answer as he chuckled. "I agree, another tuck, my Angelina." He kissed her once more before rising. Smiling back at her as she finally slept, he headed for bed.

CHAPTER THIRTY-THREE

Lana encircled her arms further around Caleb, and opened her eyes to find him smiling at her. "Time to get up, Caleb?"

"No, about two and a half hours before we meet Seth downstairs, so at least an hour before we need to get up and ready."

"That long? Somehow, it doesn't feel that way."

"Remember the later start time today. Did I mention there's an hour to spare?" He pulled her closer and kissed her neck.

"You are insatiable." She giggled.

"You're irresistible, my sweet Lana." He whispered. "As I enjoyed reminding you last night." He continued his focus on her neck, as his hands teased over her bare body.

He was right, as she went back to last night and countless wonderful nights like it. She didn't begin to know how he did it so quickly, but she loved it, as every inch of her awakened to his touch again, and reignited the fire in her. "Well, let's not waste the hour." She pulled him over the rest of the way and kissed him.

Angelina turned over to check the display. 8:50. She'd get up, but give Dante until time, considering how late she kept him awake. She emerged from her quarters, to find Alika already seated on the couch. He looked up, as she entered.

"How are you feeling?"

"Fine, despite my outburst last night."

"Good. I figured you'd manage, since I released you to Dante's watchful eye."

"Yes, he's persistent."

Alika laughed. "We said that some time ago about him. Surrender, and be done with it."

"He determined I wouldn't call him if I needed him again and took your offer. I'll wake him soon."

"He's smart too, because you wouldn't call him. What time are you due to wake him?"

"Another fifteen minutes." She noticed the look from Alika. "Yes, he won't fly out of here, since I'm the one waking him. Best I go now, if we're to be on time for the others."

She almost hated waking him. He slept soundly, with a smile still on his face. She wondered what he dreamed of now. Maybe her? Probably not. Although most of the time when he frequented her dreams, she finally slept well. *He's even gorgeous when he's asleep. Time to stop gawking at him, and get him up.* She gently squeezed his shoulder and ran her other hand through his hair, while sitting on the bed. "My Dante, time to wake up."

"Such a sweet voice and wonderful touch, first thing this morning. Come closer, would you?" He wrapped his arm around her waist, as the other hand reached for the side of her face.

"This close enough?" She smiled, and knelt her face close to his.

"Perfect." He grinned, as he kissed her gently and slowly. He had high hopes for the rest of the day, based on this start. If only ... he wouldn't think about it now. Nothing else mattered, as he enjoyed this moment with her.

"You're supposed to be getting up, Dante," she murmured, as her arms instinctively wrapped around his neck.

"I'm sitting up. See," he whispered into her lips. "I can do two things at once."

"You amazed me again," she whispered back, as she realized he gradually sat up in bed, as he kissed her.

"I'll be completely happy, if you can arrange to wake me this way every morning. What do you say?"

"We'd both be completely happy, but we know the answer."

"One day, though." What he wouldn't give, to wake up every day with her lying next to him in bed. It would mean they shared the one bond, finally, the future he longed for with her. He loved her, as if she were his bride already. However, they couldn't even be seen together now, hardly good dating arrangements, and certainly unworkable for marriage.

"One day, though." She kissed him on the cheek, while guiding him up from bed. "You're out of bed now. Almost there."

"See you in a bit?" He stood at the ship's door.

"We'll be down soon."

He gave her a quick kiss before heading for his quarters.

CHAPTER THIRTY-FOUR

"There he is," said Caleb.

"Whatever it is, I didn't do it," said Dante, as he strolled in the room.

"Maybe it's something good, Dante." Ryan grinned.

"Unlikely, if Caleb is hunting for me." Dante laughed.

"Wondering about your girl. How do you think it all sorted out last night?"

"Turned out real ugly last night, Caleb. She finally calmed down, by the time she hit the bed. By this morning, she seemed her normal self again."

Lana stammered, "I thought you were here. I mean she could only talk about it with them, but this morning you saw her?"

"We're sufficiently confused, Dante," said Seth.

"Sorry. I took her back to the ship, but I sensed it got bad. The whole connection thing. Initially, I didn't know what to do, until the Ancient One instructed me to go to her. Things were heated, to say the least, when I arrived. She was beyond angry and ended up in tears, but then she settled down somewhat. Alika offered me the extra quarters on the ship, and I accepted them, in case she needed me again. They went to bed, and I handled the rest with her. I stayed up with her for a while longer, talking and being there like usual. This morning, she woke me up, so I could come back over to get ready."

"What a long night." Ryan shook his head.

"Did you figure out what upset her like that?" asked Lana.

"Not particularly. Something surrounding the anger Trey's confrontation ignited. I came to find her yelling back at Alika and Alena, so I missed part of it. Maybe that would've cleared it up. I'm certain it's tied with her past. It's a constant trigger. What I heard seemed strange, to create such a reaction." He stopped as footsteps approached. "This will need to wait for another time."

"Everyone good this morning?" asked Seth, smiling, as his eyes rested on Angelina.

She returned his smile, as Dante wrapped his arm around her waist, and kissed her on the cheek. "Yes. Thanks to you three, for taking care of things this morning. It ended up being an extremely late night."

Caleb nodded. "Happy to help, so you could sort out the other. Grab something to eat, everyone."

Angelina spoke up first, "We're already starting late. Once we finish eating, are we set to leave for the planet?"

"Yes. We can leave immediately," answered Lana.

Dante glanced at Angelina, but she smiled back at him. She determined to put yesterday's events behind her. She couldn't manage a repeat.

Once they landed on the planet, they headed straight for medical. After the last visit, they abandoned pleasantries and found the one person they trusted.

"Good to see you again this soon."

Lana smiled. "You as well. Let's check on one of your patients from last time." She directed them back to Anna's bed, and Ryan and Caleb closed the curtain, to ensure privacy with Doctor Iban.

"How is she?" asked Angelina.

"As you left her. I wish I could actually do something for her, and the others in her state."

"You're doing everything you can for her. We're grateful to you."

Lana said, "Kate's right, but we must also ask again for your assistance. We needed to speak with you in private, as it's becoming impossible to discern who we can trust. The examination of the bodies and the blood samples proved helpful. It answered several questions, and raised new ones, but provided enough answers to proceed forward. You should sit for this. There's a lot to share with you."

He sat. "Please, continue."

Lana relayed about the differences in the blood samples, and the mark they located.

"Your group was busy."

"We were, and we worked out a plan, with a process to do this. Today is the test, to see how the process plays out in practice and to evaluate what adjustments need to happen. Part of it is an extension on the last visit, to make your area safe."

"I'm ready to hear it."

Iban listened as Lana laid it out. The others added pieces occasionally, with the doctor asking a few clarifying questions. At the end, he nodded and said, "It's well conceived, but time-consuming at the moment."

"Our thoughts too, but we're in a difficult position," said Seth.

"They secretly came in, and must be discreetly eliminated. Black Dragon can't discover we stumbled on the truth, at least not at first," said Alika.

"Yeah, they can change things fast and find another way to weasel their people past us," said Caleb.

Lana nodded. "Iban, we need three rooms near each other, meeting the specifications we covered. We'll get the bit of equipment moved to them."

"I figured out three rooms as we spoke, and all have a connecting room, as you wish, Lana."

"Is everyone ready?" asked Lana, as she stood in a room with Caleb and Iban.

"We're good in here," answered Ryan, in a room with Alika and Alena.

"Ready as well, Lana," Dante replied, in another room with Angelina and Seth.

They brought in one individual at a time into a room. It was a medical facility of sorts at present, so no one questioned the made-up story about a medical checkup from the poison hitting the planet. They were looking out for the welfare of the colonists, and anyone coming to the recently-poisoned planet. The story worked, as well as it did the last time on the planet. The group uncovered the Black Dragon agents sooner, since spotting the mark took no time, under the guise of a quick medical exam. Each agents' fate became sealed at the end of a blade, be it sunspear or sword. One in the group dragged the body to the adjoining room, and a firestone did the rest. In contrast, those belonging to the Ancient One left, believing they received a quick medical checkup, a simple precaution after what happened.

"Think it's working?" asked Ryan, as they closed the door for one of the colonists leaving. He waited, before granting the next one entry.

"Seems to be. They don't suspect anything. It's just another medical instrument taking a reading. The stamp is small, and only shows with the special lighting device calibrated as we have it, so they won't know it's on them," said Alena.

"More importantly, neither will Black Dragon. The fingerprinting is working too. They don't realize they give it to us, when they set their hands down on the pad. These are all noninvasive ways to keep our side tracked, which aren't easily compromised. Hopefully, a day comes when it's all unnecessary," said Alika.

"Our mark has an expiration date," reminded Ryan.

"Yes, but we can't fathom still being threatened by the Black Dragon's device three years from now. Even Black Dragon won't have patience to wait that long to unleash their destruction. Somehow, this comes to an end," said Alika.

"Another one." Dante shook his head, as he dragged the body to the next room and closed the door. "I'm not sure if I should hope the others are doing as well as us or not."

"Me, either," said Seth. "Thankfully, we've the element of surprise on the enemy."

"Otherwise, this is messier. Although every day of this process ..." Angelina paused. "I wonder if we don't give your group the harder task, how it'll leave your spirits." She looked down. "Time to bring in the next one."

Seth motioned the next colonist in and to be seated. She was an attractive brunette in her mid-thirties. After listening to Seth's simple explanation for the visit, she flashed them an unconcerned smile. She fixed her attention on Angelina, who took over helping Seth with the female patients, as Dante did with the male patients. Dante stood aside, watching in case, as Angelina did when it was the opposite. Angelina kept a smile on her face, as she went behind the woman, "Have you felt anything strange, after what occurred on the planet? Like anything bothering you from the poison? Such as pain anywhere, headaches, discomfort in your joints or muscles?" As she talked, she moved the woman's hair off her neck and pretended to check the area, as part of the exam. She spotted it and nodded at Dante and Seth. Preparing her sword, she circled back around to the woman.

The woman started talking. "There's no pain from the poison for me, but we both knew." She peered straight into Angelina's eyes. "I also know what you mean to do, but I'm not what you painted me to be. What if I'm not sure now? Can't I get another shot at it?"

Angelina met her gaze, unable to surmise how the woman knew. An internal alarm sounded at her own confusion, but she showed none of it. "You made your choice."

"What about the chance to reconsider? Are you sure this is the best way to do this?"

"Yes. There's no other way." It came out confidently, but inside that started to dwindle.

"Yet you wonder, wish for another way, don't you? Because what if you're wrong about a colonist?"

"I don't wonder. Then I'll just have to be wrong." An abruptness resounded in her voice, one she didn't mean.

"You can't be satisfied with such an answer, and you don't make it simple. Nothing is, in your eyes."

Her eyes? Angelina brushed it aside and continued, "And yet it is. They serve Black Dragon, and kill in his name."

"But if there's one. That one would be your undoing. An innocent colonist's blood upon your blade. How would that eat at you?"

"It would ..." she faltered, but forced the firmness back into her voice. "No, they're not innocent, and you're not either. You can't win this."

"You continue telling yourself that, but I'm skilled at playing this game and winning, aren't I? Yet back to the original discussion. It was easy when they were half machine. Now they're flesh and blood, former colonists. Can you stand the image, the vision ... yes the vision, going through your head? How would you stand it?"

There was no mistake now. "How do you know?"

"I can't imagine, but I'm not the one who must, am I? Perhaps since a multitude of images already torture your sleep, what's another added to the mix? Another one, to give you no peace? But it's always about the one you can't save, right? It gets you every time, doesn't it? The one you can't forget, despite how hard you try. Oh my, how you've worked over the years, the lengths you've gone to."

"Who are you?"

"Just another colonist, Kate." She chuckled. "But you were right before. I'm content with my chosen path. The question is, are you confident of yours? Time remains to change it. There's nothing to fear. Come, Kate."

"No, this can't be," she whispered.

"Fearing it is ..." she smiled, as she remembered the right words, "tales told to scare children, nothing more."

"H ... How?" Her face paled further, as her sword dropped to her side.

"It certainly does not lead to destruction, as you have been told. Come to me, Kate." she whispered, "Because we both know you can't kill me. You couldn't even manage to get your sunspear out now, if you wished to, Kate."

The woman spoke the truth. The sword started slipping from her hand as the woman talked. Soon the weapon would land on the floor, more useless to her than now, and no hope existed of drawing her sunspear. She tried to move the sword to kill this one, but nothing made her body do as she commanded. Faced with this foe armed with the past she couldn't leave behind, she stood absolutely lost again. Worse still, she conceded, no matter how many blades plunged into this one, it forever rose again for her to battle. Suddenly, she realized the woman sat still. New words no longer gushed from the figure, only the ones already said, echoed in Angelina's head. Finally, she registered the black goo pouring from the woman, but she didn't recall the motion at all. When did she pull her sunspear out?

"Kate, Kate, can you hear me? Listen to me, now! Kate!" Dante kept calling to break the dangerous dialogue going back and forth, but he received no response. Seth tried intervening as well, but to no avail. Once Angelina's sword slipped from her hand, Dante stepped forward with his sunspear, glaring at the colonist. "Enough. This ends now." Without hesitation, he plunged the sunspear into the colonist, as she pulled out a concealed dagger towards Angelina.

CHAPTER THIRTY-FIVE

Angelina collapsed to her knees, as Seth and Dante rushed to either side of her.

"I got her. Get it out of here, Dante."

He nodded, and dragged the body to the other room. After retrieving the data pad from it, he put it separate from the rest of the collection and threw a couple of firestones on the pile of bodies. He rushed back into the room, to kneel beside Angelina. "Please say something, anything." Not a word came from her, as her eyes were vacant as the previous day, after her encounter with Trey's spirit the first time. Dante turned to Seth, pleading for a solution.

"Stay with her. I'll tell the others."

"Of course," whispered Dante, as he stroked her back and hair, desperate to coax her from the trance.

Seth got up and moved to the side, as he kept concerned eyes on Angelina. "This is Seth. Our group is done with examining colonists. Once you finish with your current patient, we must talk."

A couple of minutes later, a voice responded, "It's Lana. Our group finished. Is everything okay?"

"Yes and no. Physically, everyone is unharmed. Let's wait for the others."

A few minutes more passed, and Alika's voice came through, "We encountered a pause as well. Something happened?"

"Yes. We'll reroute the colonists to your two groups. A situation occurred, between one of the female turned colonists and Kate. Dante finished the colonist off, before she used the dagger on Kate. Kate is fine physically, but in other aspects is in no condition to continue with this. Dante is with her now. The rest of you be careful. The colonist started out with a ploy. Despite manifesting the mark, she put on an act, claiming she had second thoughts about her Black Dragon allegiance. It became clear as she continued talking it was a lie, but it gave her sufficient time to pull the dagger on Kate. She also said other things to confuse Kate and delay her in using her sword. Dante eliminated the Black Dragon agent, just in time."

Seth's words were answered by complete silence. Everyone but Iban figured out the true reason for Angelina's current state. Iban contributed it to being the near miss with the dagger.

"Is she really okay?" asked Lana.

"Yes, what did she say?" asked Alena.

"She didn't say anything while I was there, and I don't believe it changed."

"It's like that," Alika sighed.

"What do you wish?" asked Seth.

"Everyone else continue. Kate will be fine. Seth, I'll speak with you."

After a few moments, Seth continued, "I'm here, Alika. Do you wish to talk with her, and I switch places with you? I'll follow your wishes."

"I will, if she asks. You know, as does she. However, I trust your wisdom, as you would if it were Dante in the same situation, and I spoke in your stead. Your counsel may prove more helpful, since you heard the confrontation."

"I'll speak with her as you would, and we'll send for you, if she asks."

"Thank you. I know she's in good hands, so I'll let you see to her."

Seth approached Angelina and Dante. He glanced at Dante, whose anguished expression revealed he couldn't draw a word from Angelina, despite his desperate attempts. "Time you got off the floor. Let's sit over here." Seth gently pulled her up on one side, and Dante did the same on the other side. They guided her to a chair, and she sat, as they settled in chairs on either side of her.

"You heard my words to Alika. He'll come if you wish. I'm concerned about you, as is Dante. Can you not say something, child?"

She should say something. What could she say though? No words came to ease their concern. The conversation replayed in her mind. The same questions reformed; she asked but received no answers. Yet, she understood with mounting dread, she did get them, or she already had them. She didn't want to think about it because the possibility grew too terrible for her mind to entertain. Any moment, something inside of her would finally shatter into pieces. She wanted to say none of it was true, but she couldn't. The words of Trey's spirit whispered to her, "I know you Kate, even as you wish I did not."

"I can't win," she whispered.

"One defeat doesn't mean you lose," said Seth.

"Yes, you stood up to Trey yesterday and won."

"No. He returned today in this colonist, to mock me. All is lost again. There's no victory for me in this."

"Child, you can't believe that, and let it leave you in this hopeless state each time."

"But I can. Different time. Different place. The form changes. It's the same battle from before replayed, and the result is always the same. I thought it done. Gone. But it always returns. I can't beat it. I've no clue how, but it knows everything about me, even the parts I can't bear to..." she buried her face in her hands.

"All this, from one battle which wrought such pain to your spirit. What in this battle caused your spirit to always see the shadow of defeat? To see yourself through this same shadow, child?"

"I can't. It's in the past and I ... It doesn't matter. I'll never put it aside. This colonist knew and Trey's spirit too. Everything revealed."

"You only see failure and this shadow? Do you truly believe this is who you are? How is this all you see, child?"

"Because it's who I am." Her voice broke. "You don't understand and can't imagine how possible it is."

"No, it's not." Dante got up from the chair, and knelt on one knee in front of her, staring up at her. He firmly grabbed her arms, and pulled her closer to him. "Listen to me. I don't know your past, and I don't care. I know you, though. I've seen you, your spirit, and your heart. You're the one who almost died saving my mother, who spoke words of truth in my brokenness to snatch me from death, who gave words of comfort to my father in his despair, who pours herself out repeatedly for those colonists whose hope is in the Ancient One, and who I absolutely adore and can't imagine my world without now. That's you. The only one who captured my heart, who does now, and always will." He pulled her closer, until their faces almost touched. "See that one."

"How?" she whispered, unable to leave his gaze.

"See through my eyes, my Angelina."

"I've been told before." Tears glistened in her eyes.

"Must I show you how, my Angelina? Do you truly not see it?" he whispered as he clasped one of her hands and kissed it. Then he leaned in, and softly kissed her lips.

"I do, when I stare in your eyes, and I long to keep your image, Dante. Yet, the other images come, reminding me of what can't be undone."

"What do you need undone, Angelina? Please tell me."

"I see scores of images, with pain that goes on and on. Always powerless to stop it. Your brother's murder. Your mother's imprisonment. You said I got her back, but for what? I failed to awaken her. You at the Elders Hall. It almost claimed your life, and what you endured there nearly broke your spirit. Your father. I said you would get him back, but instead the Dark Lord slaughtered him before your eyes. I sent your group to retrieve a dispersal device which turned into a fool's errand, while three planets of innocent colonists met a horrible fate. All dead, dying, or being terrified in their sleep. Their faces I watched, tormented, and their anguished cries I heard echoing, still do." Instantly, she seemed somewhere else. "It has always been that way. See the vision, but I can't stop it from happening. I was too late, and I failed. Don't you see? It was my fault. I should have ..." Immediately, she realized where she was and who listened to her. She bowed her head, and a sob escaped.

Seth suddenly remembered the colonist's words, "the one you can't save ... It gets you every time ... the one you can't forget." A question formed. "Child, who is this one you could not save, that you can't forget, which overshadows all these other images?"

Angelina stared up at Seth, realizing she had said too much. "I can't. It's my pain, my burden, even if it's my undoing in the end." She shook her head, and buried her head in her hands. Dante rose, and moved his chair to face her. He sat back down in it, lifted her entire body effortlessly over to him, and cradled her in his lap, as he whispered, "My Angelina, I'm here and won't let you go. I've not left your side and will not now. If I could take it all away, I would." His words continued, whispered promises pouring into her spirit, along with his gentle caresses delivering calm to her.

He brushed a strand of hair from her face. "Do you remember the first time we met in person, when you surprised me in my quarters?"

"I could never forget." She smiled at the memory.

"Do you recall what I said to you?"

"Every word of it. The next day, to see you couldn't come soon enough."

He kissed her on the forehead at her response. "I felt the same. I told you this couldn't be one-sided, as you comforted me, you must let me do the same."

"That's all you've done, since my arrival, Dante. It's completely one-sided, now."

"Not what I see. It's the same story as that evening. You carry burdens too heavy for you alone, and ones not meant for you to ever tote around. You aren't responsible for the things in the visions."

"That's impossible to believe, when you see them."

"Yet the things you named, like my brother's murder for starters. You weren't there and didn't know the truth any more than anyone else, until you received the vision. Besides, you were a child when it happened. How can you blame yourself? My mother too? You didn't do any of this to her, including putting her in this sleep. Why is it solely up to you to awaken her? No one believes that. The same with the others. Why put these burdens on only yourself?"

"It's complicated. I feel responsible for what happens in the visions, like I should be able to find a way to change the outcome."

"You're wrong on this one and too hard on yourself. We're very alike remember? An Elder once told me that." He smiled.

"Alika's words I believe, but we said it could've easily come from another Elder." She smiled over at Seth.

Seth smiled back. "Yes, I would say the same as Alika." He paused. "You said the one thing would be your undoing, but I'm not convinced." He gazed in her eyes and clasped one of her hands. "Dante is right. This will be your undoing, claiming burdens that aren't yours to carry and placing them upon yourself. You're not meant to bear it. You're not alone either, but you continue to be so, even when you sit in a room surrounded by those who care for you."

"There are certain things I think I understand, but the struggle of the moment snatches away the truth. I'm left back where I started again."

"And you aren't the first student to wrestle so, and I know she won't mind me sharing with you. Not long ago, Lana visited me one evening, unable to sleep. She grappled with her decision to allow Black Dragon to take more supplies, though it was necessary to obtain further intel. She encountered the same feeling of being alone, but she was not." He waited.

"The aloneness, seen through the eyes of a leader. She's not responsible for the outcome, but always a voice whispers different. The one that says she gave the last order and made the final decision." She paused. "Like with the visions. I say I'm only the messenger, but when the vision comes, it's empty words."

"No, truth remains. Constant. Unchangeable. Despite our feelings, child."

"Which is what you told Lana."

"In so many words. I also told her some lessons must be repeated many times. Although they appear simple, they are hardest to grasp at points in our journey. This is one of those truths."

"I heard similar words from another Elder only hours ago, and from the Ancient One." She closed her eyes briefly as a single tear slid down her face, but a smile finally broke through.

"It's time to take our advice. All give wise counsel. It's good we're in agreement." He glanced at Dante. "She's smiling again. A good sign, Dante."

"It is." He wrapped his arms a little tighter around her. "How are you feeling?"

Her eyes twinkled. "You make a comfortable chair, Dante."

"You are feeling better." He grinned.

"Although you must be uncomfortable by now, so I'll get off you." she laughed, as she started to rise.

"Oh, no you don't. Remember, I brought you over here." He kept her pulled down in the chair with him and laughed. "I'm good, right where you're at."

"Are you, now?"

"I am, but I figured out how to make this more comfortable."

"How's that?" She wound her arms around his neck the rest of the way.

"You're overdue for this." He closed the gap, to begin enjoying a long kiss with her.

Seth got up beforehand, chuckling in anticipation of how the teasing would go between the two. He checked on the others, to allow Dante and Angelina time.

"Kate is doing better," answered Lana.

"Yes, she's feeling better."

"How much better?" asked Alena.

"She smiled, laughed, and managed to give us a hard time about a couple of things."

"Is she right there with you?" asked Alika.

"No, she's not. She and Dante are still speaking at the moment." He glanced over and grinned, seeing them enjoying another kiss.

"I see," said Alika. Everyone but Iban picked up the unspoken in Seth's comment. Alika grinned as did Ryan and Alena in the room with him. "Sounds like she's back to her normal spirits thanks to you two, and Dante continues being an encouragement. Still the right call to end things for your group after that incident. It will be time to wrap things up for our groups soon, so we can return and evaluate the process. We'll be in touch once we reach a better stopping place."

Seth came back over.

Angelina asked, "Time to go?"

"No, still finishing up. Enjoy your time with Dante." He winked at her.

"That she can do." He smiled as she kissed his cheek, rested her head back into the crock of his neck, and wound her arms back around him. He wrapped his arms snugly around her waist again, content to have her close and calm.

"Iban, a pleasure working with you," said Alika.

Alena nodded. "Yes, absolutely. The patients are in the best care."

"We won't stop searching for the answer to help them." Angelina cast a sad look at Anna's still form.

"I know you won't give up, but you three act like you're going away forever."

Alika spoke up, "No, but Ryan needs my focus on other things, since we created a system with this, so I don't anticipate assisting with this part much anymore. For the other two, Lana mentioned other tasks she will hand over to them. Isn't that what I understood?"

Ryan momentarily forgot the cover story, but his adjustment was flawless. "Yes, he's right. My plate is overflowing with the recent developments. His help with the other is essential."

Lana agreed, "I find myself in a similar situation now. Occasions will still merit their expertise with this process." She smiled towards Alena and Angelina. "There are always unforeseen things, but their counsel is proving invaluable to me on the other necessary tasks. They'll turn their attention to those matters."

"I hoped to see you three again, but whatever they pulled you to do, it must be important. Stay safe. It appears a harder task for some of you." He glanced at Angelina.

"I'm fine after my latest mishap, but you're not the first to tell me. I'll attempt to do better, but I appreciate your concern." She smiled at him.

"I'm glad you weren't harmed, Kate. This is the group to have your back. Based on your visits, you won't be offended if I ask about you, when I see the others?" He chuckled.

"There's not a truer group of friends, and today proved that again. I earned the other, so I can't be offended. Hopefully, you won't be unhappy with their answer." She laughed.

Dante smiled. "We'll find a way yet, to keep you from trouble."

"I'm glad you were here today, Dante. You literally saved me. If you hadn't jumped in when ..."

Dante came over, but reminded himself they were in the open with Iban. With a friendly touch on the shoulder, he said, "We keep each other safe. Just relieved it ended like it did." He grinned. "I don't want to do it again, so how about you listen to Iban, Kate?"

"Just this once. I owe you that, Dante."

Lana turned to Iban. "We'll be back soon. Until then."

"Until then, Lana. Goodbye to you all."

CHAPTER THIRTY-SIX

Seth and Alika sat in one corner of the fortress room sorting the results from the colony visit.

"Everything is consistent, Seth."

"Yes, it bore out our original conclusions. If the mark appeared, the blood poured black. No mark, the prick showed red."

"Still a lot of data to track the colonists and create a manageable process to streamline it. Luckily, Alena and Angelina always had a talent for this type of work. They put it to use on more than one occasion. Now we get to help your group. They should be familiar enough by the day's end with the process."

"Agreed." Seth sighed. "We'll miss your two, for far different reasons than this."

"Yes, difficult goodbyes lay ahead. Especially for two young men here."

"I don't know if they'll let your two students leave."

"It will happen. Angelina will see to it despite her wish to stay. She won't risk overstaying her time with your group and endangering them. It's her fear."

"Alika, your young student holds many fears, many burdens, and she worries me terribly. Today, it frightened me to watch."

"I see it more times than you imagine. Let's locate the interview and listen together. I need to hear what happened between her and the colonist."

They listened in silence, to the replay on the data pad screen. At its conclusion, Alika sighed. "Dante ended it in time. The colonist rendered her unable to function again."

"Alika, she believes she can't defeat it, and says it's the same battle from before. I'm assuming she refers to the battle you alluded to, the first time we spoke."

"You guess correctly, my friend."

"You said she came through it, though it was her hardest struggle."

"I did, but what does victory look like, Seth? It's a different vision depending on the eyes of the viewer, the lenses it's seen through. Alena and I saw victory and continue to tell her, but it doesn't matter. It's what she sees, which pours into her heart and mind."

"And she sees failure."

"Something much darker. The worst possible scenarios are encompassed in her head and brought to the brink each time. What could've been, and just because it didn't that encounter means nothing."

"Because it can happen the next battle." Seth felt the weight again for her. "She blames herself for everything in the visions too. Things she could do nothing about."

Alika's eyes became sadder. "The never-ending battle with her. Her role of messenger becomes engulfed with the intensity of the vision. Some of our most severe arguments ensue because of it. She came apart that evening when she stepped on the planet and the horror of her vision's reality lay before her from the device. It brought up everything, all the visions and not being able to stop any of them. I challenged her right there, although it shattered us both to do it, and I'll never forget it. Seth, she was so angry, but so full of pain too. Somehow, she needed to make it her fault. As if it would take a piece of the suffering away, make the planet whole again."

"Yet it won't. I'm sorry, my friend." Seth paused, giving Alika time for the mist to pass from his eyes and wipe the tear sliding down his face. He asked quietly, "Who is the one that haunts her so? Who she couldn't save?"

"She wouldn't tell you, would she?"

"No, and you can't either?" Alika's face gave the answer. "Then tell me, could she save the one as she believes?"

Alika took his time answering. "The truth is, it doesn't matter what I believe, as with other facets of her world. She believes she could, and it distorts her perception of everything else." He hesitated. "Seth, there's no possibility she saves the one. She tried, but through no fault of her own she couldn't. It was too late.

She isn't to blame for any of what happened. There's the truth, but no one can convince her of it."

"How is a single battle this powerful, and visions so intense they wield this sway over her?"

"It only explains a part. With the other pieces haunting her, I'm not sure I could see differently either. Alena and I keep those pieces close." His eyes focused on Angelina, the expression changing to a father, searching for means to protect his child from what future heartaches laid in store. Yet he came up empty, and returned his attention to Seth. "I'm grateful for the counsel and comfort you and Dante provided her today. She's happy, and her spirit is peaceful again for a bit."

Ryan shook his head. "You're amazing, Alena. You broke this down enough for even me to get."

"Stop with that." She poked him playfully. "You're a smart man. They wouldn't let you go around commanding fleets, if they doubted your judgement."

"But this takes another way of thinking, and I was drowning when we got our first look. Thanks, Alena."

"You're welcome. I always have a soft spot for you," she teased and noticed him still staring at her. "What is it?"

He clasped her hand. "I'm thinking how I'll miss you."

"You got this, Ryan. I've full confidence in you."

"I'm not talking about that."

"I know," she whispered. "I'll miss you too."

"The waiting between seeing you will be terrible."

"The Black Dragon will keep us occupied."

"That doesn't make me feel better, Alena." He pulled her over, and looked down at her with worry in his eyes.

"We'll all be fine, and we must believe so." She stared back at him and put her arms around his neck. "I'm not gone yet. Let's enjoy the time I'm here. We still have this evening."

"We do." He kissed her and murmured, "We should finish this other up."

"Yes, I don't wish to get you in trouble, Commander."

"I'm too deep to escape now, if this is trouble." He laughed. "I don't wish to either, Alena." He kissed her again.

"How is she?" asked Caleb, pointing to the screen.

"Seemingly better," answered Dante, nodding he caught Caleb's motion. He pressed something on his data pad, and watched Caleb's screen again.

"Good to hear." He scanned the screen again, as they continued working and talking. "Was it that close, Dante?"

"In retrospect, yeah, but I didn't register the dagger, until I brought my sun-spear in motion. All I wanted was to stop that woman from saying another word to Angelina. Things turn out for the worst, if Seth or I weren't there. Seth moved to intervene at the same moment, but I took care of the threat first. If it's Angelina on her own, then it's no for sure. The exchange completely immobilized her, like with Trey's spirit."

"The colonist had three groups to work that ploy. Why your group? Better yet why her every time?"

"The same question bugs me too, but it wasn't about the ploy. The colonist wanted her words to render Angelina like the other day, broken from whatever this past is she locks away." Running his hand through his hair, he shook his head. "There's nothing I can do."

Caleb put a hand on Dante's shoulder. "Hey, not true. You do what you can with the pieces you get. Give yourself a break. You make her happy and calm her down. Everybody sees that. You feel helpless not knowing. That's got to be frustrating. Like if you see it all, you could do more." He paused. "Kind of like in battle, when you're forced to go in without all your intel. Maybe a layout of the place, or weapon capabilities, or as basic as who's in charge now. If you know, maybe you meet the challenge and handle the unexpected curves you find better. Sometimes we don't get it all, and who says it ends up helping. We work with the pieces we get thrown, make good with them, and it turns out to be enough. Keep working with what she gives you. She'll give you enough to help her." He grinned at Dante. "You know she's crazy about you. Half the time she can't get her words out, because of you."

Dante laughed. "You guys got to stop. She's only done it a few times now."

Caleb laughed too, shaking his head. "It's Alena's fault. She gives her more grief about it than we ever thought about doing. Your girl doesn't mind, Dante. We only tease those we like."

"She should feel well-liked."

"She is and will miss it soon."

Dante sighed. "Yeah, she will."

"She'll miss one person a lot more." He lightly jabbed Dante. "You can't convince her to stay?"

"No. Whatever this past is with her identity, she made it clear, it puts us in danger to stay for too long. She won't relent, no matter how persuasive I am."

"I believe you if you say it can't be done, since I've witnessed some of your persuasion on her. You're impressive." Caleb grinned again. "Enjoy the time she's here."

"I plan on it." He grinned back. "We better get back to this before we're in trouble with Lana."

"Won't happen. You forget I possess powers of persuasion with Lana." Caleb laughed, but focused back on the screen.

CHAPTER THIRTY-SEVEN

Lana scanned the screen and said, "I can't believe what a smooth process this is with this much data and people, Angelina."

"Yes, we did well with the time we spent, and with only our group carrying out the exams. It's a bit to manage at first, but there's a way."

"A fair number came from other places to help. It looks like many at first, but the truth is ..." Her voice trailed off as her hand went to her necklace, where a small piece of pottery hung. An image displayed on the pottery, but it was indiscernible without more of it.

Angelina's eyes followed the motion to the necklace, and then she focused on Lana's face. She finally spoke quietly, "There should be many more. I'd give anything to have them back too, Lana." She paused and asked as though she didn't know. "This necklace, reminder you wear, who is it from?"

"Emily, a little girl from the colony. She and her family perished in the attack. We saw their home or where it used to. All gone, like a thousand firestones extinguished it. Nothing left. No sign of life. No sign of Emily." Tears glistened in her eyes.

Pain coursed through Angelina, as Lana's grief opened anew. "I'm sorry. There are no words, Lana. I remember her from the monitorings. The same sweet little Emily?"

"Yes." She looked up, initially surprised, but realized she shouldn't be with Angelina. "What she told us uncovered the supply swap."

"She was helpful, but that's not why you miss her, why you hurt so for her. Tell me about Emily, this little girl." Angelina smiled and clasped Lana's hand.

"You should have met her. She was only six. She ran up to me, bursting with excitement to see me because I wasn't Lana, not like this anyway. I was Princess Lana to her. Someone I forgot existed, but that's all she saw. There was something wonderful about it. The title in itself didn't matter. It's what it meant to her, and I can't put it into words. It flowed from her, how she saw things, like an innocence still remained about her, despite everything she had seen from the Black Dragon. She stole everyone's heart with us. Commander Gabe found himself reduced to tears, inspired anew by her. He left a different person that day. His eyes still mist over now when he remembers she's gone. Dante couldn't resist her charm either. She was taken by him, her hero with the sunspear who fought off all the Black Dragon troops." Lana smiled at Angelina through her tears and Angelina smiled back, squeezing her hand.

Angelina waited, because Lana had more to tell. "She said one day she'd be brave and fight the Black Dragon, like us. She was already brave, but she didn't see it. I told her she didn't need to, because I..." Lana's voice broke, "I'd keep her safe." The tears flowed freely now. She whispered, "But I didn't. I failed her. I failed little Emily. How could I fail her?"

Angelina pulled her over and hugged her. "No, Lana, you mustn't think that." She couldn't say more, because she understood as she had always done, like no one else could. Together, they wept for more than Emily.

Ryan and Alena looked up and noticed the two, but a glance from Alika and Seth stayed them. Dante and Caleb peered up the same instant, and immediately started to go to the two. They were stopped as well, but by Alika's and Seth's physical presence. Even without hearing the conversation, Alika and Seth had watched it unfold.

Alika said, "Your heart instinctively moves you to comfort, but stand back."

Seth agreed, "They find themselves in a similar struggle, and perhaps a peace is found in the midst of it."

"But it feels wrong to watch her cry, and do nothing," said Caleb, his face wincing.

"He's right, but I trust you two." Dante whispered, "It hurts though."

Alika said quietly, "Because you both care for them as you do. Dante, Angelina once said the exact words as you did as she prepared to watch one's heart broken and many tears spill. I tell you, as I told her, 'It always does for those who walk the path and those who must watch them." He sighed and placed a hand on each one of Dante's and Caleb's back.

Dante stared back at him. He wanted to know.

"On the ship, Dante, when we arrived the first time with your mother. She watched Seth take you to the room to tell you everything, the truth of what happened on that day in your family's past. Your pain would cut deeply, and she would feel and see it with you, as only she can."

"Experience it," Dante whispered, as a tear ran down his face without warning, at the knowledge of what her seeing encompassed.

A quiet fell over the exhausted faces of Angelina and Lana. Yet their thoughts intertwined as they found their voice.

"Lana, you can't blame yourself for what happened to Emily or any of them."

"I see her there, promising her. I should've protected her. There had to be a way, should've been a way. Why couldn't I find it, Angelina?"

"Because it wasn't there for you to find, Lana." Her voice broke. "Yes, there should've been a way to stop it, but if it existed, I didn't see it either. We can go over it a billion times and never glimpse it. We're left at this same place."

"With this feeling it's my fault, because I didn't see the solution. A way to save her. It'd be easy to believe everyone, when they say the opposite."

"But it's not simple, and Emily is the one who shatters that world for you. There are those who enter our world to create such joy, but topple everything we know in the same instance. Yet we wouldn't ask to take away the moments, the wondrous time ever of them being a part of our world. I don't know how we sort it out, Lana. To be told repeatedly you could do nothing, you were helpless in the face of such misery, but everything screams to you differently."

Lana stared back and clasped her hand. "You understand, because of the visions alone, but there's more you don't tell. You feel it though, the questioning, the second guessing forever. It's horribly unfair..."

"Cruel, inescapable at moments, and it doesn't get better with time." She paused. "Emily possesses a beautiful, sweet spirit and wouldn't wish you to carry this burden. She'd never want to be the source of your grieved spirit." She took a deep breath. "Tell me, what is this piece on the necklace?"

"The only reminder left from my day with Emily. We found it sticking out of the ground where her home once stood. She begged me to remain and have tea with her that day. She had a unicorn tea set she loved, and this is a piece from it. I wish I had stayed and indulged her, but we left to pursue the answer at the warehouse. I gave her what amounted to trinkets, and promised to tea with her the next time I visited. Another broken promise to her." Lana's voice cracked again. "I never dreamed the next visit would ..." She couldn't finish.

Angelina whispered, "None of us did." She gave Lana a minute before continuing. "Lana, they weren't mere trinkets to her. I believe she treasured them, because they were from you, her Princess Lana. She grew fond of you and Dante and Commander Gabe in that brief meeting. What did you give Emily?"

"A scarf and the matching hair pin."

"Did you simply hand them over to her?"

"No, of course not. I put them on her." Suddenly it was reminiscent of talking to Seth. Angelina wanted her to see something important. "I told her she looked beautiful, like a princess, for those things to remind her of us, and to be brave if she got scared again."

"Still believe they were mere trinkets? Emily would disagree. Lana, it's what she saw each moment she wore them. It was time spent with the giver, the words of the giver, and the heart of the giver."

"Angelina, I also told her the Ancient One would protect her, and He let us help do that when I gave them to her. Can you still say such kind words of this giver?" Her voice shook, as tears threatened to fall again.

Angelina fell silent for a moment. "Only days ago, I heard one speak these dying words to his son in comfort, 'It does not always come out as we envisioned." She paused, composing herself again as the memory swept over her. "He found peace in those words as did his son. I'm still struggling to find it, with what happened to him. Ethan spoke truth, and I know that deep down, Lana. The Ancient One does protect his own. Always. He privileges us to help, but it's not how we envision, every time. Emily belongs to the Ancient One, and her life is in His Hands as it always was. Wherever she is, whether here or with Him, she's forever safe." She clasped Lana's hand. "So yes, I still say it was about only one person who mattered to Emily that day, the giver. Emily was ecstatic, because she got to see a Princess, not just any Princess, her Princess. Lana, Emily loves you, and she always will."

Lana stared back at her. She understood her, but now she sat at a loss. This one battled such inner chaos constantly, and couldn't quell her own shadows, but for others she knew their battles and poured out comfort she couldn't give herself. "Who are you, Angelina?" she whispered, as tears flowed anew.

Angelina smiled at Lana through tears of her own. "I don't know anymore," she hugged Lana, "but I'll miss you when I leave."

"I'll miss you too, Angelina." She hugged her back.

"Yet I didn't convince you to loosen that weight from your neck which rests on your heart."

"Did I persuade you to lighten your burdens from the visions?"

"We remain as we were."

"No, it feels lighter, Angelina."

"It does, but I'm not sure how. Ready to finish up?"

"Absolutely. We can't have our two guys finish before us." Lana laughed.

"Done," said Dante. Relief flowed through him at seeing Angelina and Lana absorbed back into work. "We can go help them now."

"Sure, help them. That's why you want to go over there." Caleb grinned. "Me too. Come on."

"Can we help?" Dante asked as he stood behind Angelina and massaged her shoulders while waiting for an answer.

"Yeah, how close are you to knocking this out?" asked Caleb as he perched on the couch's arm beside Lana.

"Twenty minutes, maybe?" she answered, waiting for Angelina's confirmation.

"Dante, where did you learn that?" Angelina sighed.

Caleb laughed. "You lost your help, Lana."

"Apparently."

"No, I said I would, Lana. Dante, you must stop. I can't with you doing that."

"You're sure?" he teased, leaning close to her ear as he continued the pressure on her shoulders.

She sighed again. "Yes, if I'm to finish this with Lana."

He brushed a kiss on her cheek. "I promise to finish later." He sat next to her. "How's that sound?"

"You know." She gazed at him. "What other hidden talents lay in you?"

"Stay longer with me, and find out."

"Don't I wish." She ran her hand over the side of his face. "Sit here and be good, so we can be done, Dante."

"I was being good, *very good*." He winked, winding his arm around her waist.

"Lana, let's get done before your cousin distracts me further."

"I've no command over my cousin in that area. In fact, I encourage him. You keep him smiling. Anyway, you don't wish him to stop, Angelina." She laughed.

"You're right, and he knows that too." She turned to him and lightly kissed him. Gazing into his smiling face with those soft brown eyes again, she couldn't grasp how everything reflected in them centered on her.

"How are Alena and Ryan coming?" asked Lana as the four worked together completing the rest.

"Looked like they finished a few before we came over and are talking now," said Caleb.

Angelina peered over at them. "We got this. Give them the time." Her voice softened. "Being tied to my world isn't a good thing, and she must wish ..." She stopped, realizing the words didn't remain in her head, and studied the screen again. "We're almost through."

Dante exchanged a glance with the other two, but none of them said anything. Clearly, she didn't want it addressed. She navigated a complicated world, but he was staying in it too. Nothing would cause him to regret his decision.

CHAPTER THIRTY-EIGHT

Alika asked, "Everyone comfortable with the process?"

Caleb shrugged. "Slow going now, but a couple more times at it, even with training others, yeah, we'll be good, right, everybody?"

A cascade of nods followed, and Alika smiled. "You are excellent students, and our services are no longer needed here."

"Hey, I didn't hear anybody going there," Ryan spoke up, looking at Alena.

"He's right." Dante's voice rose in alarm. "You're not leaving tonight, are you? You can't. Not yet." He turned to Angelina and clasped her hand while tightening the arm encircling her waist.

Alika answered, "Calm down, you two. Not tonight. The plan is for tomorrow."

Silence descended over the group. They had known, but hearing it spoken changed everything. The reality finally struck home. Goodbye laid only hours away.

Dante pleaded with her, "There's something keeping you here. There must be."

"There has never been *something* keeping me here. Always *someone* drew me here and creates my longing to stay." She ran her hand through his hair. "It's because I care for you, I won't stay longer. No harm comes to you or the others because of that desire."

"I wish it could be different." He stroked her cheek.

"Me too." She forced a smile. "But I haven't left yet. This evening is ours again, and we'll see each other tomorrow. Don't look sad, my Dante." She wrapped him up in a hug.

A pained look crossed Lana's face and Caleb spoke up, "Some people would like to spend tonight together, as soon as possible. Let's get dinner out to make that happen for them."

Ryan started to get up to help, but Caleb stopped him. "Hey didn't you hear me? You and Alena, and the other two, sit down. We got this. Your time is spent better here."

"Thanks, Caleb. I know Dante agrees."

"Anytime." Lightly slapping Ryan on the shoulder, he followed Lana.

Angelina moved her utensil around absently on her plate through the noodles.

Dante asked, "Are you sure you want to spend time with me tonight?"

"What? Of course, I do. Why are you asking such a thing?" She startled at the question.

"You'll never finish dinner, at that rate."

"You're right." She sighed and put the utensil down. All eyes turned to her now. "Don't you wonder how three entire planets got attacked, undetected?"

"We did find out. The colonies didn't check in when we contacted them." Suddenly, Dante gasped as he realized what she meant.

Caleb finished the thought. "Alarms should've gone off, but we never got a signal they were under attack."

Lana said, "We said their communication probably got knocked out first or jammed in some way, but looking back ..."

"All three planets, and not one stray communication slips through from an individual colony?" questioned Ryan.

"It borders on impossible, but you knew because of the vision, Angelina," Seth pondered aloud.

"Yes," Angelina answered. Dante sensed her frame stiffen as she dreaded the forthcoming questions, but an expected reaction, with the grief the visions caused her.

Seth continued, "I'm sorry to ask, but did you see anything in your vision to indicate how they managed to attack undetected?"

Dante felt her frame relax. Whatever question she anticipated didn't happen. "No. I saw all the forces, ground and air, fully engaged and visible to the eye. There's no reason they go unnoticed," she hesitated, "but we formulated an unpleasant theory to explain it."

"Let's hear it. It's more than what we have," said Caleb.

"I've no evidence to support it, and I hoped my tap into the database fragments on our planet visits would yield a clue. However, my data pad chats came up empty. I still need to go through further downloads, but I don't expect to find anything with the damage to them."

"When did you do that?" Dante looked at her in amazement.

"I always find a way. I'm afraid we discover our answer lies in the words of someone I detest, but I quote Trey, 'It has already started.' What they did screams of an inside person, inside access. It wouldn't be the first time someone pretended to be with our group, and served the Black Dragon's interests." She paused, seeming unable to accept her own words. "There's one thought."

"Your guess explains a lot, but if it's right, we're in deeper trouble than we thought," Caleb groaned.

"Exactly."

"What's the other one?" asked Ryan.

"The Black Dragon has a busy agent, at least under the Dark Lord's reign, who changes her appearance at will. She goes in and ensures communications will shut down before the attacks began. She must do this beforehand, since he dispatched her the day of the attack to deal with Abigail."

"Lana has impressive access," Caleb said.

"You all do. Any of you become excellent candidates. Honestly you don't need Lana's access," said Seth.

Angelina nodded. "Nothing close to it, which complicates things. Gain the trust of someone with some of Lana's access. Make the right connection. Once someone believes you belong to their side, they're easily manipulated. The impostor only needs sufficient access to get the rest, or to weasel his or her way over time to gain the trust of the person with all the access. For example, an administrator with the proper connections or expertise, potentially causes a galaxy of trouble." She saw eyes on her, the unspoken question. "We navigate a different environment than your group is accustomed and experience more than you wish to ever know. It wouldn't benefit you to enter it, so I won't take you there."

"If you're correct, who are we looking for, Angelina?" Seth asked.

"A most dangerous individual. Once they're all in, there's nothing they won't do to see it to its endgame, no price they won't pay. I promise, you don't want to stand near when it comes crashing down on the one, least you be buried in the rubble."

Dante watched as she looked down, and a shadow settled on her. His hand slid down her arm, and he kissed her forehead. When she looked up at him, she smiled at him, and the shadow passed from her.

Alika watched also, knowing where her thoughts retreated. "All variations of the same theory. An inside agent of Black Dragon, either one who always existed which is unknown to us, or Black Beauty, or ones newly created by the poison."

"Any of which explains it. All equally terrible, but answers won't come tonight, so enough," said Lana, as she turned to Angelina. "Go with Dante." Then she turned to Alena. "Go spend time with Ryan."

Angelina asked, "Are you sure we're done already?"

"Go now." Lana hugged her. "Don't take anymore of my cousin's time from you."

"You heard, Lana. Come on." He smiled, as he took Angelina's hand.

CHAPTER THIRTY-NINE

Dante laid the drinks on the table in his quarters, as he went to her. Wrapping his arms around her waist from behind, he rested his head on her shoulder and kissed the side of her face. His eyes closed, while he took in everything Angelina. She felt wonderful and soft engulfed in his arms, as he whispered, "What has you entranced, my Angelina?"

She continued leaning back into him as she peered out the window into the night sky. More than anything she yearned to stay safe and cared for in the protective walls of his arms. Yet soon she'd plunge back into the darkness and walk the delicate line, to get what she needed. Alika warned her at the beginning about the dangers of navigating this world she entered. She thought she did it successfully, but past scenes flashed before her with nagging doubts following them, causing her to wonder if unknowingly she had moved into the shadows. Closing her eyes and breathing deeply, she yielded completely to how wonderful Dante felt, with his arms around her. She'd give him her full attention this last night, before she left. "Nothing out there." She turned around in his arms. "You though ..." She grinned as she wound her arms around his neck and begin kissing him. It was a slow, explore every inch of his mouth seduction, and she controlled every part of it. He surrendered to her, letting himself be caught in her mesmerizing spell. He didn't realize how much, until she had already eased him down on the couch, where they had spent the previous evenings.

"How did you do that?" he murmured in her ear, as she cuddled up beside him.

"You aren't the only one with moves, and I can lead you where I wish, my Dante."

"You are sneaky."

"I'm trained well."

"I see."

"I'll never lead you astray, though, my Dante. You always have me." She stroked the side of his face.

"That I know."

"I intend no more distractions tonight."

"That won't do, because I love your distractions." He ran his hand through her hair.

She laughed. "I meant nothing distracts me from you this evening. I promise plenty of those distractions tonight."

"Good because I'm inspired to take a turn." He grinned as he pursued the warmth of her lips again.

"Any idea, when you come back?" asked Ryan as he stroked Alena's arm while she cuddled next to him on the couch.

"No. Just depends on what we find, once we dig."

"Those last operations turned out dangerously close. I wish your group would allow us to help."

"What we do is better suited for the two of us. It's an entirely separate world, as Angelina alluded to earlier. A different set of skills comes into play. She practices it more consistently than me, since she handles most interactions with the ship dealers, but we both do it with the other operations."

"What set of skills?" The way she said it put him on edge.

"Portraying a part, pretending to be someone else for the time needed. Like that of a Black Dragon troop but without becoming Black Dragon. We won't do the evil things they do, but we look the part, and our speech in every way matches it, when we're in their world. We won't make it out if not. Same with the shipping encounters. Angelina takes on the role of her environment to get what she needs, but without going too far. It's a constant balancing act, in a harsh business. Sometimes she worries she goes ..." Alena stopped. "She's the best at what she does though."

"You worry she comes too close sometimes, what it does to her."

"With the need to get the information, I do wonder. Playing roles constantly causes the line to become blurry. Like withdrawing a toll from her, a little at a time. I keep telling myself, it's because she's that good, so convincing, when she immerses herself in the role."

"Do you talk to Alika about it, or ask her?"

"Both. We discuss the findings, so we routinely check in with her. Many times she brings it up first. She doesn't cross a line in her actions. Simply because there are countless ploys for your actions to appear one way, without it being the case, in our line of work. Mostly, it's the speech matching the role which bothers her. Words leave as ugly a mark as the end of a blade, in instances. All three of us had to do it at points to our pain, and we wouldn't take it back. It proved necessary at the moment, but some stay with you despite all your efforts."

Ryan read in her eyes one stayed with her, and its recollection pained her. "What was this moment for you, Alena?"

"I can't tell you the details, but Alika and I did it and would again without hesitation. Otherwise, Angelina dies that day. Our words ended up adding to her pain. We said the opposite of our heart to save her life. Enough she ... it crossed her mind, we betrayed her."

Disbelief shone on his face. "She would never think that."

"Only crossed her mind, but we were convincing, Ryan. We had no other choice. Her life stood in the balance."

"I can't fathom how hard that had to be, even to save your best friend. Not a battle one wishes to face, Alena."

"We don't get to pick our battlefields. Rather, they come to us. With many waged, the aftermath is felt, long after we believe the battle done."

"I'm sorry, Alena," he whispered.

"Me too, but we did what we had to." She paused and stroked the side of his face. "Ryan, we know it's not a game. We'll keep doing whatever it takes."

"I just can't imagine something happening to you." He gazed in her eyes as he cradled the back of her neck and head.

"It won't. I'll come back to you, Ryan," she whispered, as he began to kiss her.

"I gave my word," Dante whispered.

"You did." She sighed, as he massaged her shoulders.

"You thought I'd forgotten." He planted a string of kisses on her neck, while continuing the pleasant pressure on her shoulder.

"Silly me," she murmured.

Dante chuckled. "You should stay with me. You'll miss me too much."

"This is another form of your seduction."

"Call it what you will. Is it working?"

"I do wish to stay, Dante."

"Let me start arranging it now."

"You would."

"Say the word, Angelina," he whispered, as he kissed the side of her face.

His warm breath on her ear, and his kisses with the unceasing massage, caused all kinds of wonderful havoc to her senses, and he knew it, too. She desired to give in and say yes to staying. She longed for normal, to grab what others had so easily. It stood there offered freely, but she couldn't accept it. Not yet. All because of the world she found herself thrust into, the one she couldn't leave. Hence, she somehow didn't give him the answer she wanted, but the answer she must, "I will when the time comes, and I can, Dante."

"I'm going to miss you, my Angelina."

She placed her hands on his and turned to face him. Placing his face in her hands, she gazed into his soft brown eyes. "I'm going to miss you too, my Dante." She wrapped him up and began to kiss him again, as his embrace engulfed her.

"I can't believe it's time." Dante pulled her cloak on her. "I should've said no leaving, until we finished all the dessert." He glanced up from tonight's empty dessert plate.

"Dante, it's like twelve slices. Maybe, two weeks from now we finish it."

"Exactly."

"You know I couldn't stay that long." She squeezed his entwined hand. "Time to head to the ship."

"Hello, you two." Alika smiled, as they walked in and sat.

"Hi, Alika." Dante forced a smile.

"I know. Alena is in her quarters, for a bit. A difficult evening for those two as well. It's expected, Dante. I don't fault you, and I won't tomorrow, when the moment arrives. Your Angelina is beautiful in every way. I'm told your father agreed." Dante's smile came easy, as he remembered the exchange with his father. "Yet, for a season it must be this way. I'll join Alena in her quarters, to go over things and give the two of you time to talk more freely this evening, take your time with your goodnight." He patted Dante on the back, as he left.

"He just put it out there, didn't he?" said Dante.

"Sometimes he uses the direct approach." She cuddled into him.

He wrapped her up and took in her closeness. "I want to stay like this. I won't be able to let you leave tomorrow."

"You must. We must."

"You told me a hundred ways why, but none of them makes sense, when I'm holding you like this. I hate letting you go back into danger."

"I'll return to you, Dante."

"You have to, because I can't do without you now." He kissed her.

They stood at the ship's entrance, as the previous nights. "Goodnight, my Dante."

"Goodnight, my Angelina." He pulled her into his arms and kissed her. He held on to this kiss longer than the previous nights, not wishing to leave her. Finally, he released her and walked to his quarters for the night.

Alika and Alena emerged, as she retreated from the cockpit window. Her tear-filled eyes met theirs while whispering, "It must be like this, right?"

Alena nodded, as her eyes matched Angelina's eyes.

"Alena, I'm sorry you chose this path with me. I take away your chance of happiness. It's not right."

Alena placed her hands on Angelina's shoulders. "Stop. You do no such thing. Our path together brought us to them. Being with Ryan the way I wish is only postponed, as yours is with Dante. It won't always be the case. We must believe that."

"I'll miss him so much, Alena."

"I know. I get it." She hugged her. "Let's speak with Alika and get some sleep."

"You all right?" asked Caleb.

"Another emotional day, and tomorrow will be worse."

"Yeah, but there's no way to make that easier. Not even your cousin can change Angelina's mind. It looked like it got intense between you and her earlier."

"It did. She keeps everything bottled inside, but somehow she pushes that aside and gives to others in a way which amazes me, Caleb." Immediately, the conversation between her and Angelina spilled out.

"To think she blames herself for everything in those visions. Those three planets alone are enough to take somebody over the edge. Then there's something else that tops that somehow for her. I don't know either, how she talks like that to you about Emily." He reached over and wrapped Lana up. "Now we do our part to keep the colonies safe. At least you two won't face anymore of those nightmares."

"What if we can't, Caleb?" She wrapped her arms more tightly around him.

"We will, with everything in us, I promise," he said as he kissed her.

CHAPTER FORTY

Where was she? Angelina surveyed her surroundings, but didn't recognize this place. Maybe an open field, but she couldn't be certain. Either night invaded it, or a fog seeped into every crevice. Yet, something more settled around her. More than the haunting appearance of the place. An unnatural stirring vibrated, through the unseen cover. Why was she here? A familiar dread crept up, as she strained to peer through the terrifying blanket hiding whatever lurked around her. Suddenly she could stand it no longer and spoke, "Come out and face me."

"I'm here. We're all here," the ghastly voice crooned.

Instantly, a figure emerged ahead of her from the sinister veil. It revealed a shadowy figure in Black Dragon attire, but it faded in and out. No, it couldn't be, but her eyes didn't betray her as the individuals changed before her eyes. Yet they were solid enough, and she knew them all. Pulse racing, her mind spun with the possibilities of why she saw them. She tried getting both in check for whatever awaited her, as she held her ground with her sunspear poised for battle. She waited for the figure to advance further, but it stood fixed on her with cold, stone eyes, displaying in its hand a long dagger.

"You escaped the end of a blade like this many times, didn't you? Seconds before it plunged in, and you were no more. Always cheating us of your life's blood. Hardly fair. Not just the blade. You writhed from Death's grasp in many ways, didn't you? Too many. How many times do you believe are left before it finally captures you? What will the snare be? Will it be the blade slowly slicing through your flesh, an explosion reducing you to your true nothingness, a plummet to shatter you into a million broken pieces, fire engulfing your body until it's mere ashes? No, it'll be creative, won't it? Because we're talking about you. My bets are, your own breaking point finally does you in. Now, that will be the sight to see." The figure laughed. "We both know it. One day, it all consumes you. Your sunspear can't help you. No one helps you. Death overtakes you, because it shadows you." Still holding Angelina's eyes, the figure stroked the dagger and stepped closer to her. "But we both know, your death is not what you truly fear."

Suddenly, Angelina sensed it. A crowd of people joined her, but no threat originated from them. In fact, she knew them in some way, several more intimately than others. She wanted to confirm it, but didn't dare leave her eyes from the figure before her.

"Go ahead. Look. I'll stand here and not harm you while you peek. I promise, this once, to keep my word." The figure grinned.

The figure would do so because it wanted her to see those behind her. Slowly she turned, keeping her sunspear poised. She saw people she knew and treasured. Some she met briefly like Anna from the colony, and they waited further back from her. In the front stood those close to her spirit. She saw Abigail, Christopher, Alika, Alena, Seth, Lana, Caleb, and Ryan. Then the one closest to her heart, Dante. She turned back to the figure, and something changed. The dagger was covered in a familiar sight. The red liquid glowed eerily, as it poured in a steady sickening stream unto the ground from the blade. Then she turned pale as she recognized the figure now bearing the Black Dragon garb, and an acquainted rage found its way into her eyes.

"Yes, your true fear. Don't I know it well? Death finding one of those dear to you. A bloody dagger. A memorable sight, is it not, my worthless daughter? You recall whose blood found its place on this dagger by my hand. A shame yours doesn't decorate it too. It's fine. With time to consider it, I concluded, better for you to stay alive, to keep reliving it. I enjoy watching it, more than killing you. Yet she's only one. What will the final count be? I wonder, is there another's blood mingled with it? You couldn't make it in time to save her. Who else will you fail, daughter? Who else's blood will be on your hands?"

Her voice shook. "No, it wasn't my fault. I tried to get ..."

His voice mocked her. "Oh, yes, we know how much you believe those words. You failed her. Now she's dead, because of it, and you can't ever undo it. A couple of minutes, and you couldn't give it to her. Such an ungrateful child. The question remains. Who else's blood is mingled in this because you don't get there in time?"

Her voice trembled further. "Enough! I would undo it, if I could. I couldn't stop you then, but you're dead now, and can't hurt anyone else."

"I can though, girl." The figure became Black Beauty. "Who will it be? Who feels death first with the dagger? Maybe I come back, and finish the one. Make Abigail bleed this time, but why stop there? Make it a family affair. Strike down her beloved son Dante, too. Do the job right, and get rid of the whole family line." She pointed with the dagger, to the two behind Angelina. "You can't be everywhere at once. One day, you won't make it, and my dagger will deal the final blow to one or more of them. You cannot stop it." Black Beauty stepped closer.

"Don't come near them! I won't allow your hands on them. I will not have anyone else taken from me." She tightened the grip on her sunspear.

"Oh, she'll succeed, because I trained her well." The figure transformed again to reveal the Dark Lord. "She failed me at the last, but now she's hungry for revenge. She'll satisfy it, and it'll come in the form of a bloody bath. She's an assassin, skilled in the art of torment. Her victim will suffer many times over, and you'll be helpless to stop it. She'll make me proud. Who will it be I wonder?" The figure laughed, as he took another step.

"Not another step or I'll take you out." Angelina dug in, but the figure stepped dangerously close now.

"They're right. Eventually, you lose." Trey appeared. "The only question is how it unfolds. Maybe you finally lose your duel with death, and the others are left for the picking. The other likely possibility is, you fail one or more of them. You simply aren't there at the moment when they need you, and their blood is laid out on the floor. You have a history of that." He waved the bloody dagger in his hand, and advanced another step towards her.

Instantly she found herself up against a rough, solid surface. Tree bark? Where did a tree come from? She couldn't move, and he pushed her against the tree further with the bloody dagger securely in his grasp. She succeeded in using her sunspear to block the dagger from penetrating her neck or chest, but made no headway getting enough space to mount any attack. He watched her in amusement, his face so close she felt his breath. "Who else's blood will this dagger boast? It holds a child's blood, little Collin, right? You thought we forgot? We didn't. Your dear mother's blood too. Who will join them, Kate? You can't protect them all." He dipped his fingers in the blade and rubbed the blood between them. A grin spread across his face. "The possibilities. Who will be the next one you can't save? The next sacrifice?"

"Noooo!!!! Never again! I won't let you!" With all her force, she moved against him with her sunspear. It still did no good with the angle he pinned her against the tree, and the figure's eyes looked beyond her to those behind her. He stared back at her, and laughter erupted from him, one fueled with cruelty and bent solely on the creation of suffering. The figure began changing repeatedly, a reminder of all her visitors. "We are the darkness. All your fears before you, and we will take away everyone you care for, one at a time. We promise you, and that is one promise no one stops us from keeping."

CHAPTER FORTY-ONE

"Alika, get over here, now!" Alena yelled as she rushed to Angelina's quarters. Alena stood in shock only for an instant, as she surveyed Angelina standing in the center of the room, still asleep, with her sunspear fully activated.

Dante woke up from a sound sleep, struggling to breath and sweat pouring off him. He turned to the display. 6:05. Something happened to her. He reached out and got no answer. Momentarily, he started to get up and leave, but halted when he received no prompting this time. He sat up in silent agony and waited.

"Angelina, wake up! It's me, Alena! Put the sunspear down!" There was no effect. "Alika, hurry!"

"I'm almost there, Alena."

"Be careful. She's got her sunspear drawn, and she's asleep standing."

"Understood."

"Angelina, you must wake up! It's only a vision. Please, hear me. It's Alena." Alena initiated her own sunspear to block a blow if necessary.

"I'm here." Alika came over. "Oh, my, it's as you described. We must safely disarm her."

"Not an easy feat, but we have done it more than once now."

"I'll get it." He returned a moment later. "Ready?"

Alena put away her sunspear. "Ready."

He sighed and shot what resembled a small capsule through the air with a tiny needle on the end. It struck Angelina's arm, and she lost her footing briefly. At the opening, Alena grabbed the loosening sunspear, while Alika caught Angelina, before she fell to the floor.

"Got it, and I'll get water," said Alena as she placed the sunspear aside. Meanwhile, Alika lifted a mumbling Angelina off the floor, put her in bed, and removed the dart object from her.

"What happened?" asked Alika, as he sat at her bedside, studying her as he brushed her hair back.

"I heard her mumbling, but nothing major. She does so in her sleep regularly you know." Alena glanced sadly at Alika. "Pretty soon I heard her yell something like, 'no you won't again.' I ran in to find this."

Angelina's mumbling increased again, with her head moving sideways more frantically. Alika said, "We must get her awake. She can't remain in this state any longer."

"Agreed."

Alika gently shook her by the shoulders and spoke firmly, "Child, you must wake up now. It's only a vision and can't hurt you. It's Alika. Come now, awaken." He sat her up and placed a sturdier hold on her. "Please wake up. We're here. You're not alone. I say you are held no longer by these false images before you. You are a child of the Ancient One. Now, hear my voice and open your eyes, my child."

With a gasp, she did. Her breaths came in pants, and her eyes struggled to focus as one unable to trust them. "Alika, Alena, you're okay." She brought them over in an embrace and cried. Alika and Alena hugged her tightly, knowing they would soon learn the terror behind her eyes.

Leaned against the wall in her bed, she sipped the water Alena offered. Eventually her hand stopped shaking to hold the cup steady. She nodded, and handed it back to Alena to set on the table.

"You saw a vision?" asked Alika.

"Not a vision. A nightmare."

"Those look similar sometimes. Are you sure?" Alena asked.

"Yes. A vision always comes true. A nightmare is a reflection of my fears, of what could be. It was the latter."

"What did you see?" Alena prompted.

She glimpsed the display and groaned. "Let's get showered, dressed, and I'll go through it before we meet the others. There's enough time. I wish it hadn't ..." she shook her head.

Alika asked, "What is it?"

"Dante is having a fit. It woke him up, like the last time. He'll be nuts, by the time we're there." She took a deep breath. "Come on. Let's get moving."

Dante caught his breath and climbed from bed. He paced the floor of his quarters, the debate ongoing in his head. Finally, the overwhelming terror from Angelina receded, but it didn't ease his alarm. Why didn't one of them call? He settled on a shower and getting dressed though the meeting time was at least two hours away.

"Alena is getting dressed now. She jumped into the shower, as soon as I finished mine," said Angelina.

"Efficient as usual. You're calm now. Considering the scene I walked into that's comforting."

"What exactly did you walk into?"

"You standing in the center of the room, completely asleep, but with your sunspear activated and poised for battle."

"Like in my nightmare. Terrific. Thankfully, I didn't harm either one of you."

"I'm sorry, but we used a dart on you." He smiled.

"Don't apologize. It's the safest way to bring me down in that situation. Feel free to do it again." She smiled back.

Alena plopped down next to her. "I'm ready."

Angelina closed her eyes momentarily, and steadied her breathing, reciting the encounter as best she could remember. They listened, visibly troubled, and clasped her hand or touched her shoulder in reassurance. Finally, with several stops and starts, she managed through the terrifying account and shook anew at its conclusion.

"No wonder you were in such a state," said Alika.

"I waited too long to check on you."

"Alena, you didn't know. You'd never rest if you got up every time you heard me babbling in my sleep. I'm accustomed to getting little sleep."

"I wish it weren't the norm for you. Quite the array of scary visitors. I'm sorry." Alena wrapped her arms around Angelina's shoulders.

"They knew everything even if they weren't present for the event, as with Trey's spirit." Alika frowned.

"Yes, my true fear revealed for them, and they echoed Trey's sentiment they knew me. Perhaps too well for the future." She stared at the ceiling.

Alika said, "That last one in the list unnerved you."

"That I'll eventually lose it? Ironic, isn't it? They wave a bloody dagger before me while threatening me with my horrible approaching death, and it doesn't bother me at all, but that one part left me shaken at my core. It's like they shone a light inside me to the darkest part and found my demons, this unending chaos I stay in, because of it all. I'm coming apart. What if it's the truth, one day?" She got up and stared out the cockpit with her arms across her chest.

They walked to her. Once she turned to them, tears glistened in her eyes. "Child, come here," said Alika, hugging her as Alena stroked her back.

Angelina murmured, "I'm afraid sometimes."

Alika said, "I know, but it's not the truth. We'll keep you together."

"You worry about protecting others, but someone must keep you safe. We will."

Angelina nodded, and she spied the display. "It's time, and we'll go through this again once we enter the fortress. I must pull it together. This isn't fair to Dante. It's our last day together."

Seth came down with Ryan, Caleb, and Lana trailing him. Initially, Dante rose from his chair at the sound of approaching figures, but sat back down with a sigh, when he recognized the faces.

"First one down again, Dante. You're ..." Caleb halted his teasing at the despondent expression on Dante's face. "What's wrong?"

"I don't know, but there is." He ran his hands over his face to entwine them behind his head briefly before resting them back on the table.

"How do you know, cuz?" She put her arm around his shoulders.

"I felt it around six. It woke me, like when she couldn't sleep, from the visit to the colony after the attack."

"You sat alone all this time?' asked Seth.

"Not entirely. I paced in my quarters until I couldn't stand it, showered, and dressed. Then, yeah."

"Why didn't you call me, so I could keep you company?" Ryan sighed. "Nothing from them?"

"Not a word."

"It's almost time for them to come, cousin. We'll know soon." She squeezed his shoulders, but cast a worried look at Caleb when Dante didn't respond.

CHAPTER FORTY-TWO

"Did we get them all?" asked Alena.

"Yes," replied Alika, holding both bags up.

"I'm glad somebody remembered." Angelina didn't manage another word, as she crossed the fortress entrance, when Dante assailed her.

"What happened, Angelina?" His hands firmly gripped her shoulders, and his eyes held hers.

"What are ...?"

"Don't what me." His voice tried maintaining calm, but frustration spilled out as he commanded an answer. "Start explaining. I've been worried sick for hours, and I asked you to call me whatever the time, Angelina."

She put her hands on his arms and said in a soothing voice, "I know, Dante. Let's all go over here, and I promise I'll tell you. Please, my Dante. This is our last day together for a while."

He sighed and melted. Without a word, he hugged her tightly and burrowed her head into his chest. A moment later, he pulled back slightly. "No more delay. We talk now. Come on." He led her to the couch.

They all sat. Dante wrapped his arm around her waist, stared up in her eyes, and waited.

"Only a nightmare."

Dante shook his head.

She sighed. "An extremely, intense nightmare."

"They're the same as your visions?"

"No, Dante, not the same. There's an important difference. A vision shows what will be. Sometimes it's not entirely clear, but it'll happen. A nightmare is one's fear coming to life in images. The hope is it's nothing more. That it never finds substance in reality."

"Whatever the images, I felt your terror. What did you see?"

"If I tell you, you must remember the entire time what I said. You all must. Do you promise me, Dante?"

"I promise, Angelina." He clasped her hand, with his free hand, and watched her with troubled eyes.

"I stood outside in an unfamiliar field. It was dark, foggy, or both, and I felt a dark presence. The figure emerged in front of me with a clean dagger, but kept changing persons. They all had one common thread. They were loyal to the Black Dragon, and all ones we killed at some point, except for Black Beauty. A few took turns speaking to me with personal conversations, mostly involving the dagger. Early in the encounter, I looked behind me because I sensed another presence. It was you all and others I met and care for in some way. When I returned my attention to the Black Dragon figure, the dagger dripped in blood, and the figure continued to step closer to get past me to those around me. The conversation continued in the same vein, but the figure intended to use the dagger on those behind me in the future. At the end of the nightmare, I positioned my sunspear up in front of the dagger between the figure and those behind me."

There was quiet. She recounted it nonchalantly, brushing aside the terror of the encounter, but Dante had felt a taste of the fear that tore through her earlier. "Who did you see from Black Dragon?"

"Many. Unnamed troops we've killed, ones from the facility ..."

"Come on. That won't work. Who spoke to you directly?"

She sighed. "Briefly the woman colonist from yesterday. The more drawn-out conversations included Black Beauty, the Dark Lord, Trey." She bit her lip and looked down.

She named off company scary enough, to have anybody sleeping with their sunspear cuddled beside them. All the worst Black Dragon agents, visited in one nightmare. Yet as he watched her something stirred, and he gently pulled her chin up. "Anyone else?" He searched her eyes and saw.

"Yes."

"Who?"

"I can't."

"Why not?"

"Before your time. I'm sorry."

He sighed, "Your past."

"Yes."

"What did they say to you?"

"All amounted to the same thing. Any of them would love to use the dagger to end me. Death will catch up to me eventually though I escaped it thus far. Pleasant Black Dragon sentiments. They concluded my real fear was one of you being killed. They vowed to get past me, and I wouldn't stop it in time, like before. I'd fail again, and they'd win again. They taunted me with which one of you it'd be this time."

"Stop it in time? Fail again? Who were they talking about?"

She froze and stammered out her answer, "Um, Collin, yeah, they said, like they murdered Collin."

He examined her face. "No, you couldn't stop that because you didn't even know."

Such a careless mistake in her words. Although she despised doing it, she'd make her inner battles serve a use. "Dante, it doesn't matter. I long established I'm responsible for many things everyone says I'm not, and I continue laying claim to it."

"But you're not, and you must stop doing so."

"I try, but they knew that about me as Trey's spirit did before. They latched onto it, and my greatest fear being I'll fail to protect one of you. I'd blame myself for not keeping you safe, if something happened to one of you. They're right. My greatest fear is losing one of you."

He stroked her cheek. "What about you?"

"I'll do whatever I must to keep you safe, whatever the cost, surely you know that."

Dante's voice rose as his hands grasped her shoulders. "Stop, Angelina. Don't you see? I do know, and it scares me to death. I don't want whatever cost to you. You tried brushing it aside, but I heard it. They threatened your life a hundred different ways in your nightmare, and you treat it as nothing. Though your life is tossed away, means nothing next to anyone else. I need you to stop, because I'll worry every second for you. Angelina, I need you to care enough to protect your own life as you do mine and those around you. Can you? Is it in you anywhere? You matter, your life matters. You are everything to me. How do you not see that by now? I need you to see, and I'm begging you. What else must I do? Tell me, show me, anything. I'll do it, I promise." He didn't realize how much he needed her to, until now.

His eyes, burning with an intense anguish, caused fresh pain to course through her heart. "Oh, my Dante, what have I done to you?" She brushed his cheek with the back of her hand and placed a soft kiss on his cheek. "I never mean to hurt you." She should've told him the truth, that she couldn't say. Yet sadly, she did tell him the truth. She always put everyone's life before her own. Anyone who got close to her saw it, so he knew. However, reminding him today of all days bordered on cruel. He needed reassurance now, not further reason to worry. "Dante, I'll protect my life because you value it, and I wish to share it with you. That promise I give you."

He whispered, "That promise I'll take, my Angelina."

Her arms eased around his neck while whispering, "And I'll seal that promise properly." She gave him a kiss.

He smiled at her when their lips parted. "I'll admit, that helped you." Brushing a strand of her hair back, he regarded her with his usual care. "Well?"

"Dante, they did know I'd blame myself, if something happened to any of you, and they mentioned Collin's death with the bloody dagger. They weren't talking about Collin on the other part though. I lied to you when you asked, and I'm sorry."

"Why did you do that?"

"Because I can't tell you whose blood."

His memory stirred. "The one you couldn't save. Is it the one?"

"The same."

He saw her wince at the memory. "Who confronted you about it?"

"I can't say anymore about that part."

Her earlier refusal to name one of the visitors must tie into this painful incident, and pursuing it further would get him nowhere. He moved on from the topic. "The nightmare came from your fears, but were there any specific threats?"

"No, just a broad threat to you all. The purpose was tapping into my fear, that they would kill one or more of you eventually to hurt me."

Dante stroked her cheek again. "And you? Anything specific on getting to you?"

The words haunted her, but she attempted pushing it aside. "Uh, nothing useful." She tried holding his gaze, but the nightmare intruded.

He searched her eyes. "No, there's something. Don't do like before, my Angelina."

She whispered, "I won't." She paused. "The figure toyed with me by rattling off possibilities of how I'd die in the future, drawing on the ways I cheated death previously. Strangely the figure wasn't a part of the encounters."

"That specific of a list?" Worry returned to his voice.

"Yeah, the list included a blade, an explosion, falling from somewhere high, f ..." she stopped.

"And?" He watched as she stared down at her hand, as though she didn't recognize it, before the moment passed.

"A couple of others got named. One from my past."

"Involving your hand."

She sighed. "I'll let you have your guess."

"The other one?"

"It's the only one that hasn't occurred." She sounded unsure as she said it. Many times she felt dangerously close. "The figure thought it amusing to toss it in the mix because of my momentary state of mind."

He watched her unsuccessfully pretend to brush it aside. Fear consumed her eyes. "It got to you, and it still does." Entwining his hand in hers, he held it against his heart. "I'm here. What did the figure say? Tell me."

She closed her eyes for an instant and gazed back at him. "The figure suggested my demise wouldn't come from one of them, because I'm the source. My death will be my own breaking point, and the figure laughed at seeing it." She murmured, "Just talk, meaningless mind games. Nothing more."

He knew she didn't believe her words, as he wrapped her up. "Yes, that's all it is. Like you said at first. We'll not let your fears find life, and I won't allow anyone to hurt you, my Angelina."

"We'll bring lunch over to you two," said Alena.

Dante gave her a grateful look as the others left them. "Angelina, you still should've called me. I almost burned a hole in the floor with all the pacing I did. You're impossible at times." He ran a hand slowly through her hair.

"Parts of the nightmare I couldn't share because of the past. Anyway, Alena walked into a chaotic scene first from what I understood. The focus became disarming me." She spotted the alarm in his eyes. "I was asleep, but standing up with my sunspear fully activated, when Alena came into my quarters."

"Angelina." All the possible disasters bombarded him, which thankfully didn't materialize. Even with Alika and Alena both stopping her, he wondered how they managed.

"Alika is always prepared with me. His aim is impressive with those disabling darts. One grabbed my sunspear, and the other kept me from meeting the floor. All in a morning's work." She winked at him.

"Couldn't leave it alone, even on your last day here?" Only she found humor at being shot down in her sleep with a dart. He pulled her closer. She drove him insane, but captivated him too.

She grinned and whispered, "Now what would the fun be in that, Dante?" Closing the distance, she brought him in for a long kiss, as she left the morning's images behind.

He murmured, "Plenty, but I'm fine spending the rest of the day like this."

"We have work today, Dante."

"What did I tell you about working constantly?" he teased, soft and seductive, on her ear.

She giggled, as he lightly tickled her side through her shirt, and his warm breath remained near her ear. "I forget, Dante."

"Four days with me, and you're encountering a memory lapse? I don't believe you, so I'm continuing this reminder."

She laughed harder, as he kept his word and managed to sneak a couple of light kisses on her neck at the same time. "You must stop. I can't breathe."

"Not the first time I left you in that state, and you never complain, my Angelina." He eased up, as his eyes took a different look now. They had that soft, intense focus to them as they rested on her, and his arms wrapped her up tighter.

"I won't ever, my Dante," she whispered as she met his gaze, and a delightful warmth passed through her. She stroked the back of his neck with her fingers. He left her breathless, countless times now, with a single kiss, and she loved it. She didn't get another word out as he did it again, delivering a kiss so intoxicating every fiber of her hummed with pleasure.

CHAPTER FORTY-THREE

Caleb chuckled, as he laid their plates on the table in front of them. "I didn't have the heart to interrupt you two earlier."

"Appreciate that." Dante smiled as he glanced at Angelina, who leaned up against him.

"Yes, I'm better, thanks to Dante." She returned his smile, and said to the others, "Dante and I can eat while we all talk."

Lana nodded. "Based on last night, our group will concentrate on formulating a way for the colonists to alert us of an attack, and do our best to protect the colonists during another attack. We'll update the commanders on the findings first."

"There's also training a group, to take over weeding out the turned colonists," said Caleb.

Ryan said, "Which may not be easy. How do you prepare someone to handle another colonist like Angelina met? Nobody is ready for that."

Angelina said quietly, "None of us expects for that to happen again, do we?" She glimpsed the apologetic look from the others, and Dante squeezed her hand. "It's okay. I accept she came for me. She capitalized on my weakness and exposed it, leaving me defenseless when she attacked. It's a long-time Black Dragon tactic."

Dante matched her subdued tone, "Springing from their master. I remember Seth preparing me to face the Dark Lord, and I didn't conceive how many ways my mind could be turned and twisted. I asked Seth if that was how the Dark Lord would attack me." He turned to Seth. "You said it was different for everybody, and told the truth. He used something else, but he got me to the same place he wanted. A place where I doubted everything I believed, and piece by piece I threw it aside. What I almost exchanged it for, I can't fathom I did such a thing." He looked down.

Angelina lifted his face. "My Dante, you aren't the first to find yourself in such a dark place. Don't keep taking yourself there. It didn't bind you, so don't allow it to take hold now. You're with us, where you belong, and our fear for you didn't become reality. Nothing else matters." She hugged him, and his arms wrapped around her too.

Alena and Alika exchanged a glance. The paradox struck both of them, as they heard words echoed they had spoken a hundred different ways to her, but it got nowhere.

Seth said, "Dante is right. There is a similarity between the Dark Lord's deception and the turned colonists. We're sometimes unaware of our vulnerabilities."

Alika agreed. "Which means though we don't expect it as a normal ploy, anyone could fall victim to the manipulation. Choose wisely your team, and train them well."

Angelina said, "We'll concentrate on locating the device, while you prepare for the worst outcome. Your group isn't immune to the poison. We saw its aftermath and those discs too, so you can't go to the planet like this." She put a hand on Dante's bare arm and tugged on his shirt.

"I thought you liked this shirt," he teased.

"I do, but the man under it I care for, and I must keep him alive."

He kissed her cheek. "You will."

"I better, Dante." Her voice held a command seldom used with him. She turned to the group. "No matter what happens, you don't meet the threat unless you're in full gear. It's the new normal for everyone. You could end up helping ground forces, even if you start out in the air. An operation to a planet can turn hostile rapidly. Enemies hide under the cover of colonists, as Trey did. You have your sunspear or sword, but they have this poison, the dispersal device, and these disc weapons. One shot in the right place, and it's over. We saw those soldiers. If not that, it's a torturous sleep for who knows how long. With more time, they could invent a new way to disperse the poison. No leaving without gear on must be the rule."

"Although I detest it, this is the new world we find ourselves in," said Lana.

"We won't be fighting for long, if we don't put on full armor, especially now." Ryan paused. "There's only one person I picture rushing out of here without suiting up."

"Me too, and I'm taking care of it now." Angelina focused on Dante.

"Me?"

"Yes, you. You can't look surprised because you know it's true."

"Why would you think so?"

"Our teachers speak true, that we're alike in many ways. It's because I know you Dante, better than I know myself at times."

"I'll be in gear before I hit the battlefield, okay?"

"Not good enough. You must promise me, Dante."

"Why?"

"Because you'll never knowingly break a promise, especially to me." Her eyes watched him, unwavering.

He sat, amazed at her faith in his word. "You're right, I can't imagine breaking a promise made to you, as you wouldn't break one given to me. I promise, I'll make sure I'm in full gear before we enter battle, or if it seems we're entering a dangerous situation. Are your concerns lessened, Angelina?"

"Yes, Dante, I'm satisfied with your answer." She kissed his cheek.

"Why do I doubt you, Angelina?" Ryan grinned.

"He can be reasoned with." She winked at Dante.

"Is that what you called it?" She prepared to move on, but he stopped her. "What about you?"

"What do you mean?"

"Don't give me that. What about you in full gear?"

"I'm always in full gear, as is Alena. The whole hiding our identity thing."

"When you do a shipping deal or get intel too?"

They all caught his meaning. "Dante, I'd mark my death going in full gear for a shipping deal or getting intel."

"But you don't know who is who now. Colonists turned Black Dragon. And you told me the other evening, the type of company you associate with who could become engaging in unpleasant ways if given ample time. Those shipping dealers are excellent candidates for Black Dragon."

She could say lots of things to him, but a seemingly inappropriate reaction emerged. She laughed. "Dante, you listen well to me."

"Usually, you consider it one of my better qualities, and what's funny about this to you?"

"This is one of the times I wish you didn't listen closely to everything I said, because it makes this difficult to maneuver out of."

A hint of a smile showed. "Thus far, you're managing poorly at it."

"I maneuver out of tight situations constantly."

"You won't from this one, despite how you distract me."

"A shame there's not time to try, Dante."

He started to give into her distraction rather than pursue the current questioning, but he begrudgingly restrained himself. "Angelina, the full uniform, the shipping deals, unsavory characters."

She sighed, "I understand your worry. It appears you're taking all these measures to remain safe, when I'm doing the opposite, but I'm not. I'm blending in with the crowd, wearing the garb of the business, and talking and acting the business to ensure safety."

"I get it, but I don't like it. Is there any way to be better protected?"

"I already do. It's worn under clothing and called armor breathe in many circles."

Dante did a double take. "Armor breathe? I know of it. It appears thin, but it's made of a lightweight metal material which appears almost woven. It's strong and resistant, blocking blades to an extent. Hard to come by. At least I thought."

"Basically correct. Difficult to procure without the proper connections which we have, but you still can't obtain a large order. We keep a supply for ourselves with backups. We secured more before we came, because I felt prompted to do so. After what we learned since our arrival, it's no longer a mystery. I'll let Alika take over."

Alika got out a couple of bags and pulled out a suit of armor breathe from one. "There's a suit for each one of you, and it'll fit with no problem. One of the unique parts of its nature is the manner it adjusts to the wearer."

"This doesn't replace the full armor in the other situations." Angelina looked at Dante.

Alika smiled at her reminder to Dante. "Exactly. In certain situations, full armor raises more suspicions as Angelina said, so this is in order. Seth can disperse these later."

Alena added, "The suit gives, like any armor, if your enemy's blade plunges hard enough, but it may prevent the death blow. Part of the armor's protection is a mental thing, since it's under you and unseen. Since they don't realize you have armor on, they usually send the strike with less force. It's an unconscious thing on your enemy's part. They expect immediate flesh and bone, but they encounter armor, and don't know why."

Ryan finished, "And sometimes the only thing separating life and death is a second to regain the upper hand, and fight another day."

"Exactly."

"I've never worn anything made with it. How does it feel? Can you move in it freely? Can you really not tell it's worn under?" asked Dante.

Angelina answered, "It's surprisingly comfortable considering its makeup. It moves with you, and it's seemingly stretchy though not in the true sense but agreeable enough many wear it straight on their skin. Alena and both found we could do it. Neither one of us preferred it, but in a short time we didn't feel it anymore. Like wearing regular clothes. Normally, we wear the lightest layer under it, called skin clothes or air clothes." She saw the looks. "Yes, the same commonly prevalent in seedy circles, but it has other purposes. Then we put regular attire on over the armor, like normal."

"There's an obvious solution." Alena grinned.

"True, seeing for oneself works better," Angelina answered. Dante watched, as she scrolled through her data pad in her usual whirlwind pace, and it jarred his question from a couple of nights ago. He'd ask her today. She stopped on something, but hesitated opening it, as she addressed the group. "I'll show you one of my trips, with me wearing the armor. Remember everything is different in the shipping world, including attire. You may have to leave in a hurry if a shipment doesn't go as planned. Attire is made to work in a real sense, but its deceptive appearance makes it seem someone's mobility is constricted. I assure you it's not. The wardrobe takes on a very snug fit, but it's the atmosphere to blend into the environment." She hid a smile. Dante's reaction could be entertaining.

The recording projected before them, with her stepping from the ship to play the shipping dealer role.

Dante stared at the projected image of her, frozen before them. She told the truth. Nothing indicated the armor underneath. She stood all in black from head to toe. He recognized her attire as the stretchy, leathery look-alike material common to those expected to always be moving. Yet as was characteristic, its appearance hinted at no give. It was indeed snug, as Angelina described. Beyond snug. With her slender figure and incredible curves, the black pants and shirt appeared molded to every inch of her shapely form. If not enough, her satin wavy brown locks cascaded down, as they caught the dancing beams of the sun, and added to her irresistible allure. Then he found himself drawn to her eyes, shining the same beautiful blue he loved, and he lost himself in them. Her expression was different, as someone preparing for a transformation of sorts. One who could go from engaging to calculating, or seductive to cold, reminiscent of how she toyed with Trey. Yet, Dante felt better by what he glimpsed, a reassurance she'd do whatever necessary to keep herself safe. If that meant going from a comfortable chat to running a sunspear through someone, she'd do it. One thing stayed the same, as his eyes continued sweeping over her image. She stood absolutely breathtaking to behold, and she was his. He became enthralled by her beauty again, his heart skipping a beat, as he tightened the arm wrapped around her waist.

He held back the urge to pull her over the rest of the way, and steal a kiss from her right there.

"You uh, I mean ... it's perfect, flawless ... you know the uh ...armor." He stumbled his words out.

"I'm glad you're impressed with what you see," she teased.

He turned to her and grinned, knowing he was caught. "You wear it well. I certainly can't deny it." He took a sip of drink.

The others couldn't hide their grins, at seeing the tables turned on Dante, and Caleb and Ryan barely contained their laughter.

Angelina asked innocently, "You look flushed. You okay?"

"It's suddenly warm in here for me, but you warned me it would happen." He pulled her closer and kissed her cheek. "You better take your image down, for my sake."

"I did forget, Dante. This demonstration served its purpose, and more." She laughed as she flicked off the image. "You're a good sport with the teasing." She brushed his cheek with her fingertips.

"No harm done. I enjoy it from you." He kissed her hand, and settled on it clasped in his. "I remembered about asking you something, when you searched through your data pad."

"Remembered?"

"Yeah, I started to a couple of evenings ago, but got distracted," he smiled at the memory and saw her do the same, "and we never returned to it."

"What has you burning with curiosity, Dante?"

"Burning for sure," he murmured and shook his head at her word choice, after the last exchange. "There were tons of transmissions and activity on your data pad the day of the attack, to retrieve the dispersal device, and the days leading into it. The three of you never said what kept you busy those days. So, what did?"

Silence held hostage the room. Angelina exchanged glances with Alena and Alika. None of them rushed to tackle the question. Dante sensed Angelina tense at it, but she reluctantly answered, "We engaged in an operation related to the situation at the time, and brought in our source we work with a great deal to assist.

Many transmissions include ones with him. There's no way we accomplished it without his help. The operation ... it ... I ... we can't disclose about it."

"You can't disclose it? Why can't you?" Dante stammered.

"We promised it would stay with us, and breaking that promise puts others in grave danger."

"You can trust us. No one in this room will betray your confidence."

"Dante, there's no one we trust more than this group, but it's like many things. The more you know, the more dangerous it becomes for you. The knowledge won't help us with any of the answers we seek. Don't ask to take on this burden. Either way, our group won't put anyone in danger. We gave our word."

"I know what your word means, so something else to add to the list of mysteries."

Ryan added, "I wish everything didn't involve people dying, if word got out. It doesn't make us feel better, about you all leaving today." He glanced at Alena.

Alena replied, "We're uncertain, too. In a sense, we're starting over. For every piece of information we obtained, we raised more questions to answer. There are several directions to chase them down, all with varying degrees of risk and time. Some yield answers. Others nothing. All take precious time, that we can't afford to waste."

Seth asked, "Where do you start?"

"Our main source first. Anyway, we're concerned for his safety, with the new and improved Black Dragon soldiers. Perhaps he's heard possible chatter, about the changed power structure at Black Dragon."

Angelina sighed, "We expect the device information will be harder to come by. It'll reveal itself in indirect ways, like changes in shipping patterns for the supplies. I'll hang out with engaging company," she heard Dante groan, "and see if something useful slips out. There are places to check from Black Beauty and downloaded information from the data pads we confiscated, including Trey's data pad. Maybe it has a useful chat, leading to where Drew wandered, and a location to the device." She saw Dante start to protest. "I get you hate the idea, but everything must be considered now. The shipping dealers may hold the key."

Caleb asked, "How?"

"Use the greed, marking this profession, to our advantage. The shipping dealers we wish to concentrate on are a varied batch. The line of morality is a strange thing. In some situations, the extent of your problems is making sure you got everything you paid for, but others you best have your weapon ready to remedy the situation. Just like that line, there are some as greedy as they are and who throw aside every scruple, they care about preserving their own skin enough they'll not do business with Black Dragon. Make no mistake, there's no loyalty to your cause either. Yet they're willing to supply someone else not afraid to deal with Black Dragon. Which brings us to that other group, the direct suppliers to the Black Dragon. They're beyond greed, all boundaries vanish before them, and they only see what's gained at the end of the deal. They live for the payoff and the rush from it, but aren't satisfied with the traditional payoffs many times. They'll use whatever means to get that elusive payoff, including a blade without hesitation and don't care that one day they'll likely be at the end of a Black Dragon blade. They ride it to that end, until it drains their last drop of blood. One or all of those could serve us as cold as it sounds."

"Wait a minute, you said you don't work with those. I won't have you go against the rules keeping you alive thus far. You'll find another way." Dante listened for as long as he could stand, before cutting in.

"Dante, I'm sorry, I didn't mean working directly with them." She rubbed his back as she addressed the group again. "If we find out which dealers supply Black Dragon, we can track where the supplies are going, as before."

Dante sighed. "Find the route to the supplies, find where Black Dragon are hanging out."

Lana whispered, "and risk walking into a whole army of Black Dragon, or one of their agents."

Caleb added, "before you get a location of the dispersal device."

"Every operation we do has that risk," said Angelina.

"You barely lived through a few of them," Dante paused, "and it's more difficult now to pick out these Black Dragon agents." He wrapped his arm around her.

Angelina settled back against him, and encircled her arms around his midsection. "Honestly, we're not too concerned about running into mutated shipping dealers turned Black Dragon."

"I don't understand."

"In a sense, nothing changes for Alena and me. Shipping dealers serving Black Dragon do so willingly, without any coercion. Exposing them to the poison and marking them is unnecessary, even counterproductive, in the world they operate. Why chance marking them, if these dealers have always done their bidding?"

Caleb finished, "Because, at some point, Black Dragon figures out that we have unraveled the mark, and if you want to remain undercover..."

Lana continued, "You don't mark everyone."

Angelina nodded. "Alena and I will continue trusting no one and using our same methods to discern friend from foe. We have warning, if we spot the mark. If there's no mark, it won't help. They could still be Black Dragon, but we simply know not to count on our blaster. We're not the only ones that can't depend on the mark." She looked at Alena.

Alena said, "Our sweep definitely eliminated the ones the Black Dragon *marked* on that part of the colony."

Ryan's look changed to horror. "Some we cleared could still be Black Dragon."

Seth sighed, "And on the loyalty spectrum to Black Dragon ..."

"Only the most," Angelina replied her voice taking a gentler tone, "As we discussed before, Black Dragon has always had those, serving them in the shadows. The poison only makes apparent what was hidden. A heart loyal to Black Dragon is with or without the mark. Yet hope remains. The Black Dragon's unwavering trust in one's loyalty doesn't always work for them, because they can't see the condition of one's heart." She smiled and looked over at Dante. "They found their deceptive hold didn't possess the strength they believed, even over years of bondage. There is a stronger claim, that broke through with the right prompting."

Dante smiled back. "Once the Ancient One claims one as his own, they are secure forever. My father and I were reminded of that."

Ryan's eyes widened. "What about Iban?"

Angelina smiled. "An advantage of the gift from the Ancient One. Iban is clear. With the time spent with him, I'd know by now."

CHAPTER FORTY-FOUR

"Did we cover everything for your group, Alika?" asked Seth.

"Yes. Lana, how about you?" asked Alika

She hesitated, and Caleb gave her a perplexed look. "I think, we're good." She peered at Angelina, who leaned contently against her cousin, with his arms wrapped around her. They were happy, so she couldn't.

Alika studied her and glanced at Seth. Seth asked, "Lana, are you certain?"

When she didn't answer immediately, Alika said, "Lana, something remains unanswered for you. We'll get it from you, as I possess much practice in this art now." He smiled.

"I feel wrong, even cruel, asking. I fear I take someone to a frightening place for my answer, and I don't wish to be the cause." Her eyes rested on Angelina.

"I believe she should decide whether she wants to answer."

Angelina smiled and said, "Lana, I know you'd never be intentionally cruel to me. Something bothers you deeply, and I won't leave you like this. Whatever it is, ask, and if I can answer, I will. I intend to wait."

Lana fingered the necklace. "In all the visits to the planets, with the countless bodies we saw either lying dead to be cleared, ready for the incinerator, or lying in a torturous sleep, there was not one child. They can't be turned Black Dragon, so they are either all dead under the rubble," a sob escaped, "or taken prisoner."

Angelina nodded to Dante and got up to sit beside Lana, putting her arm around her shoulders. "How long have you wondered? You should've asked me before."

"I didn't want to cause you pain, by asking about the images from the planet. I know you couldn't sleep from them, and blame yourself. To ask you about it, I just couldn't."

"But this is not the way, and you can't remain in this state. You wish to know what I saw with the children."

"I do. I see Emily, and I'm sorry, Angelina. Forgive me, for what I ask. I don't wish you pain." Lana's eyes glistened with tears, as she met Angelina's eyes.

"There's nothing to forgive in your request. The pain is seeing your grief, and knowing my words won't ease it. Lana, I saw nothing of the children in the visions of the attack. Not as prisoners, slaughtered, or their bodies laid out dead."

"They could be prisoners. Being tortured. Angelina, I can't ..."

"That didn't happen. The visions are more than images. They encompass feelings, impressions too. Although I didn't see the children in the visions, I'd realize if that happened."

"Then they were all ..." She looked at Angelina, pleading for another answer.

Angelina stared back at her, visibly struggling, and desperately yearning to give her something, but understanding herself unable to do it. "The visions of the attack showed me only what you saw on the planets, Lana. Total destruction unleashed on them. No one could escape it, except by the Ancient One Himself ..." She bit her lip, seeming to compose herself. "I witnessed no children in the visions, Lana. I can give no words to comfort you, and I'm so sorry." Lana sobbed openly now, and Angelina hugged her as Lana's grief poured through her, as the previous day. Caleb's eyes glistened with tears at his wife's grief, and Angelina nodded to him. He pulled Lana to him, as Angelina released her. Angelina closed her eyes, and put her head in her hands, hating herself for what she had done. She could do nothing for Lana, and yet... no, Lana must continue to shoulder this grief. But for how long? Instantly, Dante settled beside her on the couch, and wrapped his arms around her in comfort. She allowed his solace to soak through her, as she fell into his embrace.

"Should I feel better or worse, Angelina?" asked Lana, with a weariness to her voice. "If they were prisoners, they'd be alive, but in the hands of Black Dragon. Is not death the kinder of the two? At least one is with the Ancient One, in death."

"Death seems a better fate, Lana, but the next time I wonder of the outcome."

"What do you mean?"

Her eyes swept across the room at the others. "This will sound cold, but I'm looking from a Black Dragon viewpoint. With three planets to get through in one day, they were on a tight schedule, to test out the device and its effects, as well as securing more soldiers, courtesy of the poison. Prisoners, particularly ones they considered," she stopped to regain her composure, "helpless, needy, and demanding excessive attention couldn't happen. Children would constitute nothing but multiple irritations, with the occasional rebel mixed in, to make it worse."

"On another day, another attack," whispered Ryan.

"They attack leisurely, the aim akin to their normal. It's not lack of cruelty keeping them from taking children prisoners to torture them, train them for Black Dragon, or use them for leverage to bend the will of another. There are many ways the mind of Black Dragon cruelty twists." She looked down. "We were saved from seeing it another time."

"What do you mean, Angelina?" asked Seth.

"There were no children, when they used the colonists as human shields."

Lana whispered, "Maybe they thought the children couldn't carry the boxes."

"Do you believe that, Lana?" Lana's eyes reflected her answer. "Me either. The squadron leader couldn't wait to wet his sword. A child becomes the preferred choice because the squadron leader finds an excuse to end the life sooner." Her next words were spoken in almost a whisper. "I believe our answer lies elsewhere."

"Where?" asked Caleb.

She turned to Dante, her eyes moist. "With Ethan."

"My father?"

"Yes, Dante. I couldn't read his thoughts, until that day in the Elders Hall. Yet I sensed the Ancient One's whispers to your father's spirit becoming louder, digging deeper into his heart, as the time drew near to your meeting with him. Your father's true heart gradually emerged again, but we didn't recognize it."

"My father intervened on the plans, kept the children from harm that day, though he couldn't later."

"Yes, my Dante, I'm sure of it." She hugged him.

"I miss him, Angelina," he whispered, as he found his comfort in her arms.

"I know, Dante, I know."

"Now, is there anything else?" whispered Alika.

Lana shook her head and spoke quietly, "Everything is answered. The day passes quickly."

"We can get a snack, and decide where to go from here." Caleb suggested.

Alika nodded. "Let me confer with these two, momentarily, to ensure everything is in order, and we'll join your group."

The three retreated to the far side of the room, as the others set out a snack. Angelina's eyes trailed Lana's figure, before turning to Alika and Alena. "My words only grieved her more. Emily is her undoing."

"You answered her question," said Alena.

"Yes, her exact question I answered, but that I answered her question..." She shook her head.

"There were no children in your vision," said Alena.

"But we know why."

"You did what had to be done," said Alika.

"As always, right?"

Meeting her gaze, his voice softened, "You did well in your answers, and they did not come easy, child."

She stared at them briefly, before continuing, "The day will come. A question gets answered a certain way or we say something and it falls apart. They'll realize it. When that day comes, what will they do?" She closed her eyes, unable to imagine the look in their eyes.

"We'll see to it then." Alika sighed.

Alena said, "It was not our choice to make."

"I still can't reconcile it. How will they ever, when the day arrives?" she whispered.

"Only with the Ancient One's help, my child," Alika whispered back. He hugged her at seeing her glistening tears, and Alena wrapped an arm around her shoulder. "No more talk of this, as another comes to comfort you."

Dante glanced over, and read Angelina's body language immediately. The look from Alika and Alena confirmed it. He held back until they embraced her.

"I'm sorry, but is everything okay?" His face fell, at the expression on her face.

"The upcoming goodbyes, I expect. Take over, Dante." Alika whispered, as he released Angelina, and Dante wrapped her up. Alika and Alena joined the others.

"I'll miss you, Dante." Running her hand through his hair, she wound the other arm around his neck.

He whispered, "I don't see how this happens today, either." Not knowing whether she lived or died at each day's end is what would drive him insane. He stroked her cheek, and stared back into her eyes. They drew him in and held him captive, like the enthralling emerald blue ocean scene in her quarters. "You're absolutely beautiful, my Angelina." He pulled her over, and kissed her long and deeply. Not to comfort or reassure her, but because he needed her with everything in him.

"You leave me breathless," she murmured.

"And you still leave me speechless," he murmured back. They leaned sideways, close together against the wall, to look out the window displaying a picture-perfect day. For a moment, they shifted to join the others. Dante caught a look from Caleb and Ryan.

"You two coming for dessert at least?" asked Caleb grinning at the two as Ryan chuckled.

Dante grinned back. "I don't know. I have it pretty sweet over here."

Angelina laughed. “You guys finish without us.” She whispered, her voice teasing, “You’re right. Why go there for dessert, when I have you right here?”

Dante laughed too, as she brought him over, and he tasted the sweetness of her lips again.

CHAPTER FORTY-FIVE

"That will be all for now." He sat back in the Black Dragon commander chair, as he flashed the screen off for a bit. A massive amount trailed across it, in the course of a day. He took for granted how much the Dark Lord tracked, when he ran everything, even with the Black Dragon Commander and Black Beauty to help ensure things went smoothly. Those were the ones everyone knew anyway, by the Dark Lord's design. There would always be others, like himself, hidden away in the shadows, to further the Dark Lord's cause in more subtle ways. Some played the role better than others. A handful excelled in it, and the Dark Lord recognized such talent by elevating their roles at the proper time. Yet the Premier Black Dragon never dreamed of finding himself in this position. He unconsciously sat straighter in the chair and smiled, as he stared across the expense of space before him, the planets dotting it, ready to be mastered by him now. A surge of heat blazed through him, and radiated from him, until it spread to every corner of the room. For an instant his breath forsook him, but it was exhilarating. It returned renewed, with a power filling him, and his eyes became drunk with intoxicating visions of domination playing before him. He murmured, "Oh yes, you will all be mine. I am the one to see this through to the endgame. All will kneel before me, or die."

He closed his eyes, infatuated in his delicious galactic vision for longer, before considering the information they brought him. Everything appeared to be going as planned at the proper pace. The Freedom Fighters made the expected visits to the planet and would start putting pieces together. All for nothing, as they fought a losing battle. Too much in motion already to be halted, and it stretched over a longer time than they could imagine. Yet, he was reminded of what happened a week ago. Although he faulted the Dark Lord's downfall to his loose reins and inattention to the operations at times, the Dark Lord had built a powerful and terrifying realm over time. The Premier Black Dragon couldn't complain either, being the recipient of it now. Despite all the Dark Lord's supreme power and masterful scheming, he met his demise, along with the Black Dragon Commander. That part interrupted the Premier Black Dragon's perfect images. He wanted to know, what happened at the Elders Hall? What brought the fall of such power? He wondered. Perhaps it was time to summon two individuals back for a discussion. Black Beauty insisted the man she dragged before him was the Dark Lord. He wasn't, but she sounded convinced. Undoubtedly, she dabbled somewhere. He suspected that day, but as he pondered it further, a theory began to form. The impostor stood here calmly, with not the slightest fear in his eyes, mocking Black Beauty throughout the entire encounter, as he enjoyed her humiliating plummet from power. He didn't look like the Dark Lord, but in many respects his behavior was reminiscent of the fallen leader. Yes, the more he examined the situation, he became more certain Destroyer could provide him insight, on what transpired at the Elders Hall. Who knows what other information might be forthcoming, maybe valuable knowledge the Dark Lord ran out of time to convey? The Premier Black Dragon would continue to walk a delicate line because he didn't want Destroyer forgetting who commanded Black Dragon now. "Yes, I'll bid them first thing in the morning, let it be their wake-up call. They can be useful, sooner than I anticipated." He laughed.

CHAPTER FORTY-SIX

"I'm afraid it's time." Alika smiled at Lana and the others with him, as he glanced at Angelina and Dante in one part of the room, and Ryan and Alena in another part. "At least they received a bit more time today." Alika rose slowly, to deliver his message.

"Sorry to interrupt, but it's the agreed upon time, Angelina," said Alika. He came with the others, after already retrieving Ryan and Alena.

"Of course, Alika." She turned to Dante. "A story to finish another time, Dante?"

"Suppose so," Dante replied unhappily, as he helped her up.

Angelina said to Alika, "I must say goodbye to Abigail, one last time."

Alika nodded. "Of course."

They all stood in Abigail's room, but Dante and Angelina sat on the side of her bed.

Angelina took Abigail's hand in her own, as Dante's arm reassuringly encircled Angelina's waist. *What if she never awakens? Will she be the same mother Dante remembers, if she does? After all, she endured the Dark Lord's torture for so long. I can't think like that. Dante has lost everyone else already.*

"Abigail, I got to see you again. I wish you to awaken, to find your way back to us. I saw your kindness, your sweet spirit, your love for those around you, the strength of your spirit. Visions only take us so far. Some things can only be experienced in person." She looked over at Dante, before turning back to Abigail.

Her other hand traced the outline of Abigail's face for a moment. "Abigail, I long … please hang on. We'll find the means for you to be with us again, not imprisoned in this sleep. I'll undo the Dark Lord's evil on you, span whatever galaxies to uncover the answer. I promise, I won't fail you." A tear slid down her face.

Dante heard the truth in her words and the determination fueling them. He should be comforted, but inside he feared the lengths she'd go to obtain the answer. As much as he sought the answer, he didn't want to sacrifice the life of the woman he loved in the process. The thought of losing her too … Instinctively leaning in closer to her side, he kissed her on the top of her head.

"I leave you in safe hands, surrounded by those who care for you, especially Dante. I see you and Ethan reflected in him. One of many reasons I care for him more with the passing days." Dante encircled his other arm around her waist from behind, to have both arms wrapped around her. "Look after him while I'm gone. I leave him with many difficult things to do with the others. An unfortunate pattern with me for him. You'd help him, if only you were awake. I'll miss you, Abigail." She kissed Abigail's forehead and whispered, "I'll keep my promise to you."

She turned and wrapped her arms around Dante's neck, burying her face there. "Angelina, we'll find the way, but it's on us all. You forget. And yes, you leave me with many tasks, but not all as you said." He pulled her back, to look in her eyes. "We made countless pleasant memories in these few days, to look back on until you return, and we hold on to those. One day my mother awakens, and I'll show her all the wonderful reasons you have my heart. The moment she meets you, she'll see why I care for you as I do." Kissing her on the forehead, he eased her up with him.

With a last look at Abigail, she and Dante walked out hand in hand, as the others followed them.

They stood out beside the two ships, for the dreaded time.

Alika said, "My intent is to mostly send these two to manage things, likely making my absence longer." He turned towards Caleb and Lana first. "Caleb, keep things running smoothly, as you do with this group. Take care of her, especially. She is a keeper."

"I knew the instant I laid eyes on her, Alika." Caleb grinned.

"I observed from the first visit. You two give me hope. There are few couples as devoted to each other. Lana, lean on him. Allow him to bear some weight you feel. Also, it's easier, if you don't place the planets' fate on your shoulders."

"Me, do such a thing? Where did you get that idea, Alika?"

"I learned to recognize the look, and I'm still breaking another one of the same. Lana, remember from Whom you draw your strength."

"I will, and I'll miss your company and counsel." She hugged him.

"Seth, your hands will be full. With the perilous days ahead, they need your help and guidance, as never before." He peered over at Ryan and Dante. "Some require a different sort of counsel, and more immediate."

"I believe so, too," Seth said as he cast a sideways view at the two men. "I enjoyed your company, Alika, as you always encourage me when you come."

He chuckled. "Refreshing to hear, considering I've commenced each past visit in the middle of a dire situation. I do understand your meaning, and you're a true friend to me as well, Seth." He hugged Seth goodbye.

Alika turned to Ryan and Dante, whose face mirrored the same expression. "No delving necessary to know your thoughts. Nothing I say makes this easier. Their past track record is a continuous shipwreck." He placed a hand on each of their shoulders. "But I promise, I'll do everything in my power to ensure they return to you each time."

Both of them nodded. Ryan sighed. "We know you will, Alika. You'll call, if they need help, right?"

"I will, Ryan. We'll do much better with that."

"Okay. Thank you for everything, Alika." He managed one of his smiles, and hugged Alika.

"Ryan's right, but Angelina is difficult to keep ..."

"Reined in." Alika grinned.

"One way to describe it. But there's the other stuff she deals with. All of it together ... she worries me, and I've witnessed it firsthand now. What if it comes at a crucial time?"

"I see now. Dante, in all this time of training her, a vision never occurred during an operation. The colonist immobilized her in the one situation, but either you or Seth intervened before that dagger found its mark. Alena and I will persevere through every vision with her, in whatever form they take."

"I sound like I doubt you, but I don't. I'm sorry, Alika."

"No reason for apologies. Your words are spoken from a heart of concern, for the one you hold close. I wouldn't trust you or Ryan to spent time with my students as you do, if it were not the case," he teased.

Ryan and Dante both laughed, and Dante said, "I'll miss you, Alika, and I don't even mind the double lessons from you and Seth."

Alika smiled, perceiving the sincerity shining from Dante's eyes. He knew Dante recalled those talks from the first visit, and before the encounter at the Elders Hall. He hugged Dante. "I'll always be here for you, young Dante, and will miss you as well."

Meanwhile, Alena and Angelina started with Caleb and Lana too, saying their goodbyes.

Caleb said, "Stay out of trouble. At least the kind beyond Alika's expertise. We're fond of you two, but my best friends over there ..."

"We know, Caleb. Keep them too busy to worry about us," Alena teased.

"I'm not that good."

"At least keep them focused enough, so they don't end up hurt," answered Angelina.

"They'll focus where they should during battle because they know the cost if they don't."

"They do, but ..." The memories of her chilling encounter with the dark spirit, in the form of Trey and the turned colonist, resurfaced. Thankfully, Ryan and

Dante didn't share her inner chaos. "Sorry, anticipating shadows that don't exist again."

Caleb and Lana exchanged a look. Caleb said, "We got Ryan and Dante. You two keep your end of the bargain."

"We'll try our hardest, Caleb," said Angelina, and Alena added, "Yes, thank you, Caleb." They reached over and hugged him.

"My husband is right. Despite just arriving, it's like I've known you both for much longer."

Alena said, "We felt the same, in the time spent with you."

"Some moments spent are beyond any vision to ever capture." Angelina smiled.

"I wish you two could stay. My spirit felt lighter, in these days with you both." She caught Angelina's look. "Even though some were far from lighthearted, and the conversations brought their share of tears, I didn't feel hopeless at all. I felt ..."

"Like you weren't alone," whispered Alena.

"Like you were understood," whispered Angelina.

Lana nodded, and her eyes misted over. "I'm going to miss you two." Alena and Angelina pulled her over at the same time and hugged her.

"A familiar scene with you two." Seth smiled.

"It seems to be," replied Alena.

"I recall fears voiced the last time, but they proved unwarranted. For one, this visit took an unexpected, but pleasant, surprise," he smiled at Alena who grinned back at him, "and for the other it proceeded as everyone always knew it would, did it not?" he stared at Angelina.

Angelina whispered, "It did, Seth."

"Let's make this the beginning of many times to see you two here. You know, you are no longer just Alika's two students. You can always come here, and we'll make sure you're safe."

"We know, and we eagerly await your added imparted wisdom to us when we return, Seth," teased Alena.

Seth laughed. "I have time, then. Appears I'll need it with you. Alena, keep yourself safe from the darkness around you and your younger sister. You're invaluable to her. Don't take that for granted. Your spirit is strong, as is your unfaltering trust in the Ancient One. You're treasured by us all, but especially by a certain commander."

"Your words encourage me, and I definitely found more than expected. I couldn't be happier." She winked at Seth, as they both glanced at Ryan. "Keep him from harm's way, Seth." She gave him a hug.

Seth focused on Angelina, and clasped her hands. He stared into her eyes, realizing how much lay behind them. It amazed him at points, saddened him at times, and caused him fear the next second. "What shall we do with you, Angelina? You remain mysterious to us, but your spirit draws everyone to you, as it inspires and comforts them. Yet, you don't see this from yourself."

"My eyes see through different lenses. I'm told I occasionally view through a shadow."

"More than on occasion. You must see things through another's eyes, as he said. You're strong in many ways, but your shoulders are smaller than what you envision. They can't bear the weight I watch you place upon them, and you pile more. Don't continue doing so, child."

"I keep receiving this counsel from more than you, Seth," she whispered.

"Child, I beg you to heed the words because it's too many fears for one person."

She nodded, struggling to find words. "Your words are kind, as always."

He knew there was much held in those words, but she couldn't convey them now as her eyes glistened with tears. "You're not alone, but surrounded by those who care for you. There's one who will not cease thinking of you for a second. Do not let whatever this shadow is claim victory."

Overcome with emotion, she hugged him tightly and whispered, "Seth, I'll fight it, I promise."

Alena smiled at Dante. "Be safe. Full gear every time. She'll find out, and you'll not hear the end of it, Dante."

"She means business on that. It's the closest she came to issuing me an order." He chuckled, before the concern returned. "Be careful too, Alena. We can't have anything happening to you."

"Same to you. We'll guard Angelina from her crazy schemes. Alika and I must approve these operations too, and all the shipping deals are monitored, by me on the ship, and Alika from afar. I'll jump in, if she gets in over her head, but thus far she hasn't needed assistance. She's confident of her abilities in that realm, and rightly so."

"I know. I just can't stop ..."

"Because it's mere words. You'll worry, as we do for you all, as we did for you, with your battle at the Elders Hall."

"Yeah, like that, and I'll watch after Ryan for you."

"Thank you, Dante," she whispered.

"Keep each other safe."

"We will." She hugged him goodbye.

"You better be careful, Angelina," Ryan said.

"Always."

"Heard that before from someone else. Right before he put a hole in his back from an exploding tank, almost got squished by one, and the whole trip to the Elders Hall. You two don't comprehend the meaning of careful."

"I'm afraid I don't boast the record to reassure you, either."

"You're right. Yours is as terrible as his. No staying behind for downloads, hanging out of a ship sending detonators, jumping off rooftops ..."

She laughed. "I got the idea, Ryan. Your memory isn't serving me well now."

"If I remember so well, it's imprinted forever on someone's else heart." He heard her sigh. "If something happened to you, we'd be, well you know, but he'd be ... I don't want to think about how it'd leave him. He'd be in pieces, Angelina." He looked her straight in the eye.

"I hold his heart in my hand, in a whole other sense, and that one scares me." She bit her lip, as her eyes moistened. "You found the other part of your heart with this visit, and I've never seen Alena as happy as she is now. You must stay safe too. I'm fond of you, but you command her heart now, Ryan."

"I'll handle it with all my care, Angelina," Ryan whispered.

"I know, Ryan. I promise to do whatever it takes, to keep her safe and bring her back to you."

He held her eyes, at her comment. "Both of you, Angelina. We saw the footage, and she won't leave you behind. Remember what I said about Dante, too. Your life is not your own." He paused. "I know you'll keep her safe."

"She always gives so much, in agreeing to help train me. Today, she gives again. I wish things could be different, Ryan. That she could remain with you." She looked down.

Ryan put his hands on her shoulders. "Today is hard enough for us. Don't do this to yourself. She never regretted training you, but understood what it meant. She told us one evening. The four of us will make this work. It's too valuable not to."

"I'm sorry it must be like this, Ryan."

He hugged her and said, "None of us believes it'll always be this way. Have faith, Angelina."

CHAPTER FORTY-SEVEN

The others stepped back, as the two hardest goodbyes arrived.

Ryan wrapped his arms around Alena's waist as she slid her arms around his neck. "I didn't believe it possible in such a short time, but I ..."

"I've no doubts, either. You kept your word, Ryan."

"About what?"

"The evenings. I'll expect more of the same, every time I visit you." She tried putting a teasing tone in it, but her eyes glistened.

"Guaranteed." He leaned his lips to her forehead. "Perfect is the only way to describe every single moment spent with you. I've never cared for someone, like I do you. You gained total sway over me, Alena."

"I'm not even a commander."

He whispered, "Your powers of persuasion are superior to any commander, sweet Alena." He kissed her.

She murmured, "I'm glad they worked on you."

"I never stood a chance, but I wanted to be persuaded to your side, from the moment I saw you," he groaned, as he hugged her, "Oh, I'm going to miss you."

"I'll miss you too, Ryan." She pulled back slightly and touched his cheek. "Please stay safe. It only takes one shot, one of those discs. You saw."

"There's a whole fleet behind me. I don't like your odds, when you run into trouble. Two against an army, and I can't lose you, Alena."

"What we do is suited to our numbers. I'll be okay. We must trust. We just found each other. It's too soon to ..." she stopped, as tears rolled down.

"Say goodbye, but it's time, right? At least for now." He pulled her as close as he could against him, as he kissed her. This time, it was a long, deep kiss, and she tightened her grip around his neck, as she returned the kiss with the spirit he loved about her.

"Until next time."

"Next time, sweet Alena." He reluctantly released her, and let her hands slide out of his at the last.

"How did we think we could do this?" Dante wrapped Angelina up in his arms, and stared down into her eyes.

"We have to, for you to stay safe, Dante."

"I should be protecting you, but I won't know if you remain safe each day. How can I do that?"

"You were doing it before. Nothing changes." Tears sprung in her eyes.

"Everything changed. Don't you see?" He stroked her cheek. "You're no longer a mysterious connection I'm sorting out, or an unknown messenger, or just this incredible fighter I stand in awe of for rescuing my mother. You're mine, my beautiful young spear-bearer, the keeper of my heart, the longing of my spirit, the center of my entire world now. Nothing is as before, my Angelina."

Her eyes widened in wonderment, at his words to her. "Which is why I can't lose you, Dante. I can't be the reason something happens to you because I'm all that to you. I care for you too much. Please, Dante. It must be this way." Her voice broke, and she buried her face in his shoulder.

He pulled her over and held her. She would come back. He told himself, but with the goodbye here, it didn't work. All his fears of what could occur in the interim screamed to the surface, and overpowered every logical argument in his head. "I'm sorry. I'm not trying to make this harder, but I can't let you go now." He lifted her head to look in her eyes. "You aren't the only one with fears. I'm scared too, Angelina."

"We got through so much together already, Dante. At the end of the battle, we always end up at each other's side. We cling to that image. It must chase away the others, or you can let them take control if you allow them. I know a lot about that." She forced a smile. "We made many pleasant images from the last few evenings to draw on. Just like you said. We focus on those, right?"

"They were wonderful images, but it's not working now."

"It's like saying goodnight to me for the evening."

"The difference is, I won't see you tomorrow."

"You will, a tomorrow in the future. My Dante, you must meet me halfway."

She was right. He caressed away her tear with his hand. "Be safe, please. Goodbye, my Angelina."

"Goodbye, my Dante."

He wrapped her up completely, and kissed her. It was a long kiss, as one trying to stretch the moment out as much as possible, both knowing the end of the kiss truly meant goodbye. If only they could stay in that kiss. But they couldn't forever. They sighed in unison, as they backed away from each other, and their hands let go.

Alika walked towards his ship, as Alena and Angelina did the same towards theirs. Angelina started to step on the ship's ramp, when a yell rang out, accompanied by the running of footsteps.

"Wait, Angelina, please!"

Angelina turned around. "Dante, we must part."

He engulfed her trembling body in his arms again, as a sob escaped her. Scattering soft kisses on her cheeks, he replaced the tears running down her face. "This is where you belong, my Angelina. I've never been so sure of anything in my life."

How she knew as well, but she still had to leave. "Dante, we ..."

"You care for me?"

She realized he knew the answer, but needed to hear it again. "You know how much I care for you. Never doubt that. All I do is because I care for you. I gave you my heart, when you were but a vision to me. You have been my Dante, for longer than you imagine. There is no one but you." Pulling him over the rest of the way, she kissed him slowly and deeply.

"I'm selfish to want both now."

"No, selfish never described you, and it doesn't now. I'd say the same as you, if I viewed through your eyes with the pieces you have, but I glimpse the other pieces you can't. You have to trust me."

"There's no way now?" He ran his hand through her hair.

"No, but one day, I hope. Dante, our bond saw us through everything already. What is between us has been created and tied by many bonds of care connected with your heart and mine." She stroked the side of his face. "There are many bonds created through our lifetime, this incredible one we're building, others we already formed, and new ones crafted, ones of friendship and family. They are precious bonds, ones we fight to protect at all costs. Yet, not every bond is forged of the same metal. Rather, they are forged of darkness, of cruelty, and of suffering. We witnessed it. Your father, Dante. Years of such a bond imprisoned him, before we freed him. Your mother is asleep, burdened by the chains of another one. The others on the planet share the same chains. These colonists, turned Black Dragon, serve a bond of darkness they don't fathom. Yet they oblige it, and the destruction they leave behind will be terrible. For it is a master demanding more, though he takes everything already, including their life's blood. These bonds forged of darkness, they must be broken, my Dante. If not, they destroy the treasured connection, our link created with the bonds of care."

"We'll say goodbye for a bit, because this bond between us is worth fighting for," Dante whispered.

"Yes, my Dante." She smiled, through her tears. "I'm never far from you, in truth. Because ..."

He held her eyes. "Between us is a bond,"

She finished, "that cannot be broken."

"This is only goodbye for a moment."

"Yes, only goodbye for a moment." She continued, smiling, knowing his next words. How she loved him.

"Try to make the moment brief, because I long to see you again, my Angelina," he whispered.

She whispered back to him, "It cannot be brief enough, but I will try for you, I promise, my Dante."

This time they moved towards each other in the same moment. It was a long, passionate kiss, infused with words of care and reassurance from the bond they shared, perfectly translated by their two hearts. A happy sigh escaped Angelina, as their lips finally parted. Dante smiled as he heard it, and noticed her breathless state from the kiss again. This time, he found himself in the same condition, and she knew it, as she smiled up at him. If they had to say goodbye for a bit, this was the way to do it. Slowly, they released each other, until their hands only remained clasped together. Staring up at him, she brushed her hand out across his cheek, as the first night. He smiled, as he turned his face to brush his lips to her hand, and he finally let her go.

Alena and Angelina flashed one last smile at Ryan and Dante, as the ship door closed.

Alika's voice came through the ship's communication system. "I'll take off after your ship, whenever you two are ready."

The two sat in the cockpit chairs, staring out.

"All right, Alika," murmured Alena.

"We'll come back, like we promised?" said Angelina, but it came out a question.

"We will." Alena grasped Angelina's hand. "We will, Angelina."

"Then why am I..." She closed her eyes.

Alika's voice came through with a gentle reminder. "The ship will practically fly itself. Might I suggest using the feature? All the turmoil is within the ship's pilots, today."

"Always wise counsel," replied Alena.

"We're doing it, Alika." Angelina made a couple of swipes on the console and leaned back in the chair. The ship lifted off and headed for the portal, as the two stared out the cockpit, to the two men dominating their thoughts.

CHAPTER FORTY-EIGHT

They sat at the table inside the fortress, with the attempt at normal conversation proving pointless. Dante and Ryan didn't respond beyond yes or no, as their eyes drifted to the empty spaces next to them.

"Time to give this up," Caleb said.

"What, I ..." Ryan snapped to attention.

"Yeah, I mean ... what did you ask?" Dante stumbled, startled from his thoughts.

"I stated the obvious."

"I'm sorry. We need to focus." Ryan sighed.

"Me too. Sorry as well." Dante ran his hands through his hair, and slumped further in his chair.

Seth rose, and put a hand on both of the two men's shoulders. "No, Caleb is right. This is a lost cause tonight, and perfectly understandable. Alika is probably mustering nothing useful out of his two, either. Give yourselves tonight."

Lana looked at the two in sympathy. "Yes, we'll start over tomorrow. The other commanders arrive early tomorrow afternoon. We don't wish to see either one of you down here until lunchtime, unless you need something beforehand. Call us, if you do."

"Thanks, everyone." Ryan stood, forcing a smile.

"Yeah, tomorrow we'll be better."

"Think that will be the case?" asked Lana, as she watched them leave.

"Normal, no. Well enough, yeah," Caleb replied as Seth nodded in agreement.

"This will be a long evening, Ryan."

"No kidding." He read Dante's look. "Yeah, me too. Probably, tomorrow night I'll be up to talking."

"I had to offer. You're my best friend, well you and Caleb, but I feel the same tonight."

"Thanks, Dante, for always being there. I know the offer stands, if I change my mind and want company tonight."

"We always got each other's back."

"We have to, some of us literally." Ryan's face broke out into his normal grin.

"You couldn't resist?" Dante grinned back.

"It's me, right? You won't ever live that down. Goodnight, Dante." Still grinning, he turned to his quarters for the night.

"Goodnight, Ryan." He shook his head, as he laughed.

"Decided to put that down yet?"

"What ... no ... I'm looking at ..." Angelina almost dropped the data pad on the table at Alika's voice.

"Share what you found, because you examined that same screen for the last forty minutes." He sat beside her.

"I couldn't tell you." She laid the data pad down.

"Lay it aside, as Alena did, because she knew it a pointless endeavor tonight. Time for you to admit the same. Tomorrow, you'll be clearer again, and you wished to speak with Christopher."

"But there's much to sort out from those days. More questions. The vision bothers me still. Not for the reason it did you and the others. It's the puzzle, of who she used the dagger on. The Ancient One took me all the way back to the Elders Hall to show it to me, and anything Black Beauty bloodies her hands in is a reason to be frightened." She struggled to find the words. "Alika, I have my disturbances at times, but I was drowning. It was so ..."

"Continuous?"

"Yes, as though they all found me at once, and I couldn't recover before the next one tore at me. This can't be the new normal because the nightmare is true. There is a point..."

He clasped her hand. "Which you won't reach. We'll trust it reflected a strange string of occurrences. With the events that just transpired at the Elders Hall and the three planets alone, it triggered things from the past and the emotional turmoil you went through a few days before. It overwhelmed your broken spirit and left you vulnerable."

"You make sense, Alika. Your counsel is sound on the other, too. I can only think of Dante tonight. No matter what I do, I won't make him happy. The one arrangement he desires, I can't give him, and I don't know if I ever can."

"No one knows the future, but we both know you don't believe it's an if thing. I also disagree about the happy part because I caught smiles on Dante's face countless times during our stay." He leaned over to her, as his eyes twinkled. "You discovered multiple ways to make young Dante happy, and I spied numerous smiles on your face too, which are to his credit."

She grinned back at Alika. "He does possess an undeniable charm about him, and he used it on me from the first. Something you can't appreciate from a vision."

"I always suspected as much from Dante, and his charm continues." Alika produced a box and an envelope from beside him. "He told me to give this to you tonight, and for you to open the box first, and then the envelope."

"When did he have the chance? I never saw." Her eyes shone, as she took the items.

"He ensured they reached me. I'll leave you to them."

"No, stay at least for the box. It's cold. What could it possibly be?" She stared at it.

"Open and see, silly." Alika laughed.

She unsealed the silver glimmered box, to reveal a smaller light blue box. Around it laid matching blue colored tissue paper and a scattering of what resembled light blue beads or water droplets. She realized though the arrangement was beautiful, the beads also served to keep the contents cool. Opening the box, she gasped and understood. The box contained three compartments. One had a small card, another a little fork, and in the center a large slice of dessert. She pulled the small card out, and read it silently.

My Angelina, I wish you were here to share dessert again with me this evening. When you enjoy it tonight, I hope it reminds you of me and the sweetness of the time we spent together.

Missing you,

Your Dante

She slid the card over to Alika.

"Are you sure?"

She nodded, unable to read it aloud, as her emotions swelled.

His face registered understanding, and he slid it back to her. "Every evening, a piece of this dessert?"

"Yes, he got a whole thing of it once he knew I was returning the next day."

"I agree. He's charming and masterful with courting you, and we'll gladly give him our blessing, when the day comes." He winked at her as he headed for bed. "Enjoy your dessert. I'll let you read the other in private from him."

She read the card again, and laid it aside for safe keeping. She opened the envelope to find a letter from him. He took care with this in every way, knowing she'd read it repeatedly. He wrote it on scribe paper, as it's often called, and used the ink known as Forever Imprinted Ink. They were both normally employed on things needing to withstand lots of handling and retain their print. Elders kept all the items handy, but for everybody else not the case. Dante didn't go far to find a helpful Elder to secure the items. She chuckled and read, while she ate her dessert.

My Angelina,

I don't know where to begin. These days and evenings with you are like nothing I could ever imagine, as being caught up in the sweetest dream. When I look into those incredible blue eyes of yours, I become lost in that world, a future built only for us, my Angelina. Don't shy away from it, because of whatever else you endured in your past. We'll topple those other images, no matter what it takes, with my words of reassurance to you, and one kiss at a time if need be. I won't abandon the future I'm creating with you, and one day we'll claim it all. I won't forsake this path with you, my Angelina. We are together, side by side, in this journey now. I care for you so much; I feel my breath taken away at times. I long to be with you, to hear your voice speak my name, to talk the evening away with you, to hold you close, to kiss you.

My Angelina, I see this amazing woman I can't get enough of, who has taken a hold of every part of me. A woman of such strength, who has seen a world so painfully difficult, and has not only endured it, but fights with a fierce passion, that won't let it take her captive or anyone else. Yet, also a woman of such gentleness, who reaches out to comfort in a way that touches my heart to its core. It's with that same gentleness you speak my name, wrap me up in the most wonderful embraces, and kiss me sweetly. I wish to have you here, to do so now. I miss you already, my Angelina, but I'll have you in my arms again soon. Until then, I hold you in my heart and will not cease to think of you. Your beautiful image, and the time we spent together, stays before me. Come back to me soon, my beautiful Angelina.

With all my care,

Your Dante.

Tears streamed down her face as she finished reading. She lost count how many times she reread it, but each time warmed her as much as the first. She whispered, "I will, my Dante. I love you, my Dante."

Dante stood lost in the middle of his own quarters, clueless with how to spend his evening. It felt all wrong. He changed for bed, turned the projection on, and pretended interest on the display. "Why not?" he murmured. A supreme waste of time, but he needed a distraction. "Who am I kidding? There's only one distraction I want tonight." He grabbed a piece of dessert, a drink, and put both on the table. His attention focused on something behind the small pillow, as he sat on the couch. "What is that?" Slowly he retrieved the envelope to discover the outside read, "My Dante." Immediately her familiar sweet fragrance tingled his senses, as he brought it nearby. Once he opened the envelope, the sweet fragrance intensified, and he enjoyed the pleasant images it invoked. Inside he discovered a letter, and he smiled, as he noticed the beautiful blue paper and ink. She knew he'd read this repeatedly, as he anticipated she would his letter. It was on paper, and written in ink, to stand repeated handling and the test of time. He read the letter, while eating dessert.

My Dante,

Hopefully, this eases your sadness about the message I erased from your data pad. I hope you prefer this one.

No matter how much I thought I knew you in the visions, there are no words for what you brought to my world, in these days with you. There is a happiness I didn't believe possible, until I was with you, staring into your eyes, being held in your arms, kissed breathlessly by you. It's a bliss I can't fathom; I know there were things that happened, which were far from what anyone normally describes as happy. Yet I'll gladly take those times too, because I wouldn't trade one moment spent with you. Even those times, you were there to give comfort, such words of care to my spirit, and hold me, as only you can. Your words touch me to my core, in a way no one can, my Dante. I can't imagine my world before you, and I don't ever wish to.

My Dante, I wish there were words enough to tell you how I care for you, but they will always fall short. You leave me stumbling over my words, but I don't mind in the least. I could listen to you forever, and each time your words to me leave me in awe. I can't understand, how I captured the heart of such an incredible man as you, my Dante. You always give, pouring into me your care and reassurance. Always knowing what I need, when I don't know myself. A patience, insisting ever sweetly, until my spirit is calmed. There's no one but you, my Dante. You shook my world at its center, but in the most amazing way. I wish it to never end now. I long to be back in your arms, to share yet another kiss with you, to hear the words I feel come through with every one of them. I already miss you, my Dante.

I will remember every sweet word you spoke to me, every gentle touch you gave, and every breathtaking kiss from your lips, until the next time I see you. When I see you again, you will not wait long for the next kiss, my Dante.

With all my care, from the only one who ever caught your eye and captured your heart,

Your Angelina

He grinned, as he read it several more times. He'd know it in his sleep soon. His heart galloped, and warmth encircled him. He closed his eyes, and for an instant she laid snuggled up against him on the couch again. The memories from the last few evenings flooded over him, and the warmth continued encasing him. He murmured, "You're right. You won't wait long for that kiss when I see you next time. I do love you, my Angelina."

Angelina cleared everything from the table and picked up the letter and card to put away for safekeeping. She peered out the window, as she headed for bed. It unveiled a beautiful night, and her thoughts remained fixed on Dante.

Dante took care of everything, but made a stop before turning in. With letter still in hand to put away securely, he went over to the window. A clear night sky stretched out dotted with a multitude of stars. He wondered what she was doing now. Probably still up for a while or maybe not. Normally, she kept long hours, but he felt she turned in early tonight. Hopefully, his package and letter lifted her spirits.

As she continued to gaze into the lustrous night, she smiled and whispered, "Goodnight, my Dante."

Dante stared out into the twinkling display and whispered back, "Goodnight, my Angelina."

ABOUT THE AUTHOR

Elizabeth Lavender is the author of the Sunspear series. Originally from the Alabama coast, she currently lives in the Dallas area with her husband, Jeff, and her two children. She has a Master's degree in counseling from Dallas Baptist University and has studied psychology and English.

She enjoys science fiction and fantasy and hopes to bring some of that same enjoyment to others. She also enjoys suspense novels. However, as long as the storyline is intriguing, she will give it a try. Her reading spans from Les Miserables to Shakespeare to the Percy Jackson series to anything written by Ted Dekker or Frank Perretti.

She works full-time and has been at the same company for over twenty years happily. She is a huge football fan and has a decent throwing arm, despite what her oldest son says when he practices with her.

Although she enjoys Texas, she does love going home to Alabama to visit. Besides visiting family and friends, it is nice to be back near the water again, where the seafood is the best.

Find more books by Elizabeth at:
https://elizabethlavender.net

www.ingramcontent.com/pod-product-compliance
Lightning Source LLC
Chambersburg PA
CBHW030626310726
48979CB00003B/896
9781951741082